The Queen's Bastard

Also by Robin Maxwell

The Secret Diary of Anne Boleyn

Virgin

The Queen's Bastard

A Novel

Robin Maxwell

Arcade Publishing • New York

FIRST ARCADE PAPERBACK EDITION

This is a work of fiction. Names, places, characters, and incidents are either the products of the author's imagination or are used fictitiously.

Library of Congress Cataloging-in-Publication Data

Maxwell, Robin, 1948–
The Queen's bastard : a novel / by Robin Maxwell. —1st ed.
p. cm.
ISBN 13: 978-1-55970-475-5 (hc)
ISBN 13: 978-1-55970-848-7 (pb)
1. Leicester, Robert Dudley, Earl of, 1532?–1588—Family—Fiction. 2. Great Britain—History—Elizabeth, 1558–1603—Fiction. I. Title.
PS3563.A9254Q84 1999
813'.54—dc21 98-50502

Published in the United States by Arcade Publishing, Inc., New York
Distributed by Hachette Book Group USA

Visit our Web site at www.arcadepub.com

10 9 8 7 6 5 4 3 2 1

EB

Designed by API

PRINTED IN THE UNITED STATES OF AMERICA

For Max

Acknowledgments

I owe a huge debt of gratitude to my husband, Max Thomas, for the book's concept, as well as for his endless input and editing during the writing of it. His tolerance and patience with a wife who was living, for great swaths of time, more in the sixteenth century than in the twentieth was nothing short of heroic.

The character of Arthur Dudley was inspired to a great degree by Monty Roberts, who in his book *The Man Who Listens to Horses* wondered whether there were young boys in centuries past who, like himself, had discovered the "language of the horse" and the compassionate art of gently "starting" horses rather than the torturous conventional method of breaking them. Interestingly, it was Her Majesty Queen Elizabeth II who brought Roberts's work to light and has shown him continuing interest and support.

As if by magic, perfect books presented themselves to me at every turn in my research: *The History of Horsemanship* by Charles Chenevix Trench and *Dark and Dashing Horsemen* by Stan Steiner, *The History of Warfare* by Viscount Montgomery of Alamein and *Elizabeth's Army* by Charles Grieg Cruickshank, Winston Graham's *The Spanish Armada,* Marcelin Defourneaux's *Daily Life in Spain,* Paul Johnson's *Elizabeth I,* and any number of A. L. Rowse's works on the Elizabethan Age, as well as Lacey Baldwin Smith's *Portrait of a Queen.* Peter J. French's biography of Dr. Dee, Lady Antonia Fraser's of Mary Queen of Scots, and an entire chapter on Francis Englefield in Albert J. Loom's *The Spanish Elizabethans* were all invaluable.

I thank Billie Morton, David Hirst, Butch Ponzio, and Jillian Palethorpe for their reading and comments during the writing process. Robert Patton provided me with crucial information about ancient British ritual and translations of Celtic chants. And special thanks to Philip Daughtry, who, on a moment's notice, wrote *Cum Rage!,* John Dee's powerful incantation used to ward the evil off England's shores.

I will always appreciate the support of my agent, Kim Witherspoon, and my publishers, Jeannette and Richard Seaver. I also thank Ann Marlowe, my excellent copy editor.

Finally, thanks to my mother, Skippy Ruter-Sitomer, who taught me the meaning of love, and has never stopped believing in me.

Book One

One

My Father is dead and my Mother is Queen of England.

The handwriting on the first page of the blue leather journal was bold in stroke and plain in design. The author, a tall, powerfully built man, gazed out across the vast expanse of sea, his red-gold hair whipping sharply round a strong-boned jaw. The face was deeply lined and ruggedly handsome, with searing black eyes that blazed with a fine intelligence. As he steadied the volume he held upon his knees, he hoped the ocean would remain calm and the winds too, for he was unused to such writing, and was hard pressed enough putting his thoughts to paper without this tilting ship sending his inkwell flying or the pages flapping about in the breeze.

Far off to starboard a flock of gulls in straggling formation caught his gaze. Probably making for the Canary Isles, he thought, but a long way for gulls to be from land. Dipping his quill in the inkwell at his knee, he began again, considering each word before committing it to the vellum page.

My name is Arthur Dudley, he wrote. *These are words which ring to my own ears as strange and ungainly, but they are nevertheless good and true. That which follows is not a diary, for until the events of several years past I had thought so little of my own life and condition that the conceit of journal keeping had entered my mind never once. Instead, this document constitutes the twenty-seven years of my history as best I remember it. A memoir. Tis odd that such a plain life as my own should be worthy of remembrance. But as I have said, I am the son of a Queen and therefore mentionable.*

The creak of the sails on the mizzen as the wind shifted pulled him sharply back to the deck, the day, the sun dipping toward the western horizon. He sought the flock of gulls, but they were no longer off to starboard, nor were they dead ahead where he expected they would have traveled. How could this be? The birds had been in the air a moment before. He scanned the sky round him. There! The flock was a diminishing speck still flying low, but off the *port* side.

"I have been lost," said Arthur to himself, "lost within the words I have been writing." Time, he realized with a pang, had simply vanished, gone whilst within the thrall of memory — a bit of natural magic. Arthur Dudley smiled with the thought. Each day of his voyage to the New World he could write his life, and for those few moments would become a conjurer of time.

Two

"He is here, Your Majesty." Kat Ashley's voice was grave, and she made no attempt to hide her displeasure. The fifty-two-year-old waiting lady observed with annoyance that the young queen, who now primped before her dressing table, bothered equally little to suppress her delight. "If you do not mind my saying so, Madame . . ."

"But I do mind, Kat, I mind very much indeed. I have no need to be eminded of the scandal over Amy Dudley's death. I know it quite well al-aeady."

Kat Ashley snorted. "Your favorite wears his mourning black all right, but he struts about, a peacock all fine and glowing with good health, like man just back from taking the waters instead of a widower come from a funeral, not to say a suspect in a murder inquest."

"Would you have my loyal friend looking grey and ill, then?"

"Never, Your Majesty." Kat realized winning an argument with the Queen was impossible. "Never in a thousand years. Shall I show him in?"

"No . . . just one moment more." Elizabeth took stock of herself in the silver-framed looking glass and prayed her nervousness would not be apparent. She looked well enough. The three months of her lover's enforced absence — enforced by herself — had been a strain, certainly. She had suffered more than her share of migraines and head colds. But now her eyes were bright, her skin beautifully pale and opalescent, and her red-gold hair a wavy halo round her perfectly oval face.

Elizabeth's long graceful fingers unconsciously sought a large silver locket she wore at her throat, one she'd recently taken to wearing, and she grasped it for comfort. 'Twas no ordinary bauble, this, but a valued keepsake. Not a soul knew that inside it nestled a miniature of her long dead mother, Anne Boleyn, and a lock of that lady's dark silky hair.

Her black taffeta and brocade gown heightened the whiteness of the Queen's flesh, but this day the choice of attire was dictated not by vanity but by respect for the dead — Amy Dudley — and the return to Court of Amy's husband. Elizabeth's favorite. Her Master of the Horse. Her beloved. Robin Dudley.

Elizabeth rose from her dressing table. She was tall for a woman, almost unnaturally tall, but her father King Henry had been a giant of a man. She was slender as a reed, and the stays and underpinnings of her heavy gown held her torso rigid. The only allowances for graceful effect were her arms and hands, the tilt of her head, and her rich, modulated voice.

"This will be the last day of mourning attire," she suddenly announced to Kat Ashley. "Have Lady Sidney see to my wardrobe after she's had a moment to greet her brother."

"Yes, Madame. And which gown will Her Majesty wish to wear first," inquired Kat, her voice acid with sarcasm, "the scarlet one?"

"Katherine Ashley!" Elizabeth's eyes flashed furiously.

"I'll show Lord Robert in," murmured the unrepentant waiting lady and bustled from the Queen's bedchamber.

It was the longest Elizabeth had been without him. Since her accession to the throne two years before, she had insisted that Robin, her dear friend from the age of eight, be at her side continually. His appointment as Horsemaster had guaranteed his close company, and their passionate love affair had borne him on a great wave of aggrandizement at her hand. But it had gained him more jealous enemies at Court than friends. He had nevertheless weathered his raising with good nature and astounding grace, and despite the barbs and criticisms from every direction, Elizabeth had never once questioned his love and loyalty.

Then his wife Amy had died under mysterious circumstances, and the hated courtier had fallen under suspicion. With leaden heart, Elizabeth had banished him from Court to his house at Kew until the coroner's inquest would, hopefully, establish his innocence beyond a reasonable doubt.

Elizabeth had endured their separation in a wholly disquieted state, for she had only recently completed the reading of her mother's secret diary. Filled with revelations shocking to the young queen, the writings had illuminated the nature of the deceiving and ambitious men who had destroyed Anne Boleyn. And for the first time, unbidden but undeniable doubts had arisen in Elizabeth's mind about Robin Dudley's motives.

In his absence Elizabeth had visited her mother's unmarked grave under the floor of a chapel in the Tower of London. Lost in grim musings, she had imagined the corpse, its head severed from the body and laid at its side in a rude arrow box — for that was all Henry had cared for his once beloved wife — and pondered the treachery of men. In that moment and the terrible empty days that followed, a strange and unthinkable idea had been forged in her mind, and like the blacksmith's white hot sword plunged into a trough of water, it had hardened into steely resolve. *She would never marry any man,* not prince nor king nor subject, never relinquish the vast power she had legitimately inherited from her father, Henry VIII. It was outrageous, she knew. The natural order of things was for a woman to marry, bear children. And for a queen, imperative. To the thinking of all Englishmen of conscience, the only reason for Elizabeth's existence was to bear heirs — princes for the succession, princesses to be sold into marriages of alliance.

But now, despite the "death by mischance" verdict that freed Robin from official responsibility, Elizabeth could not be moved from her course. She might play the game of courtship, pretend her intention to marry, but she would never ever give in. Not a soul knew of her decision. Least of all Robin Dudley.

The bedchamber door opened and there he stood in somber black doublet and hose, all stately carriage and grave countenance. 'Twas said of Robin Dudley — even by his enemies, those who derisively called him the Gypsy — that he was the most reserved man of his time, and carried a depth not to be fathomed but by the searchers of hearts.

My God, thought Elizabeth, how beautiful he is! She wished for nothing more than to fly into Robin's strong embracing arms. But she was determined this day, resolved to dignity and restraint. There were so many problems lying heavy on her heart and mind. Problems of politics and diplomacy and religion, some a result of this disastrous affair of Amy's death.

"Your Majesty." He spoke quietly and, at an almost imperceptible nod of Elizabeth's head, moved to kneel before the Queen and kiss her hand. Then he rose to his full height — over six feet tall, the only one of her men to whom Elizabeth was forced to look up.

"You are welcome back to Court, my lord," she said, willing her voice to calm steadiness. With these words Robin Dudley's face exploded into a smile, and he instantly pulled Elizabeth into an embrace which she resisted for less than a moment before returning it in kind. They held thus entwined until he pushed her to arm's length, stared in through her eyes to her soul, and kissed her hungrily on the mouth. She yielded to the kiss and moaned with the familiar pleasure of his touch. But this sound of pleasure she suddenly heard as an alarm, and wrenched away perhaps more violently than she had intended.

"Elizabeth, what is it?"

"What it is, Robin," she said, pulling herself together, "is a disaster. My reputation in Europe is sullied beyond imagining, some say beyond saving."

"But why!" he demanded hotly. "I've been found innocent of any wrongdoing in Amy's death. 'Twas an accident, so say a jury of the country's most able men. Men of integrity!"

"And know you what my Scottish cousin Mary says? That the Queen of England is going to marry the Master of her Horse, who has killed his wife to make room for her!"

"Mary is bitter. She no longer has a place in the French royal family since her husband's death. And she has nothing to come home to in Scotland but a pack of Protestant nobles who'd best like to see their Catholic queen disappear. She has every reason to slander you, Elizabeth. She wants your crown!"

"And she may get it if I cannot salvage my reputation and strengthen my position."

"You exaggerate, Elizabeth. The Scots queen has no power. Her mother-in-law de Médicis is well rid of her and has too many problems of her own in France to support a Scottish invasion of England. You are talking nonsense."

"*I,* talking nonsense!" Elizabeth bristled. "When have you ever known me to talk nonsense?"

"When you are angry with me," he said quietly, holding her with his eyes.

Elizabeth groped helplessly for a retort. Robin was right. She was still furious with him. Furious for destroying the dream she had harbored from the bright January day of her coronation, as he rode proudly beside her, till the moment the messenger from Cumnor House had knelt before her and with trembling voice announced the death of Amy Dudley. "She was found at the bottom of the stair by her servants when they came home from the fair," the courier had said. "Her neck was broken, but her death seemed not from the fall. Her headdress was never disarranged. They are calling it murder."

Murder. And Lord Robert Dudley, scandalously embroiled with the Queen of England for all the world to see, hoping for his way to be cleared to marry Elizabeth, had been the prime suspect.

Perhaps, thought Elizabeth, he had nothing whatsoever to do with

Amy's death. Perhaps he was entirely innocent of that crime. But of the crime of ambition Robin Dudley was wholly guilty. It was in his blood. His ancestors before him — grandfather, father, brothers — had died for the sin of ambition, and though she knew he loved her truly, she did not know if he loved the dream of becoming king of England more. She had been told that when Robin, still in exile at Kew, learned she had angrily slashed to ribbons the patent granting him the promised earldom of Leicester, he had raged and thundered at the unfairness of it. But now, only grateful for his return to the Queen's good graces, he made no talk of anger or bitterness.

"Whilst I was banished at Kew I knew only the deepest misery, Elizabeth. I missed your sweet company most of all, but I worried, too, that I was unable to discharge my duties as Horsemaster. I knew not how you would be attended when you rode abroad, if the right horses would be chosen, if you were safe from harm. For no one knows or cares for your person as deeply as I do."

With his words Elizabeth felt her anger recede like an outgoing tide, for she knew them to be true and utterly sincere.

He went on. "Those months away, awaiting the verdict, I felt I was living in a strange dream from which there was no waking. My only relief, and I thank you for it, were the visits from Secretary Cecil, who was, despite the sour feelings I know he harbors for me, very kind. I want . . ." Dudley stopped as if he could not find the words to go on. "I want you to forgive me, Elizabeth. This is no admission of guilt for Amy's death. I mean forgive me for causing you, by my very existence or circumstance, any misery or grief. I wish only the best for you, you know that. I want your reign to be long and glorious, and I mean to be at your side in whatever capacity you allow me. I am your subject and your servant, Your Majesty, but I do and will always love you."

Elizabeth's eyes had suddenly filled with tears, and she quickly turned away that he should not see them. "Very well," she said with forced levity. "You are forgiven." And with the suddenness of the sun emerging from behind a black thundercloud to brighten a dull day, Elizabeth felt her soul lighten. Her love had returned to her. She faced him with a piquant smile. "Faithful servant, would you care to see your new apartments?"

"Have I new rooms?" Robin's features softened with surprise.

"Come," said Elizabeth lightly.

He looked puzzled as she moved to a curtained wall and pulled back the heavy arras to reveal a door. With the expression of a bemused child Dudley opened it. A short unlit passageway lay ahead.

"You may lead, Sire," she said teasingly.

Taking her hand, he headed into the darkness, and not ten feet beyond found another door.

"Open it," Elizabeth commanded.

Robin Dudley stood staring in at his new rooms. Not overlarge, they were nonetheless sumptuously appointed with a great canopied bed fit for a king, a fine silk-threaded tapestry of mythical beasts on one wall, and on another his family's coat of arms — the red and blue field upon which rose the bear and ragged staff. A fire blazed welcomingly in the hearth.

He was overcome and, for once, speechless. This gesture from the Queen — adjoining apartments — was certain to infuriate her councillors and his enemies, further scandalize gossipmongers . . . and solidify his position as Elizabeth's favorite. Was she not but a moment ago venting her fury at him and bemoaning her tainted reputation in the European courts? What could she be thinking of? But of course, thought Dudley, changeability was Elizabeth's chiefest foible . . . or virtue, depending upon one's perspective. It drove her advisors wild and kept her friends and playmates breathlessly entertained.

"Elizabeth, this is impossible!" he cried with obvious delight. He turned to find Elizabeth smiling mischievously at him.

"I am the Queen, and I do as I please," she said resolutely, then thought to herself, I may choose never to marry, but I shall not be without pleasure in my life.

At the same instant each took a step toward the other, and then in a moment they were in each other's arms. In quiet ecstasy Dudley breathed in Elizabeth's natural perfume, delicate and powdery like the rarest of white birds, and she his familiar masculine scent tinged with a horsey musk. Then in Robin Dudley's kingly bed, he made long-awaited and passionate love to the Queen of England.

Three

On this eve of the New Year of 1561, thought Lady Mary Sidney as she put the finishing touches to the Queen's toilette, Her Majesty could only be compared to a precious gem — a fine cut diamond, brilliant and lustrous, reflecting off her many facets all the light round about her, but burning with a fire from within as well.

Lady Mary, herself a beautiful woman with features as fair and delicate as porcelain, adored her mistress. Mary's special fondness, she had to admit, stemmed in good measure from the love Elizabeth bore her elder brother, Robin Dudley. She and the Queen shared a common bond in Robert and enjoyed lavishing upon him all manner of affection.

Mary thought, too, that she liked the Queen well in her own right. 'Twas a joy to intimately attend such a magnificent woman, so lovely to look at, the fine white skin, pleasing aquiline features, and that unruly sunburst of hair. Elizabeth, despite her tempers and exasperatingly capricious moods, was bursting with vitality, exhilarating to be around, and very kind to her friends.

"All right, Mary, let me have a look at myself," said Elizabeth finally. Mary Sidney stepped aside and the Queen swept past into her mirrored bathing chamber. She enjoyed this ritual — clothing herself in the most opulent silks and velvets, brocades and furs, with glittering jewels, painted fans, and elegant slippers, then standing in the center of the floor-to-ceiling mirrors to admire the exquisite sight from every direction.

Tonight, thought Mary as she watched Elizabeth examining herself, the Queen must realize that she had quite outdone herself in brilliance.

"I'm very vain, am I not, Mary?" said Elizabeth, coyly freeing a fraction more of her small, pale breasts from the top of her satin bodice.

"You are indeed, Your Majesty. But you deserve to be vain, for you are very, very beautiful."

Elizabeth smiled broadly, her small teeth gleaming in the candlelight like pearls. She did so love to be admired. "Will our Robin think so?"

"He will be overcome," said Mary with grave sincerity.

Elizabeth turned and grasped her lady's hands. "Isn't it wonderful having him home, Mary? The Court felt dead to me, empty without him. I haven't been myself. I feel that I can somehow breathe easier knowing he is here."

"I too, Madame," said Mary, warmed by the Queen's words. "I too."

"Well, let me look at *you,*" said Elizabeth, turning her gaze on Mary. "You're looking lovely tonight. Your husband should find you very fetching. But I think" — Elizabeth strode back into her bedchamber, where several other ladies were putting away the gowns and jewelry she had chosen not to wear — "you are missing something. Come here, Mary."

Mary Sidney followed Elizabeth to a small chest filled with glittering ear bobs and watched as the Queen picked out a pair of sapphire teardrops mounted in gold filigree. Elizabeth held them up against Mary's blue velvet bodice.

"A good match. Here, put them on."

"Thank you, Your Majesty," murmured Lady Mary, deeply touched. She was aware of all the other ladies' eyes upon her, the waves of petty jealousy usually reserved for her brother now directed at herself. Mary straightened her back, and as she fastened on the sapphire ear bobs she suddenly understood how Robin was able to bear the hatred directed against him: Elizabeth's love, like a great cleansing wave, swept away all that was foul and malicious, leaving nothing but the undivided devotion of those who truly cared about her. Mary Sidney turned and smiled graciously at the gaggle of scowling ladies, then followed Elizabeth out her bedchamber door.

A festive group was now assembled in the Presence Chamber — the Queen's inner circle. When Elizabeth swept in, a stunned silence fell over the guests. She looked this night, as Mary Sidney had observed, radiant, indeed almost otherworldly. The men bowed, the women curtsied, and Elizabeth, releasing them from the initial moment of formality, began moving amongst them. The Queen was overflowing with good humor, genuinely happy to see these loyal friends and relatives. She moved first to her devoted secretary, William Cecil, who knelt and kissed her hand.

"I'm glad to see you've left your sober faces at home tonight, Sir William. We are here for a celebration, are we not?"

"Indeed, Madame. We have much to celebrate in this New Year. A hard won peace with France, a reformed currency, religious settlement. No mean feats for any monarch."

"And especially a *woman,* he did not add," teased Elizabeth, dandling Cecil's collar playfully.

She next turned to Mary's husband, Sir Henry Sidney, a man of soft voice and soft-edged features that belied a sharp mind and a firm, upstanding character. He doted on his beautiful wife, and she on him. Elizabeth was very fond of the pair and now accepted Henry's obeisance with a compliment to Mary for her especial tenderness in caring for the Queen's person.

With a gentle word to Kat and John Ashley, her guardians since early childhood, Elizabeth moved on to a group whom she recognized as her Boleyn relations, all newly raised to positions of honor in the Court since her reading of her mother's secret diary. The sudden and unexpected elevations of Lord Howard of Effingham, Francis Knollys, and young Lord Hunsdon had proven a pleasant shock to them. Until her accession, Elizabeth had not spoken her mother's name for more than twenty years. She had always accepted Queen Anne's appalling official reputation as traitor and adulteress, and had distanced herself from the shame of her ignominious death. The Queen's maternal relatives, who for the safety of their families had buried their connection and laid a cloak of silence over Anne's memory, were now lifted by Elizabeth's loving hand to high office. This evening their greetings to her were effusive and most sincere.

Finally Elizabeth approached her lover, who stood with his only living brother, Ambrose, a slighter version of Robert Dudley but every bit as handsome and graceful, and sharing in his comely reserve. In unison the brothers executed their lowest and most theatrical courtiers' bows, which wrenched a laugh from the Queen's throat.

"My lords Fric and Frac. Have you a little jig to go with your performance?"

"For Your Gracious Majesty we will invent one," replied Ambrose Dudley.

Elizabeth caught and held Robin's eye.

"What is your secret, Majesty?" he asked. "Each time I think you could never appear more beautiful, you outdo yourself once again."

"If I told you, Robin, it would no longer be my secret. Therefore," she said, caressing his tanned cheek with her long white fingers, "I shall remain an enigma."

With a gallant gesture Robin Dudley offered his arm to the Queen, and together they led her nearest and dearest into the eve of the New Year.

The congregation in the Great Hall was gay and glittering, buzzing in anticipation of the Queen's coming. Her entourage this night would include the infamous Dudley, a man more hated than loved, more feared than respected. The Tudor court was always a place of divers gossip and scandal, but this evening all the talk boiled round Robin and Elizabeth . . . and Amy Dudley's death.

Near the specially erected stage where a play would soon be performed stood a group of ladies and gentlemen, their heads tilted together, keeping their voices discreet.

"They say Lady Dudley drove every servant from the house to go to the fair, leaving her all alone," said Lady Norbert. "A strange thing for a woman so ill to do."

"I'm told she had a strange mind," added Lord Mayhew. "'Tis very suspicious to me. I say it was suicide."

"Aye, her closest servant, Pinto she is called, claimed the lady prayed daily on her knees to God to deliver her from desperation," offered Mrs. Fortescue, fanning herself furiously as though the gossip were making her perspire.

"There was much to be desperate about," said Lady Norbert, as cool as Mrs. Fortescue was overheated. "The cancer in her breast. Her husband waiting for her to die."

"I think he did not wait for her to die," announced Doctor Fortescue, a portly, ruddy-faced gentleman. "Dudley is a man too single-mindedly bent upon marrying the Queen to have left it to chance."

"You give him too little credit, Fortescue," insisted Mayhew. "Dudley is a clever man. Why would he risk such an accusation if his wife was bound to die sooner rather than later?"

Lady Winter, whispering to make her opinion seem more important, interjected, "I've heard tell of a woman with that same malady whose neck had turned so brittle it *snapped* when she walked down a step. And Amy Dudley was found at the bottom of a long stair."

Across the Great Hall a rather more grave argument was in progress. These men of the Privy Council had all eyes fastened upon a tall, blond Swedish prince glittering in a gem-studded doublet of cloth of gold. He was surrounded by his own delegation as well as English courtiers currying favor.

"Now that Dudley is back," observed Lord Clinton, "Prince John will have no more luck gaining Elizabeth's hand than his brother Eric had."

"Less," said Lord Arundel morosely. "For now the Gypsy is free to marry, and 'tis said the Queen's affection for him is intact."

"Well, she must marry and she must marry soon," insisted Lord North. "She will certainly choose one of the Spanish archdukes."

With mention of the Spaniards, all eyes naturally sought Bishop de Quadra, the short, squat man robed in black and red, ambassador from the court of Philip II of Spain. He was listening with tightly knit brows to a conversation between two ambassadors from Brussels. The bishop was a good listener — some thought too good. It was well known that de Quadra was Philip's spy, and wrote copious dispatches to the king daily, filled with official intelligence as well as backstairs gossip regarding the wholly unsavory heretic queen and her court.

"She is stubborn," pronounced Lord Clinton, resuming the Privy Councillors' conversation. "The past two years have proven as much."

"Even she must realize the urgency of producing an heir," reasoned North. "She claims to love England, but without a successor the threat of civil war, or worse, Spain and France fighting on English soil, hangs over all of our heads!"

"She will try to marry Dudley," growled Arundel, "and we know that Dudley will die trying to marry her."

Norfolk, ablaze with the highness of his lineage and title — England's only living duke — spoke very quietly, and everyone leaned close to listen. "There is not a man in England who can suffer the idea of Robert Dudley as our king. I tell you, if he does not abandon his present pretensions, he may not die in his bed."

At that there was a flurry of murmuring and whispers, even some laughter.

Lord Suffolk, himself a man of unquestionable lineage and no little importance, spoke with authority. "You all know I have no love for Robert Dudley. But I say we must let the Queen choose after her own affection. We know that children are more readily conceived within the midst of passion than without. And if what England so desperately needs is a child of the Queen's body, does it not seem wise to let her take a man whose sight arouses her desire? That, I tell you, is the surest way to deliver us a blessed prince."

A fanfare of trumpets cut short the gossiping as the Queen and her intimates arrived in the Great Hall. Even those amongst them who had reason to grumble were overwhelmed by the radiant splendor of Elizabeth this night. Guests of a certain age could not help but compare the Queen's presence and physicality to her father's. Only the oldest of her Boleyn relatives did perceive any resemblance to her mother. Each and every one, nevertheless, found himself drawn into her gossamer web, spun of wit and grace and magnetic charm. The year 1561 had not yet been born, but its promise was as resplendent as the Queen of England herself.

Four

Robin Dudley, still clad in a fine lawn nightshirt, sat motionless as Tamworth snipped his master's red-brown beard. The manservant had laid out in readiness across the bed Lord Dudley's work garments — buff hose, leather vest and doublet rubbed soft with use, and thigh-high riding boots.

'Twas a perfect day, thought Dudley as he stared out the mullioned window at the crisp winter dawn, perfect to put his intrigue into play. Though remnants of ugly rumor about his involvement in Amy's death persisted, the affair was well and truly over. Robin Dudley was a free man now, and higher in the Queen's favor than any courtier had been before. His determination to marry her had never been so fierce nor so sharply refined. He was, self-admittedly, ambitious to a fault and would have been lying had he claimed he did not wish to be king of England. But, he asked himself, who better for the task? He was an Englishman of noble blood, had proven himself a brave and resourceful soldier during Queen Mary's reign, and, even his detractors had to concede, was a brilliant administrator.

More important, thought Robin as he stood and allowed Tamworth to pull the nightshirt off over his head, he loved the Queen truly, lusted for her even. The words of endearment that he whispered in moments of private passion — as well as his public protestations of devotion — were utterly sincere. Elizabeth moved him as no other woman had, her mighty intellect stirring him as greatly as her physical attraction. She was not a beauty in the traditional sense. She was too tall, too thin, too angular. But the fire in her spirit had become the fuel to his own flame, and he fully believed that Elizabeth Tudor was his great and fortunate destiny. All obstacles that had come before, all that would be thrown up before him, were meaningless, for he and his childhood friend were decidedly meant to be husband and wife.

A sharp knock at his bedchamber door sent Tamworth scurrying to open it. Dudley's brother-in-law Henry Sidney, attired for riding, brushed past the manservant with a minimal greeting. Sidney was all business this morning. Too overwrought to sit, he paced as he talked.

"How do you think he will like it?" began Sidney nervously.

"Bishop de Quadra? I think he will be intrigued. I stand well with the Spaniards. King Philip regards me with high esteem for my military service to him in the Neapolitan wars."

"But for Philip to throw the whole weight of his support behind your marriage to the Queen . . . ?"

"His reward would be far greater than his expenditure of favor," said Dudley, lifting one leg and then the other for Tamworth to pull the boots over each well-muscled calf. "After all, what Philip desires above all else is an England under his control once more, a Catholic country as it was when he was married to Elizabeth's sister."

Tamworth strapped on Dudley's sword and dagger, making final adjustments to the Horsemaster's attire. Outfitted thus, he was as virile and handsome as any man at Court . . . and he knew it.

"See to my purple velvet costume for this evening, Tamworth. I'll need fresh linen and new hose."

"Yes, my lord."

"Come, Henry, I have business at the stables before de Quadra arrives for your ride."

As they strode down the palace corridors, they kept their voices discreetly low, their eyes ever alert for spies upon their conversation. There were men who would pay handsomely to be privy to the business of the Queen's favorite.

"Are you quite sure you have the Queen's consent for this plan, Robin? I myself see no harm in Catholicism being restored, and papal authority renewed, but Elizabeth has struggled so fiercely to establish the New Religion in England. Would she now let Philip dictate policy on English soil, as your plan supposes, or put down Protestant heresy? It means her begging and groveling to Spain, all for the honor of marrying you."

"I know it sounds mad," whispered Dudley. "But do you think the Queen has installed me in the apartments adjoining hers for no reason? She loves me truly, Henry."

"I do not doubt it."

"And she has told me countless times that she is the Queen and will do as she pleases. When she lies in my arms she swears over and over again that she will have no other man."

"And as we all know she must marry . . ." added Sidney.

"She will marry *me!*" said Dudley with quiet conviction.

They had arrived at a long low brick building that housed the royal stables. Equerries and stable boys snapped to attention at the Horsemaster's approach, and as he passed, Dudley acknowledged each with a smile or a slight nod of the head.

"But at the price of Spanish domination of England?" persisted Sidney. "I cannot help but think . . ."

Dudley stopped and turned to face Henry Sidney squarely.

"'Tis simply the way to accomplish my goal, Henry. A means to an end. I am a Protestant at heart and have no wish to be ruled by Philip or Rome. But I do know that once Elizabeth and I are married" — he seemed overcome with the thought — "*everything* is possible." Robin approached the stall of a handsome grey mare and entered it, sidling up to the horse and stroking its powerful neck. "And besides," he added flippantly, "treaties are oftentimes broken."

"Broken treaties provoke wars," insisted Sidney.

"Jackie," Robin called to a grubby young man spreading hay in the next stall, "bring Great Savoy round for Sir Henry, if you please."

Dudley began brushing the mare with a stiff brush, and she nuzzled him affectionately. The man did have an extraordinary way with horses, thought Henry Sidney. Elizabeth's appointment of him as Horsemaster was most fitting.

"So you will *not* speak on my behalf to Bishop de Quadra, then?" Robin inquired, seemingly unperturbed.

"I haven't said that. I simply require some assurance that I'm not stepping into a hornet's nest. We know that the queen bee's stinger is long and very sharp indeed."

"I take it my sister is still annoyed with me over the affair of Archduke Charles," said Dudley.

"Mary's forgiven you because you are her brother and she adores you, but she was humiliated and mortified by your involving her in your devious marriage intrigues," said Sidney as the stable boy returned with a magnificent stallion. "She'll not likely involve herself again — and she has no idea what I'm about to do."

"Then you *will* help me!" cried Robin, clapping an arm round Henry Sidney.

"I've said I will and I'm good for my word. I swear, Robert, you charm me as handily as you do women."

Dudley led both horses outside just as the diminutive black-clad Spanish ambassador approached.

"Good morning, Bishop," said Robin with a respectful bow.

"Good morning to you, Lord Robert, Sir Henry," replied de Quadra, his accent thick as Spanish honey.

"Your mounts are ready, gentlemen," announced the Horsemaster.

"You have given me Speedwell again, I see," said de Quadra, stroking the beast's muzzle and examining the taut muscle of her right front leg.

"You liked her well the last time you rode," said Robin, "and her foreleg is healed altogether. You'll have a fine ride."

Henry Sidney had already mounted his horse, and Robin himself gave the Spanish ambassador a leg up.

"Godspeed, gentlemen!" cried Dudley as the men took off at a fast trot. "And good luck to you, Henry," he called after them. But the pair were already out of hearing.

Once they were out of sight, Robin saddled his own mount. He needed a place to give his mind free rein, to dream about the good news his brother-in-law would soon bring him of his fate and future. And for Robin Dudley that place was the back of a horse. He flung himself gracefully onto the beast's back and with the merest coaxing — for his communication with these animals was exquisitely refined — they were off, flying at a full gallop out the gates of Whitehall Palace.

Five

'Twas the season's first water party and Dudley, Grand Master of the Revels, had once again outdone himself. Weather had obliged, the March sun spreading its warmth and light over the Thames. Hundreds of small, gaily festooned vessels wound with the tide on its curved course down from Greenwich through the reedy water meadows toward the sea. A large sailing fleet of white swans cruised in majestic escort alongside the royal barge, giving the Queen an extra measure of delight in an already exquisite day.

On the foredeck Robin stood with Henry Sidney gazing out over the clear water, which sparkled like a broad basket of jewels. The men were smiling, full of confidence, pleased with the results of their latest efforts. At Henry's urging, Bishop de Quadra had written to King Philip, and the Spanish monarch had indicated his support for Dudley's marriage to Elizabeth. Even now de Quadra sat with the Queen on the poop of the barge, her special guest this day, for viewing the entertainments and water games.

"The bishop tells me Elizabeth has said she shall have to marry someone, and that she believes her subjects wish her to choose an Englishman," said Henry in a low confidential voice. "And better still, the ambassador claims that Philip would be especially pleased if the Englishman were yourself, as he has always been very fond of you."

Dudley could not help but puff with satisfaction. "How close I am to success," he whispered fiercely. "I think only Elizabeth's timidity holds her back now."

"I say you should take the manly course, entreat the Queen in a headlong manner to marry you before Easter."

Dudley inhaled deeply. "Wish me luck then, Henry. 'Tis as good a day as any."

As he reached the poop, Robin could see de Quadra and the Queen sitting side by side, heads together, sharing a laugh. He could hear that they conversed in Spanish, a tongue Elizabeth spoke as fluently as English.

"Perfect," said Dudley to himself. "They are of good cheer. Let me just find my way into the matter —"

"Lord Robert!" called de Quadra heartily, spotting Dudley. He continued to speak in Spanish. "Come join us. We are very much enjoying this entertainment of yours."

"Did you see the mock battle of the frogs and fishes?" Dudley inquired, referring to the colorful floats manned by outrageously costumed aquatic figures.

"If the frogs were the French," asked Elizabeth tartly, "then who were the fishes?"

"Who won the battle?" said Robin, answering question with question.

"The fishes," replied de Quadra.

"Then the fishes were English, of course," said Dudley with a charming grin.

They all laughed merrily, and suddenly Robin Dudley, gazing over the rail into the water, found that his prayers had been answered. From the raft of swans to starboard, two birds had pulled ahead, gliding side by side as though leading a stately procession. Dudley acted quickly. There was no telling how long the formation would last thusly.

"See the happy couple," he said, directing Elizabeth's and de Quadra's gaze to the swans. "The bride and groom and their wedding party."

Elizabeth looked up at Robin with startled eyes. He held them brazenly for a long moment, then plunged into the boiling cauldron.

"Bishop de Quadra, you and I and the Queen are all present on this already marvelous occasion. Why do you not marry us here and now?"

Elizabeth's eyes blazed, and Robin could not discern if they flashed with anger or excitement. Elizabeth smiled and took de Quadra's hand in hers.

"My lord bishop," said the Queen carefully, "what think you of my sweet Robin's proposal? Would you marry us?"

Dudley's heart fluttered strangely and he hardly dared to take his next breath.

"But I wonder," she added coyly, "that you may not have enough English to perform such a ritual. And of course, it *must* be done in English."

A clever feint, thought Robin. Neither an assent nor a rejection.

Dudley's suggestion at such a time in such a place had startled the bishop somewhat more than it had the Queen. He became serious then, and addressed her directly.

"Heretics continue to despoil England, Your Majesty. Rid yourself of them," he urged, pressing her hand between his own. "If you and Lord Robert will restore the True Religion, Philip will bless your marriage, and I . . ." He was barely able to speak, so overcome was he with the thought that in this moment he might give his king the one gift he most ardently desired: a Catholic England. "I shall be honored to be the priest presiding over that ceremony."

The smile never left Elizabeth's face, but Robin wondered, as he watched her, what lay behind that smile. He had made his bid as boldly as a man could have done. His suit was supported by the King of Spain as fully as he had dreamed. "Elizabeth," Dudley cried silently. "Elizabeth, consent. Make me the happiest man on earth!"

"You are very kind, Bishop." The Queen looked up warmly at Robin, grasping his hand. "You know of my deep feelings for Lord Robert. I shall give both your proposals some good thought. Ah, look there!" Elizabeth pointed to a seaweed-covered barge coming alongside them where mermaids and mermen lay about surrounding an enthroned Poseidon. The god-king raised his mock gold trident to the Queen, and she raised her hand to him, a triumphant salute.

"I do so love my subjects!" Elizabeth exclaimed.

'Twas a passion, Robin observed with a sinking sensation, that would have been far better directed at himself. The Queen had managed once again to outsmart him, evade him, slip through his hands like a wiggling eel.

"Damn her, damn her!" he cried inwardly. Then affixing a pleasant smile on his bemused face, Lord Robert Dudley regathered his wits and resumed the intricate courtier's dance.

Six

On a morning dark as dusk with the gloom of heavy rain, the royal carriage rumbled down the rutted highway. Men of the Queen's guard muttered curses against not the wet but the cold of this Easter storm. The winter had been interminable, the Thames frozen over many times. In weeks past the warm days had heralded spring, trees rioting with pale green buds, delicate wildflowers poking up in patches of soft grass. And now this. Numbing cold rain and Her Majesty refusing to postpone the journey to Mortlake.

Inside the carriage its occupants felt neither the wet nor the chill nor suffered the bone-rattling ride, for they were snug in cheerful good company. The Queen, attended by those dearest to her — Robin Dudley, Lady Mary Sidney, Henry Sidney, and their seven-year-old son Philip — was in high spirits. So comfortable and boisterous were these five, with ideas and arguments tumbling from their mouths like water from a fountain, that they shouted over each other to be heard, then laughed good-naturedly at their own rudeness.

"John Dee seeks nothing more than educational reform!" cried Robin Dudley.

"Reform? He seeks nothing less than revolution, Robin! He would, if he could, change the entire curriculum at Oxford and Cambridge, discarding classical humanistic studies, imposing Hermetic sciences and, worse, *mathematics,* which, as our childhood tutor Roger Ascham would say, is a little suspect, mayhaps even diabolic."

"And *my* tutor Doctor John Dee —" Robin persisted.

"And mine —" added Mary Sidney playfully.

"And soon to be mine —" piped in young Philip.

"*Our* illustrious tutor taught us" — Robin wrapped an affectionate arm round his little nephew — "and will soon teach you, Philip, not only mathematics but practical *applications* of that science."

"Even you must admit, Your Majesty," added the mild-mannered Henry Sidney, "that counting and bookkeeping with Roman numerals is more clumsy and time-consuming than with arabic numbers."

"I have no quarrel with practical mathematics, Henry, but Dee and his brothers in Hermeticism make wild claims that 'number' is the key to truth itself, that without it one has no understanding of the universe. Preposterous!"

Certain that his next words would provoke an explosive reaction, Robin spoke directly to Elizabeth. "I agree with Doctor Dee that, in fact, 'number' was the pattern of God's mind during creation."

"You cannot believe that, Robin!" said the Queen.

"But I do," he replied evenly. "I have all good faith in John Dee. He is the most brilliant mind in England and I know you agree."

"I do, but —"

"And you were so mad with anticipation for this visit to his home that nothing — not a headache yesterday nor foul weather today — could keep you from it."

"I have the deepest esteem for Doctor Dee. He is a great philosopher and scholar, navigator and cartographer. He has written an elegant translation of Euclid's *Elements* and finds many ways to serve his country with his learning. Only last month he offered up an interesting plan to reorganize our entire fishing industry. More important," she added, "he has the most magnificent library in all of England. Four thousand books! Oxford and Cambridge together have less than one quarter that amount." Then her expression changed to something close to disdain. "But of his beliefs in occultism, apocalyptic numbers, cabalistic formulas, and magical inscriptions, I do have serious doubts."

"So you have *not* come to see his gazing table, and will refuse to let him tell your future?" teased Henry Sidney.

"Do you mean his magic mirror, Father?" asked Philip Sidney. "Does he really have such a wonderful thing?"

"I'm told he has," answered the elder Sidney. "And if he does, we shall all soon see it."

The little boy clapped his hands with excitement and the others smiled indulgently.

"I think the Queen makes light of her interest in the occult sciences," offered Robin, intent on reviving their argument. "She did, after all, have Dee cast her horoscope to find the most auspicious day for her coronation."

"On *your* insistent urging!" Elizabeth retorted. "And besides, one can hardly count astrology as occult. 'Tis common knowledge that the stars affect man's fate and fortune." Elizabeth thought of but did not mention something she had read in Anne Boleyn's diary — a prophecy given her mother by the half-mad Holy Maid of Kent, one that had steered Anne's fate, and therefore Elizabeth's own. It was a seeing that told of Anne's becoming queen, the birth of her "Tudor sun," and that child's reign of four-and-forty years. The first two aspects of the prophecy had come to pass, mused Elizabeth, but any well-informed person of that time might have guessed that the dark-eyed beauty so hotly pursued by King Henry might become his queen and would almost certainly bear a child. As for herself reigning forty-four years, Elizabeth was extremely dubious. She was already twenty-seven. A woman still reigning as queen at age seventy? She thought not.

"You would do well to be more discerning about these Hermetic beliefs, my dear Robin, and not follow so blindly after every word this man proffers."

"Do you believe in the teachings of Moses, Your Majesty?" asked Mary Sidney.

"By all means, Mary," replied the Queen, startled by her waiting lady's question.

"Moses himself was instructed in the ancient Egyptian and Hermetic texts which say that magic is simply the knowledge of natural things. He was a man who had power in both his words and his works, do you not agree?"

Elizabeth realized with sudden annoyance that she had blundered into a trap. But it was too late. Mary went on.

"Therefore if Moses, who was simply a learned man, practiced magic, why then should a learned man such as John Dee not do the same?"

Elizabeth slumped back into her cushioned seat, defeated. "There are four of you and only one of me," she groused. "I shall never win this argument."

"Will you keep an open mind at least?" urged Robin Dudley. "Accept the possibility that mathematics and the occult have a true place in philosophy?"

"When have I ever lacked an open mind, Robin? I will give our Doctor Dee every chance to convince me of his strange sciences."

"Look!" young Philip suddenly cried, pulling back the curtain. "The rain has stopped."

Indeed, the downpour had ended and the air wafted round their faces fresh and sweet. They could see trees still dripping with moisture, and the sun peeking through what remained of the black clouds. Robin thrust his head out the coach window for a moment, then turned to his friends.

"We've arrived at Mortlake," he announced with a smile. "The adventure begins."

An ancient and rambling farmhouse of many pieces and several levels, all cobbled together haphazardly, came into view. Waiting to meet their guests at the door stood the great man himself, his wife Katherine, and their eldest son Arthur, thirteen. The carriage clattered to a halt and Elizabeth had a glimpse of the spindly, middle-aged Dee, his long triangular beard and piercing blue eyes. The Queen's men scrambled down from their mounts to take up positions near the entrance, and footmen pulled open the carriage doors, helping the passengers to alight.

There was a flurry of excited chatter and warm embraces all round between the Dudleys and the Dees. To the Queen her hosts offered their most sincere obeisance. But Elizabeth, happily informal with her previous company, desired to extend that same informality to the Dees, and so they were in good cheer as they entered the farmhouse, all weariness of the journey forgotten, and shut the heavy wooden door behind them.

Dinner of mutton pie and roasted quail was served almost immediately after their arrival, for it was the plan that they should have as much of the daylight hours as possible to wander amidst the doctor's libraries and laboratories. Conversation and argument continued over the meal as it had in the carriage — lively, loud, good-natured. For Elizabeth this was an especial delight, to be far from the rigid protocol of Court, the constant malicious gossip, the never-ending responsibilities. Here she was a girl in the classroom again, with no need to impose her will or always have her way. It was, she concluded, a great meeting of minds at this table — brilliant men, intelligent women, even interesting children, all participating, all exchanging information and ideas.

Young Philip Sidney and Arthur Dee had become fast friends the moment they'd clapped eyes on each other. Philip, younger by half a dozen years and still a beautiful child with wavy dark hair and searching brown eyes, was razor sharp, brimming with wonder and anticipation of the day ahead. Arthur was self-possessed for his years, naturally well-mannered and already exuding the inquisitive air of a scholar. Certainly he was in awe of the Queen sitting at his family's table, but the young man took little time to realize that he could speak his mind as freely as with his own kin.

"Not sixty years ago," said Arthur Dee gravely, "we thought the circumference of the entire world was twenty thousand miles, that we could get to the Indies by sailing west, and that the sun and all the universe revolved round the earth."

"I take it, then, that you subscribe to the teachings of Copernicus, Arthur," said the Queen with equal gravity. "That neither biblical evidence nor God's own voice speaking through his church prove that the earth is the center of the universe? That the firmament moves because the earth rotates?"

"I do believe full well in the theories of Copernicus, Your Majesty," he pronounced firmly. "His calculations showing the earth rotating on its axis, and the planets revolving round the sun, are most logical."

"Indeed," said Elizabeth with a smile, "we live in wondrous times. First the shape of the world is called into doubt, and now the shape of the heavens themselves. We must be very brave to meet the future, for we have little idea what our explorations might bring us."

"I pray they bring us no more destruction such as Señor Cortez visited upon the conquered peoples of the New World," grumbled John Dee. "The Spaniards burned the ancient Mayan libraries, saying the books contained nothing but superstitions and falsehoods about the devil. *Think* of what was lost to us in that one act of idiocy."

"Unpardonable. Like the Turks when they burned the library at Alexandria," added Mary Sidney.

"Oh, oooh," moaned Dee, seeming almost in physical pain at the thought. "What we might have learned from those texts . . ."

"Come, John," crooned Katherine Dee soothingly. "What's done is done. You'll upset your stomach crying over lost libraries."

"Speaking of libraries," said Robin Dudley with determined cheerfulness, "might we begin our afternoon's pleasures in yours, Doctor?"

"Yes, yes," said Dee, pushing back his bench and regathering his good spirits. "I've added a new room to the others, you must have noticed when you drove in."

Everyone stood, Philip nearly knocking his stool over in excitement.

"I've done — I should say Arthur and I have done — a great deal of work on our collection, have we not, boy?" Arthur Dee puffed with silent pride at his father's approbation. "We've separated the books and manuscripts into those of philosophy, science, mathematics, Hermetic sciences . . ." Dee, churning with enthusiasm, was already out one door through a curtained archway into another room when Robin Dudley offered the Queen his arm. With an anticipatory gleam in her eyes Elizabeth took it, and together they strode into Doctor Dee's fantastical world.

Even at the height of the afternoon the light was faint in the musty rooms of England's greatest library, for the doctor had, besides the neat rows of books lining the shelves, so many volumes stacked on tables and in piles on the threadbare Turkey carpet that the small windows were nearly blocked by them.

Elizabeth's senses were at once alive with the musk of vellum and leather and ink in her nostrils, the hushed and whispering tones most naturally assumed in the presence of such splendor, the muted colors of the wood and paper, the sizes and shapes of books — some small enough to fit inside a lady's hand, others when opened covering the breadth of a table. Here was an illuminated medieval manuscript lying open to be studied, here a parchment scroll in Hebrew text, its curling ends held down by carven Egyptian stones, there a mariner's map of the African coast.

The library was not one vast chamber, rather a warren of small rooms and alcoves and window seats, all crammed with books. John and Arthur Dee shadowed their guests, holding up mirrored candles for extra light as they roved amongst the stacks quietly reading titles, perhaps choosing one to be pulled down from the shelves and reverently laid upon a table for perusal.

For Elizabeth, and she knew for the others as well, such a place as this conjured up childhood memories of the schoolroom, the first brilliant moments of a young mind's life of learning — seeking, thirsting, feeding greedily upon the words and ideas of the great masters, ancient languages. Even now Elizabeth spent an hour or more daily translating Greek and Latin texts as a joyful pastime. Here amongst such a vast treasure of man's greatest works she felt not so much a mighty queen as an overawed child.

Over the top of the volume she held, Elizabeth gazed at John Dee helping Lady Mary, now ensconced in a window seat, with the translation of a passage from Homer. It occurred to her then that this was a man whom she should keep close to herself, for whether she countenanced each and all of his pursuits or no, Dee was a person of eminent power and resource, and a true friend of England.

Now Robin had joined his sister and Dee, and the three were conversing ever more animatedly. Mary's eyes flashed, Dee gesticulated broadly as he made a point. Elizabeth's curiosity too much to bear, she replaced the volume she was reading on the shelf and moved quietly to the window seat.

"'Tis no wonder you've collected so many enemies, John, both Protestant and Catholic," observed Robin, "if it is true that the Hermetic texts glorify man as magus and, by virtue of his divine intellect, equate him with God."

"Yes, yes!" cried Dee. "Through intellect alone man can perform marvelous feats! The divine order is no longer man *under* God, but God and man standing shoulder to shoulder."

"You are a mystery to me, Doctor," interjected Elizabeth. "You are as pious and filled with Christian humility as a man can be, yet you are entirely arrogant in your claims of equality with God, and your pagan beliefs in magic."

"In Hermetic philosophy, Your Majesty, man is raised from awestruck observer of God's wonders to one who uses the hidden energy and power of the cosmos to his own advantage." Dee's eyes grew suddenly unfocused and he seemed almost to recede from them. "Energy is manifested in circular rays," he whispered, his hands unconsciously demonstrating his words. "Emitted from everything in the universe . . . circular rays . . ." His voice trailed off.

"And is it through the working of this 'hidden energy' that you perform your marvels, John?" Elizabeth inquired.

The question seemed to bring him back to them. Dee turned to the Queen. "*You* will perform marvels in your reign, Your Majesty," he uttered portentously, "through the coalescing of natural forces within your imagination. See the thing in your mind first!" he commanded her. "See it very clearly, and eventually it will come into being, yes!"

Elizabeth felt giddy, entirely bereft of words. Robin and Mary stared in amazement at Dee, this man who dared to speak so audaciously to a queen. He went on, his voice rising.

"You must build a great navy, yes! Advance exploration and expansion into the new territories to the west. You have examined my genealogical tables outlining your family's historical claims. Through your father, King Henry, you are come from Wales and descended from the line of Great King Arthur, Majesty. 'Tis your sacred duty to build a British empire as he once did!" Dee was trembling with emotion. "Your claim to the Atlantean lands which the Spanish call America, those lands are *yours,*" he ended, his voice rising still further.

"Father," said Arthur Dee, and placed a quieting hand on John Dee's arm.

"Forgive me, Your Majesty," mumbled Dee. He dropped to his knees before Elizabeth and took her hand in his, kissing the coronation ring and bowing his head. "Forgive me."

"There is nothing to forgive, John. You spoke plainly from your heart and mind, and I like what you say. My father laid down the great shipyards at Newport and Plymouth. Mayhaps I should put them to better use. Come, rise."

John Dee stood and Elizabeth took his arm. Together they strolled through a low archway into the science collection. Robin and Mary smiled with relief, listening to the Queen ramble on about her man Francis Drake and his first successful voyage to the New World.

"One calamity averted, dear sister," whispered Dudley. "But what adventures await us tonight in this den of pagan idolatry?"

The afternoon had passed without further incitement. All were nestled cozily amongst the great books, happy in their quiet pleasures. John Dee, in one of his practical laboratories, extolling the virtues of applied science, had demonstrated the concept of invisible energy with a large magnet, and the importance of optics, which made far-off things seem near and small things great. But he had drawn sniffs of disbelief from even his most ardent supporters when he described how a vacuum, and air pumped from a cauldron, could be employed to keep a man under the sea for a time.

The rain had begun again after a light supper, but since the party would lodge at Mortlake that night there was no alarm, and the evening proceeded at a leisurely pace.

The boys abed, John Dee cleared his throat loudly. With an almost mischievous grin showing his long ivory teeth, his bony fingers thumping his chest, he inquired, "Would you care to taste a little of the magic arts?"

Where the friends had sat moments before were now but empty benches, for they had risen as one, and with such enthusiasm that there was great laughter all round. They walked back through the nest of library rooms and reassembled at the closed door of an as yet unexplored chamber. Dee unlocked the door and, with a twelve-pronged candelabra in hand, led his guests into his famous magic laboratory.

This odd room had five equal sides, the floor painted with lines from corner to corner in a five-pointed star. The chamber was devoid of furniture or books, save one overlarge volume which lay open on a pedestal and appeared ancient and well worn. Dead center in the room, within the pentagon formed by the lines of the star, was an object four feet square, waist high, covered entirely by a black silk drape painted in red with mystical symbols.

"The magic which I practice, Your Majesty," Dee began, ignoring the group's quizzical stares at the object, "*Hermetic* magic, is none other than the science of the divine. 'Tis a direct revelation from God, you must understand, and therefore cannot possibly be evil. You may not know that Hermes Trismegistus — the most pious of Egyptian priests who lived before the time of Christ, and whose original treatises form the basis of the Hermetic tradition — actually foretold the coming of Christianity, yes!" Dee paused only long enough to take a breath. "As you have noted, Majesty, I am a religious man, and you should know that the highest attainment I seek through my magic is salvation through divine abilities . . . albeit *without* the church's intervention and with only God's help."

Elizabeth refrained from replying, from acknowledging Dee's apology, or otherwise speaking, for she knew this was the lecture of a great teacher, and she was humble before him.

"'Tis common knowledge," he went on, "that the stars influence everything on earth, bathing all in their heavenly effluvia. The magus performs his many marvels by manipulation of those effluvia. A magician such as myself could, theoretically, change the stars themselves, even control the heavenly powers, yes!"

Elizabeth was thunderstruck at the boldness of Dee's statement but she forced herself to remain silent.

"My body, however, would be entirely destroyed in the attempt," he added with a wry smile, "so I will refrain from such an experiment this evening."

At that there was a flurry of relieved laughter, and now the man strode purposefully to the center of the room where, with a great sweeping gesture, he flung the black silken drape from the object hidden beneath it. There were low gasps all round, for in the many years of the Dudley family's friendship and tutoring they had never been allowed the sight of Doctor Dee's magic accoutrements.

The object was a four-sided claw-footed table of normal height, though that was where the normalcy ended. Painted in an astonishing kaleidoscope of brilliant colors — vermillion, royal blue, pea green, violet — its carven sides were covered in characters, hieroglyphs, and esoteric names written all in vivid yellow. A seal had been placed under the four claw feet, and a great seal was set in the center of the table. The tabletop itself was covered in bright red silk, and upon the central seal sat a smooth, perfectly round black crystal gazing glass.

As everyone stood gaping at the sight of the table, Dee had been lighting a multitude of candles set round the room's perimeter, so that now the gazing glass blazed with a brilliant reflection.

"Move back . . . if you please," said Doctor Dee to his guests as he pulled two benches up to opposite sides of the table. "Madame." He gestured for Elizabeth to take a seat on one bench and, with no fanfare, took the other. Then he reached across and grasped each of her hands in his own.

The room was suddenly still, those assembled loath even to breathe too heavily. There was portent in the air, for the Queen of England sat before the greatest magician in the land, conjuring visions of King Arthur and his magus Merlin. Robin could see the round tops of Elizabeth's milky breasts heaving rhythmically, and a single bead of sweat forming at her temple. She bit her lip to stop it trembling.

John Dee closed his eyes and began to drone in measured verse a Hebrew chant in a strange, low and guttural voice that bore no resemblance to his own. Over and over he sang the words. They ran together and the unintelligible babble filled the listeners' heads with endless sound, endless sound. . . . Outside, thunder rumbled in the distance. Eyelids grew heavy. Elizabeth's were the last to close.

When John Dee spoke next, it was neither his usual voice nor the guttural one of Hebrew chanting. It was clearly the voice of a young woman. First there was a great exhalation of breath, almost a cry, "Iieeee!" Then the words, clear and simple, "I hold the hands of a queen."

There was silence. Robin Dudley, Mary and Henry Sidney, mildly startled at the woman's intonation emanating from Dee's mouth, awaited further utterances, for the words themselves had so far been unremarkable — a simple statement of fact.

But Elizabeth's eyes flew open as a shuddering bolt of recognition shook her, body and soul. These were the words, the very words spoken by the young Holy Maid of Kent, when Anne Boleyn sought to hear her future in the Convent St. Sepulchre almost thirty-four years before! How? How could it be that this man could know, could utter in that voice a prophecy given her dear mother all those years ago? The first words of the very seeing that would impel Anne to cast her fate into King Henry's hands and lead her to her doom? No one knew of it but Elizabeth and old Lady Sommerville, who had brought the diary to Elizabeth. And that lady . . .

no, 'twas impossible! The Queen peered round at the others in the candlelit shadows, their eyes still closed. No one knew her turmoil. Could they not hear her heart thumping wildly in her chest?

The magus exhaled once more, long and slow. Elizabeth held her breath, terrified of what Dee would next say. Should she stop him from continuing? No, she could not. The man, the magus, was certainly involved with the manipulation of celestial effluvia, reasoned Elizabeth. If she should interrupt him at such a time, might his body not be destroyed? She could never be responsible for such a thing!

But John Dee had grown quiet. Mayhaps, thought Elizabeth, he had finished with his seeing. Mayhaps she had imbued the simple words he'd spoken with far too much importance. He had, in fact, been holding the hands of a queen. And the young woman's voice . . . who was Elizabeth to say 'twas the Holy Maid of Kent's voice? She was simply overwrought.

But now the room had begun to change. The air had somehow thickened. There seemed to be a strange humming, though Elizabeth could not tell if it was inside her head or coming from a great distance. And suddenly her nostrils were assailed with the unmistakable scent of fresh flowers, the delicate spicy fragrance of roses . . . Tudor roses. But the room was closed. And there *were* no roses in bloom. Elizabeth began to swoon. John Dee was yet blind to the world. She looked to Robin, who stood swaying slightly, his eyes still closed. There was an almost questioning look about his beautiful face. Was he smelling the roses too?

"Ahhh," moaned John Dee.

Elizabeth turned and saw a smile soften the magician's face.

"A life," he whispered. "A soul."

What was his meaning? she wondered.

"Within you, Elizabeth" — he answered her silent question — "a child is growing."

Her heart heaved. No, he could not mean . . . Impossible! She dared not meet Robin's eyes.

"A son," cried Dee. "A son, yes!"

"Enough!" roared Elizabeth, wrenching her hands from Dee's, uncaring now of breaking a celestial spell. 'Twas a hoax, this magic! Robin and Mary Sidney rushed to the Queen's side, patting her hands and trying to comfort her. The magus, though glassy-eyed and startled with the suddenness of his return to present reality, seemed otherwise intact.

Elizabeth attempted to compose herself. Had the others heard? Did

Dee himself remember that, a moment before, he had announced that the Queen of England was pregnant with an illegitimate child?

She pushed back her chair and glared down at John Dee and his infernal gazing crystal. He was aware that something had gone terribly wrong. The Queen, he could see, was very, very angry. But helpless and momentarily weak, all he could do was lift his hand in a silent supplication of forgiveness.

"John Dee," she said finally. "I have accepted your gracious hospitality this whole day long and I am grateful for it. You are a friend of my friends and of England too. But I do not approve of your magic, for it is false, and causes you to speak falsely in its name. Good evening to you all."

She turned and, pushing out the door, was gone.

With a look to his dazed companions, Robin followed. He reached her as she marched through the darkened library.

"Elizabeth!"

"I do not wish your company."

"Please, listen."

"Listen? To what? More lies? I am not pregnant, Robin. Can never be pregnant. I do not bleed like other women. You know that."

"Yes, I know. Where are you going, Elizabeth?" She was heading to the front door of the farmhouse.

"I'm going to Greenwich."

"Tonight? Are you mad? The storm is peaking. I will not let you go!"

"You cannot make me stay."

He stood defiantly blocking her way.

"Call my carriage or I will call it myself. I will send a coach for you all tomorrow."

"Why does this upset you so? If you say you are not pregnant, then you are not. 'Twas a false seeing, my love, that is all. No need to rush away so angrily. Poor John is beside himself. He meant you no harm!"

Elizabeth felt suddenly cold, and Robin, who sensed her moods and temperatures keenly, wrapped his gentle arms about her and rocked her trembling body.

"Stay, please stay, Elizabeth. I have been dreaming of this cozy night abed with you, under no royal roof, no disapproving eyes spying on us, gossiping. Just to wake with you on a sweet spring morning in the country surrounded by friends, oh stay!"

"I am not pregnant," she said quietly but firmly.

"You are not pregnant," he replied dutifully.

"And we shall not speak of it again."

"Agreed."

"Would you make my apologies to the others?" she said more mildly. "I'm suddenly tired."

"No need. They will understand. Here, let me show you to your room." He smiled the crooked smile she so loved. "Our room."

Elizabeth felt good humors flowing back through her veins in a warm rush. 'Twould indeed be lovely to lie in a warm bed with her love this night.

"Come, Robin," she said, taking his hand. "Show me the way."

Seven

"The chin a bit higher, Majesty."

Elizabeth rolled her eyes in irritation at Master Thomas Rhys, the timid young portrait artist whom Robin had convinced her to hire, then thrust her chin skyward at an extreme angle.

"Like this?" taunted Elizabeth.

The poor young man, entirely discomposed by the uncooperativ queen, was careful to refrain from speaking impertinently.

"'Tis a bit . . . high, Madame."

Elizabeth fought the temptation to drop her chin to her chest and further upset the painter, his paintbrush suspended impotently in midair but restrained herself and leveled her chin to the perfect haughty angle she knew he desired.

"Beautiful, beautiful!" cried Rhys enthusiastically and with obvious relief.

Elizabeth felt herself flush with the compliment and was suddenly contrite. She knew she'd been irritable of late and unreasonable in the extreme. All of her servants and councillors, even Robin, had been treading lightly in her presence, but she'd made no attempt to change her behavior and continued acting the spoilt child. Kat and Lady Mary Sidney, sitting silently to one side with placid countenances staring straight ahead, dared even not exchange glances when Elizabeth was in such a temper.

With a sharp knock the Presence Chamber door opened. Sir William Cecil and Sir Nicholas Throckmorton moved forward and presented themselves to the Queen.

"Secretary Cecil." He nodded, and she then skewered Throckmorton with her gaze. "And how does my ambassador to the French court?" Elizabeth's question was sharpened to a fine edge.

"Well, Your Majesty. With much news to report."

"'Tis clear from Sir Nicholas's intelligence that we must pay strict attention to your cousin Mary, Your Majesty," offered Cecil. Alone amongst her men and ladies, William Cecil showed no fear of Elizabeth even in her most difficult moments, having served her from the earliest days of her reign, and possessing the most finely honed instincts of all her councillors. He was trustworthy, loyal, and generally unflappable.

"Now that Queen Mary's husband is dead and she is merely queen dowager in France," Cecil went on, "she is far more dangerous to you than before. A wild card. For she is still queen of Scotland and may, in her widowhood, be played in one of many directions."

"Speak to me, Throckmorton," said Elizabeth, turning to her ambassador. "Tell me the good news first."

Throckmorton hesitated, knowing full well he was riding into an ambush, with Elizabeth the entire raiding party. For what was good or bad news to the Queen depended entirely upon her mood, and her mood, he could not help but be aware, was entirely foul. He feigned an optimistic tone and began.

"Since young King Francis's death —"

"A death not unexpected," interrupted Elizabeth peevishly. "He was always feeble, always sickly. A pathetic creature, stunted in growth, a child whom his mother de Médicis was always reminding to blow his nose. He was, I am told, not a capable man at the time he married my cousin."

"The rumors were that the couple were intimate, Your Majesty. You are aware that they were childhood friends — grew up in the same household. They loved each other dearly. But no, he was by all reports not yet . . . capable. 'Twas said that Mary might have many, many children, but not by Francis."

Childhood friends, mused Elizabeth, like herself and Robin Dudley, and yet Mary's and her upbringings had been as different as they could possibly be. Her own motherless youth had been miserable. Elizabeth, rejected as a bastard by her father and the court, had been stripped of her title as princess and banished to a poor and distant household. And despite her great charm and intelligence, she had suffered from an overwhelming sense of unworthiness mitigated only by the constant, blessed love and devotion of her servants Kat and John Ashley, the Parrys, and finally her father's sixth and last wife, Catherine Parr. This upbringing she could not help but compare to her cousin Mary's. Henry VIII's own great-niece, crowned queen of Scotland at nine days old, was by some standards — Catholic standards — more deserving of the English crown than Elizabeth, child of the great whore Anne Boleyn. Henry had, in fact, attempted to betroth the infant Mary to his own son, Edward. Had the Scots nobles allowed that marriage, and had her dear brother Edward lived, thought Elizabeth with equal measures of relief and regret, Mary Queen of Scots would have been her own sovereign.

Betrothed at four to the dauphin, heir to the French throne, Mary had been brought up at the sumptuous Valois court, pampered, pleasured, embraced as one of the royal family, adored by her young husband-to-be and loved, always loved. The little queen had sailed blissfully through childhood on gossamer clouds, comfortable within her place in the world. When Francis's father, King Henry II, had died suddenly and tragically, the young couple had ascended the throne effortlessly. Mary, thought Elizabeth with a raw pang of jealousy, had never had to fight simply to survive as she herself had had to do.

"Go on, Throckmorton," commanded the Queen. "You were saying that since Francis's death . . ."

"Yes, the queen dowager has seemingly begun to know her own mind on matters —"

"As she had *not* previously, taking all guidance from her mother's family, as well as her mother-in-law de Médicis," interrupted Elizabeth again.

"She was, after all, only sixteen, her husband fifteen. But now she is showing the greatest modesty and excellent wisdom for her years."

"How so?" demanded Elizabeth.

"By thinking herself not too wise, and taking good counsel from learned elders on the matter of her remarriage . . . a great virtue in a queen, Your Majesty."

No one was prepared for Elizabeth's violent outburst as she sprang from her chair and rounded on Throckmorton, nearly knocking him off his feet.

"You blatantly contradict yourself, ambassador! First you have the queen knowing her own mind, and one breath later claim she thinks herself not too wise. That she no longer takes counsel from some, but now takes counsel from others. Which is it?"

"I am sorry, Your Majesty," Throckmorton mumbled.

"And is your estimation of the most modest Scots queen being wise to take counsel on matters of her marriage a comment on your own immodest queen refusing to do the same?"

"No, Your Majesty, never!"

Throckmorton held himself rigid to control the trembling Elizabeth's outburst had produced in him. The others seemed to fade into the walls, hoping the Queen's wrath might not be turned in their direction.

"Methinks," continued Elizabeth, pacing the room, glaring at her unfinished portrait as she passed behind the artist, now quaking in his shoes, "that Mary is a fool. She is undisputed queen two times over, yet she is eager to hand her power to men below her. Well, whom is she considering marrying?"

"The suitors are many," replied the ambassador. "Don Carlos of Spain, Philip's heir, is her first choice."

"Don Carlos!" shouted Elizabeth in outrage. "Don Carlos is an idiot, a more wretched oaf than her first husband! Small, crookbacked, cursed with the falling sickness and a lisp! He is known to fly into maniacal rages and attempt murder! Is she mad?"

"I do not know, Your Majesty. I can only assume she places dynastic considerations before personal ones."

"Who else?"

"The Earl of Arran —"

"A Scotsman," spat Elizabeth. "She will never marry a Scotsman."

"Her Valois brother-in-law Charles."

"De Médicis would never allow it. She will be rid of her darling daughter-in-law as soon as it is seemly, of that you can be sure."

"And Lord Darnley, Your Majesty."

"My cousin, Lady Lennox's son?" Elizabeth asked, perplexed.

"He holds a weak but definite place in the succession, Majesty," added Cecil quietly but firmly.

"God's death!" cried Elizabeth. "Does Mary believe that two weak claims to my throne together make a strong one? So, is she still demanding that I name her my successor?"

"*Demanding* may be too strong a word, Your —"

"And does she still refuse to ratify the Treaty of Edinburgh which Cecil negotiated last July?"

"She has declined only until she might consult with her council in Scotland, but she indicated her answer will then be favorable to you. She wishes above all else, your Majesty, to meet with you personally to discuss your differences and solidify your affection as cousins and friends."

"Does she? My cousin Mary. I hear she is overlarge for a woman. A giant," said Elizabeth, "with large floppy ears."

"She is nearly six feet tall, Majesty, but delicately boned and willowy."

"Willowy. . . . And is she as lovely as they say, Throckmorton? Tell me the truth."

The ambassador found himself suddenly speechless. Whilst his previous reports had soundly angered the Queen, he knew a truthful discussion of her younger cousin's physical attributes would drive Elizabeth to paroxysms of fury, for it was widely held that Mary was the most beautiful queen in Europe. Throckmorton chose his words with extreme care.

"Her hair is reddish gold like your own, Madame, and her eyes are the color of amber. Her skin is very pale. They say it was whiter than the white veil of mourning at her husband's death."

"Her features, Throckmorton."

"Some say her nose is too long." The ambassador was pleased to be able to report that. "And, as you say, her ears are quite large. The eyes slant upwards a bit, and her mouth . . ." Throckmorton had blundered into dangerous territory.

"Go on."

"Her mouth is well formed with a pretty curve to it, and her speaking voice" — he drove on with no road of escape — "is considered very sweet indeed."

"Unlike the voice of your harridan queen!"

"Your Majesty," interrupted Cecil. "You are acting most unreasonably with your good ambassador. You asked for a truthful report —"

"And what I have gotten . . ." Elizabeth stopped midsentence with a suddenly confused look spreading across her face. She had gone a shade paler than her normal alabaster skin tone. Her hand groped blindly for support, finding it with Cecil's arm. Kat and Mary Sidney had instantly leapt to their feet and surrounded the Queen, Mary fanning her briskly and Kat patting her cheek.

Elizabeth's lips were pursed tightly together and Kat Ashley could see that the Queen was fighting nausea. Mayhaps this was the onset of one of the Queen's migraines.

"Come, Elizabeth," Kat crooned soothingly. "Let us get you to your bed." But before the Queen could take more than a few steps toward the door, she fell into a dead faint.

"No!" shouted the Queen, slapping away Kat's ministering hands. "I am not pregnant!"

The elder waiting lady sat still as stone at Elizabeth's bedside, her expression almost as horrified as her mistress's. Mary Sidney stood a few paces away wringing her hands in silence, but otherwise the royal bedchamber was empty, all waiting women sent far from sight and hearing.

"I have seen too many pregnant women to be wrong, Your Majesty. You have all the signs."

A wild-eyed Elizabeth looked to Lady Mary for reassurance that Kat was somehow mistaken, but Mary stood firm, meeting and holding the Queen's pleading gaze. "John Dee foretold it, Madame. And the symptoms are there," she said.

"Damn the symptoms!" cried Elizabeth, then suddenly, with one hand slapped to her mouth, gestured to Kat for the basin. The Queen vomited prodigiously, then lay back on her pillows and began to weep.

"I warned you, Elizabeth," scolded Kat sternly. "Warned you time and again that no good would come of this untoward passion. Now it is too late, and all that you have fought your whole life to have, that which you and I, my husband, the Parrys have sacrificed and nearly lost our lives to secure, is forfeit!"

"Not forfeit," sobbed Elizabeth, wiping her mouth.

"No? And how do you suppose you should save your crown? Rush into marriage, as if that were possible, with the prince of Sweden, or Archduke Ferdinand? Pretend the baby is premature and pray that it does not resemble your lover too closely?"

"I will not marry them, either of them," whispered Elizabeth.

"Ah, then the Queen of England will give birth to a bastard child. That should do wonders for her already besmirched reputation," hissed Kat. "Her loyal subjects will no doubt be delighted to have a harlot queen for their —"

"Silence!" thundered Elizabeth, suddenly in command once more. "You will not speak to your queen in such a tone again, Katherine Ashley, or you shall find your head on a pike on Tower Bridge!"

Silence there was. Mary Sidney stood quivering in horror at Elizabeth's words. Kat simply stared at the Queen in disbelief. In all her time with Elizabeth, from the earliest days of childhood when Kat had been the only human being who cared if the little girl lived or died, through all the years of Kat's outspoken opinioning and impertinent scolding, Elizabeth had never spoken so harshly. And now this, for simply stating the truth.

"So you'd have me beheaded, is that it? Bowels ripped from my old belly? Drawn and quartered too?" Kat sniffed indignantly and rose from the bed.

"Kat . . ." Elizabeth grabbed her lady's hand, immediately contrite. How could she have uttered such a terrible threat to her dearest friend and keeper? But her waiting woman had unknowingly touched a painful wound in Elizabeth's soul, the memory of her mother — by repute England's harlot queen, in truth a headstrong and honorable woman who had fought courageously against all odds so that Elizabeth could one day wear St. Edward's Crown.

"Forgive me, Kat. I'm out of my mind with worry. Please sit. And Mary . . ." Elizabeth looked to Mary Sidney, who had yet never moved, hardly breathed for some minutes. "Come close to me. I need your loving counsel, too." Mary approached the bed, sat down at Elizabeth's feet. "We must think, be reasonable."

The three women were quiet for a long moment. When Kat spoke again her voice was so low Elizabeth had to lean in to hear.

"I can speak to Treadwell, the apothecary. He need never know for whom the potion is meant."

"No," said Elizabeth. "I will not do away with this child. I mean to have my baby."

"But, Elizabeth . . ." moaned Kat.

"May I speak, Your Majesty?" said Mary Sidney. Elizabeth nodded her consent. "Are you not forgetting my brother?" Mary could feel Kat stiffen next to her, but she went on. "He loves you so, from the depths of his soul . . . and you love him. No one would make you a better husband than he. And there is already some support for such a match, both here and abroad. You have no less than King Philip's blessing on a marriage with Robin. Even Lord Suffolk is said to support it. Robin is an Englishman and the true father of this child. The ceremony could be performed quickly so that appearances could be preserved — the child conceived immediately after the marriage, born prematurely. You might even announce that you have been married secretly for some time. There is rumor to that effect already. I see no better solution to your dilemma, Majesty."

"Let me think, let me think!" cried Elizabeth.

She was a Christian queen, Supreme Governor of the Church of England. Her reputation for strength as well as piety would in the future determine the measure of power she wielded amongst the monarchs of Europe. She reflected with a shiver of awe that in this day and age women ruled a vast portion of the known world — de Médicis in France, Mary in Scotland, herself in England and Ireland. A child born out of wedlock now would brand Elizabeth once and forever as a whore, a prince ill suited to reign . . . a weak woman.

But what of the promise she had made to herself on her mother's grave, that she must never marry? What of the perception that to give her hard-won power away to a husband, no matter how beloved, no matter how trusted, was as good as a sentence of death? If not death of the body, thought Elizabeth, then death of the spirit. For that part of her which lived for her country and her subjects, marriage and the relinquishment of her duty as queen was as mortal a sin as treason.

But she was young still, thought Elizabeth. She could not allow the world to know her mind's true turnings. Her subjects would think her mad. Rebellions and civil wars would boil up to topple the lunatic queen who refused to marry and bear heirs. Crucial foreign alliances would be lost. Robin, her darling Robin, might desert her.

Now was the moment, Elizabeth knew — and John Dee had foreseen it — when England should sail forth into the future, not as the meek and tiny island nation it had always been but as a mighty vessel bound to conquer the world. And she, Elizabeth, standing alone at the helm, should be its captain. For this to happen she must let them all go on believing that she might yet marry. She must play for time. Yes, that was what she needed most of all. Time.

Elizabeth gazed first at Kat Ashley and then at Mary Sidney, who sat with eyes downcast, allowing Elizabeth the privacy of her own thoughts. Wild and grandiose schemes, she mused, of a mad queen pregnant with an illegitimate child. Her child. Dudley's child. A child of her body. The idea was staggering.

"Your Majesty, please," Kat began. "We must think what to do."

"I know what we must do," replied Elizabeth, forcing herself to remain outwardly calm.

"Tell us, Majesty," said Mary Sidney. "What have you in mind?"

"The progress," she said. "We shall make our summer progress as expected. And all will then be revealed."

Eight

"God bless my grandfather Henry Tudor," swore Elizabeth, settling back into the red leather seat of her coach. "These roads are excellent still, fifty years since their building."

"Aye," agreed Kat Ashley, herself well pleased with the smooth ride. "Not even the plushest of cushions can save a rump from the ruts of a foul road."

Elizabeth, always passionate when the topic was her kingdom or her people, clung to the subject like a terrier with a bone. "Unlike my father, my grandfather had nothing in him of vainglory. He did for his country what was good and wise with little unnecessary spending."

Kat glanced sideways at the Queen. 'Twas the first time in all their many years together she had heard from Elizabeth's lips an iota of criticism of her father.

"Do you know," Elizabeth went on, "that when my grandfather died he bequeathed two thousand pounds for the making and repair of his highways and bridges between his principal houses?"

She thrust her head and shoulders far out the window for a better look, and had to shout to be heard. "Look at this, Kat, how well and substantially ditched they are on both sides, how nicely graveled and raised to a goodly height! And in most places two carts may pass one by the other with ease!"

"Elizabeth, come in from there! 'Tis unseemly for the Queen of England to be poking from her carriage window like a turtle from its shell."

Elizabeth pulled back in, her face flushed and moist.

"Unseemly to whom," retorted Elizabeth, "the sheep?"

Indeed, the royal carriage, four hundred lumbering wagons and carts overladen with bag and baggage, and the full complement of Elizabeth's entire Court — the Queen's summer progress — now traversed the wild meadows and silent soggy backwaters of rural England, inhabited more thickly by herds of cattle and flocks of kingfishers than human beings.

Kat peered out at the desolate landscape made even gloomier by the grey and threatening skies. "'Tis as rough and inhospitable a place as when Caesar found it, I daresay."

"'Tis beautiful to me, Kat."

"I'm hoping our lodgings tonight are far from any swampland. They are unhealthful, harboring poisonous vapors. Breed the plague. We haven't come this far from London to . . ."

"Hush, Kat, your complaining makes my head ache. My harbinger reports the house to be large and rambling, with sweet and airy chambers overviewing a deer park round about it. And the village, he claims, is free from plague. So have no fear, we are well taken care of. Now let us hope it begins to rain."

Kat grumbled quietly at Elizabeth's last comment. Rain indeed. 'Twas all part of the Queen's most fantastical and secret scheme for concealing her pregnancy — a scheme, Kat was forced to admit, which had until now worked marvelous well. Few were privy to the plan — herself, Secretary Cecil, Robin Dudley, his sister and brother-in-law the Sidneys. Elizabeth insisted it was elegantly simple and foolproof if followed to the letter. Kat found it agonizingly complicated and contrived — and riddled with opportunity for exposure. All it would take was one misstep, one unexpected glimpse by a pair of unfriendly eyes, one tiny mote of foul luck. But blessedly, luck had so far been on their side.

After only a month of nausea, which was put down to the flux, Elizabeth had regained her good health and cheerful disposition. Since she had never bled with the moon's cycle, her lesser waiting ladies were none the wiser. The idea had been to begin the progress in late June, heading out for stays of a fortnight or more to the Queen's several residences — Oatlands, Richmond, Eltham, Hampton Court — and also to the closest country houses and estates owned by her most important nobles. Here she had shown herself publicly, in the earliest stages of her pregnant condition, before it had become apparent.

Kat recalled Elizabeth's almost childlike enthusiasm as they had approached Richmond Palace, its towers and pinnacles rising like a fairy castle from a cloud of pale pink blossoms, for the cherry orchard surrounding it was enormous. They had passed the gilt aviary filled with exotic birds from many lands, and arrived at the front gate ablaze with heraldic decorations to a joyful welcome of song and dance accompanied by pipe and tabor.

The entertainments at Richmond had been magnificent, the already fabulous royal residence outfitted for sheer pleasure. Out of the storehouses came bedsteads of marble and gilt, cloth of gold window carpets latticed with diamonds and silver. Each meal was more lavish than the one before. A single course might consist of chickens, pigeons, dotterels, peewits, gulls, pastries, and oysters. Food appeared in elaborate shapes — castles, animals, even human forms. And wine was overflowing. Elizabeth, who generally partook most sparingly, enjoyed her food with great gusto, surprising and delighting the castle cooks.

But most magical — and what Elizabeth loved above all, a remembrance from childhood — were the dozens of palace towers, each capped with a bulbous onion dome and a tall vane, which, together in a high wind, became like the strings of an Aeolian harp. The Queen had woken each morning of her stay hoping for a storm, and was finally granted her wish on a dark afternoon in July. As the gusting increased, Elizabeth had hastened out the front gate, and despite Kat's and Mary Sidney's many pleadings had stood, hair and skirts flapping wildly about her, beneath the marvelous instrument made of the castle towers, and listened to the strange and otherworldly music, entirely enraptured.

Elizabeth was slender, and her belly had hardly swollen until her sixth month. Wearing clever padding in the stomacher, and other rigged undergarments routinely worn by ladies hoping to conceal their delicate condition, Elizabeth had been able to maintain the appearance of normalcy, though curtailing the most strenuous of exercise, until well into August.

The second stage of the scheme was then begun. The Queen, with Robin Dudley's assistance, had laid out her route of travel with the utmost precision. From August on, she would limit the number of her immediate entourage to the chosen few. She avoided as many great houses as possible, those whose lords and ladies knew her intimately and might construe her behavior as strange or untoward. Happily, the nature of the progress was such that the royal harbinger might ride out to a great estate or a more humble residence and announce the Queen's impending arrival on the following day. With such scant warning, the equally honored and horrified hosts were then required to scramble into hasty preparations to bed, feed, and lavishly entertain the Queen's enormous retinue. With but a few notable exceptions, no one in the kingdom actually *expected* her arrival, so she could wander at will through the countryside, make arrangements and cancel them, compensating her disappointed and no doubt relieved hosts with a generous gift. When she was forced to personally appear at an accommodation, great commotion and feigned illness upon arrival could spirit the Queen to her rooms without much ado. Sometimes Mary Sidney, in Elizabeth's clothing and high-heeled shoes to approximate Elizabeth's height, and swathed in veils, played proxy whilst the Queen elsewhere sought lodgings as a plain lady with her husband, Robert. Thankfully, most stays were but a day or two.

She made much use of a canopied but otherwise open-sided carriage in which she could ride, waving to her subjects, through gaily decorated villages, watch a country dance, or a pageant presented by a town of weavers, listen raptly to a child's sweet recital of verse, or sit through a morbid morality play. No one ever suspected that this gracious and beloved queen was heavy with child.

As her pregnancy became undeniable, and because the planned route was unable to avoid several great estates of the high peerage, the third and most dangerous stage of the Queen's scheme was brought into action. Today, thought Kat with trepidation, Elizabeth would be welcomed at Fulham House, where she was to lodge with Lord Clinton and his family for a fortnight. 'Twas a frightfully audacious plan, and it rested wholly for success on the weather's turning rainy. Though the sky was threatening, there were too few miles before they would reach Fulham, and the rain had not yet begun. Kat peered up at the sky pleadingly and then at Elizabeth, unable to hide her worry.

"I know, Kat, I know," she said soothingly. "But we still have miles to go."

"But what if it doesn't rain!"

Elizabeth sighed in exasperation. "Then I shall stop the progress and call for a picnic. Then it will most certainly rain! Come, Kat, please be of good faith. All has gone well and will continue so."

"How are you so sure always that things will go your way?"

"Because," replied Elizabeth evenly, "this child is meant to be born. 'Twas written in the stars — and foretold by a great magician. My son . . ."

Elizabeth's voice trailed off, but Kat Ashley did not press the Queen to continue. For she wished to hear no details of the strange fate and future of this bastard child — some mad intrigue to send him far from Court to be raised by Elizabeth's distant but trusted relations, to live secret and unknown until the time the Queen deemed it safe and politic for him to be brought forward and acknowledged. Sweet Jesus, they were all a heartbeat away from disaster!

The coach came to a sudden halt, and at once Robin Dudley on horseback reined up beside Elizabeth's window. "The advance guard from Fulham has arrived to escort us the final distance to our lodgings, Your

Majesty. Two hundred liveried horsemen. Lord Clinton's household is in prodigious readiness." He flashed a conspiratorial smile at the Queen. "And the rain has begun up ahead."

"Good. Are your sister and brother-in-law ready for the play to begin?" she inquired of him with a sly grin.

"As you would have them, Madame." Dudley reached down impulsively and kissed Elizabeth's hand.

Kat looked away, exceedingly annoyed. They were all acting like willful children playing a dangerous game. They were *enjoying* themselves. Well, thought Kat Ashley, this game could have no happy winners. She would have to take these unruly children in hand.

The rain was streaming in sheets across the landscape as the procession neared Fulham House. Though Elizabeth knew that Lord Clinton's waterlogged welcome would be disappointing to him, she was most gratified that the weather was complying with her own well-laid plans.

Lord Clinton, his family and retainers, and a choir of singing children stood under canopies upheld by liveried servants as the Queen's royal guard, a regiment of equerries, and a dozen carriages carrying her chamberlains, Privy Councillors, and the Archbishop of Canterbury with fifty of his own horsemen approached and moved beyond the front gate. There followed a coach with Cecil and the Sidneys. And finally, attended by Horsemaster Robin Dudley, Elizabeth's own carriage clattered to a stop in front of their hosts.

Robin swung down from his mount and, when a footman opened the door to the royal coach, was ready with his hand as the Queen emerged in a voluminous, hooded leather rain cloak. There was a flurry of activity as Henry Sidney and William Cecil descended from their carriage and helped Kat and Mary Sidney down, each lady wearing a rain cloak similar to the Queen's, as though it were a new fashion.

With only a brief nod to a chagrined Lord Clinton, Elizabeth and her retinue swept across the moat bridge into Fulham's courtyard. 'Twas a pleasant enough brick house with the typical Tudor jumble of towers, gables, and chimney stacks, but Elizabeth hurried past the gathered household staff huddled under waxed tarpaulins, through the front door, and into the vestibule.

Lowering her hood but retaining her cloak, Elizabeth waited for Lord Clinton and his family, who gathered near the Queen in a rush of warm greetings and courtly obeisance.

"Your Majesty, we welcome you most heartily to Fulham!" Clinton stretched out his hand to take Elizabeth's to kiss, but she pulled back so sharply he was startled.

"I am terribly sorry, my lord Clinton, but I fear I am unwell," said Elizabeth with an expression of sincere regret.

"Unwell?" cried Lady Clinton, a stout, plain-faced woman whose rich attire could do nothing to improve her appearance. "Selby!" The house steward appeared instantly at her side. "Call Doctor Williams here at once. Your Majesty, our physician may be a rural man, but he is well known for his —"

"You do not understand, good lady. My symptoms are consistent with smallpox."

There was a general sharp intake of breath in the vestibule. Elizabeth could see several people discreetly step back from her. Admirably, Lord and Lady Clinton stood their ground, though their faces had gone suddenly pale and stricken.

"Unhappily I must therefore command you all to vacate this household with haste," announced Elizabeth. "My people will see to me. Wish me well and be off as quickly as you are able. My apologies for your inconvenience."

"But, Your Majesty, we could not possibly leave you —"

"Lord Clinton, I will not be responsible for any illness in your household. Have your steward show us to our rooms, and our cooks to your kitchens. My retinue will lodge in tents outside."

Elizabeth's eyelids fluttered and she staggered slightly, reaching for Robin Dudley's ready hand.

"Please, I must take my rest now."

"Of course, of course," murmured Clinton, bowing and moving backwards from the Queen. "If there is anything at all I can do . . ."

But Elizabeth and her intimates were already moving up the great staircase.

"Pray Jesus she does not die here," muttered Lady Clinton to her husband. "What a curse that would be."

"But if she lives, 'twill be a blessing," said her husband, "for she will remember this house with affection."

Lady Clinton leaned close and whispered so that no one else should hear. "We shall save five thousand pounds just on the entertainments," she said.

As the family and servants dispersed to gather their things and be off, Lady Clinton noticed a solemn and faraway look clouding her husband's face. "What is it, John?" she asked.

"If Elizabeth dies," he answered, "she dies without an heir. Things will go badly for England. Very badly indeed. Assemble the family in the chapel at once, Margaret. We must pray for the life of the Queen."

"Well done, Your Majesty!" cried Mary Sidney as she removed Elizabeth's cloak, which had admirably concealed the now prominent bulge of Elizabeth's belly.

The royal entourage behind the closed doors of Fulham's upstairs apartments were preparing to take their rest from the long day's ride, and collapsing with relief after the Queen's undeniably polished performance.

"Summon my physician!" cried Elizabeth with a theatrical moan. "I've broken out in spots!"

"Poor Lady Clinton," said Mary Sidney, unable to suppress a smile. "She looked rather disgruntled."

"Think you? I wager she's counting the money saved on the entertainments and feasts she'll not be lavishing upon us," said Robin, making a survey of the spacious bedchamber, checking its windows and doors, looking carefully for any secret compartments or hidden passageways.

"Come, Elizabeth," said Kat. "Sit you down or, better still, get into bed for a proper rest."

"I'm not tired in the least, Kat. I feel wonderful," replied Elizabeth.

"You're a pregnant woman and you have had a grueling day. You shall rest, Madame, if I have to sit atop you and hold you down."

Robin and the Sidneys burst into laughter at Kat's rude familiarity, knowing the Queen forgave such trespasses. Finally Elizabeth relented and gave herself over to Kat's ministrations.

"Gentlemen, leave us. I'm about to be untrussed and put to bed by my lady Ashley. See to our supper, Robin. Ask the cook for simple fare — some poultry and a cold pie."

Robin and Henry kissed Elizabeth's hand, bowed low, and left the Queen with her women. As they began unlacing and unbuttoning her gown, Elizabeth gazed down at the extra panels hanging loose over her bulging belly and smiled.

"A child of my body," said Elizabeth in a hushed whisper. Even if she had spoken the words more loudly she doubted whether Kat or Mary Sidney would have heard, for they were deep asleep on their pallets at the foot of her bed, exhausted after the long day's journey to Fulham House. But the Queen was hardly weary. Indeed, she had of late been infused with a startling vitality, an ever-present wakefulness and clarity of mind that all about her wondered at it. But Elizabeth understood. 'Twas the thing John Dee had seen in his black gazing crystal — a life, a soul, growing within her, which made her something more than herself. She was, in this body of hers, two people, and it gave her new strength.

Many months before, when Dee had foretold that she should bear a son, Elizabeth had balked, shunned the truth of it for fear that it would forever brand her a wanton or, if she were forced to legitimize the child, trap her in an unwanted marriage. Either eventuality could weaken her position irrevocably, wrest the hard-won monarchical power from her hands.

But in the months following the seer's revelation, as the babe grew within her, so grew a new determination, a strength of purpose. And so grew a love that knew no bounds, a love over which the Queen, who had long ago mastered her emotions, had no control. She knew this was irrational. Irrational, too, was her unshakable belief that she would survive the delivery, that this child was fated to be born and live long. So many women miscarried their babies, so many infants and mothers died in childbirth or soon after. Her own mother had miscarried three times.

Where once, in the early days after the revelation, had festered confusion and worry at the decision to have Robin Dudley's child, one day in early summer, as she felt her son move within her, her mind grew suddenly calm. A plan had begun to take shape, as a complex strategy of battle might form in the dreams of a great general.

Destiny, she realized, had timed the pregnancy for the months of her summer progress. Had it been otherwise, Elizabeth, wintering in the rigid confines of her court, would have found it impossible to conceal. As it was, her precisely delineated plan had worked brilliantly. Of course, it had required considerable help from the Fates and from her friends. But that had materialized unfailingly — if not always, in the latter case, altogether wholeheartedly. While Robin and the Sidneys — party to John Dee's prophecy — had become willing participants in her scheme, Kat and William Cecil had fought tooth and claw against it. Elizabeth had been forced to bring all her queenly strength, even tyrannical powers, to bear.

'Twas after all a mad scheme, even Elizabeth had to admit. Hard enough to bring to full term a secret pregnancy during five months of grueling travel. But she then must spirit the child far from Court to sanctuary with her Boleyn relations to be raised quietly, and contrive to see the child as often as possible till the time when she felt strong enough to acknowledge him and proclaim him her successor.

It was this last portion of the scheme that made Kat and Cecil most skeptical. Granted, Elizabeth might somehow conceal the pregnancy by use of proxies, feigned illnesses, and disappearances into the deep countryside. But to keep a royal bastard undiscovered for years? It would require profound and unerring loyalty from too many people for too long. Intentions might be good, but any number of things — a conversation overheard by a disgruntled servant, one of the Queen's secret assignations with the child observed and questioned — might lead to exposure.

Elizabeth's trust in her plan was based, as Kat's or Cecil's could never be, on her belief in destiny. As her own birth had been foretold by the Maid of Kent, her child's had been similarly prophesied by John Dee. The man nun had seen that Anne Boleyn's "sun" should shine for two score years and four, and where once Elizabeth had doubted that she would reign so long, she now knew in her heart that it was so. She would live to be a powerful old woman who would rule a vast empire over the western sea, as John Dee had said, and in that time she would gain the power she needed to bring forward and proclaim this child of her body as heir. She *would* have the power. Of this she was certain.

Elizabeth lay trembling with exaltation, hands upon her great belly. Suddenly her mind flew to thoughts of her sweet Robin, flew as swiftly as a London kite might fly to the safety of its nest atop a high castle tower. For only with Robin was her heart truly safe. In his presence alone was Elizabeth other than queen. She was, simply, a woman.

She groaned inwardly to think her love, father of this child, willingly joined in her scheme in ignorance of the true nature of his role. He believed, for Elizabeth had sworn, that once their son was born and lived she would, in time, marry him, make him king, proclaiming to the world they had been wed in secret, as her father had wed her mother after Anne had become pregnant with herself. Yet Elizabeth would not marry Dudley. She could not. Her heart ached with guilt, and with the fear that he would forsake her once the truth was known. How could she blame him? The one clear desire of his life — to marry her and be king of England — seemed finally within reach. Yet his sweet devotion to his wife-to-be and child all rested on an illusion, a bitter conjuring, a cruel deception at the hands of his beloved. 'Twas a cold plan forged in the mind of a hard, scheming queen, she thought ruefully. Hard and cruel, but necessary. For Elizabeth must rule alone. Nothing could move her in this conviction. Not pain, not guilt. Not love. She was one with England, and when she died her son Arthur, descended as he was from the great and legendary king, would rule gloriously after her. She must gather her strength and courage, for the road that was her destiny was long and hard and dangerous unto death.

Nine

It had been a nerve-fraying race against time, thought Kat Ashley as she ripped clean sheeting into wide strips — such devious maneuvering as she in her life had never before, and hoped never again, to perform. Seated outside the Queen's bedchamber, where within Mary Sidney attended Elizabeth, Kat smiled to think how she had deceived them all, smart as they were — Elizabeth, Dudley, Mary and Henry Sidney. At any moment Cecil, her only ally in the plot, would be returning with the midwife, Agnes Hodgeson.

A bolt of lightning seared across the darkening afternoon sky, and Kat worried that the vagaries of weather might imperil her well-laid plans. An almost immediate crash of thunder announced the storm's nearness.

Kat remembered the moment just two weeks before when she had discovered how she could take control of this dreadful travesty in which Elizabeth had entangled herself, and save her misguided charge from tragedy.

On that fine late-summer Wednesday Kat had ordered the coach and gone to the nearest village for some sweet plums which Elizabeth had requested. For Kat, accustomed to being always at the Queen's side to do her bidding, it had been lovely out on her own, driving through the bustling market square with its shops and gaudy stalls, vendors hawking ripe country fruits and vegetables, live squawking poultry hung up in reed cages, piles of rough breads and manchettes, kegs of ale. Rowdy children pinched apples from a barrel, and a drunken shepherd drove a flock of black-faced sheep down the main thoroughfare, knocking over a dozen carts and stalls. Kat had gotten out and gone happily about on foot, her basket tucked beneath her arm like a country goodwife and not first lady to the Queen of England.

There at a rude table outside the half-timbered apothecary's house she overheard two women talking, and stopped nearby, pretending to examine some leather sandals. They were both midwives, so it seemed, the wizened older woman, Agnes, regaling the younger with some wisdom about the inducement of labor and its benefits.

"If in the eighth month the choild be large and the mother small in her places, then she best be served by an early birthin'. Otherwise she can be torn so badly ye can do naught but watch her bleed and die. The babe might live, but what good is it without a mother?" said the crone.

"And what be the potion, then," asked the younger midwife, "and what amounts be given to bring on her labor?"

As measures of strangely named herbs and concoctions which meant nothing to Kat's untrained ear were exchanged, she found herself reflecting that Elizabeth was nearing the eighth month of her pregnancy. She was even now awaiting the next downpour, during which she would don her great leather cloak, bid Lord and Lady Clinton fare-thee-well, thanking them for their comfortable home in which she passed through the outbreak of smallpox with, Jesus be praised, no ugly scarring, and be on her way to the final destination of Cumberland Manor. There some distant maternal relatives, Boleyns or Howards whom Elizabeth deemed loyal and trustworthy, would oversee her lying in and foster her bastard child.

Kat had grown more certain with every passing day that once the babe was born and out of her hands, disaster was sure to follow. The Boleyns and Howards were anything but trustworthy. They were as ambitious and conniving as any family in England. Their womenfolk — Anne Boleyn and Katherine Howard — had been queens to Henry VIII and both had died for acts of treason and adultery. Kat had always believed, secretly, that Elizabeth's wild blood and tendency toward wantonness was her mother's. If she could only take the child in her own hands, give it over to someone truly trustworthy, truly loyal, someone with no ambitions save a quiet and God-fearing life . . .

The two midwives had risen from their table in the market square and bid each other good-day when Kat approached the older of the two with a friendly smile.

"You're just the woman I need to see," she said, locking arms with Agnes congenially. "Is there a quiet place we might talk?"

As Kat sat outside Elizabeth's bedchamber now remembering that day, she realized that the lightning and thunder had not abated but worsened. With the dark came a fierce wind. Hearing a commotion in the courtyard, she peered out the upstairs window to see that all members of the summer progress were being ushered hurriedly into Fulham House. The tents must have blown down in the wind, thought Kat. They'd all be entering with misgivings. Smallpox was a far more terrible threat than a good drenching. Still, they needed shelter. 'Twould be a foul hall with such a crush of bodies. Now behind the last of the servants Kat could see the horses being herded into the courtyard. It must be a more furious storm than she could discern from this protected place in the house.

"God in heaven!" swore Kat under her breath. The entire court just below them during the birth. Elizabeth might cry and scream in pain, or the baby when it was born. . . . Sweet Jesu, would her own tampering with the Fates lead to the very outcome she had worked so assiduously to avoid? Where on earth were Cecil and the midwife!

It had been almost unbearable waiting for word from Agnes Hodgeson that their machinations might begin to go forward, and, too, for the next rain. But in the late morning of this day, as soon as it was apparent that a storm was approaching, Kat had administered the potion to bring on Elizabeth's labor. She had mixed the herbs into the gravy of the Queen's favorite meat pie and watched her eat, holding her breath lest Elizabeth, whose appetite had become large but whose senses were nevertheless refined, might notice something amiss. She had always found strong smells and flavors repugnant. At her own coronation she had recoiled in disgust at the foetid odor of the holy oil with which she'd been anointed, and had insisted on bathing thoroughly before donning her gown for the feast. But Elizabeth had eaten her meat pie this day with great gusto, perhaps too busy barking out orders for immediate departure from Fulham to notice.

Kat and Lady Mary were in the midst of packing the Queen's trunks, Elizabeth hovering over them with endless annoying instructions on how her things should be arranged, when the labor pains had begun.

"God's death!" cried Elizabeth, choking back a sudden cry of pain and clutching the bedpost with one hand, her great belly with the other. She looked to her waiting women, her face a mask of terror. "But it is too soon."

"'Tis soon, Madame," said Kat soothingly as she helped Elizabeth lie down, "but not dangerously so. Mary, go tell Cecil and your brother it has begun."

As Kat pulled a nightgown from a half-packed chest, Mary bent and whispered in her ear, "We are not prepared at this house, Kat. Who will — ?"

"Have no worry, child. I have in fact prepared for this eventuality.

There is a midwife in the village whom Cecil will fetch. Our queen has been so certain of her great plans, but not everything can be left to chance. Go quickly now!"

"Yes, Kat."

"And scour the cabinets for clean linen sheets and bolts of muslin. If they are not here you will have to search the laundry."

Mary Sidney nodded and bustled out.

"Kat," moaned Elizabeth, "come hold my hand. I'm afraid."

"No need, my darling. Everything will be fine. The child will be smaller, 'tis true, but the birth will be easier for you."

"But he must live. . . ."

"That is in God's hands, Elizabeth, God's hands alone."

Kat had smiled at the Queen with calm reassurance, but her smile had been one of secret pleasure as well. After so many years of service to Elizabeth, Kat Ashley was once again in charge.

But as the storm grew in fury outside the window, the smile faded and only worry creased Kat's face. What if Cecil could not find the midwife? What if the old woman had hidden in fear? Agnes knew she would be attending the Queen of England — there could be no hiding that. Mayhaps the payment for her services and yet more to keep her mouth shut were still not enough. Once the bargain had been struck — the midwife's reward sufficient to keep her in comfort till the end of her days — Kat, with a coldness she had not known she possessed, had sealed the bargain with a threat. If word of this birth ever came to public knowledge, she swore, the midwife would know a terrible death indeed. Had the threat frightened the woman away? What if Elizabeth should . . . ? No, she must stop this senseless rumination at once. Elizabeth would not die, could not die!

With a flash of lightning that lit the chamber bright as midday, and a crash of thunder that seemed to shake the very walls, the door opened. William Cecil, dripping wet, accompanying a figure enshrouded in one of the hooded leather rain cloaks, entered and shut the door behind them. Kat sagged with relief as Agnes Hodgeson pulled off the cape and revealed herself, scowling and cursing, carrying two large cloth satchels, one of which bulged and clanked with the fearsome tools of her trade.

"Did anyone mark her arrival?" Kat demanded of Cecil.

"In that stinking nightmare down below? There is such confusion and so little space 'tis difficult even to find a place to sit. One driver did recognize the cloak and bid greeting to yourself, but that was all."

"I'll need hot water and clean linen torn in strips," ordered the midwife to Kat. She was not one for pleasantries, thought the waiting lady with irritation. But neither was Mistress Ashley to be ruled by this bad-tempered old crone.

"'Tis done and ready," said Kat, nodding smartly to the pile of neatly folded bandages and a kettle boiling atop a brazier. She moved close and whispered in the midwife's ear. "Have you brought —"

"I have all that I need," Agnes answered abruptly. "Set me up a screen over there near the door, with a table behind it, a basin, and another brazier. Lay a pile of the rags there too."

"Where is Robin?" cried Elizabeth weakly. "Why has he not come?"

"I failed to find him, Majesty," replied Mary Sidney, clutching the Queen's hand. "Mayhaps he is helping secure the horses, for the storm is worsening and there is insufficient room in the stables."

"Find him, find him!" Elizabeth wailed hoarsely. Then just as she screamed again in pain, the bedchamber door flew open and Robin Dudley, followed by his brother-in-law, entered and strode to Elizabeth's side. Her arms went round him, embracing him as though she meant never to release him.

"Will ye for God's sake get all these men out of here, and do it now!" Agnes ordered Kat with an impatient growl. "'Tis a birthin', not a barn dance!" Her words were punctuated by the most frightening explosion of thunder yet.

Robin could barely be torn away by Henry Sidney from embracing Elizabeth and kissing her face bathed in tears and sweat.

"I'll pray for you, my love, you and our son," he cried.

"Robin!"

As the men exited the bedchamber, Cecil, the last to leave, exchanged a fraught look with Kat.

"Be ready," she whispered. "And pray that all goes well."

"Let her scream, why don't ye? 'Twill do her good," muttered Agnes to Kat, who, with jaws clenched determinedly, placed a clean roll of bandages between Elizabeth's teeth to stifle her shrieks. She pressed a cool wet cloth to the Queen's forehead. Her skin was nearly as white as the lawn sheets, and she moaned deliriously.

"Just do your work, woman, and keep your opinions to yourself," snapped Kat, wishing that she had found any other midwife in the wide world than this querulous hag who now toiled between Elizabeth's outstretched thighs.

"Aye, her parts are small," said Agnes, pointedly ignoring Kat's command for silence. The midwife knew she could afford a smart word or two, for in this room it was she and she alone who stood between life and death for the Queen and her child. "'Tis a good thing we —"

Kat gave the woman a vicious pinch on the soft part of her upper arm to silence her, for although Elizabeth was beyond hearing, Mary Sidney hovered close by and must never know what Kat had conspired with this old woman to do.

"There's its crown. 'Tis comin' now. O Jesus help us, I think a hemorrhage has begun!" Agnes glared at Kat and gestured with her eyes toward Mary Sidney.

"Mary," said Kat urgently, "run down to the laundry for more sheets. And tell your brother to fetch that physician Lady Clinton spoke of. We may have need of him."

There was panic in Mary's eyes, but she held herself bravely together. Before dashing away she grabbed Elizabeth's hand and kissed it, then was gone.

"Robin, Robin," moaned Elizabeth, only half conscious.

As the door closed and Kat locked it behind Mary, Agnes smiled a rotten-toothed smile. "Ye done yer part well, milady. Now she must do hers." She peered at Elizabeth from between her angled knees. "Yer Majesty . . ." Elizabeth just groaned deliriously. To Kat the midwife said, "Ye must slap her face, bring her to. I need her to bear down, and I need it now."

Kat went to Elizabeth's side, gritted her teeth, and gave the Queen a smart slap on each cheek. Her eyes fluttered open. They were dull with pain and exhaustion.

"Elizabeth, 'tis time. The babe is coming, but you must bear down when Agnes tells you." Then, lifting her skirts, Kat Ashley climbed upon the bedstead and squatted behind Elizabeth's head. "Here, give me your hands."

Elizabeth obeyed, raising her arms above her head and clutching Kat's with her own.

"All righty," said Agnes with fierce determination. "Let us bring this choild outta ye."

Whether because of Agnes's skill, the smaller size of the premature babe, or simply the Fates cooperating once again, Elizabeth and Dudley's son emerged with a lusty cry from the Queen's body not five minutes after

Mary Sidney's departure for the laundry. While the hemorrhage had been a mere pretext to afford privacy, and Elizabeth had come through the birthing with little damage or tearing, she was nevertheless dead with fatigue and pain. She never questioned the midwife as she snipped and tied the umbilical cord and retreated with the bloodied creature behind the screen. Elizabeth managed a weak smile as Kat wiped her face with a cloth.

"Is he beautiful, Kat?" she whispered.

Kat squeezed Elizabeth's hand, and tears welled up in the older women's eyes. This was the moment she had planned so diligently and dreaded so terribly. For a moment she thought she could not go through with it, had not the strength. How dare she perpetrate such a foul deed on the sweet woman who trusted her so completely? But now Agnes had stepped out from behind the screen with a tiny bundle in her arms and was moving toward the bed, a grim look on her wrinkled face. Too late, thought Kat. Too late now.

Elizabeth saw the midwife's expression and turned to Kat, her eyes suddenly wide with alarm.

"I'm sorry as I can be, Yer Majesty, but the boy was born dead."

"No, he was not! I heard him cry out as he was born!"

"Naa, 'twas yer own screamin' ye heard."

"Kat, you heard him! Did you not hear him?"

Kat fought to keep her face from breaking apart with the agony of the lie. She shook her head slowly, but did not trust herself to speak.

"Let me have him!" Elizabeth demanded of the midwife, still not believing.

Agnes placed the bundle in the Queen's arms.

Slowly Elizabeth pulled back the linen to reveal the tiny face, the sweet wrinkled face so still and peaceful. She touched the velvet cheek with the tip of her finger. It was warm. Elizabeth began to weep helpless, bitter tears.

"Take the child, Agnes," Kat managed to say, but Elizabeth slapped the midwife's hands away.

"No! No, I want to hold him. I must hold him till his father . . . Oh, where is Robin, where is my love . . . ?"

Kat had never seen such copious tears from Elizabeth, not at the death of her father, of her beloved brother Edward, of the only woman she'd called mother, Catharine Parr. It was breaking Kat's heart to see Elizabeth so distraught, and she prayed to God for strength to see her plan through. It was, she told herself over and over again in a solemn litany, "for her own good, for her own good, for her own good . . ."

*   *   *

Through the darkened hallways and backstairs of Fulham House hurried William Cecil, holding close to his body the bloody bundle which he could hear mewling faintly beneath the muslin wrapping. Moments before, standing outside the Queen's chamber, trembling with trepidation at this mad act in which he had been persuaded to play a part by Kat Ashley, he had heard the knock from inside and opened the door. Agnes Hodgeson had thrust the bundle at him unceremoniously and turned back to her table behind the tall screen. He'd seen her lift the body of a dead newborn from her second satchel and place it in the basin of hot water to warm its cold skin. Looking up to find Cecil staring, the midwife had riven him with an expression of disapproval bordering on disgust before closing the door in his face.

Blessedly the wind had begun to lessen, but the rain continued a deluge. Cecil splashed through the base court past the barns, stables, slaughterhouse, and smithy, and found standing under the moat tower a lone woman, coarsely dressed, boots muddied to her ankles. As he approached he could see the once pretty but prematurely aged face, the unutterably sad eyes. She would be the mother of the dead babe, the woman whose stillbirth Agnes had awaited to give signal to Kat, and, for the next weeks, wet nurse to the child he held in his arms. William Cecil handed the countrywoman the Queen's bastard, and without a word she turned and disappeared into the stormy night.

Robin lay full length beside Elizabeth, cradling her in his arms. As dawn broke sweet and clear after the dreadful storm, they had finally allowed Kat Ashley to wrest their son's body from their embraces. Elizabeth and Dudley had each had in their lives many losses, innumerable tragedies. Their families had been decimated by violent, sometimes meaningless death. And yet today, despite their long experience with grieving and the common understanding that childbirth as often ended badly as well, they were beyond consolation.

As the candles Elizabeth had demanded be lit round her bed flickered, they had spoken little, cried not at all. Just carefully laid the child between them and unwrapped the muslin sheeting to reveal his tiny body. As they caressed the silken hair on his head, held the delicate limbs in their hands, examined the tiny buds of fingers and toes, they knew this was not the way men and women mourned the loss of their children. Death amongst newborns and infants was too common, too expected. Parents inured themselves to it. Even if the child lived, mothers and fathers often withheld any affection at all until the babe had reached the age of one or two.

But their son, Arthur, as he grew and thrived in Elizabeth's womb, had been no ordinary child. He had been a dream come into flesh. A promise brought to life. A bridge between a man and a woman. A torch to illuminate the future of England. And now he lay dead and cold in his shroud.

"They are saying," said Robin finally as the sun's first rays slanted in across the bedchamber floor, "that it was the most fearsome storm England has ever known. That the world was at an end, and the days of doom had come. Floodwaters carried away houses. The winds tore down ancient trees. Townsfolk gathered for protection in the village church until a bolt of lightning struck its steeple, which broke apart and collapsed the roof. Some people died."

"My people," murmured Elizabeth. She had, despite herself, been drawn into Robin's telling. "My subjects died in this storm." And then, remembering the lifeless body that had lain between them, she looked up into Robin Dudley's eyes. "For some the apocalypse has already arrived."

"Elizabeth . . ." Robin cupped his hand round her pale face. "'Tis not the end. We can have another."

"No, my love. That was the child with which destiny gifted us and which it saw fit to withdraw."

"Then I defy destiny!" he cried, pulling Elizabeth into a crushing embrace, burying his head in the soft damp hair at her neck. She felt his body heave once, then again and again, and knew that he was weeping. Weeping for the sweet impossible dream which they had together lost and which could never, despite their most fervent prayers or diligent efforts or royal commandments, ever again be found.

Elizabeth laid her head on Robin's and wept with him.

Ten

"Well, my good Secretary, I see from your dispatches that my cousin Mary has finally returned from France to that bleak arse of the world she calls home."

Ever despairing of Elizabeth's vulgar tongue, William Cecil frowned as he observed the Queen, still in her nightclothes, riffling through state papers at the silver-topped table in her bedchamber. He was concerned for Elizabeth's health, which had worsened since her lying-in two months before. She was thin as a rake, her skin so pale and delicate as to be almost transparent, and her obvious attempts to seize control of her wayward emotions had failed miserably. Even her normally unflagging affection for Robin Dudley had receded noticeably.

"She has, Your Majesty," replied Cecil mildly. "Mary's arrival in Edinburgh was celebrated with great rejoicing by her Scottish subjects, both Catholic and Protestant, though I have serious doubts that the lairds of the great clans be sincere in their welcome."

"Indeed," said Elizabeth. "Those men are the true rulers of Scotland, and not their queen, for 'tis the clan leaders to whom the low ruffians of that country give their allegiance. 'Tis strange to me how each particular family's ambitions and fortunes obscure all else, even the Protestantism they fought for and won. It may be Scotland's greatest weakness."

Cecil never failed to be impressed by Elizabeth's grasp of each and every detail of her government. She read on.

"I see that Mary hears Mass in her private chapel, since she may not do so in public. And yet her people still complain of it."

"They do," he agreed, "though Mary, while ardently Catholic herself, does appear to be agreeable and accommodating with respect to her countrymen's religious beliefs."

"Has she a choice if she wants to keep her crown?" asked Elizabeth.

"Your Majesty will be pleased to know Mary has had a visit from our good friend John Knox."

Elizabeth laughed aloud at Cecil's sardonic jest, and the councillor was graced by the first smile from his Queen in many weeks. Her eyes shone with wicked glee.

"Do tell me, Cecil, what said our anti-Papist fanatic to our most Catholic cousin?"

"He was very bold, Madame. I am told he braced himself as if he were meeting the devil incarnate and not a young girl of eighteen."

"One of his 'monstrous regiment' of women monarchs he so despises. What was it he wrote to describe us?" Elizabeth searched her memory and in a moment extracted the quote from Knox's tome as handily as a cherry picker might pluck a ripe fruit from the tree. "'Weak, frail, impatient, feeble and foolish creatures who rule, contrary to God and repugnant to nature.'" Elizabeth chuckled. "And now one of them is sitting on the throne of his own country."

"Apparently Knox agreed to tolerate her for the time being, as long as the realm was not laid low by her femininity, and would allow her to rule, provided she did not 'defile her hands by dipping them in the blood of the saints.' He then proclaimed her subjects' right to rise up against any unworthy ruler who opposed God's word."

"Good Lord! And what was her reply to this outpouring of venom?"

"I am told she shed some tears, but that on the whole of the matter she disported herself proudly and with quick wit. Your cousin is crafty, Your Majesty, and 'tis my opinion that you must never ever underestimate her."

The bedchamber door opened and Kat Ashley entered carrying the Queen's fresh linen. She pottered quietly as Elizabeth and Cecil continued his morning's audience, but when she observed a natural pause in their dealings she moved to Elizabeth's side and made a small curtsy.

"Yes, Kat, what is it?"

"I am begging your leave, Madame," said the waiting lady quietly.

"Begging my leave? For what?" Elizabeth seemed quite as mystified as she was annoyed.

"My aunt in Suffolk is very ill and I feel it my duty to see to her. She is very aged and has no one, Majesty."

Elizabeth stifled a great sigh. "How long must I be without you?" she asked, keeping her voice calm even as she felt panic envelop her. Kat, even more than Mary Sidney or Robin Dudley, had been her main solace in the weeks since the tragedy at Fulham House.

"A month, perhaps more, depending upon the roads. The rains have begun early."

Elizabeth looked directly into Kat's eyes. The sparkle of youth had long gone, but this was the first time the Queen had noticed a rheumy dullness there. She prayed to God that Kat herself was not ailing.

"You have my leave, but only with the promise that —"

"I will return as quickly as I am able, Your Majesty. You may be sure I will."

"Must you leave immediately?"

Kat nodded.

"Go, then. Tell Mary Sidney to attend me closely in your absence."

"I shall, Your Majesty, though we both know she needs no telling."

Fighting sudden tears, Elizabeth turned back to the state papers. She did not, therefore, notice the conspiratorial look that passed fleetingly between William Cecil and Kat Ashley before she backed out the door.

"May the Lord forgive me for what I've done," said Kat to herself as she stared forlornly out the window of the coach that rumbled down the road toward the east coast of Suffolk. Her guilt was increased as much by the plushness of the carriage Elizabeth had especially provided as by the lusty cries of the infant nestled in the arms of the wet nurse, Ellen, sitting opposite Kat.

"He's a sweet lad, he is, and the hungriest child I ever knew," said Ellen. "I swear I have scarce enough milk for him."

Kat could hardly bear to look at him or even say his name silently. Arthur — Arthur Dudley. He had his mother's and father's reddish hair and his mother's fair complexion. The newborn's blue eyes had quickly turned the deepest brown, almost black in some lights, and his cheeks were pink and chubby, a tribute to this lowborn woman who had suckled him so diligently in the place of her own dead child.

Too, there was the sinister gift from Arthur's grandmother Anne Boleyn. Kat refused to think on it. The child would soon be gone out of their lives.

"I cannot help myself, milady," said Ellen suddenly. "I've grown powerful fond of the little tyke, I have." The wet nurse looked up and Kat saw tears spilling from the corners of her eyes. "I shall be hard pressed to give him up." She fondled his red curls. "Sweet boy," she cooed.

"Now, Ellen, you'll go home and have your husband give you another child. You'll forget this one soon enough," said Kat, trying to keep the annoyance out of her voice. Kat reminded herself that Ellen, though she knew only that the babe's mother was a highborn lady, had been paid almost as handsomely as Agnes Hodgeson for her sacrifice and silence.

She watched the babe now suckling contentedly at Ellen's breast, the woman not daring to look down at him, as though she were putting distance between them even as they were linked in that most intimate of embraces.

Kat Ashley thought of what lay ahead up the road — *who* lay ahead — and her heart began to ache anew. Was there no end to the pain that this innocent child's birth had caused them all — caused her? She was bound in one hour to face the man she had once loved and lost, Robert Southern.

Oh, how long ago that had been. She'd been just a girl — Katherine Champernoune, fifteen years old — when that gentle soul, that smiling, open-faced lad had stolen her heart. Unheedful of their families, Robert and Kat had courted, lovestruck and blind. It had come like a thunderbolt from a blue sky, therefore, when John Ashley, the man her parents had chosen for her to marry, appeared hat in hand in her father's house. Kat, not yet strong enough to resist, and Robert, with nothing to recommend him in fortune or family, had bowed to the will of their parents and tradition. But not without tears. Many tears. And a vow that had been their only defiance — that they should in any case, and in secret if need be, remain good friends for life.

For her part Kat had been fortunate. Her marriage to John Ashley had been a happy one. He was a mild-mannered man, and after several years together she had confided the painful ending of her ill-fated courtship with Robert Southern. Knowing Kat's character well, knowing she would never betray him, John Ashley gave her leave to write occasionally to the man Kat called her "everlasting friend."

Robert had not been so lucky in the ways of the heart. Third son of a yeoman farmer, he had inherited almost nothing, and his apprenticeship to a cattleman afforded him no money with which to get a wife. He had, however, an uncanny skill at husbandry, claiming with a poke of fun at himself that he was more comfortable with animals than with men — or women.

Robert Southern's fortunes had overnight changed when his master had died a widower and childless, leaving his farm and cattle to his, by now, beloved apprentice. Robert had worked and prospered largely, never losing his humble ways, always praising God for delivering him some property of his own. Just six years ago Kat had received a letter from

Robert announcing that he, so long a bachelor, had taken a wife, Maud. Now there were three children.

Robert Southern, thought Kat as they rumbled toward their destination, was the only person in the world outside of her kin and her loved ones at Court that she fully trusted.

Driving an open wagon far ruder than the conveyance in which Kat Ashley traveled was Robert Southern. Back straight as a rod, he wore the same grim expression as his old friend now riding to meet him at the Drury crossroads. He would not meet the eye of Betsy, the young woman sitting next to him. She was just a wench, a "slut" his wife would call her, a poor unmarried girl who'd gotten with child and mercifully lost the babe in childbed. She was, thought Robert ruefully, not so different from his milk cows, for that was soon to be her purpose — to wet-nurse this child Kat was bringing into his life.

"Good Christ, what have I gotten myself into?" he asked himself, flicking the reins to hurry his team along to his destination. He had sworn loyal friendship to Katherine Champernoune Ashley more than thirty-five years before, but he'd never in his wildest dreams expected to be asked a favor such as this. A favor that, he knew as surely as the day was long, would wreak havoc in his own house.

In Kat's defense, he reasoned, she could not have known the recent circumstances that had befallen him. And he had never troubled Kat with the truth about Maud. He had only said, in his occasional letters to the woman who had become the Queen's first lady, that his wife was beautiful, that his farm was flourishing, and that his children thrived. How could Kat know of their misfortune — the recent outbreak of cattle fever and the death of more than a third of his herd? Above all, how could she know of the rift that divided him from Maud? Sometimes their differences seemed like an ever widening chasm, the kind that in a nightmare opens before you, altogether impossible to leap across. 'Twas ironic, he thought morosely, for the rift was made of the simplest stuff — her ambition, his lack of it.

Seven years before, finally prosperous enough to call himself a yeoman and afford a wife, Robert, with the help of a matchmaker — for he had no family for the purpose — had scoured the parish for a proper girl. Several with decent dowries had been offered, but one spring Sunday after church, as the younger men scrimmaged rough and tumble at football outside the churchyard, gentlemen, yeomen, poorer countrymen, and all their wives chatting in the sunshine, pretty, dark-haired, brown-eyed Maud Copely had caught Robert's eye. He had been smitten, and despite urgent pleas from the matchmaker, who wailed that the girl had no dowry and would be "marrying up," Robert Southern could never thereafter be unsmote.

Maud had wed the prosperous dairyman gladly. He was old, surely, but not decrepit. And, as Robert later learned, she had plans, many plans. When they took the vows he had barely known her, never realized what he was getting in the bright, perhaps overtalkative, but charming bundle of energy. Maud, he found, had been to grammar school. Could read. Was even clever with numbers.

She had determined early on to become Robert Southern's helpmate, take his prosperous farm, and make them wealthy. Once wealthy, she dreamed — oh, how she dreamed — they would move to London. Live the life of wealthy merchants in Londontown. Perhaps be asked to Court. Meet the Queen. Did he not once have a friend now in the Queen's circle?

Maud saw herself, she told Robert one winter afternoon daydreaming in front of the fire, wearing a fine blue brocaded gown with silver embroidered sleeves, curtsying to Her Majesty, and the Queen bidding her rise to compliment her sparkling eyes. And maybe, just maybe, the Queen would think: What a pretty thing to have for my waiting lady. When Robert had asked what would become of *him* in such a grand life, Maud had quickly added that of course Robert should go to London too. He would have a fine suit of clothes to meet the Queen. "But what would I *do* in London?" he persisted. "I am a man who knows and works best with animals." Becoming cross, Maud had shaken her pretty head and blustered, "There are animals in London! Horses, chickens, pigs. There must be animals!" She'd stormed off, her dreams compromised by a bumpkin husband.

Shortly thereafter Maud had begun having babies. A boy had been first, and despite her grandiose schemes the child, John, had brought Maud as well as Robert great joy. Two strong girls in quick succession had kept Maud busy. She always insisted, as wives of yeomen and gentry were wont to do, on hiring wet nurses to suckle her children. So Maud, between her household chores, schooling the children, teaching them their letters and numbers, and supervising the servants, had found time to establish a cheesemaking factory on the farm, producing great rounds of rich cheese which she with her clever ways contrived to sell most profitably across the Channel. She had never lost her dream at all. Simply postponed it. Enlarged it, even. Only God and Maud knew what grand London mansion on the banks of the Thames the girl had settled them in, which high lords and ladies she had invited to dinner. The dream had remained intact. Until now.

The cattle fever had scuttled Maud's plans as surely as a great sea wave might scuttle a small skiff, thought Robert. All profits were lost as they scurried frantically to keep from sinking altogether.

And then the confidential letter had arrived from Kat.

He had thanked the Lord that Maud had been elsewhere when Kat's man Roger brought it, but as he read the missive his heart thudded thick and hard in his chest. Kat was asking him to take in Queen Elizabeth's bastard child by Lord Robert Dudley. A child whom the Queen herself, owing to Kat's machinations, believed to be dead.

'Twas folly, thought Robert Southern, treason even. But worse still than the terror of a traitor's death, was the thought of Maud's rage. Kat had specified that no one, not even his wife, could know the child's lineage. Not that Robert wished to tell Maud, for if she knew the identity of the babe's parents, 'twould only feed her unattainable dreams. But when he brought a strange child and its wet nurse into their home demanding — for he must demand it — that the boy be accepted unquestioningly, what on earth might Maud think? That he was Robert's own bastard child, of course. No good amount of explanation, no talk of a distant family member in trouble — for Maud knew all of his meager family — would suffice. Lord, now of all times!

Robert groaned aloud, and Betsy turned to him with a look of concern. "Are you unwell, Mister Southern, sir?"

"No, no, I'm fine."

"Are we almost there, then?" she asked, shading her eyes to look down the narrow highway that cut through flat marshlands dotted with sheep and cattle.

"See up ahead, Betsy, where the road meets with another road? The sign has been pulled down, it appears, but that is the road to London."

"London? Is the babe come from London, then?"

Robert cursed himself silently. Betsy had shown considerable curiosity about her position with the dairyman's family since her clandestine hiring, and he wished her to know as little as possible. He would not even have brought her in sight of his meeting with Kat Ashley, but for the child needing a caretaker once the exchange had been made. Besides, he did reckon, Betsy could have no way of knowing who Kat was, this girl who had never once left the confines of her rural village in the sixteen years she'd been alive.

The milk wagon clattered to a halt at the crossroads, and they waited. It should not be long. Kat had estimated the time from the previous night's inn to the meeting spot as less than four hours.

Perhaps, thought Robert Southern with a twinge of hope and guilt combined, the child had died, God rest his little soul, and Kat would arrive alone to say, "Thank you, my friend, for agreeing to this favor but, alas, the Queen's bastard has met his Maker." Then they would sit amiably, hold hands as they chatted, exchange idle gossip as friends do, and leave each other with a chaste kiss goodbye.

His hopeful musings were shattered by the distant unmistakable rumble of a carriage approaching down the London road.

The coach Kat Ashley came in was large and elegant, a transport that would surely incite talk. 'Twas not the coach of any local lord or gentry, and by the next day all in the village would know of the fine carriage come from London and who had met it at the crossroads. But Robert had plotted their meeting so far from his own home that, even if it were to be seen, the village abuzz with gossip would not be *his* village. And unless luck was dead set against him, Maud would never hear how or when he had acquired the child.

As the coach clattered to a stop a hundred paces from the milk cart, Robert Southern took a deep breath, straightened his jacket, and climbed down. He was strangely aware that the road under his feet was hard and uneven, and he felt, with less foreboding than he imagined he might have, that he was walking toward his destiny. Perhaps this was good fortune for them all, and consequences be damned! He would deal with Maud, quiet her fears. He would take in this royal child, much as Sir Ector, centuries before, had raised the boy Arthur as his own until the day the lad had pulled Excalibur from the stone and been proclaimed king of all England. All would be well, he told himself coming abreast of the carriage, all would be well . . .

Kat and Robert dared not tarry overlong. She had immediately sent Ellen out to give the child over into the girl Betsy's keeping. Kat did not wish to be witness to the scene and hardened her heart against Ellen's pain at losing the infant who had for many weeks soothed the ache of her own stillborn babe.

Kat and Robert sat in the fine coach opposite each other and spoke — not unlike he had imagined — sweetly, companionably, trying to fit too many years apart into one half hour. He had not, however, reckoned how greedy he was for the sight of her, how he searched the face, now crisscrossed with fine wrinkles, as if it were a roadmap of their past and perhaps, too, his future with the boy.

They did not, at first, talk of the child. The details had been arranged by letter. But the time to part approached and it was only fitting that some words be spoken of this strange bundle being passed into his life. Yet no words came, no questions formed in Robert Southern's mind. He groped in agonizing silence and Kat, good old friend that she was, sensed his confusion.

"His name . . ." she said finally.

"His name?" said Robert uncomprehendingly. Did she wish to know what he would name the child? "Oh, of course. What is he called?"

Kat looked away out the coach window, perhaps remembering that terrible stormy night, the pain, the blood, the betrayal. . . .

"The Queen called him Arthur."

Kat grasped Robert's hand suddenly and fiercely. He moved to sit beside her, his arms going round her. As she leaned into them and cried bitterly, Robert Southern wondered at the Fates that had once again brought two lovers together, and a new child into his life — a royal child called Arthur.

Maud Southern could barely contain her excitement. She had finished her day's chores — overseeing cook's preparation of the dinner meal, sewing the sleeves into Meg's new Sunday gown, scolding the buttery workers for their slack pace, and haggling with the merchants from Plainfield over the price of her best cheese. Yes, she was weary, but like a buzzing bee her marvelous idea had flitted here and there inside her head, and even seemed to make her heart beat faster at the thought of it. Oh, where was Robert! She was trembling with anticipation to lay the scheme before him, watch that always sober countenance crinkle into a surprised smile of joy.

She envisioned herself seated across the buttery table from him detailing her plan to sell the dairy *now,* before more cows sickened and died and they lost any more of their holdings. She would spread before him the money she had secretly squirreled away from her buttery operation, and describe how she had contracted with local Suffolk cheesemakers, and some others from across the Channel in France and the Low Countries with whom she had negotiated to import rather than export cheeses.

The family would move to London, to a modest address, and open a white meats shop selling eggs and butter and cheese, with cheeses shipped in from all over England and Europe. Robert's friend in the Queen's entourage would help them get the license they would need for business. 'Twould at first be a small operation. They would be Lesser Merchants, to be sure, but news of their fine products would spread to all parts of London and beyond, and surely come to the Queen's attention. They would move up in the world, become Great Merchants with a better address in Milk Street and perhaps a home separate from their shop. Young John would have the finest education and the girls large dowries. The family would rise from yeoman class to gentry. John would become a man of substance, perhaps study law, perhaps hold public office. Oh, 'twould be exciting, a life in London, sociable and satisfying! How could Robert possibly say no?

Maud bustled up the stairs and peeked in the nursery where their servant Barbara sat suckling Maud's youngest girl, fair Alice, just two years old. Meg, who played quietly with her new kitten, was three. She resembled her mother, with dark eyes to match her hair, and was a pretty child. Meg would have no trouble finding a good husband, with her looks and a rich merchant father. She might even marry up. And what, indeed, was "up" from the gentry? Maud smiled contentedly and turned to the room she shared with Robert.

The bedstead, the finest piece of furniture in the house, was good sized, with a canopy and even some carving in the headboard. The muslin sheets were the best they could afford for now, though she always wondered how it would feel to slip in between fine lawn sheets. Well, she would know soon enough.

Maud moved to the small mirror to see how she looked for Robert's return and glimpsed John, almost five, from the window. The boy was chasing chickens round the barnyard and shrieking delightedly at the ruckus he was causing. He looked the way she imagined Robert had looked as a boy, the same fair ringlets framing the same high forehead, the toothy smile, large ears he would never quite grow into. John was her firstborn and Maud adored him, glad that he had inherited his high spirits from her, and not the quiet seriousness of his father.

The boy stopped in his tracks, then streaked to the farm gate. Robert must be home. Maud peered into the mirror, tucking a flyaway bit of hair behind her ear, and bit her lips to redden them. Despite three children in a few short years, she still retained her girlish prettiness. But now she must look neat and professional — like the proud tradeswoman she would present herself to be.

Maud sent the servants scurrying after the children, so that when Robert Southern entered the buttery door they were quite alone. She was sitting behind the wooden table, erect, her hands folded neatly in front of her. Her pert, enigmatic smile drooped slightly with the first look at her husband's face. Always serious, he was this afternoon very somber indeed, with what appeared to be a perplexed expression. Maud decided she must proceed nonetheless.

"Robert. I've been thinking a good deal of our situation here at the farm, the dairy and such, and my cheesemaking. I've thought, too, about the cows and their illnesses, and how we do depend so dearly on them for our feast or famine."

"Maud, we must talk together."

"I know that, Robert. But I tell you I have done a good bit of talking to myself, sometimes as if I were talking to you, so —"

"You don't understand, Maud."

"What do I not understand? Why you've walked in here with a face as long as a rope? More cattle have not died, have they?" she asked, suddenly alarmed.

"No, no cattle have died, and no one we know has died."

"Well, that's a relief, then. What *is* it, Robert? Tell me quickly, because I'm bursting to tell you my news."

When he did not answer, Maud followed his gaze out the buttery window and saw the girl sitting in the milk wagon holding a bundle to her breast. Maud squinted. "Who's that out in the cart? It looks to me like . . . Betsy Newman." She looked at Robert quizzically, but he had not yet found words to begin. "Is she not the slut that birthed a little bastard last week?" Maud peered more closely out the window. "But she's holding a babe in her arms, and I heard the child died. Why is she sitting in the milk wagon in our yard, Robert?"

"'Tis Betsy Newman indeed," he said in a strained voice.

Maud waited for Robert to go on. Then she asked challengingly, "Have you brought that slut for a visit to our home?"

"'Tis a babe she holds in her arms . . . though 'tis not her own, for hers did die," Robert finally said. He could see that Maud was becoming very alarmed, but he could only push the words out one by one. "'Tis not Betsy Newman so much . . . who has come to our home . . . as the child."

"The child? Whose child is it? And why has it been brought here? Robert, I'm beginning to feel very cross, so I pray you speak to me smartly now."

"'Tis the child of a friend," he lied — the first lie he had ever spoken to his wife — "though I will not tell you what friend. And I mean for us to take this child into our household, with Betsy Newman for his wet nurse."

"What are you saying? We have no money for a ward in this house. We have barely enough for our children and servants. And what mean you that you will not tell me which friend!" Maud's face had turned red and blotchy with growing anger.

"I do not mean for the child to be a ward —"

"I should hope not," Maud spat.

"I mean for us . . . to adopt him as our own."

Maud sat at the buttery table, eyes downcast, biting at her knuckles as she tried to make sense of her husband's senseless words.

"Have you heard me, Maud? I want Betsy to bring the boy in now. It's cold and getting colder out there."

"No," she said quietly.

"Maud . . ."

"No, I don't want another child. And whose is it! Is it *your* bastard, Robert?"

"No, Maud, I swear 'tis not my child."

"We are having no more children now, Robert. We are moving to London. That is what I meant to tell you this evening. We are selling the farm and —"

"What nonsense are you talking, woman? We have no such plans."

"But we do. *I* do!" Finally Maud moved from her chair. She sprang to the cabinet, flung it open, and pulled a small chest out. Her movements were so wild by now that she knocked open the chest before setting it down, so its contents spilled out across the floor and tabletop. Robert's eyes stared uncomprehendingly at the coin and paper. So jumbled were his own thoughts, he could make neither head nor tail of Maud's.

"A white meats store, Robert, in London, with cheeses imported from everyplace — and sold to the Queen herself! You've seen the success I've made of the business here. I'll do the same in London. I'll run the shop, trade with the wholesalers, keep the accounts. We'll do fine, I swear to heaven we will! But we must go soon. We cannot afford more cattle dying. The dairy will never sell!"

She was growing frenzied. Robert knew he must move, bring the babe inside against the cold, but when he went to the door, Maud leapt at him and barred it like a madwoman.

"No, Robert!"

He fixed her with a stare she had never before seen, a stare that spoke of past transgressions of hers — sullen humors, fits of temper, irrational vexations — that he had chosen to meet with mildness and acquiescence.

But now he was a man decided, and he would not be moved. As gently as he was able, he pushed Maud aside and opened the door.

"Betsy," he called, "bring him in."

Stock-still Maud watched the slut, her teeth chattering, and some unnamed bastard boy cross the threshold of her home. The wet nurse looked to Robert for instructions, and he pointed to a door into their great room.

"Warm yourselves in there for now," he said in a kindly voice.

Betsy chanced a small smile at Maud and was rewarded with a hatred colder than the November night.

"Yes sir," said Betsy, and disappeared with her silent bundle.

Maud was rigid, refusing to meet Robert's eye, for she had been roundly chastised by him for the first time in the entire length of their married life. And she knew not why. How could he conceive of such a plan without her consultation? And who had so much power over him that he might risk the happiness of his hearth and home?

Robert had also remained silent, collecting his thoughts.

"Maud . . . I do not wish for you to be angry, and I know you are. Perhaps you will like the rest of this."

"There is more?" she asked with dread in her voice.

"I know you wish to be raised to the gentry."

Maud listened, afraid to breathe.

"With this adoption" Robert continued, "comes a reward. A position. We will be moving . . ."

"Where?"

"Closer to London," he said carefully.

"How close?"

"Two days' ride."

"'Tis still the country!"

"I know, Maud, but I shall be the keeper of a great chase — Enfield Chase, a fine parkland. One which the Queen herself comes to visit and hunt in. We shall have no more cows, Maud, but beautiful horses instead, and wild game all round us."

"Still the country, full of bumpkins and rowdy fools!"

"Think you London has no bumpkins and rowdy fools? Then you are a fool yourself, Maud Southern!"

"How comes this post with this child? One of your high friends, is it?"

"We shall not talk of it, Maud. I have said that, and I mean it."

She fumed. Her fists clenched, and her jaw. Robert thought then that if a person could explode, Maud might do that now. He was suddenly frightened, for he had seen a man once, angry like this and bursting with rage, who had fallen down with a stroke and died.

Robert put a soft hand on Maud's arm.

"Please, Maud. I have asked very little of you in our marriage. I have given you free range for your thoughts and ways. I have fostered your ambitions. I have never struck you, not once." He looked away. "But you must let me have this boy, and you must go with me as my wife to the new post. And never . . . never ask me about it again. Do these things, and you will shortly find yourself a gentlewoman. I'll give you leave sometimes to go to London if you wish, though I have little love for the place myself. Perhaps, even, John can be schooled there when he's older."

Maud watched her husband as if from a great distance. He was smashing to pieces the beautiful confection she had created, and demanding she be grateful for the crumbs he now scattered before her. She supposed he expected her to love this child, this highborn bastard, destroyer of her whole life's ambition. Well, thought Maud as she turned to face her bleak future as a country wife, Robert Southern had better think again.

Eleven

For as long as I can recall
Twas a horse whose affection
Held me in its thrall

A poor poem, that, but the only verse I confess ever to have writ. Poor, but a true sentiment all the same. A horse and a boy together — the story of my life. What was my age? Which of those good friends was the first? I cannot say, but I was very small, this I know. I remember neither the beasts name nor color nor markings, whether twas stallion, mare, gelding. What I do recall is straddling the wide back, seeing before me the high proud head, muscled neck, breathing in the rich musk, hearing the sweet sound of nickering and blowing. Above all I remember the graceful rock and rhythm which soothed my senses, all the while bringing them sharply to bear. My tiny fingers are splayed round the leather pommel, my fathers great paw atop my smaller one. He and I are riding thro the greenwood, a slow clop, clop, clop, me nestled back against his large comfortable frame, gazing this way and that, for we are the protectors of the forest and all its wild inhabitants.

This Heaven on Earth in which I was, with my family, so happy to reside, was Enfield Chase. Twas a Royal grant and license given to my Father, and with its acquisition came a great raising of our familys fortunes, just after my birth. The property was a large wooded expanse, well stocked with red and fallow deer — the noblemans favorite game. Wild boar were imported from France. Hare, hunted by gentlemen and yeomen, ran in smaller circles than the stag and were slower, but they were good quarry none the less with their cunning, and gave the hounds a run for their trouble. Fox were abundant but inferior prey, no better than vermin.

The far end of the Chase went to marshlands, and there resided numerous ducks and mallards and geese which were hunted. On some farmland in the south quarter of the property, our tenants grew the oats, wheat, rye and sweet hay which they baked into horsebread to feed the livestock. The trees were many of them ancient, but there was new growth which showed the health of the forest. The trees were thickly grown, tho the whole of the wood was crossed with sufficient old and wellworn paths as to make travel within it — even hard riding — most pleasant.

On the estate was a small manor house which I always thought very grand, tho my Mother complained of its age and dampness, and its nearness to the barn and stables which she said gave the house a stink of animals. This was not untrue, tho me and my Father chuckled together in private, how we liked the smell a far lot better than the French perfumes she sprinkled about.

For it was, from a tender age, the stables that were more homely to me than the manor house would ever be. We kept thirty mounts — English Great Horses, Arab, Spanish, Barb. And more than just the keeping of them to be rented for hunting and hawking and several for racing, we backed and trained young horses, and taught equitation to local squires, their wives and children. All of those must be skilled riders, for horsemanship — to ride surely and cleanly — was part and parcel of every gentle and noble persons education.

I should not forget the running hounds that we raised and kept, but I must admit that tho I felt a fondness for dogs, they were nothing in my mind compared to horses, but merely the necessary companion of hunting. I saw, tho, how there was a great bond twixt the two — the hounds inspired by the trampling hooves, and the sharp cry of the dogs urging the horses pursuit. The music of the hunt.

My chores as a young child were mucking stables, feeding horses and grooming them, even sewing feed bags upon occasion. I soon learnt the differences in breeds, their temperaments and shortcomings — tho I must admit I rarely called any behavior in a horse a shortcoming. Twas simply that steeds own manner of mind. I saw, even as a child — albeit no one I have ever known to this day agrees — that each horse was born with a mind. Whilst not the mind of person, surely tis a mind none the less. The temperament and dis-

portment of a wild horse before backing — that cruel science which must be endured by all pleasure and hunting mounts — changed and grew different after it had been saddled, its mind broke and remade to civility, now more a mans than a horses.

Enfield Towne was two days ride from London. Some city folk made the journey, for our Chase was known widely for its beauty, greatly stocked wood and fine horses. A good inn known as Stags Head, in the village, made the visitors stay most comfortable. There came, too, high lords of manors a days ride away, and local nobles and gentry, and they all partook of the bounty of Enfield Chase. Together with the rents collected from our tenant farmers, my Fathers fortunes rose. We lived well, though my Mother was wont to grumble that the Queen never came to hunt at Enfield, but my Father said she only rode out when on Progress and had not seen fit to come into our part of the country yet, but she would presently, he was sure.

My brother John was four years older than me, and my Mothers favorite. This was as it should be, loving most greatly her firstborn, she always said, but to her disgruntlement he was not also my Fathers favorite.

"John is your heir," I would hear her say when she saw my Father being merely kind to me.

He would say, "I know that, Maud, and John is the rightful inheritor of Enfield Chase under law, but I mean to provide for <u>both</u> my sons. Young Arthur needs to learn a trade, and he takes well to my own, so if I keep him close to me and school him in husbandry and game keeping it is most natural, so please do not interfere."

"Satans child!" she would mutter in a low curse, and my Father would flush red with fury.

"He is no such thing! A tiny nub of extra flesh on the outside of his hand is nothing . . ."

"There is a nail in it, John. Tis an extra finger! A witches mark, you know as well as I."

"If I were prone to superstition maybe, but I am not. Tis no more a witches mark than the great brown wen on your thigh."

"I say we bring the surgeon here," she said, ignoring my Fathers reasoning, "and let him have it off."

"And I say you mind your business, woman, and leave the boy alone!"

To cover the offending digit — a strange thing to be sure — I was made always to wear a small glove. My Mother instructed me to say to curious folk that I had badly burnt the hand in a fire, and wished to hide my disfigurement. The glove came to be a most natural part of my apparel, and I thought little of it as the years went by.

For Johns part, he was a reasonable brother in my younger years. Sure he felt our Mothers bitterness towards me, but he was just a plain lad with few leanings in particular. He learnt his numbers and letters well enough but cared little for them. He rode, but then all young gentlemen did. He fished in the marshes, played at dice and other games of chance. No passion stirred him, but then twas not a necessary thing, for he would without question, and despite his behavior inherit all of Enfield Chase upon our Fathers death. Twas the law of primogeniture.

My sisters Meg and Alice, sweet girls, doted on me. My wet nurse left our employ when I was two, and to my great advantage my sisters — only two and three years older — were my little mothers and I their little doll. They would whine and wheedle those times my Father came and whisked me from the nursery to take me riding, claiming he took away their favorite plaything. Our Mother treated Meg and Alice well if not lovingly. Dressed them in pretty dresses, braided their hair, talked endlessly about the good marriages she would one day make them, the fine dowries their Father would provide.

I have long since forgiven my Mother the beatings she gave, those which she proffered with switch, broom handle, leather strap or fisted hand. But I do remember that when they were freshly meted out to the small tender boy that I was, they were in deed cruel. They injured my flesh, I think, less than my emerging spirit, and yet did help to form the man which I became. For, I reasoned, if I were beaten by someone I loved, I could never then beat someone whom I loved. And as I did love horses, I learnt a kind of friendly intercourse with them shared by few men and distained by many.

In my family I was the only child to attract my Mothers fury. I was perplexed, for my behavior I saw as not so different from my brother Johns. But I received all punishment stoicly, and in the way that children sometimes do, came to believe I was deserving of it, that I had somehow erred, that when I was older I would come to understand. For Parents are sacred, small Gods to a child and can do no wrong. I saw my Mother in those times as an Angel — she was quite beautiful to me — whose violent tempers were caused by a Devil spirit temporarily inhabiting her body, whispering bad things in her ear about me. For when my Mother was good she was very good indeed. Sharp and bright like a fine blade, flashing and brilliant in the sunlight.

She read us Scripture twice daily in a voice filled with meaning, not the dull droning I had heard in other Godly households. She schooled us well, taught us right from wrong in all things, gave us our numbers and letters, and was patient with my brother and two sisters, tho less with my self. But as I have said I saw her as having good excuse to beat me, and in schooling that much more so. Whilst I was not slow, I had scant interest in schoolroom learning. I wished only to be abroad with my Father, helping him tend Enfield Chase, learning all manner of husbandry, doctoring sick beasts, building shooting towers and blinds for the companies of noble folk who would come to hunt in our little Paradise.

And to be riding my horse — that most of all.

Twelve

The high rhythm of a French galliard resounding in her ears, Elizabeth found herself for a brief, brilliant moment airborne looking down upon her dancing partner. Then the same brawny arms that had thrust her upwards caught her fall. The moment her slippers touched the ground James Melville spun the Queen full round, and she landed with a whoop as the galliard ended. Melville was laughing, glistening with exertion as were all on the floor of the Great Hall who had shared the dance and the excellent music of pipe and tabor.

"By God, by Christ, and by many parts of his glorified body, I do love dancing!" she cried.

"Ye leap as pretty as a fine young goat, Yer Majesty," answered Melville with a low bow.

"And you as high as a roebuck, Sir James."

Offering Elizabeth his arm, Melville walked her off the floor, but the Queen declined to be seated. Though she wished to dance the next dance, she could see that Sir James wished to talk. The Scottish ambassador this evening had heeded her advice only to make merry, and had steered away from subjects of a serious cast. But he clearly enjoyed, as much as she, two bright and educated minds newly joined, discovering through light banter territories yet unexplored. In the past week Elizabeth and the roughly handsome and imperturbable emissary from the court of Mary Queen of Scots, who stood out from her peacock courtiers in a kilt of the muted tartan of his clan, had covered much and varied ground. Whilst she knew his purpose to be the penetration of her mind, and relaying the intelligence there discovered to his sovereign, Elizabeth smiled inwardly to know she had penetrated his mind equally. Besides queries about the Scots queen, from trivial gossip to matters of serious statecraft, she had asked him what books he liked to read and questioned him about the countries to which he had traveled — for she herself had never left England — and the peoples he had chanced to meet there.

Was she flirting with Melville? Elizabeth asked herself, accepting a cup of wine from him and taking her first full breath in what seemed like hours. She liked this man. She had admitted as much the moment she met him, and was complimented by Mary's choice of ambassadors, sure that the decision had been carefully and cleverly taken. Melville had proven to be not only a well of information about her mysterious cousin but wise, kind, and wholly sincere. He wished for nothing more than his mistress and Elizabeth, young cousins by blood, to finally meet and come to happy accord, particularly with respect to the succession. But the Queen also sensed that Melville felt a genuine esteem for herself, and would no doubt relay the same to Mary.

"I am told Mary loves dancing as well as I do."

"Aye, she claims a close contest between her favorite pastimes — playing music, dancing, and hunting."

"She rides well, then?" asked Elizabeth.

"Oh, she's a fierce rider, Yer Majesty. She's recently returned from Balmoral, where on one morning a thousand Highlanders came out to beat the bushes for stag, which she and her lords made sport of all the day long." He bent down to whisper to Elizabeth, for he was tall as well as brawny. "I tell ye, Yer Majesty, the two of ye'll be fast friends at the end of the first day ye meet."

Elizabeth smiled coyly. "You make your case well, Melville. Somehow you've contrived to take the sting out of my recalcitrant cousin's refusing still to sign the Edinburgh Treaty, and her neverending insistence that she is the true queen of England. I am almost inclined to agree to this meeting. But they," she added conspiratorially, indicating a gaggle of older, bearded ministers across the room, "are in doubt of this meeting's worthiness. Some fear it. In any event 'twould be a great undertaking, a farther journey than I have ever made — and I am but recently returned home from my summer progress. Traveling that way is a complicated affair."

"Then do it another way, Majesty."

"Another way, Sir James?" said Elizabeth, her curiosity piqued.

Melville whispered even more quietly, "Disguise yerself as a lad — my page. Accompany me back to Scotland. Cross the border and slip into Holyrood Castle incognito with nobody the wiser."

Elizabeth chuckled but found herself silently contemplating the outrageous plan. "Are all Scotsmen as bold as you are, Sir James?" she said, pinching his earlobe playfully.

"Ye come to Scotland and I'll show ye a passel of bold men and a bold queen to boot."

Lord Clinton had shouldered close to Melville and begged a word. As Elizabeth gestured that he was released from her company, she spied Robin Dudley inviting her pretty cousin Lettice Knollys for the next dance, and found herself troubled with confusing emotions.

Pain stung the back of her eyes with the clear remembrance of her and Dudley's poor infant lying between them, and Elizabeth's dream of a life with her love growing colder, even as the babe's body took on the chill of death. She was stung, too, by a terrible guilt. Despite her and Robin's continuing liaison, despite the very real love and care that they shared still, despite the great honors and estates, licenses and pensions she had heaped upon Robin, building him into a powerful New Man, she knew that he refused to believe, chose to be blind to the truth of her motives.

Not a month before there had been the incident with the Swedish ambassador. When he had come courting the Queen on behalf of King Eric, Robin had thrown obstacles in his path to herself, threatening the man with imprisonment, even with physical harm. When Elizabeth heard of the disgraceful incident, she had raged wildly at Robin before all the assembled lords, cursed him for interfering with her diplomacy, and screamed that she should never ever marry him. He had been humiliated publicly and injured privately. In a blazing quarrel he had begged her permission to leave the Court, go to the Continent to lick his wounds. Elizabeth had granted him leave, believing the separation might be wise. She hoped the injury to his pride would finally force him clear of his hitherto faithful but hopeless pursuit of marriage to herself. But it had not. He had thought better of removing himself from Court when he knew himself held in disfavor, and after a reunion both tearful and passionate, Robin had renewed his efforts to wed her with ever more cunning stratagems.

Was she herself evil? she wondered, watching Robin and Lettice — a pretty couple — swirl and bow and march with the elegant measured steps. How could she continue to let him believe she might yet marry with him? How could she keep him tied jealously to herself? Ah, thought Elizabeth, the answer within the question. Jealousy. She could not bear to think of him in another woman's arms. He was hers alone, since childhood, and despite his marriage to Amy Robsart, Elizabeth had always owned his heart and he hers.

There were worse fates for Robin, she suddenly thought. Worse than standing as the Queen's favorite man, gifted with castles, honors, riches, and power — unheard-of power for a mere subject, son and grandson of traitors to the Crown. Worse fates indeed. No, she would not marry with him, bestow upon him the Crown Matrimonial, though she might lead him to believe one day she would. She was Elizabeth, Queen of England, and she had a kingdom to rule — to rule well. That would be uppermost in her thoughts, though she would never banish her own pleasure altogether.

Elizabeth seized her lingering guilt with both hands and flung it away over the heads of the dancers. When the music ended she glided imperiously across the floor and came squarely to face Robin. He smiled at her then, as much with the tenderness of their many years together as with the fire of a brand-new lover. And she was smitten all over again. Wordlessly, she took his arm and as the drums and pipes swelled to their tune Elizabeth and Dudley, in perfect and joyful harmony, began to dance.

The Queen's hawking party sped through the open meadows behind Hampton Court, racing for the ground beneath which the great bird soared in silent pursuit of its prey. The red hawk had been a fine gift from her cousin Mary, delivered earlier that week by Melville, who now galloped beside her. Robin, his brother Ambrose, and Henry Sidney brought up the rear. The ground trembled under so many thundering hooves. Elizabeth rode in the new fashion for a lady, a practice begun by de Médicis, right knee hooked round the pommel. The cold morning air lashing her face, flanked by her favorites, Elizabeth knew herself as whole and well contented as she had been in many months.

She had shared Robin's bed this night past. Before he'd discreetly disappeared from Robin's chamber, Tamworth had filled the room with braziers of red hot rocks against the winter chill, and the place had glowed with lovely warmth so that they could lie perfectly naked in each other's sight. All sadness and fear had been banished, and the feel of his hands and lips upon her body had been exquisite. She had cried out as he'd entered her, and gripped his hard back and tensile flanks as they rode together, coupled in rhythm and pleasure.

This morning, again the Queen, reins firmly in hand, she had renewed diplomatic intercourse with Melville on the subject of her cousin Mary and was, though no one but the ambassador knew, actually contemplating his audacious scheme to take Elizabeth across her northern border in disguise.

Head angled to the sky, Elizabeth saw the swift in-flight kill. She ran her horse to a stop and waited, gloved arm outstretched, as a light rain of the prey's feathers floated down from above. A moment later the hawk swooped down and, dagger-clawed feet first, massive wings outstretched, lit gracefully upon Elizabeth's heavy leather gauntlet. She took the limp pigeon from its powerful beak and handed it to Melville. Searching the magnificent creature's eyes for only a moment, the Queen pulled the tiny plumed hood over its head.

"You may tell my cousin I like her gift almost as much as I like her choice of ambassadors," said Elizabeth.

But Melville was prevented from his courtly riposte by the sight of a lone man of the Queen's royal guard galloping at breakneck speed toward the party. When he had reined to a halt, Elizabeth gave the breathless messenger leave to speak.

"The Duke of Guise has reportedly ordered his troops to fire on a Protestant prayer meeting, Your Majesty. Four hundred are dead. The Huguenots are massing for retaliation. France is on the brink of civil war."

Elizabeth sat straight and still in her saddle. She was suddenly aware of the chill on her cheeks, and she felt in this moment as though, through the actions of a single murderous man on a continent so far from here, her whole life had suddenly, irrevocably changed.

"Sir James," she said finally to the Scotsman, who himself was clearly grappling with the dire implications of this news, "I deeply regret that I can no longer consider a meeting with a sovereign whose own uncle has handily murdered four hundred of his innocent countrymen." She turned to Robin, Ambrose, and Henry Sidney. "Come, we have much business to attend to." Then she kicked her horse and sped for Hampton Court.

Not an hour had passed since Elizabeth had hooded the hawk in the meadow. She still wore her riding clothes as she and the Privy Council, together with the Dudley brothers, debated the intent and consequences of the Duke of Guise's actions, and England's response to the same. The Privy Councillors were wary of the presence of her casual companions, but Elizabeth had been adamant about their inclusion in the meeting.

Despite his newness to the inner circle of policymaking, Robin spoke boldly. "The moment the French Huguenots are granted religious toleration by the House of Valois they are slaughtered like animals," he said earnestly. "We have no choice but to throw support to our Protestant brothers when the Guise faction is clearly planning their extermination."

"Is that so?" Elizabeth asked, skewering Robin with her eyes. She might love him passionately, but he was not exempt from her scathing sarcasm. "'Tis curious in the extreme, my lord, that you not so long ago were prepared to sacrifice our country's resources for the Catholic cause. I wonder if you are now treating with the Huguenots for *their* support in our marriage."

Elizabeth saw with satisfaction that Robin Dudley flushed red under his tan. Well, if he meant to be included in policymaking he must learn to bear the sharp sting of her lash, as all her Privy Councillors were forced to do.

"What say *you,* Secretary Cecil?" Elizabeth inquired more mildly.

"I am inclined to agree with your Horsemaster," replied Cecil, placing emphasis on Robin's lowly title. Cecil was deeply offended that Elizabeth should include the man in a decision of such import, for as sincerely as he tried, Cecil could not stomach the Queen's lover. "If Guise feels free to murder Huguenots in France, and if he then consolidates his position, I fear England would be his next target. He will do everything in his power to put Mary Queen of Scots on your throne and marry her to one of Philip's sons. Therefore, the French Protestants who oppose Guise must be supported by their English brethren."

"And how do you suppose we should aid them?" asked Elizabeth, throwing the question out to all of her councillors.

"We must protect our northern borders against invasion from Scotland," offered Lord Clinton. "After all, your cousin Mary is herself a Guise. I propose the Duke of Norfolk, perhaps Northampton and Rutland, with several battalions to ride to the Scottish border."

"Good," said Elizabeth. "Have my cousins Hunsdon and Huntingdon ride with them. What else, my lords?" She looked round at her men.

"May I suggest using this as an opportunity for Her Majesty to recover from the French our port city of Calais?" added Cecil, knowing the suggestion, though audacious, would heartily please the Queen. The loss of England's last stronghold on the Continent by her half-sister Mary had always been a bone in Elizabeth's throat.

"As you know, I have never coveted nor fought for any territories not my own," said Elizabeth. "But Calais belongs rightly to England, and regaining it would certainly protect our eastern coast from a French invasion."

Throckmorton spoke up. "Let us not behave too rashly, Your Majesty. I believe we should attempt mediation first."

"Military intervention is the clearest solution," interrupted Robin insistently. "Meet force with force. Let them see we will allow no aggression to go unchecked."

"I must agree with Lord Dudley," announced Elizabeth. Then as he smiled triumphantly, she added, "I therefore appoint his elder brother, Ambrose Lord Warwick, as captain general of the expedition."

There was a long moment of silence as the implications — the raising of Ambrose, the slight to Robin, and the magnitude of Elizabeth's commitment of military force — framed and reframed themselves in her councillors' heads.

The silence from Robin, observed Elizabeth, was complete, and his restraint almost superhuman. She knew he was furious, hurt, bewildered. Yet she had acted of necessity. Of course he wished, as all men did, to distinguish himself on the battlefield — 'twas the surest way to elicit respect from one's peers. But she needed Robin at home, by her side for good counsel. Too, if she were entirely honest with herself, she was reluctant to send him into battle. She could survive his ranting fury in private, but she could never bear the thought of him wounded. The thought of him dead.

"So, my lords, 'tis decided. Speak amongst yourselves. Send for the Huguenot envoy and let me hear the details of your plans." She moved to the door, then turned back to her councillors. "And see that Sir James Melville has safe conduct across the northern border. Cecil, will you send him my good wishes, and regrets that I shall not see him before his departure? 'Tis a pity to end our negotiations so abruptly," said Elizabeth. "He was as toward a gentleman as I have ever known."

The doors of the Privy Chamber swung open and Elizabeth swept through them, disappearing in a great rustling of skirts.

Ambrose Dudley broke the silence.

"Calais," he said with force and deliberation. "Let us speak of the return of Calais."

Robin Dudley strode down Hampton Court's long corridors and bounded up the broad stone stairs to the upper floor. He was stiff from the sixteen hours in which the council had just met without cessation. Meals had been brought into the Privy Chamber from the basement kitchens as the greatest minds in England plotted the kingdom's future. Plans for garrisoning English troops in the French port city of Le Havre with Lord Warwick at their head and sending three thousand soldiers to help defend the Huguenots were discussed and formulated.

The moment the meeting concluded, Robin had exploded from the chamber, pent-up anger surging through his limbs, the necessity of confronting Elizabeth with her perfidy uppermost in his mind. When he had spoken so boldly about resisting the French, he had clearly envisaged himself leading the troops gallantly into the fray. It had been many years since he had seen battle, and it was the surest way for a man to attain greater glory.

Robin barged past the guards of Elizabeth's antechamber, but was stopped short at the sight of his sister, Mary Sidney, exiting the Queen's bedchamber door looking pale and frightened. When she saw him, she at once began to cry.

"What, sister? What is it?"

Mary choked back her sobs. "The Queen . . ." She could not go on.

"What about her? Mary, speak to me. Tell me what's happened!"

"When she came from the council meeting, she said she felt uneasy and asked for a hot bath. Afterwards she claimed to feel better, then insisted on dressing again and taking exercise in the yard. Kat begged her to stay and rest, but you know how the Queen is. She cannot abide being still for long. When she returned from the outdoors she was burning with fever."

"A fever . . ." Robin sagged with relief. "By Christ, you had me alarmed. Elizabeth has had many fevers."

"Robin!" She gripped his arm. "She has all the signs of smallpox!"

"Smallpox?"

"The rash has yet to appear," Mary went on, "but it will come on soon. She is very, very ill."

"The council have not been informed," he said, bewildered. "I have just come from them."

"She would not let us send word. She said you were all engaged in serious negotiations and must not be disturbed."

"Oh, Elizabeth!" He moved toward the bedchamber door.

Mary blocked his way. "She does not wish to see you, Robin. Her orders were most specific. She loves you too dearly to risk your infection. You must go back, inform the council."

"They will be wild. She has never named her successor. Should she die . . ."

"She will not die, Robin," said Mary Sidney, her eyes set in steely resolve. "I will not let her die."

Robin pulled his sister to him. He held her in a fierce embrace and they trembled in shared fear and misery.

"I must keep my head," Robin told himself, "think what is best for England. The kingdom without a ruler . . . all the council's fears come to pass . . . factions, fighting, civil war . . . utter disaster." But as he strode from the anteroom and retraced his steps down the long corridors, there surged most relentlessly through Robert Dudley the instinct for self-preservation.

The Privy Council had been meeting now for the better part of a week. The Queen's condition had continued to deteriorate. She had slipped into unconsciousness the evening before, though there had been no showing of the angry red spots, the natural course of the disease. The mood was particularly grim this morning, for news that the Countess of Bedford had died of the pox earlier that day had reached them just as Cecil and the others were taking their places round the long council table. Elizabeth's death seemed imminent, and they were no further along in their deliberations than when they'd begun.

The claimants to the succession were dismal indeed. Lady Catherine Grey had been discussed most heatedly, as her claim was the clearest. She was sister of the ill-fated Lady Jane Grey, helpless fourteen-year-old pawn of ambitious courtiers, who had worn the crown for nine days and lost her head for their treachery. Jane and Catherine Grey had been included in Henry VIII's will, and named successors to his own offspring were they to die childless. But Catherine had recently disgraced herself by marrying without the council's consent and had borne a child by her husband whilst lacking legal proof of their marriage. She had been a prisoner in the Tower with this bogus husband and, unrepentant, had for a second time become pregnant by him.

Elizabeth's distant cousin Lord Huntingdon's claim was thin, and the one thing the Council had unanimously agreed upon so far was that Mary Queen of Scots should under no circumstances succeed. Cecil's only consolation in this terrible tangle was that Robin Dudley had been strangely absent. The Secretary has assumed that the Queen's lover, included in the original war council, would have insinuated himself — though he was not a member of the Privy Council — into the delicate negotiations on the succession. The council would have hesitated to disbar the favorite for fear of incurring Elizabeth's wrath should she live through her illness. Cecil's fears had proven unfounded as day after day Dudley had failed to intrude.

"We must come to some satisfactory conclusion today, my lords," announced Cecil gravely, "though each choice is more disastrous than the one before. Certainly London is staunchly Protestant, but to the north Catholics are abundant, and might rise against us to place the Scots queen on the throne."

The Privy Chamber door opened and a man of Elizabeth's personal guard moved briskly to Cecil's side, handing him a sealed letter. There was silence as Cecil stared at the folded parchment, loath to open it, fearing the worst. He scanned the faces of the Privy Councillors before breaking it open and reading. His eyes widened with surprise, and the great lords of England knew from Cecil's expression that the Queen had not yet expired, but that the news was in some way as terrible as it was encouraging.

"Tell us what has happened," demanded Lord Clinton. This nobleman had been, since the announcement of the Queen's illness, in a state of great confusion, for during her stay at Fulham House the year before on her progress, she had claimed to be suffering *then* from smallpox. Once stricken by that disease, as all knew, a person did never succumb a second time. Though he and his wife had discussed the strangeness of these circumstances between themselves, Clinton had not yet revealed Elizabeth's curious behavior to his fellow councillors. Cecil had still not spoken, his lips pursing and unpursing as he tried to make sense of what he was reading.

"What does it say, Cecil!" urged Lord Clinton.

"Robin Dudley," he said slowly and uncomprehendingly, "has in the space of five days raised an army of six thousand fighting men to defend the Queen from all usurpers."

"God's blood!" muttered Lord North. "Do we curse the man or praise him?"

"I declare, there is no one in the kingdom like him. No one with an ambition greater," said Lord Arundel.

"No one," added Cecil, who rankled with this admission, "who loves the Queen more."

"How did he manage such a thing?" Lord North demanded to know. "From where come six thousand armed men loyal to Robin Dudley?"

"That, my lords," replied Cecil, "is a question we would be wise to ponder."

"Thank Jesus he is on our side," added Lord Clinton.

William Cecil folded his hands to keep them from shaking as he intoned gravely, "Know you this and never forget it. The only side that Lord Robert Dudley is or will ever be on . . . is his own."

* * *

Doctor Burcot had been pacing before the door of the Queen's bedchamber for several hours waiting to be admitted. Both Kat Ashley and Lady Mary Sidney had come out to discuss with him the Queen's condition, but Her Majesty, who had still not broken out in the rash of lesions accompanying smallpox, had in her semidelirium refused to see the physician. He wished fervently to be allowed to minister to her, for in recent months he had had good success with a new treatment, and the Queen was said to be near death.

Finally the door opened and Mary Sidney beckoned him in. Picking up the large parcel at his feet, Burcot entered the Queen's bedchamber. He could not help but be overawed by the magnificence of the place — the enormous carven canopy bed, the sumptuous tapestries, window coverings of cloth shot with silver thread, cupboards groaning with gold plate. But all his attention must now be directed to saving the life of his Queen. She lay ghostlike and stick thin under the bedclothes, the famous red-gold hair flared out round her head like a large halo. As he bent over her lips he could hear only the faintest of breath. He lifted her still unblemished white hand and put two fingers to the pulse at her wrist. Then he turned to Katherine Ashley, who, though rumored to be ever a tower of strength, now appeared small and shrunken with terror that the woman she had tended since the age of four was dying.

"Mistress Ashley," said Burcot, "please to place several logs on the fire and stoke it till it burns with a great heat."

The doctor's confident demeanor spurred Kat to immediate compliance.

"Lady Mary, will you assist me? I wish you to uncover the Queen's body entirely."

Mary looked questioningly at the physician, but his expression compelled obedience. She pulled the bedcovers down to reveal the Queen's motionless body in a simple white gown. Opening his parcel, Burcot removed a large bolt of bright red flannel and, with Mary's help, proceeded to wrap the Queen's body from head to toe in the cloth, leaving only her face and her lower arms unbound.

"I need a soft mattress or several long pillows set by the fire," he announced.

With a look between them, Mary and Kat brought covers from the bed and made a soft lying-down spot before the hearth, which was now blazing with white heat.

"Come, ladies, help me lift her."

With his directions and strong hands guiding, the three of them carefully moved Elizabeth's red-cocooned body onto the makeshift bed near the fire.

Bustling back to his parcel, he now removed several flasks and bottles and set them up on Elizabeth's silver-topped table, forcing himself to ignore the Queen's pained moaning. Kat and Mary fluttered in subdued panic, for they had abetted this man's ministrations, and knew not whether he would cure the Queen or kill her. If he killed her, the blame could fall on their heads. Kneeling at the Queen's side, the ladies watched as Burcot poured and mixed powders and viscous liquids in a cup. He stirred the potion with a metal rod, first one direction twelve times, and then the other. When he seemed satisfied with his brew he approached and knelt between the Queen's women.

"Your Majesty," he whispered in her ear, "I believe in some part of yourself you can hear me. You are very weak and ill, as the infection is bound up inside your body, refusing to move outward into your skin."

With his words Elizabeth moaned piteously, and the doctor seemed to understand her wordless cries.

"I know, I know you fear the blisters and pockmarks, but if we cannot bring them to the surface you will certainly die. And what, Majesty, are a few spots and scars compared to your life? I beg you, drink what I have in this cup. Let me lift your head." He did this with the utmost care, placing the cup to Elizabeth's shriveled lips. She obeyed the doctor, her eyes fluttering open to peer into his face as she did. Mary inched forward as the Queen took the last drops of the liquid, and she thought she heard Elizabeth utter the words "very comfortable." Burcot laid her back down and urged her to close her eyes, rest, and let the heat and the medicine do their work.

He beckoned both women close and whispered, "I will stand vigil for now. If you are to be of any help when the Queen moves into the next phase of her illness, you must be alert, and I see you are both light-headed and utterly exhausted. Take your rest, good ladies, and as you lie yourselves down, pray for the Queen, for her fate is surely in God's hands."

Ten hours after Doctor Burcot had entered Elizabeth's room the men of the Privy Council, Mary and Henry Sidney, and Robin Dudley milled about before her bedchamber door, chatting in low nervous tones. They had, in fact, been summoned by the Queen herself. She had climbed laboriously from her stuporous condition to a state of consciousness within moments of breaking out in the angry red spots of smallpox. Whilst Doctor Burcot seemed guardedly pleased at the results of his treatment, the Queen's condition was still grave indeed, and she had insisted on speaking to her council on the chance that she might still succumb.

The bedchamber door opened and Kat called the assemblage inside. They grouped themselves round the bed where Elizabeth again lay. 'Twas hurtful for them all to see her in such condition, the once perfect skin inflamed with welts beginning to blister — spots they all knew might transform the lovely face into a grotesquely disfigured mask. Her voice was so weak that they were forced to come nearer. Though each of them felt a moment of fear for his own life, nonetheless they remained dignified as they strained to hear Elizabeth's words.

"Forgive me, my lords, for so inconvenient a council, but I fear the thread of my life is thin to breaking, and I have not yet given you direction should I die."

Thank Christ, she is finally naming her successor, thought Cecil, breathing so deep a sigh of relief he worried that all might have heard it. The weight of the decision, be it wise or foolish, should rightly fall upon the shoulders of the Queen and not on the men of the Privy Council.

"I wish to name" — she cleared her throat and took a long ragged breath before continuing — "Lord Robert Dudley as Protector of the Realm."

There was not one soul in the room, including Dudley himself, who did not gasp or start or blink uncomprehendingly at the Queen's pronouncement. She went on, either unknowing or uncaring of the great storm of emotion she had produced in the hearts of those assembled.

"Give him a title. Give him a pension of twenty thousand pounds a year, and to his servant Tamworth five hundred a year for the rest of his life."

This was, for William Cecil, too much to bear. He was forced to turn away in order to compose his features. Elizabeth, even in her dreadful condition, could not help but notice.

"William, my faithful Secretary. My good friend," she whispered. "Come, look at me."

Cecil strove to quiet the raging fury that shook his body and made his eyes water. He willed himself to turn back to the Queen.

"I know you are angry with me, Cecil." Then she went on, moving her eyes round to the other faces surrounding her, "But I tell you, my lords, with God as my witness, that although I loved Robert Dudley with my heart and soul, nothing improper ever did pass between us."

William Cecil's head was spinning. Here lay a woman, a queen he did love and admire and whom he had served with loyalty. A woman whom all in this room knew unquestionably to be the lover of the man she had moments before, in an outrageous act, named Protector of the Realm. And then, as if to add insult to injury, she had bequeathed an unbelievable pension to the servant of her lover's bedchamber, keeper of their most secret comings and goings. Did she take them all for fools? Elizabeth Tudor lay there on her deathbed and, with God as her witness, lied in so barefaced a way that Cecil thought he might himself be struck dumb for the rest of his days. For a fleeting moment it occurred to him that this was his punishment for spiriting away Elizabeth and Dudley's living child and replacing it with a dead one.

But then a new thought displaced the first — that even in extremis Elizabeth, Queen of England, was indeed the ultimate prince and statesman. She knew that long after the men in this room were reduced to dust, history would record her words for all posterity as the truth. She, like her father Henry VIII, did hold herself, if not above God, then shoulder to shoulder with him, and she dared fearlessly to lie in his name. Her will, in any event, would be done, and in death she would be remembered as she desired — as good and virtuous, the Virgin Queen.

Cecil was so beguiled by his wayward thoughts that he never heard Elizabeth commend her Boleyn cousin Lord Hunsdon to the council's kindness, and all the members of her household as well. Then she asked them all to pray for her, bade them farewell, telling them she loved them every one, and sent them away — all of them but Robin Dudley.

The Privy Councillors filed out, shoulders sloping with shock and defeat. Kat and Mary, too, could see that the Queen wished a private moment with Dudley. She had lifted a weak arm in his direction and uttered her private name for him, her Eyes.

As he moved to Elizabeth's side he crossed paths with his sister. They stood close, communing in silent pain. Suddenly Dudley's eyes widened in alarm. Mary Sidney saw his gaze shift slightly to her forehead, then to her right cheek. A cold thrill ran through her, and without her brother uttering a word she knew the truth. The pox had befallen her.

Dudley made to embrace Mary, but she backed away. "No, no," she whispered, her voice trembling with fear, fear she had not known in all the days she had nursed the Queen. "Protect yourself, Robert, for you are England's Protector should she . . ."

"She will not die, Mary. And neither shall you." He strode to the bedchamber door, called Doctor Burcot to him, and whispered, "Good

Thirteen

A most glorious occasion, this, thought Robin Dudley on the opening of Parliament. A glittering morn with trumpets blaring, crowds cheering, him riding his great white charger behind Elizabeth — so reminiscent of her coronation day. She, however, came not in a litter through the festive streets of London as she had then, but rode, resplendent in crimson robes, high and proud on horseback for all to see that she lived and thrived despite her close dance with the Reaper. While Elizabeth had come through her siege largely unscathed by the disfiguring pox, Robin's beautiful sister Mary had been monstrously scarred and pitted with oozing sores, so that she had begged the Queen's leave to go from Court and remain in seclusion for the rest of her days.

"Robin!" he heard Elizabeth shout above the ruckus. He spurred his horse forward so they rode side by side, and she graced him with her teasing smile. "What say you to all this, my lord, riding so high beside your Queen?"

"That I am grateful beyond imagining, Your Majesty."

"And well you should be, for I have passed the pikes for your sake, and proven to all how I hold you in the greatest esteem."

"And never was a man more proud of a woman's love than I am of yours, Elizabeth."

She turned away so suddenly that Dudley was left confused. Surely there had been nothing in the exchange or compliment to arouse her ire.

But the reason for the Queen's evasion of Robin's eyes was not a fault of his making, it was her own fault of vanity. Since her miraculous recovery he had remained steadfast in his protestations that her beauty was untouched, that she was as lovely to him as she had ever been. But though she believed that beauty lay in the beholder's eyes, neither did her looking glass lie. Her once flawless white skin, smooth as the petal of a Tudor rose, was, since her illness, mottled and rough. For the first time in her life Elizabeth had ordered her maids to grind a mixture of powdered eggshell and egg white, alum and borax, and paint her face with it. Though this was indeed the fashion of ladies young and old, 'twas more Elizabeth's purpose to hide imperfections that were, to her own mind, intolerable. Yet whenever she found herself sinking into self-pity, she thought ashamedly of Mary Sidney. This, of course, compounded her misery, as she had infected her friend.

With a great trumpet blast and roll of drums Elizabeth arrived at St. Stephen's Chapel where the Commons met. Great cheers rose all round as she was lifted by Robin from her horse. The Privy Councillors, all puffed with importance, greeted her and led her inside.

The hall was already close with the sweat of so many knights and elected burgesses, who now strained for a look at their monarch. Most of them loathed the fact that a woman ruled them, and despaired of how they should treat her. Subservience was due her as queen, but they were, particularly the gentry, not opposed to standing against her.

Head high, expression grave and steady, Elizabeth marched down the center aisle to the far end of the room, looking at no one. When she reached the throne, she turned and stared out at the sea of faces, trying to read their expressions. There were the Speaker and Privy Councillors on her right, bishops, judges, and officers of state on her left. The less senior members hovered over their benches waiting for her signal to be seated. Elizabeth took her chair and with a great rustling of fabric — from the finest taffetas of the lords to the roughest fustian of the burgesses — they sat and Parliament came into session.

When Elizabeth spoke, her voice strong and commanding, some of the older members marveled at the likeness of the daughter to the father. Report was made of the grave news from France, where Ambrose Lord Warwick's garrison in Le Havre, supporting the Protestants, had been defeated. In a rare demonstration of French unity, warring Catholics and Protestants had understood they hated their ancient enemy, England, even more than they hated each other. Joining forces, they had ousted Elizabeth's troops from their shores. Worse still, plague had broken out in the English garrison. Forced to admit that her first foreign incursion was an unmitigated disaster, Elizabeth had called Warwick and his troops home.

The discussions went on about a subsidy for the royal navy. Each and every time Elizabeth was addressed or complimented by the gentlemen of Parliament, she would rise from her throne and sink into a low curtsy of exquisite grace, or instead execute a great and stately sweeping gesture with her arms, both of which had the effect of transfixing the congregation with her feminine charm and magisterial power. It seemed to Elizabeth that she had established a fine balance of control and reciprocal affection with her men.

She was therefore startled when one Thomas Norton rose with no introduction and, bowing low to her, said, "We of the Parliament, with all due respect to Your Majesty, do petition you for the appointment of a committee to determine the succession."

Her gracious smile was instantly leveled, and she felt as the victim of an ambush must surely feel. Though it had not been explicitly raised by Norton, the real topic was her marriage plans — a matter intricately and irrevocably bound to any discussion of the succession. She grew very still, hardly breathing, seeming to draw all her forces inwards. Then she spoke.

"My lords and gentlemen." Her voice was charged with cool passion and no little drama. "When I lay ill not so long past, death possessed almost every part of me. But I was, in each conscious hour, worried in my heart and aware of my great responsibility to England."

She felt all those eyes fastened upon her, every man challenging her, daring her to falter. Her mind raced, for she knew beyond doubt that she could never allow Parliament to legislate the succession. If they did, they would certainly rule out her cousin Mary's claim, and for the moment Elizabeth was inclined in the Scots queen's direction.

"How," she inquired, moving her gaze from face to face, "shall I make such a decision? If I should choose a Protestant claimant, or if my successor be Catholic, do I risk losing the religious unity which I have striven so hard to establish in my reign? How shall I know what is right? If I choose wrongly, I hazard to lose not only my body but my soul — as I, unlike yourselves, am responsible to God. And I know, for I have seen in reigns of monarchs before me, what foul actions accompany the choosing of an heir in that monarch's lifetime. Hear me now, I have little desire to choose my successor quickly, for in doing so I should be forced to hang my own winding sheet before my eyes! God has placed me on this throne and trusted me with the carriage of justice and so, gentlemen, should you do the same!"

With that Elizabeth stood and, accepting no help from the many hands that were proffered, stepped down from her throne and strode from the hall. Being well away, she never heard the explosion of frustration and argument that began as the great door slammed shut behind her.

Fourteen

'Twas a day for which Robin Dudley had waited long and patiently, and he full believed he deserved as no other man in the kingdom the great title he would soon be granted. He now bathed in a copper tub before the fire, allowing Tamworth to scrub his whole body from foot to head with a rough cloth which burnished his skin to a rosy glow. This was, thought Robin Dudley as the steam wafted round his head in a fragrant cloud, a ritual bath — one that would wash away all vestiges of his previous life as a minor lordling, the remaining whiff of scandal over Amy's death, and the stubborn stench of his family's unsavory reputation as a tribe of traitors. With his raising to the peerage of England, and with the Queen's gift of noble Kenilworth Castle and its fabulous one hundred acres of lakes and meadows, Elizabeth had announced to all the world that Robin Dudley was indeed a great and loyal man of the realm. More important, he had come to believe, the new title was a sure sign that she was, after all her hesitation and indecision, finally preparing to marry with him. He closed his eyes and saw a vision that went beyond this day's investiture as earl — the moment he would be crowned king.

A sudden splash of water up his nose brought Dudley out of his daydream, ready to box Tamworth's ears for his clumsiness. But when his eyes opened he found himself staring into the grinning face of his brother Ambrose, looking much like a mischievous child whose prank had succeeded excellently well.

"Dreaming about St. Edward's Crown on that fat head of yours again?" said Ambrose with a smirk. Robin, stung by the truth of the accusation, splashed back, very nearly soaking Lord Warwick's fine yellow doublet with bathwater. Ambrose laughed as he lurched backwards and then clomped with his gold-tipped walking stick to the bed. The wound he had sustained during the Le Havre fiasco had healed poorly, and Robin feared his normally robust brother would limp for the rest of his life. Well, at least he *had* his life, Robin reminded himself. Nearly half of the soldiers of the English garrison had contracted the black plague, and many had died of it. The Spanish ambassador Bishop de Quadra had been among those who had lost their lives.

"I," intoned Robin in mock grandeur, "have far too many weighty matters to consider to be daydreaming."

"Will the soon-to-be-great Earl of Leicester deign to discuss these weighty matters with his poor brother?" inquired Ambrose with equal gravitas.

"Aye," said Robin, falling into a rolling Scottish brogue. "I'm told the Queen has been closeted with the brawny Melville since his arrival a week ago. They say she's entertained him in her very bedchamber, displayin' a miniature portrait of meself, and danglin' a great ruby in front of his nose, with fine promises it, and all the rest of the kingdom, will one day be Mary's."

"What *I've* heard is that Mary's marriage plans are in great disarray," said Ambrose, massaging the painful thigh under his honey-colored hose. "She still speaks longingly of the alliance with Don Carlos of Spain, though his madness becomes more apparent with every passing day. I think she must be even more hungry for power than our own dear queen."

Robin rose from his tub and water streamed from his sleek, muscular nakedness. He allowed Tamworth to rub his skin dry with a length of thick muslin. "I have heard," he said, "that Mary's subjects and councillors attempt to involve themselves with her choice of husband just as our countrymen do Elizabeth, and that the Scots queen is every bit as irked at their interference." Robin took the silk undershirt from Tamworth and pulled it on over his head. "Mary would do well to take guidance from her cousin on this account, for no matter how sternly Elizabeth's Parliament harassed her on the matter, she evaded and outsmarted them at every turn."

"I was privy to a prodigious duel of wit between the Scotsman and the Queen. You know, brother," Ambrose added slyly, "I think your Elizabeth likes this Melville too well. I see the way she smiles sideways at him."

"On with your story," interrupted Robin, more jealous and annoyed than he wished to appear. "What did you hear?"

As Tamworth began dressing his master in a rich surcoat of royal blue, Ambrose lay back on the bed, his head propped on the pillow of his arms, and began relating with great relish the intelligence he had gathered.

"Well, firstly, Melville demanded to know if Elizabeth was, in fact, dangling promise of the succession before Mary's eyes, with the stipulation that the Scots queen meekly submit to England's choice for her husband. Elizabeth feigned horror at the thought, then countered with the accusation that Mary was plotting blackmail with her threats of marrying a Catholic husband and inciting civil war in England. Melville must have sensed they were treading on dangerous ground, so he quickly quoted Ambassador Throckmorton's quip that he dearly wished one of the queens were a man so they might marry each other!"

Dudley and Ambrose roared with laughter at that, but in a moment Robin became serious. "I think we must keep our eyes fastened on Lady Lennox and her long-legged, lady-faced son Darnley. I am amazed she schemes so openly for a marriage between Mary and the boy," said Robin, "begging Elizabeth's leave to send him to Scotland so he can be flaunted before the Scots queen's eyes."

"Mary and Darnley are the same age, both Catholic, and he does have a fair claim to the throne of England — Henry the Seventh's own grandson," reasoned Ambrose.

"Indeed," said Robin, slipping into a pair of soft Moroccan leather boots. "And Lady Lennox loses no opportunity to flaunt the same before Elizabeth."

"And Elizabeth has herself considered the match, no doubt, though today she calls such talk treasonous. I think Lady Lennox should curb her tongue or watch her neck."

"Speaking of necks," said Robin, now magnificently clad in his investiture costume, "how think you the peer's mantle will hang about my own?"

"Proudly," replied Ambrose Dudley, rising from the bed to admire his brother in all his glory. "And indeed hard won."

He had a hundred times been admitted to the Presence Chamber, but now as he stood waiting outside the door flanked by two high lords of the realm, Robin Dudley found his heart thumping in his throat. Suddenly the doors swung inwards, giving him sight of Elizabeth directly ahead, seated regally upon her throne under the great Canopy of State. She was flanked on one side by the French ambassador and on the other by James Melville, who wore for the occasion not his kilt but a fine brown doublet in the English style. There, too, stood William Cecil, clutching in his hands a rolled parchment. They all wore looks of the gravest decorum, and even Elizabeth lacked her usual smile.

As Dudley and his companions entered and moved down between the two rows of spectators to the staid march of a single trumpet, Lord Hunsdon fell in before them carrying over his outstretched arms the peer's mantle, a cloak of scarlet velvet lined with pure white ermine. From the corner of his eye Dudley could see on one side the tall, slender Lord Darnley, holding the Sword of State. Standing behind him was his mother, Lady Lennox, whose sly, conniving character was mirrored in her weaselly countenance. Opposite Darnley stood Ambrose, proudly holding another ceremonial sword and baldric.

The moment Dudley entered, Elizabeth had fixed her eyes upon him. It seemed the orbs were like two great magnets pulling him to her, drawing him toward his destiny. As he fell to his knees before her, and the solemn intoning of the ceremony began, Robin Dudley lost all sense of time and place. Though he saw William Cecil move to the Queen's side, heard the Secretary read from the patent, and was aware that Lord Hunsdon had brought forward the cloak, all movement round him was vague and blurred, the droning Latin phrases running together in one long benediction.

"*Creavimus* Lord Denbigh." The words were suddenly sharp and clear: We have created Lord Denbigh.

Robin looked up into Elizabeth's eyes as she lifted the heavy mantle and fastened it round his shoulders. Still there was utter solemnity in her face, but before her hands left he felt to his delight and surprise her cool fingers tickling his neck. He stifled a smile, though he could see by their expressions that the French and Scottish ambassadors had witnessed the affectionate gesture, one Elizabeth had taken no pains to hide. At her nod, Lord Warwick stepped forward with the sword he held and presented it to the Queen. Now as Cecil read again from the parchment, naming Robert Dudley earl of Leicester, Robin wondered what the somber secretary's thoughts might be at this moment — thoughts of this raising, and also of Robin's recent appointment to the Privy Council. These could not but rankle.

Now came the *cincturum gladii,* the girding of the sword. Moving carefully with the unwieldy blade in its baldric, Elizabeth placed it about Robin's neck, the point secured beneath his left arm. Finally when she'd laid about him his cape and coronet, and handed him the rolled parchment of his two patents, she allowed herself a demure smile. Robin had hardly the time to return it before a dozen trumpets began blaring. The Queen rose, Robin stood aside, and she swept grandly from the Presence Chamber, with all bowing deeply as she passed.

Now in a great rush everyone surrounded the newly made Earl of Leicester to lend their congratulations. Whether friend or enemy, each knew that this bold and arrogant lord was, for better or worse, their queen's own creature, and a man with whom they would be forced to reckon.

Dinner was served in the Privy Chamber on the day of the earl's making. He sat to Elizabeth's right, and Melville to her left. It had been a splendid meal, one fit for a king . . . and for his Queen, thought Leicester, already accustomed to the name he would henceforth bear. The conversation, between the many rich courses, had waxed at times light and fanciful, then swung pendulum-like to matters weighty and political. Finally, inevitably, talk had turned to the marriage plans for Mary Queen of Scots. Giving little warning, Elizabeth had shocked the room into silence with a loudly announced revelation that she had known since the day of his arrival at Court of Ambassador Melville's secret negotiations with Lady Lennox for Darnley's marriage to Mary. Robin Dudley suppressed a smile of pleasure as the normally unflappable Melville blanched with embarrassment, and Lady Lennox shrank with fear. In a wholly unconscious movement, her fingers went round her neck in a protective gesture. But Elizabeth was not yet finished.

"Whilst you have been plotting and scheming behind my back — though happily neither out of my sight nor hearing — I have found an eminently suitable husband for my cousin Mary, one whom she cannot help but find attractive both as a man and a political asset."

Elizabeth stopped and looked round the room at the faces of her guests, each and every one puzzled, for all possible candidates had been discussed, nay argued over, ad infinitum. Who on earth could she mean? Robin again subdued his smile, knowing that Elizabeth, his brilliant Elizabeth, would stun them all with the perfection, or at least the outrageousness, of her choice. When she spoke, her voice was strong and steady, though her gaze seemed to focus on no one in particular.

"I nominate for my cousin Mary's consideration, with my full and passionate blessing . . . the most honorable Earl of Leicester!"

Fifteen

Lions and roses, thought Kat Ashley as she gazed up at the underside of the canopy of the Queen's bed. Or were they gryphons? she wondered. In all the years she had cared for Elizabeth, she had never once seen the canopy in this way. Lying motionless within the fine lawn sheets and velvet coverlets, her eyes fixed on the ancient carven images above, she wished to say aloud how beautiful it appeared to her, how lovely a sight it would be to see such a thing upon waking each morning. But the stroke she had suffered had rendered her speechless. All the words and ideas she might form inside her head became a senseless jumble as they passed through her lips.

In the chaos of her collapse during a meeting of the maids, and afterwards with a frantic Elizabeth summoned to her side, Kat had been fully conscious and entirely without pain. She had heard the Queen's terse instructions to lay her lady in the great Bed of State, and the waiting ladies' shocked whispers that no such thing had ever before been done. Kat felt the many hands gently lifting her flaccid body, though she had no sense of her right side whatsoever. The royal doctors had taken her pulse and somberly offered their opinions.

The Queen's old servant knew that she was dying, but as she lay contemplating the riot of interlocking mythical beasts and vines and garlands of Tudor roses above her, she realized with sweet surprise that she was not at all afraid of death. She had lived a fine life of privilege, first lady of the chamber to Elizabeth, whose reign, after a faltering start, appeared to be steadying. Kat's marriage to John Ashley had been a good one, and she oftentimes thought it was well that they had never been blessed with children, for their union was entirely steeped in service to the Queen.

Her Elizabeth . . . Kat's thoughts floated effortlessly down a long corridor of their years together. She found she could gaze into chambers as she soared ghostlike past their open doors, overlooking moments as if they were captured in time — the first day the sad-eyed toddler had been placed in her care, the heartbreaking audiences Elizabeth had endured with her father, Henry, the schoolroom at Hatfield Hall where the child had dazzled Kat and her tutors with the brilliance of her mind, and the strange passion they had shared for Thomas Seymour, husband of the dowager queen Catharine Parr.

The girl had become, more than Kat's charge, her duty. She had quickly become kin, the child she had never borne of her body, the greatest love of her life. John, bless his heart, had endured this without jealousy. A lesser man might have felt betrayed. *Betrayed.* The moment that word crossed her mind, Kat's dreamy state was shattered into a hundred pieces. Guilty thoughts and judgments crashed pell-mell in her head, making her squirm under the bedclothes and moan piteously. Lady Rochford hurried to her side and took up her hand with soothing noises, but Kat was overwhelmed with emotion.

The one troubling act of her tenure in Elizabeth's service had been replacing Dudley's and her child with a dead infant. Kat's reasoning and reassurances to herself had at the time seemed sound enough. She had done it in the name of good sense, for the good of England. The bastard's existence would, despite the Queen's best efforts, some day have come to light and destroyed forever what was left of Elizabeth's reputation and chances for marrying properly as, of course, she must. But now as Kat lay helpless in this bed awaiting the Reaper, that act seemed the lowest of betrayals. She had withheld the Queen's flesh and blood from her. Surely this was God's domain and His alone. What had she done! She must right this wrong. 'Twas not too late. She must tell Cecil to hie to Enfield and bring the boy back to Elizabeth. Then she and the Secretary would beg her forgiveness. She must speak to Cecil! She tried to call out his name, but her lips and tongue disobeyed her, and only unintelligible syllables emerged. Trapped in mortification and guilt she could not confess, she writhed with frustration.

The door opened and Elizabeth swept into her bedchamber. With one gesture she cleared the room of waiting ladies and physicians, and moved to Kat's side. Her face was a mask of misery, and it occurred to Kat that the Queen's earlier concerned expression had been replaced by one of utter resignation.

"Lord Cecil . . ." Elizabeth began.

Kat clutched Elizabeth's arm with her still functioning left hand and again tried, unsuccessfully, to speak. Elizabeth's face twisted with anguish.

"Lord Cecil is with his wife in the country. He has been sent for, Kat." She gazed down at the woman looking so frail under the coverlets. "Can you give me a sign that you are comfortable?" Kat squeezed the hand that Elizabeth held with a force that surprised a smile out of the Queen. "Good, good." Elizabeth sat down on the bed then and reclined against the headboard, gently draping her arm round Kat's head and shoulders, cradling her. Thus Kat could not see the Queen's face, but could only hear the words she was crooning in a soft voice in her ear.

"I cannot believe that I am losing you," she said. "You have been ever present in my life from before I can clearly remember." Elizabeth was silent for a long time before she spoke again. "God has been good to me, Kat. I have had three mothers. Catharine Parr saved me from oblivion and bastardy. She was kind beyond imagining and gave me my queenly education, and in return I betrayed her, lusting after her husband. Young and naive though I may have been, I had no excuse for it." She was silent again for a very long time, and when she spoke her voice cracked and wavered.

"I have come to know the mother who gave me life." Kat tried to make sense of this. Anne Boleyn had given Elizabeth life. Anne Boleyn had died before Elizabeth was three. "For so many years I knew nothing of her," continued the Queen, as if answering Kat's silent questions. "I could not recall her face nor her voice nor the time we shared when I was very small. But soon after I took the throne an old woman — perhaps you remember her, Lady Sommerville — brought me my mother's own journal, a secret diary which she had kept her whole life . . . till the day she died." More silence, as though Elizabeth was finding it difficult to piece the words together coherently.

"She was a good woman, Kat. Not the vile creature and witch we were all led to believe she was. She did never take those men nor her brother as lovers, that carnal crime for which they all died. She was innocent, and my father *knew* she was innocent. But he wanted her dead. And why? Because . . . because I was born a girl and not the son he required. For all I adored him, sought to please him, reveled in my likeness to him, my father never loved me, Kat. But my mother did. She loved me. She died for me." Kat could feel Elizabeth's body trembling, hear her ragged breathing to hold back the tears.

"But of all my mothers, Kat, you have been, by far, the most faithful." Now 'twas Kat attempting to hold back the tears, but she found she could not. They began to run in silent rivulets down her cheeks as Elizabeth went on. "You were there for me, Kat, always there for me. You bathed me, dressed me, scavenged for me in the years we had no money from my father. You cared for me tenderly in my illnesses, you suffered with me, rejoiced with me. You put my good always before your own. Under threat of torture you were loyal to me, Kat. You never ever betrayed me."

Kat had been lost in Elizabeth's affectionate litany until the uttering of that terrible word. She prayed the Queen would return to the comfortable truths of their love for one another, leave this poisonous subject, but she did not.

"When I lost my child," she went on, "something inside me withered, some soft part of my womanhood, and I was utterly bereft. Only you gave me the comfort I needed to go on living. Only you. So of all my mothers, Kat, you are the one I have loved the most. And I cannot bear . . ." Elizabeth was weeping now, her body heaving with great sobs. "I cannot bear losing you."

Kat began with all her will and all her might to speak. Elizabeth felt the woman straining in her arms, and moved so that she might see her face, understand her communication. The lips moved and weak sounds did emanate from Kat's throat. But all of her valiant efforts proved fruitless. Elizabeth was left to interpret the piteous utterances as best she could.

"I know you love me, too, Kat. I know you love me."

But the words, if the Queen had been somehow able to decipher them, or Katherine Ashley to more properly enunciate them, would have conveyed the desperate message she truly intended.

"Forgive me, Elizabeth," she would have said. "In God's name, forgive me."

Sixteen

The year that I was eight we all suspected my Mother was going mad, and the Queens visit to Enfield Chase during her Summer Progress for a day of hunting seemed destined to realize our fears. From the moment we received the letter from the Earl of Leicester announcing Her Majestys intention to inspect and partake of the incomparable woodlands and rich game of her royal property, each member of our household was engaged in fervid preparations to provide our beloved Monarch with a visit she would long remember. And whilst we all keenly appreciated the honor, and strove in our way to create a worthy show, Mother spun wildly and uncontrollably like a top, with an invisible hand winding her up again and again with no stopping.

Her preparations were frantic and endless. Directions and orders to children, husband, servants were not spoken but shrieked. She moved like a whirlwind thro her domain — the manor house, the yard, the kitchen, the buttery and laundry, kicking hapless chickens out of her way, swatting a maid for the tiniest imperfection in the fold of a napkin, or a cook for lumpiness in a sauce. She slept little, ate less. Her eyes glittered with an unnatural brightness, and her cheeks hollowed. The gowns she wore began to hang on her bony frame. She hired the neighborhood seamstress to tailor the dresses to her skeletal body, proclaiming shrilly that this was the fashion, that the Queen herself was thin as a reed.

I came in for more than my share of punishment, for Mother was most insistent that we children shine before the Queen like fine cut gemstones. Her Majesty loved music, so the girls would perform on lute and recorder, singing a duet as well. My brother John and I would recite — John a passage from Euripides and I some verse, blessedly in English, as I had shown neither facility nor interest in reading Latin or Greek. This fact, that my education was in sore need of broadening, had never before caused my Mother consternation, for I was the second son and, too, the child she loved the least. But on this occasion, when our performance would reflect directly upon her self, she prevailed upon me to perform with a murderous intensity. And I could never please her. I stumbled with the words, stuttered and failed to speak loudly enough to be heard. When I faltered under her scathing glare she shouted at me, berating my ignorance and clouting me sharply on the head. She shouted at John and the girls too and once slapped Meg when she dared excuse her failure to practice because of two broken lute strings.

We were fortunate at least in that my Mother had other matters to attend to in this great preparation. A feast to be planned and executed, the manor house hung with new draperies, cushions recovered, rickety furniture repaired, every surface scrubbed spotless. We would all heave a great sigh of relief when Mother would throw up her hands in disgust with us children and stomp from the nursery to see to her other chores. But then, whilst John and my sisters would repair to their various rehearsals, I would sneak away for my private preparations.

Father had given me a horse for my own and Charger was the name I gave him. He was a bay stallion — the most perfect color for a horse — with a pretty whorl of white between the eyes and one at the base of his tail. He was smallish, just fourteen hands high, but I was only eight and so I sat in good proportion. My Father always cautioned the gentlemen who came for his advice never to mount a horse too small. That however handsome or magnificent a man might be, a little horse would make him appear insignificant. Riding a high horse showed the quality and superiority of a man.

Charger was a lively beast, sound of foot and leg with good speed and action. He was docile, hardy and owned a good mouth. I, of course, thought him most intelligent. Best of all I saw in Charger a keen willingness to please me, a generosity of spirit. We had not broken him at the Enfield Stables, and my Father believed that his breaking must have been done with a gentle, temperate hand and not in the usual manner.

Twas a cruel business, backing and training young horses. A circular pit was first dug in a plowed field, and the horse set to treading the ring. Sometimes fetlock deep in mud he was tethered to a lunging rein, flogged round and round and beaten between the ears with a stick. Those animals of high courage were beaten more severely. This punishment they called correction. Once all disobedience had been discharged the backer would attempt the mount. If the horse resisted, the voice was used to rate and scream threats, with more hard beating on the head.

And there was worse. If a horse mulishly refused to move forward, an iron bar set with prickles might be suspended from his tail and passed tween his legs linked to a cord. When correction was required the device was drawn up to cause pain. Sometimes a knotted cord was tied to the horses stones, and some trainers applied fire to the tenderest parts of the poor beasts anatomy. Harsh bits studded with spikes were nothing less than instruments of torture on a horses mouth, and nosebands made of twisted iron tormented and mangled the tender gristle, wearing it to the bone.

You could always tell a horse who had been cruelly used by the look of resignation in the eye, and a skittishness or sullenness that would occasionally afflict an otherwise tame animal, as tho the thin veil of habitation and training had momentarily slipped away and defiant memories overtaken them.

Charger was happily not such a horse, but retained the proud nature with which he had been born. He was hollow backed and took well to the saddle. The carriage of his head was high and stately when trotting, but in a bolt or gallop his neck and head stretched into a great long arrow. To feel that muscular machine pounding in hard rhythm tween my thighs, the wind whipping my face, was the purest and sweetest of sensations, and it was there and there alone that I felt Gods hand in the world.

My horse and I trained and practiced daily. Truly if I had not been forced to eat and sleep, study and complete my chores, I would have done nothing else in my life but ride him. Sometimes I rode so long that my hams ached me fiercely, and John needed to help me into my bed. Sometimes I took him far afield where no one might come upon me and removed Chargers saddle and my own breeches and rode bare upon his back. My skin hardened from such use and I found with practice and some good sweat — both Chargers and my own — the best grip to be had on my horses sides.

I worked at the skills of a cavalryman too — or what I <u>thought</u> those skills might be. I became a horse soldier from other times, *other lands. A Crusader fighting the Turks in heavy armor which I fashioned of discarded metal from the smithy dump, lashed together with rawhide thongs. I became a shaggy headed Knight of the Temple who, under strictest supervision, could not even tighten his horses straps without permission from his superior. I hurled javelins overhand like some barbarous Frank, and rode home victorious with the stinking heads of my enemies hanging from my saddle bow.*

But as the day approached for the Queens visit my training came full about to the practice of manège. Twas an art, my Father said, a difficult but satisfying form of equitation whose highest purpose was to ride in best show before a Prince. For Charger, who had heretofore known nothing but of the commonest sort of riding, manège was a curious sort of exercise. On the first day of that training he stood transfixed, and all my strange commands seemed to be falling on deaf ears. Once he cocked his head with such consternation that I laughed aloud. But with much kindness and cherishing, touching and reassurance on my part, he soon learnt the movements and came to be in great union with my self. He even seemed to take pleasure in them.

My Father had none of these skills, being a dairyman by trade, and only the keeper of the Chase and stables through a Royal grant. But he had in his employ a horseman named Barlington who had once lived in France and there learnt the art of manège. Barlington had very little time in his days of riding instruction and leading the hunts to teach a young boy so exacting a skill. But I begged him and he complied. I was like a soft cloth set in liquid, soaking in each word, each studied movement, and locked it away so that it need never be taught again.

Manège was taught with the voice — words of urging, "hey hey" or "now now"; words of helping, "back boy, back I say"; words of cherishing, "so boy" and "holla holla." The tongue was used clicking against the palate to encourage stopping or turning. The crop was used gently, touching the horse on different parts of his body as a signal — on his forelegs to rein back, near his eye to turn, or the crop might be whipt thro the air to tell a horse to quicken his pace.

Charger and I learnt the volte, turning in a circle on the haunches, the curvet, a haughty, high headed raising of the forehand in half rear while prancing in cadence behind, the figures of eight, and what Barlington called "the airs above ground." These were indeed difficult movements to perform, as all four of the horses feet were required to be, when properly accomplished, altogether off the ground. A horse would be made to contain his fear so he might raise his forehand, and also to yerk, which was kicking both legs out behind. When practiced together the beast would bound aloft, his two feet yerking in a goatlike leap — the capriole.

I was bound and determined to display our heroic talents — mine and Chargers — before the Queen, but in fact twas another whom I wished more heartily to impress with our skills, the Queens Horsemaster, the Earl of Leicester. He was the most famous horseman in all of England, renowned for his knowledge of horseflesh, his strength and manliness in the saddle. Night after night I envisaged the moment I would ride out before him and the Queen to prance and leap, kick and turn with all the grace and brilliance of a lordly knight. She would clap delighted, and he would address me man-to-man in all dignity and respect.

So my life became practice with Charger, and learning to stay out of my Mothers vision, for whenever she caught me she found something always — an unfinished chore, a poorly rehearsed verse — to punish me for.

My Father was meanwhile attending calmly to his preparations for the visit. His administration of the Chase had always been so diligent that little extra work was needed. From the first sight of the parkland my Father had found his love. Cattle and the dairy had been his profession since apprentice days, but the great sprawling woodlands, the grace and beauty of wild game, had soothed his soul and set alight a piece of his spirit never before kindled. He gloried in his role as Keeper of the Forest, and protected its inhabitants from poachers with a fierceness I saw nowhere else in his being.

He was good to me, more kind and giving than a father was wont to be to a second son. He allowed me my weaknesses and gloried in my strengths. We found shared pleasure in the study of animal husbandry, and I became his willing apprentice. Though John would, thro law, inherit Enfield Chase, my Father claimed my skills would travel well, and in time and with luck I would one day be the keeper of some other parkland.

Of my Mothers abuse to me he said little. Twas something I never did understand. He was a true man, and kept his wife to her place in all other ways. But when he saw a storm brewing tween my Mother and me he seemed to dissolve into air, disappear so that he never saw the beatings, never heard my cries, tho I know he knew of them. Only once did he see me incur her full and furious wrath for some imagined trespass. As she fell on me with a broom handle, and before he slipped silently out the door, I saw on his face what I can only now describe as resignation mingled with guilt. Twas the family history, all of us knowing that Mothers unhappiness had waxed large with the move from dairy to Chase, and that even her raising from the yeoman class to gentry had never enlarged her country contentment. But why I should have attracted her particular anger, and why my otherwise strong and fair minded Father would allow such behavior, baffled me always.

The day of the Queens visit dawned grey and threatening, which served to stoke my Mothers frenzy to a wild blaze. She feared now that rain would kill her perfect roster of festivities, and certainly the hunt could not go on in a downpour. She had writ a great list of final preparations on our schoolroom hornbook and strode round the manor shouting out orders and harassing servants. As I snuck out to the stables to groom Charger I quietly passed her in the kitchen as she roughly shoved aside our faithful old cook sweating over a dozen kettles, berating her efforts and insisting she could do a better job her self.

When at nine the harbinger came galloping through the gates into our yard with news that the Royal Procession would arrive in three hours time, the sun was endeavoring to chase the dark clouds from the sky. This should have quelled my Mothers fears to some degree, but in fact the appearance of the harbinger made the Queens visit only more real, and her unfinished chores more unsettling. She began running from room to room calling for my Father who was elsewhere occupied, and raged that he had left her to fend for her self.

And then she called the children for final rehearsal of our performances. Meg and Alice, already trussed into their fine gowns, and John tolerating — but barely — his confinement in velvet and starched ruff, filed down and stood for the inspection. The girls clutching their instruments looked pretty and even Mother could find no fault with their appearance or their duet. Then she turned to John who stood stiffly with Euripides in hand, and of course expected to find me with him. I was not. When she demanded of them my whereabouts, their sweet loyalty kept them silent at first, but with my Mothers threats of drawing and quartering if they did not tell her the truth — threats which those children full believed would be carried out — John finally stammered, "The stables."

I had nearly finished a vigorous brushing of Charger whose coat now gleamed richly, when I felt a sharp pain on my ear. I was spun suddenly round by that sensitive appendage to face the Medusa her self.

"How dare you defy me!" she shrieked, her face distorted with a terrifying rage. "Look at you, filthy little wretch!" She picked up my hands. "Twill take hours just to get the dirt from under your fingernails!" She slapped me hard and then her eyes fell on Charger. I began to tremble for I knew that whilst I could withstand her physical abuses, if she took away privileges with my horse I would surely wither and die. I did never expect the words she then spat from her hateful mouth. "Tis this bony nag of yours which puts the Devil in you, yes I can see that."

"No, Mother!" I cried. "Charger is a good friend. There is nothing evil in him, I swear it."

"Oh you swear, do you?" She glared at my horse and blessedly he remained calm, staring back with those sweet brown eyes. "Then how is it he keeps you from your family chores and prayers and other Godly work?" she demanded. "What power has this horse to keep you occupied with him when the Queen is coming here in two hours! I say he is the Devils incubus!" She was shrieking now and the stablehands had all made themselves scarce. I prayed that Barlington or Father would appear, but I knew they were making a final round of the woodland trails and I had no savior in them.

Without warning my Mother picked up a shovel laying against the wall and before I could put up my hands to stop her, she swung it at Chargers head. His reaction was swift and her aim was poor. The shovel blade smashed into the stall door with such force it knocked her off her feet and she fell heavily into a pile of stuff recently mucked from a stall. She sat there with a look of surprise for only a moment before pulling herself up and grabbing me by the hair. Thus she dragged me from the stables across the yard to the manor, muttering her intention to have Charger hacked into a hundred pieces.

Up the manor house stairs we went, my knees banging the steps, my head burning with the hair wrenched by its roots. I vaguely recall seeing the faces of my horrified sisters and brother as I was carted to the nursery. There I was required to drop my breeches and bend over the table. I never saw what the instrument of punishment was, but the lash felt like thin leather strips — perhaps she had grabbed some reins from the stables as we left it. The pain was excruciating, and she held back nothing of her strength. She must have forgotten in her madness that I was a child of eight and not some Devil possessed ruffian who claimed to be her son.

Twas only thro the bravery of my brother and sisters that she did not beat me to death. They ran into the nursery and pulled her bodily from her task. When she saw them gathered round her all dressed in their finery she suddenly calmed. Then Meg said, "Mother, tis time that you dressed. The Queen is coming. Come, let me help you. I shall do your hair the way you like it." They led her away out of the nursery, never letting her eyes fall on me — a pathetic filthy boy curled whimpering on the floor.

There I lay for what seemed like hours, and only John peeked in to see me, furtive and afraid of being caught. Never the less, seeing my condition he hurried in and lifted me carefully, inspecting my poor bloodied flanks and wincing at the sight. He said that Mother had become strangely docile, even kind, and that Father had finally come in from inspecting the forest to bathe and dress, but that the children were under strictest orders not to mention my punishment. I was not, under any circumstances, to show my face to the Queen, with my excuse being illness.

A commotion in the yard announced the advance guard of the Royal Progress, and John reluctantly left me to my solitary misery. I craned my neck and chanced a look at the ruins of my buttocks. The skin was badly bruised and flayed to bleeding in many places. I could move, but only stiffly and with great suffering. I cried then, tho the tears were shed less for the pain of my injuries than the unfairness of my "correction", and the frustration that all my efforts of training with Charger in manège had been wasted, that the Earl of Leicester would never witness our virtuosity.

A great clattering of hoofbeats and creaking of many wheels, shouts of riders and servants filled the yard. I limped to the window which overlooked it and saw a spectacle I might never in my life see again — the Queens Court, fine coaches, splendid mounts caparisoned in rich cloth and worked leather saddles with gold and silver trimming, great lords and ladies, Dukes and Archbishops, all disembarking at my doorstep. I could see my family and our servants standing at the entrance in welcome. All eyes looked towards the gates, and now the finest of all the carriages — painted red, carven and gilt, with a team of matched white palfreys in white feathered headdresses — sped through the gates and came to a stop. Footmen scrambled to the door and out stepped Queen Elizabeth.

She was a sight burnt permanently into my memory — the ghostly pale skin, the bright red hair twisted and braided into shapes and piled atop her head. The broad smile and pearly teeth, the extreme grace and majesty of her movements, the long long white fingers she extended to be kissed. And, unexpected, the look of pure joy to be so welcomed by her subjects. The gown she wore was like nothing I could ever have imagined, yellow and orange silk all embroidered with intricate designs. My head spun and in the stunning vision of my Queen, I momentarily forgot that other Noble Personage who had captured my imagination — the Earl of Leicester.

But now he came riding, a lone horseman on the most magnificent stallion I had ever laid eyes on — enormous, jet black, and the saddle in the Spanish style, black moroccan leather with silver fittings. The man too was apparelled all in black, more dashing and rakish a figure than in all of my dreams.

I was suddenly filled with an anger so sharp and bright I was blinded. A tight knot had formed in my belly and I found my balled fist ready to smash the window glass. But I held back, for a conviction was growing in my head like a spring seedling under a warm sun. I saw that I had incurred more than enough injuries for one day and would need as many of my parts in good order as I could manage. I turned from the window and forced my self to look in the mirror. The figure that peered back at me was a sore sight in deed. Red rimmed eyes, filthy tearstreaked face, dishevelled hair, torn shirt, naked legs dripping blood.

I moved to the copper tub wherein my brother and sisters had bathed and found the water still tepid. Unaccustomed to immersing my body — only once before had we bathed in such a manner — I stept gingerly into the tub and lowered my self down. I had decided I must ignore the pain, and tho my resolve was strong I gasped as the water touched my raw flesh. Once in I dunked my head and lathered it well with lye soap and scrubbed my hair. I washed my body quickly and did not tarry in the tub one moment longer than was needful, then grabbed a bedsheet and blotted my self dry. I located the suit of clothing and hose and slippers my Mother had had made for this occasion and very carefully dressed my self in them — except for the velvet slippers. Instead I put on my best cordovan riding boots, the ones my Father had gifted me on the last New Year. I had grown so much they were already tight, but they would have to do — my everyday boots a disgrace.

Now the image that peered back from the looking glass was a sight better than before. My red hair shone and my eyes had cleared of tears. In fact they glinted like obsidian in the sun. The blue velvet doublet hugged my slender torso perfectly. Finally I slipped on my best leather gauntlet to cover my deformed hand. The picture was almost right . . . but something was missing still. A smile. I knew that children should be sober, but I wished now to be dashing. And the Queen had smiled. I could smile too. I thought myself a fine and handsome boy and fit for any challenge. But when I turned from the mirror pain shot through my body in every direction. I gulped a breath, found my courage and moved to the nursery door.

I could hear below me a quiet crowd, the end of my sisters duet, and enthusiastic applause. Then my Mother announced they were all welcomed into the Great Hall where a light repast would be served immediately. Twas dangerous, I concluded, to descend the stairs, so moved to the nursery window and without a second thought climbed out. I had many times escaped down the ancient ivy trellis, and only a few bored footmen and drivers now were there to witness my descent.

I was on the ground in moments and running pell mell to the safety of the stables. The grooms and stablehands greeted me with their normal friendliness, mixed with amazement, for I had but lately left them as my Mothers piteous and terrified prisoner. Now I looked a fine young gentleman, and I added to their incredulity by bowing to each and every one of them with an exaggerated and haughty bow which made them laugh and jibe goodnaturedly.

But there was little time to lose. I went quickly to Charger in his stall and he greeted me with a series of soft nickers and an approving stamp of his hoof. Taking care not to soil my clothing I finished grooming him and braided his glossy tail, then bridled him, saddled him and led him from his stall.

The stablehands all occupied with last minute arrangements for the hunt which would succeed the dinner, stopt their work and stared as I led proud Charger down the aisle. Each of them as I passed, dipped their head in silent respect to me. One came forward and gave me a leg up. As I took the saddle I felt the pain but as tho from a distance. There would be, I thought to my self, time enough tomorrow for pain, but this day for Charger and me would all be for glory. We rode out into the perfect day, for Old Sol had banished the clouds entirely. With a click of my tongue and the slightest pressure of my thighs to his sides, Charger sped from the stableyard in a great and defiant cloud of dust.

I waited hidden behind the kitchen, the front door of the manor house in my line of sight. The Queens party had decided that to take full advantage of the parkland they would forgo a stationary hunt, shooting from a blind. They would instead follow the hounds for stag and end with a wild goose chase. The noonday meal was therefore light and rather brief, yet the wait seemed interminable. As it came the hour the Royal carriages were driven away and our stablemen came leading our finest horses into the yard all dressed for the ride. Our dog keeper released the pack of yapping hounds into their midst, so the great and joyful racket of the hunt began. My heart began to gallop, and I lay down on Chargers comfortable neck, whispering encouragement in his ear. He seemed to understand, remaining so calm and still, and this helped to quiet my own senses.

Finally the door opened. Her Majesty and the Earl of Leicester were first out, followed by the lords and ladies of the Court all thrumming with excitement for the coming hunt and laying down wagers and side bets, no doubt on their horses performance but on the wild goose chase as well. They had changed into riding clothes, the Queen in a violet velvet gown of narrow measure, simple and with no frills that I could see. They moved directly to the mounts to examine and comment on the fine horseflesh. Then I saw my family follow the hunting party out the door, but they looked none too happy. My Father was quietly rating my Mother, she staring straight ahead refusing to meet his eye. My brother and sisters were giving each other sideways looks, and I knew Father was demanding to know my whereabouts. But he had not time to pursue this for everyone was choosing their mounts and twas my Fathers duty to be in the forefront. He strode to the Queen and Leicester and began horse talk with them so that they might decide which to ride on the hunt that day.

This was my moment, before they departed for the chase. I sat up tall in the saddle and urging Charger with the merest signal, raced from my hiding spot out into the manor yard. The suddenness of our approach took them all by surprise and when Charger lifted his forehands into a grande levade, he let out a loud enthusiastic neigh which seemed to speak for us both. As we began the program of elegant manège, progressing from one intricate maneuver to another, I chanced looks at the Queen and her Horsemaster. She was smiling again, her eyes glowing with delight, and the Earl was nodding with silent encouragement, for he knew very well the difficulty of our movements. Charger barely needed direction. The lightest tap of my crop near his eye caused an immediate half turn and levade. We executed a tight and perfect figure of eight, and followed immediately with curvet and pirouette. He pranced daintily on his hindquarters for a full half minute turning round and round, pawing the air like a dancer. The grand finale — the "airs above ground" — was a spectacular series of high leaps and sharp kicks which elicited even louder shouts of encouragement and excited applause. As we descended from the last capriole Charger turned round to face the Queen, knelt and dipped his nose to the ground in a graceful bow which provoked shouts and more clapping. With this I leapt from Chargers back and breathless with exertion made my own courtly bow to Her Majesty.

I rose to see the Queen laughing with delight. She was flanked by Leicester and my Father, who was beside himself with happiness at my surprise appearance.

"May I present . . . my son Arthur, Your Majesty." His voice trembled with passion as he spoke, and I stood a little higher in my boots.

"Is this the child who is ill?" the Queen asked incredulously. When my Father stuttered his reply she went on. "For if he is thus when he is ill, I should be very glad to know him when he is well. Tell me, Arthur," she said fixing me with her eyes, "what is the name of this magnificent beast?"

"Charger, Your Majesty." I blurted the word so loud and quickly that I worried I had blundered. But then she smiled again and repeated his name. Coming from her lips it sounded a blessing, and I suddenly thought it fitting that the first word I should speak to my Queen was the name of my horse . . . and my very best friend.

I felt a sudden arm clap round my shoulder and turned to see it was the Earl of Leicester.

"Well done, my boy. You are very young but I see you already speak the language of the horse."

I found myself entirely overcome, hearing from my hero the greatest praise he could ever have offered me.

"Ride next to us on the hunt," he added, referring to himself and the Queen, then gracefully mounted a white stallion from my Fathers stable.

"May I, my lord?" I stammered, overcome and hardly believing the honor.

"I command it," said the Queen. She was looking down from her mount, and I saw to my amazement she was seated astride and not sidesaddle as the other ladies were.

Twas my Father who gave me a leg up onto Charger again, and it was then he noticed the caked blood on my breeches. He ground his teeth together with a grim look but said nothing, only grasped my hand tightly for a brief moment before turning and mounting his own horse.

That summers afternoon was the best of my young life. There I rode, flanking the Queen with Lord Leicester as we pounded thro the park, dogs ecstatic voices echoing in the green groves. Knowing the woodland trails well as the back of my hand I sometimes took the lead to show Her Majesty a short cut and give her the advantage. Other times I saw her riding against me and so I met her challenge, galloping fast and tough, and with slips and turns foiled her, only afterwards remembering I had bested my Queen. The Earl was a handsome sight mounted — strong and supple in the saddle, as great a horseman as his reputation allowed. I saw how, on a horse strange to himself, Leicester managed the beast as surely as if the two were dear old friends.

When after several hours the arrow pierced stag had fallen, and twould seem the hunt was done, my Fathers stouthearted long-winded horses, goaded by these nobles with undying appetite, began in earnest the wild goose chase after a hare. We rode then cross country in Follow My Leader fashion. The Queen or Leicester always led the chase and I, not far behind, could see the game they played most joyfully, one with the other, as tho many times they had played it before. She would take the fore, holding a hard hand on her horse, making him gallop softly at great ease. But then the Earl would advance from behind and ride so close that his mounts head would touch the buttock of the Queens mount attempting to overtake her, at which sight she would spur her horses side and wheel him suddenly half about on her right hand to foil the attempt. Later she would easily let him slip by her and lead the chase.

By the hour we returned for my Mothers feast the mounts were well spent and could barely set one foot before the other. But I knew these animals, knew how well their keeper my Father had fed and exercised them, and how in two or three hours time they would be as fresh and courageous as if they had never been labored thus. My Mother in a different new gown, greeted her guests at the manor door, and all the lords and ladies of the Court, drunk with the pleasure of exertion, dismounted and went inside. Still on Chargers back, I could feel my Mothers eyes upon me angry and threatening. But then I saw my Father gaze upon me — a look of pure triumph in my honor — before they both turned and went indoors.

The Queen too had gone in and the stablehands now led the horses two by two from the emptying yard. All that was left was the Earl of Leicester who stood talking quietly to Barlington whilst gratefully patting the neck of the mount he had ridden. He saw me then and walked to me. So as not to be higher than such a high lord I was forced to dismount, but that was not easily accomplished, for my wounds which until now had been forgotten, suddenly made themselves all too apparent. The pain and stiffness of my hindquarters caused me to tumble gracelessly out of the saddle, and had not the Earls strong arms caught me I would have fallen sprawling in the dust at his feet.

He could not help but see the agony in my expression but he graciously refrained from inquiring of its source, instead regaling me with praise for my skills, claiming that in his own estimation I had "won my spurs". He could not have known what such words meant to me, that more than my hideous pain those words were close to bringing tears to my eyes. Leicester went on to tell me his thoughts on the moral virtues of horsemanship. Twas the foremost way to employ the mind, form the body and add grace and strength to activity and character. Men, he said, were better when riding, more just and understanding, more alert and at ease with themselves, and that close knowledge of horses proved a balm for the health of the man and his soul.

I must have looked a dunce, staring up at that great man with nothing of my own to add, but then he asked me of my education and I found myself, worse than silent, stuttering. I could not lie. I told him I was a poor student, not for lack of understanding but lack of desire to learn the bookish lessons. All but horses bored me silly.

He laughed then, which much surprised and horrified me, for I believed he was laughing at me. But he saw by my face what I thought and quickly returned, "Arthur, listen to me. I was once eight years old and hated my schoolwork and only wished to spend my time riding. Like you, twas the only thing I loved. But I was of such a family and position that it was required of me to do my labors in the classroom. And I was blessed with good tutors. One of them was the same that taught the Queen herself. And so I learnt my Greek and Latin grudgingly, mathematics with somewhat more joy. Twas a test of courage as much as learning with a horse to leap hurdles . . ." He looked away. ". . . or persevering in battle when badly wounded." When he looked back at me his eyes were shining as if with a new idea. In deed, he suddenly patted my arm and said to wait where I stood.

I saw the Earl stride to a cart which was piled high with the Queens baggage. He located a large carven chest, opened it and rooted thro the belongings therein so casually that I determined the chest was his own and not the Queens. He slammed it shut and with a smile approached me once again, now holding a smallish volume.

When he thrust it at me I could see it was old and very well worn in deed. But the words on the cover were writ in Greek letters.

"Do you know enough to read the title?" he demanded.

I squinted at the book and tried my best. "The . . ." was as far as I got.

"Well, that is something," said Leicester archly.

"No, no," I cried, "this word, is it not 'art'?"

"It is," he agreed.

"The Art . . . of . . ." I could not make out the final word. My Greek was appalling.

"Horsemanship," the Earl finished for me.

"The Art of Horsemanship?" I echoed stupidly.

"Composed by a Greek cavalry general named Xenophon, nineteen hundred years ago. Tis the finest book on equitation ever writ." I had opened it and was staring in wonder at the meaningless words on its pages when he added, "I am giving it to you."

I looked up at him, and so enormous was my gratitude and equal bewilderment that he laughed again.

"Right! You shall have to learn Greek in order to read it."

"Thank you, my lord," I finally managed to say. "I will. I shall learn Greek and Latin and mathematics . . ."

"Gently now," he teased. "I would not want you to ignore your horses."

"No Sir, that I will never do!"

Leicesters face softened then, more than I imagined such a masculine man could do. "Go and tend to your injuries, Arthur. Your presence will be missed at supper, but I shall make your excuses to the Queen for you. She will understand."

"Thank you, my lord," I said, the words catching in my throat. "And thank you for the book."

He had made for the door, then turned back and called to me, "When you are a grown man come and see me if you like. I shall find a place for you in the Queens mounted guard." Before I could reply, if in deed I could have found the words to do so, he had disappeared inside. I sagged back against Charger, then turned to him laying my head against his warm muzzle and wept with joy.

What followed that evening made the sweetness of the day only sweeter still. I had taken my horse back to the stables to groom him after his exertions but Barlington seeing my exhaustion and pain, offered to settle him for the night, which offer I gratefully accepted. I stumbled up the stairs hearing the commotion of the feast under way in the Great Hall and took my self to the nursery. Quite alone, as all the servants attended below, I carefully peeled my blood caked breeches from my tortured flesh, trying not to cry again for there had been, I thought, quite enough crying for one day, no matter what the cause. Naked from the waist down and having no strength left to tend to my wounds, even had I been able to reach them, I lay face down on my bed and fell instantly asleep.

I do not know how much time had passed before I was awak-

ened by a gentle hand pulling the hair back from my brow. I hazily thought it was my sister Meg. But when my sight cleared I saw my Father sitting on the bed near me, his sad eyes fixed upon my flayed buttocks.

"I am so very proud of you, Arthur," he said quietly. "And I have been a coward. Forgive me, son. Forgive me my weakness. Your Mother . . ." He stopped at the word, a peculiar unsettled look in his eyes. "She will never touch you again, Arthur. Never. By Jesus I swear it."

Maud's feast had gone splendidly, she in her glory as hostess, seated at the groaning board by the Queen and Leicester. The music and jugglers she had provided for entertainment seemed to please her guests well enough. Robert Southern, at the Queen's right hand, observed his wife, haughty chin lifted as she flicked her fingers to call for servers as if she had been a grand lady her whole life through.

He saw the high spirits and clarity of mind slip away as the final courses of sweets and savories were served and the departure of the royal party inexorably approached. When the Queen stood, thanking her hosts for a day of most excellent sport and amusement, Robert could see an odd mixture of pride and panic in his wife's eyes. But he was unmoved by her discomfiture. He led the lords and ladies from his hall, bidding them *adieu* and Godspeed on their progress.

In the torchlit courtyard they were helped back to their waiting carriages, and Robert watched as one by one they rumbled out through the gate. He was therefore startled to find William Cecil standing quietly beside him.

"My lord," said Robert, "I thought that you had already gone."

"I have not," he replied. "I wish to speak with you privately." There was a strange tentativeness about the Queen's secretary which Southern marveled at, for this was one of the highest men in the kingdom, newly raised to the peerage.

"Let us move to a quieter place," offered Robert, and led Cecil to the far end of the manor and round its corner. There were no torches there, and in the moonless night they were blanketed by darkness, though the commotion of the departing Court still could be heard where they stood.

"My condolences on the loss of your dear old friend Kat Ashley," Cecil began.

"Thank you, my lord," replied Robert with surprise. He'd no idea that Cecil had even known of his and Kat's friendship. But in that same moment, watching Cecil's shadowy figure fidget in the darkness, Southern knew unquestionably that the Queen's closest councillor was party to the secret that had bound him and Kat together in the last years of her life. Robert waited for Cecil to continue. The discomfort of the Secretary was so extreme, however, that the pair stood in silence for an embarrassingly long time.

Finally Cecil spoke. "Your son . . ."

"Arthur," replied Robert quickly to assure the man that they were riding along the same path of mind — that he did not suppose Cecil referred to his firstborn, John.

"Yes, Arthur," said Cecil. Robert thought his voice was as haunted as his eyes would have been, had there been light enough to see them. "I helped Kat Ashley to . . . remove the child from the Queen's . . ." He could not go on.

"You have no reason to fear for his welfare, my lord. All this" — Robert Southern indicated the Chase with a sweeping gesture of his hand — "was gifted to me as reward for my taking him in, and I am more than grateful."

"He seems well and happy," said Cecil, "and a true artist on the back of a horse."

Robert Southern winced at the recent memory of Arthur's bloody wounds, and a bolt of guilty pain shot through him.

"But is he . . . does he feel in any way . . . different?" queried Cecil.

"Something in him knows that he is different from us in our family. And as he grows I think that knowledge will grow stronger. But I assure you he knows nothing of his true lineage."

"I have a son named Robert," said Cecil almost wistfully. "He is being trained for service to his Queen. His mother and I love him more than life."

"My lord," said Robert Southern gently, "know that Arthur was a great gift to me. I do love the boy as if he were my own flesh."

Cecil's arm went round Southern's shoulder, and even in the dark Robert could feel the gratitude flowing like a great circular river between them.

"You must keep me informed of him," said Cecil. "If there is ever anything he needs . . ."

"Thank you, my lord. It does my heart good to know there is someone else in this world who cares for Arthur."

As the two men strolled back out into the torchlit yard they did not say, but surely felt, that Kat Ashley, for all her faults and weaknesses and the sin of taking God's will into her own hands, had indeed chosen wisely and done well by the Queen's bastard son.

All the members of the royal progress were finally gone. Maud was in the Great Hall standing over the servants, shouting orders to set the room back to right. Robert entered and in a quiet voice directed the workers to retire for the night, thanking them heartily for the fine effort they'd made that day. They wasted no time and beat a hasty retreat before Maud could stop them.

"Robert!" she said irritably, "I wanted it done tonight! I'll not have —"

"These people are exhausted, Maud, can you not see that? Let them have their rest and they will finish tomorrow."

"Well, it will not be you having to look at the mess tomorrow. You'll be out in your greenwood." She spat the last word as if it were poison in her mouth. Then she began angrily folding up the long carpets she had laid on the trestle tables, using her fingernail to scrape off bits of food spilled on them. There was something frantic in her movements, and her voice was tinged with acid.

"I'll tell you something, Robert Southern. Your son Arthur is in a pot of hot water now. How dare he defy me? How dare he humiliate me in front of the Queen and make me out a liar! I've punished the little brat for his disobedience, but there's more where that came from, you best believe it. And the next time I send him to his room he will stay there if I have to tie him hand and foot to the bedposts!"

Maud was so absorbed in her words and work that she did never notice her husband standing like a tall mountain, dark storm clouds coalescing round its peak.

"And that horse of his. I'll not have him —"

"Maud." It was a single word spoken amidst a venomous stream of invective, but Robert's tone was such that his wife stopped her work suddenly and turned. She was startled to see that he now was looming above her. Robert Southern was still as he gathered up the pieces of his anger and strength, some from many years past, others from the deepest rivers of his soul.

"I will speak to you calmly, Maud, and clearly so that you should know my meaning and I shall never have to speak these words again. Arthur may not be your son, but he is mine."

"And he has bewitched you, that's the truth. You think very little of that extra finger of his, but I see the Devil in that boy, and he has blinded you!"

Robert Southern reached out and grasped Maud by the hair at the back of her neck and pulled her face close to his.

"I fear you are not yet understanding me, Maud. What I want you to know is that from this day forward, for every hand you lay on that boy, I will lay ten of the same on you."

"You would not," she said contemptuously.

"Oh, but I would," he said, and tightened the grip on her hair, twisting it till she cried out in pain. "So, are we agreed, Maud?"

Her eyes flashed with the hatred of the powerless.

"Are we agreed?"

"We are agreed," she said finally through clenched teeth, and Robert released her. Furious tears filled her eyes but she did not dare to speak. Instead, holding his gaze defiantly, she straightened her gown and her hair, then turned and strode from the room.

Robert Southern stood alone in the Great Hall of Enfield Manor, feeling for the first time in his life a truly honorable man.

Seventeen

By the time of my fourteenth year I was, if not an enthusiastic student, an adequate one. In Enfield Towne there was a free grammar school, and tho my Mother wished to hire us children private tutors, my Father thought such a plan too grand and the grammar school a fine enough institution for his boys education. Fine enough in deed! We were made to speak naught but Latin all day long, from six till eleven in the morning, and one to five in the afternoon. I was taught to write a fair hand, to cypher and cast accounts. We had every day our prayers and a good bit of Scriptural studies, reading from King Henrys Bible, and arguing with Calvinistic fervor its passages and doctrine. We studied its maps and descriptions of the Holy Land and Garden of Eden, and then and there I began to dream of sometime travelling to distant and exotic lands.

The schoolmaster, one Jarrett, grudgingly named me the best at languages, crediting some inborn ability, since my diligence to their study was at best unremarkable. My gift was, he said, so distinctive and my ear so sharp he taught me French, and some Spanish as well.

My only joy in all that education was the Greek, for it enabled me to read, as the Earl of Leicester had promised, the finest book ever writ on equitation. I found in Xenophon, that man of ancient times, such a kindred spirit that I mourned never knowing him in the flesh. For he believed as I did that gentleness with a horse was the road to greatest success. Be firm not harsh, and lose your temper never. Reward the beast when he has followed your wishes, and admonish him — but never harshly with a whip — when he disobeys. Fear of certain objects, he said, was only increased by the whip, and the horse would come to associate pain with that object which he feared.

Xenophon taught of the art of the cavalryman, not only the proper maneuvers of battle and care of ones mount on campaign, but a way of thinking, for both man and horse. At times, in his wisdom on what might alarm a horse and how to calm him, he spoke with such a strange authority and seemed to know this animals mind so well I believed he had once himself been a horse.

Sadly my poring over Xenophon was as close to my faithful friend Charger as I got most schooldays, except to ride him to and fro, and to quickly feed and groom him, muck his stall at night. But on Saturdays and Sundays after church services we never left each others sight. I was all his and he mine, and we gloried in the practice of the military arts Greek style.

We rode cross country as tho in pursuit of the enemy — never, of course, in retreat — practiced jumping streams and ditches and small stone walls, riding at speed up and down hillocks and steep slopes. In my homemade helmet and light armor we practiced skirmishing and mounted combat. Charger trotted to within fifteen yards of the enemy and halted whilst I threw my javelin, wheeled round and allowed my imaginary second rank to move forward and do the same.

We practiced charging home at a full gallop sword in hand, either held high, or with my body slung along Chargers neck, the blade low and horizontal. I became proficient at "taking a head." For the enemy I used a pigs head set upon a pole. Galloping at full speed I would pierce it with a lance or shoot it with a pistol. Sword fighting on horseback I practiced with my brother John, tho he was most times otherwise occupied, and I was forced to battle with thin air.

I thought myself a fine soldier but alas, there was no war to be fought for England. Sure there was a bloody war of religion in France, and I heard tell that some of my countrymen, mercenary soldiers of fortune, fought on the Protestant side, and others for the Catholics. But they were few, these soldiers, for the French hated us marvellously. Twas an old hatred, I learnt from Mister Jarrett, tween the English and the French. Frenchmen, he said, believed truly that the English were born with tails, and the French believed the English the filthiest people in all the world.

I would have gladly fought for my Queen and Country had the need arisen, for I loved her truly as a subject. Since that day we had met I harbored so deep a sense of faithfulness and honor, I would gladly have died a thousand times in her service, and dreamt of the day I would take up the Earls offer and join her Royal Guard. I heard my parents and my teacher, too, speak of the Queens reign, now sixteen years since accession. How she had surprised them all with her strength of rule, good economy and aversion to war. How she had unaccountably brought peace to longtime warring religious camps. She had somehow charmed the men and women of her Court with her stately and majestic deportment, this despite her vulgar, mouth filling oaths and habit of boxing her councillors ears when angry. Twas said she was more feared than her sister Bloody Mary and ruled as absolutely as her Father Henry. And all this of a woman. That was the shock of it. None thought a female, unmarried at that, could ever rule this island and rule it well.

Some still chafed against her. There were those who opposed her cutting down of the oak forests to build great ships. Many — mostly Catholics — disparaged her treatment of the Scots Queen. But most Englishmen heeded her laws, for they were such that only strengthened England, like wearing hats made of felt to aid the felt industry, and eating fish on Wednesdays and Fridays and Saturdays to keep our fishing industry sound.

Meanwhile life within the Southern household had continued, and tho my lot was bettered since that day of Her Majesty and Leicesters visit, and the strengthening of my Fathers resolve, my Mothers mania had attracted other victims. Upon her departure the Queen had uttered a few fateful words, "I hope to return someday to your gracious home and hospitality." All but my Mother accepted the phrase as no more than polite sentiment. Maud, however, interpreted it with as much seriousness as a good Christian believes the Gospel is the Word of God, and therefore determined that the manor must be smartly refurbished before the next Royal visit or the family would be disgraced beyond endurance.

"If we fail to improve our lot the Queen will think us common!" moaned my Mother, pointing out worn places on the wooden floor planks and decrying the fact that the manor was made of daub and wattle, not herringbone brickwork.

"We are common," replied my Father mildly, reminding her how far up the family had risen already. But she would not listen. Despite our past we were finally proper gentry. We had had a visit from the Queen her self. The Southerns were a great family now, she declared,

and must needs affirm their importance with rich tapestries and a good lot more furniture — at least one joined table, not a mere plank laid on trestles, and six joined stools. She would have oak panelling on the walls of the Great Hall, glass windows in every casement, a cushioned bench neath the window. She even demanded a new wing be built so the servants could sleep separate from our family. And rugs. Scattering the floor with rushes and fragrant herbs would no longer do. She required Turkey rugs and woven straw mats, and that was that. She would not be humiliated the next time the Queen visited, not her! My father obliged only moderately, for tho we had in class been raised to gentry, we were never the less at the lowest end of that class, and my Fathers income from his properties was no higher since the Queens visit.

When her ranting failed to conjure up the rugs and furniture and herringbone brickwork, my Mother turned her attentions on her daughters, both of whom she was determined to marry "up." Her success was questionable in the case of Meg. Sure Squire Crenwick was a local gentleman with some property, but he was no nobleman as Mother had dreamt. He was an old man and stone deaf at that. But Meg knew better than to argue with our Mother and went obediently to her wedding like a lamb to slaughter, and her dowry nearly broke our familys accounts.

Alice was next, and tho she went agreeably to her private school for gentlewomen, learning the arts of embroidery, dancing, manners, treble viol and harpsichord, in addition to all housewifely chores, she secretly — to my self only — rebelled against her miserable future.

Late one Saturday afternoon she returned to Enfield Manor after a daylong visit with her married sister at Crenwick Hall. She had brought her horse and cart back to the stable where I was putting Charger down for the night. As I brushed his still sleek body she began a litany of woe, not her own but her sisters. The old man Meg had married was too decrepit to walk properly and only shuffled about in fur slippers, but once under the bedclothes the lecher demanded all his husbandly due. Meg had tearfully complained to Alice that he smelt — foot, breath and body — that his hair crawled with enough lice to stock a parish, and when she cried with pain or displeasure in the marital act, his deafness prevented him from hearing her. Her only hope now was that she might be pregnant, for during those nine months the nuptial duties were suspended. She talked of suckling the child her self — a practice rare amongst gentleladies — knowing it would extend that period of abstinence till the babe was off the breast. Poor Meg. She was a wretched girl in every way.

Her sad tale caused so great an outpouring of sympathy, disgust and fear in Alice and my self that a dialogue ensued — one of rare depth and detail on a subject little spoke twixt a brother and a sister. But we were well met and curious, and each having some intelligence of our own sexes nature, and knowing full well we would not receive the same from our Parents, agreed to speak freely. I had never yet lain with a woman and had only known pleasure, as all boys do, within the grasp of my palm. And of course Alice was a virgin. So as the light grew dim I lit a lantern and set a saddle blanket upon the stable floor. We sat shoulder to shoulder and pulled more blankets round us and spoke sometimes in whispers like devilish children, sometimes laughing boldly like a couple of bawds.

I began by reporting of a book a boy had smuggled into school. Called "Aristotle's Masterpiece or Secret of Generation," twas in Greek, and so the boy had brought it to me, the best translator of that language, and I therefore knew its entire contents. My report to Alice, unhappily, was that that ancient scholar either knew not, or refused to share, the methods and variety of enjoyment before the act, coital positions and ways to enhance ones pleasure. True, he gave great detail and description of the male sexual organ for which we boys had little use, having the actual protuberance tween our own two legs. More attention was paid to a description of the females parts and something called clitoris, which Aristotle claimed was the seat of all venereal pleasure in women, and without which they neither desired nuptial embraces nor enjoyed them. In that dim stable I swear I saw my sister blush, and that was confirmation of the truth of it.

Alice too had had occasion to view a manual of erotic lore, but hers was Italian and therefore useful. Called "Postures," by Aretino and Romano, it brimmed with graphic texts, numerous and most explicit illustrations, leaving nothing to the schoolgirls imagination. When Alice tried straightforwardly explaining several of the postures to me, we ended falling about in gales of laughter. We were none the less both sobered by the vastness of possibility where, before her reading of the book and then her telling it to me, we had each suffered under a misconception common to the young — that sexual congress had but one or two plain variations.

She was quick to add, and resolved that I should clearly know, that it was not the male alone who required satisfaction but that women too suffered from a lack of such. This news did in deed interest me, and so I pressed her whereby she gave me a shock, with intelligence that a woman may be satisfied again and again in a short space of time.

"Is that," I asked, "what Wythorne meant when he said 'Though a woman be a weaker vessel yet they will overcome two, three or four men in the satisfying of their carnal appetites'?"

"Wythorne," replied Alice tartly, "may be a fine musician, but he is a hater of womankind, so says my tutor Miss Hopewell. The truth is, if a man be wise in the ways of love, his wife should need none other." In the silence as I contemplated that thought she continued, but shyly, "So, brother, it seems from what you say that you have not yet bedded a girl."

Twas my turn to blush and stammer. "I . . . I . . . well . . . the truth of it is, you see . . ."

"I suppose you will have marked how our Mother hires only ugly servant girls, so as not to tempt her husband and sons, tho I daresay a sour puss never stopped a lad who was keen enough." Seeing I was still cringing with embarrassment at being found out a callow virgin, she went on. "No worry, Arthur. You are young still. Time enough for the sport. John is eighteen and only took it up last year."

"Aye, and has been cunt struck ever since," I added in all seriousness.

Alice cackled loudly at the truth as much as the vulgarity of my words and suddenly stood, throwing off our covers and dusting herself off. "I shall die a spinster before I marry with a man like Crenwick," she announced.

"Or you could marry to suit Mother and take a lover too," I suggested.

"Tis as daft a suggestion as ever you've made, dear brother," said Alice giving me a playful clout on the head. "A cuckolded husband is a dangerous man, for if he is found with his horns showing he is punished as heinously as his wife. His honor is gone, his virility questioned, his name defamed. I shall strive, if not for true love in my marriage, at least for a companionable man. Come, Mother will be wondering where we have got to."

*　*　*

By Tuesday supper John was still not arrived home and our Mother was beside her self. She grew wilder and more tearful with every hour, tore at her hair and chewed at the bottom of her lip till it was raw and swollen as a purple plum.

Alice and I passed a signal, eye to eye, at the supper table and when after evening prayers — this in large part my Mothers loud wailing to Jesus for Johns safe return — we met in the stables, a small secret caucus to hatch some scheme for bringing John home. My intelligence, gathered as I rode back from the schoolroom that afternoon, was that our brother was not and had never been since Sunday morning at our local publick house which he was known to frequent. I wondered aloud if he had perhaps gone home with some hedge whore, drunk himself silly with ale, and now lay babbling and cupshotten in her bed. But Alice, who claimed from John the greatest share of affection in our family, said he had talked of a trip to Maidstone, a shire town of good size and industry some six hours ride from Enfield. There, he said, he had heard he would find some pastimes and pleasures unavailable in our rustic surroundings.

So with some gnashing of teeth — for we knew my absence would further alarm our Mother — twas decided I would go and fetch John home. When we had returned to the manor house I claimed fatigue and went up to bed. Gathering a few articles of clothing for extra warmth I went into Alices room where she plied me with the few shillings she had. Added to my own, they came to very little in deed. But she had stolen some food from the larder and packed it in a cloth sack for me. With a kiss from my sister I quietly left the house as I had the day of the Queens visit — down the nursery wall trellis — and using the shadows of the yard under a near full moon as my protection, stole to the stables, dark and still. In the light of a single candle I whispered my plans to ever ready Charger and quickly saddled him. As tho he understood the need for secrecy he stepped with light and quiet hooves into the night, out the gate and onto the country road.

Twas a sweet and solitary journey under the stars. My fears of murderous highwaymen were never met. In fact I saw for the first four hours of the ride not a soul. I was glad for the bright moon and cloudless sky, and I grew so accustomed to the dark, twas as comfortable to my eyes as the day. I had never come so far this way before, and found my self at several crossroads needing negotiation.

But the town of Maidstone was so large that signs pointed the way from a great distance off.

As the sun rose on a fine day I began to pass farmers and their carts slogging into Maidstone Market. Some had pumpkins and melons, some carrots and parsnips. Others carried great loads of squabbling chickens in wood stick cages. By far the largest transports carried hops, for the city was famous for its brewing.

The old and stately church spire could be seen pointing up to Heaven, and by now the crowd of country folk on the road pouring into Maidstone was a great river, I and Charger a mere droplet in the flood. As we approached I felt my heartbeat quicken at the newness of it all. I had prayed that I would find John at the end of my journey, but now as the bustling city lay before me, I cared less for my original task than the great adventure awaiting me therein.

I passed thro the heavy town gate, craning my neck to see two local constables posted high upon towers on either side of it. They watched closely all who entered, I supposed for low vagrants, unsavory characters or criminals wanted by the law.

I must admit that in the first moments after our entry into that great town, riding high in my saddle like a fine young gentleman down the thoroughfare, my eyes bulged as if growing off stalks, at all the sights. My ears throbbed with the unaccustomed cacophony of city noises, and my nostrils were assailed by odors both foul and appetizing. Unlike our little village the road here was paved. The shops and houses, many of them stone, were in long rows, all two and three storeys high and joined by common walls. After many houses another paved street crossed the one I was on. If I looked side to side down that thorofare I saw there buildings as far as the eye could see. So many shops! They all had painted signs and glass windows in them showing their various wares. Mercers, drapers, goldsmiths, carpenters. And the people were as numerous as ants on an anthill. There were of course the farmers with whom I had entered the town but others whom I deemed residents. They stood clustered in twos and threes talking sociably in front of a bakery, a Flemish weavers shop or soap house, watching the throng pass by. I saw a dog officer hauling two mangy bitches off to an unhappy fate, and a toilworn woman with a great brick of a baby riding her hip as she pushed a small cart piled high with pasties, still steaming hot in the cool morning air.

I passed several stately buildings, one very grand with columns and carvings and many windows which I supposed was a county government house, and some great lovely private residences, tho I was struck at how they sat just next to much poorer ones. I heard many dialects and several foreign languages too. There were old and ragged beggars, and ladies very fine, and men I took as city officials in the way they strode here and there with strong purpose. But most of all there were many young men. I supposed they were, like my self, the younger sons of families come to town to make their fortunes where none at their country homes could be found.

Twas time, I thought, to start the search for my brother. I was riding down the High Street now, which was dedicated in full to victuallers of every kind. I saw and smelt bakeshops wafting the sweet scent of gingerbread, passed butteries, white meats shops and butchers with all manner of slain carcasses hanging in the window. At one corner I saw a line of women outside an unmarked shop door, each one waiting patiently with a basket on her arm. Tying up Charger at a post I climbed down, tested my wobbly knees — for I had been long in the saddle — and neared the line of women. They each carried in their baskets some raw joint of meat or several gutted fish, or a pile of uncooked but cut vegetables, as if for a stew. I thought this curious and so in my politest voice asked a young woman who by her dress I supposed to be a plain housewife, why she and all the others did bring food to this shop in such a state. She replied twas a "cookstore," that all the homes in this town did not have stoves to cook their family meals, and this place was a service to many neighbors. She was friendly enough, so I asked her where I might find the nearest ale house. She looked at me with a withering eye and turned away in a great huff.

By now feeling the pit of my stomach hollow, having long since consumed what Alice had provided, and relishing all the food stuffs round me, I decided to avail my self of something to eat, and at the same time learn the whereabouts of the towns inns and taverns. I led Charger down the street till I saw a victuallers, which seemed the most thronged with customers and so, I reasoned, having the best food. Several workmen were leaving with their midday meal in a sack as I entered, and so the way was cleared for me to see the counter, piled with meat pies, whole salted fish, slabs of cooked bacon on a plate, some half loaves of bread and a circle of hard yellow cheese with wedges already gone from it.

Before I stepped forward I glanced round, taking in all the scene, marking the details of a man or womans clothing, the dialect they might be speaking, eavesdropping on their conversation, even smelling the odor emanating from their person. From these observations I would fashion a small fantasy, a story of that man or womans life. In the country there was scant variety to choose from, as I knew all the manor and village people too well. But here was a feast for my imagination!

I had just invented a rather lewd story about a well dressed gentleman and a priest when I felt myself jostled rudely from behind. Three youths, not much older than my self were making gangway through the shop door. I heard enough of their glib talk to know they would know all the ale houses in this town, and when they might open. So whilst they chose their grub I queried them of it.

"O ho!" cried a short wiry one, his large smile showing two broken front teeth. A brawler, I thought to my self as he continued, "He wants not just one tavern but all of them!" He stuck his face close to mine and I smelt the odor of raw onions on his breath. "Will one not satisfy yer thirst? And maybe a dozen bawdy houses for yer pleasure, too!" Everyone in the shop turned to stare at me — the vicar gave me a beady look in deed — and the boys all laughed at my embarrassed flush. But I found them good natured and said I was looking for my brother.

"Well, tis a good place for your search," said the tall skinny one with long lank hair, "for in this town there are no less than six and twenty ale houses and nine proper inns."

"Truly?" I asked with what must have been such innocence that they all roared with laughter.

"And ye need not wait to start either," said the third youth who was about my size and sturdy built, "for they all open up at dawn."

"Do you want some company on your rounds?" asked the lanky boy. "Being new here, you will not know your way."

"Aha!" cried Broken Tooth to his companion, "What a good Samaritan. Or might ye be thinking on an early start on yer own daily swig, now?"

"Nothing of the kind," he replied. "This young gentleman could use a few guides to our fair town and that is a fact. Is it not a fact?" He turned and looked at me.

"Aye, it is," was my quick reply, for it seemed a good thing to have friends in a strange town, even if I might not trust them as far as I could throw them.

"Let us be off then," said Lanky Hair, slapping two pence down on the counter for his food. "We have three dozen taverns to visit and four bellies to fill."

Had I set out to find the perfect guides to the quaffing establishments of this handsome town, I could never have found better than these, which had come to me by chance. Putting their heads together they made a plan to cover the whole of Maidstone, section by section, street by street, so that each inn and ale house was duly visited in turn, leaving none uninvestigated. They cautioned me with great seriousness that they had no way to guess the comings and goings of my brother, and that we might visit a tavern where he had not been seen, then leave it for the next only to have him arrive unbeknown at the first and miss him altogether. I answered with equal seriousness, saying that we could only do our best, and that if we failed I would not hold them responsible. Besides, I would by the end of the day have the distinction of having visited every drinking establishment in Maidstone, and thought that a fine enough accomplishment. They heartily agreed. By this time I was enjoying my self completely, glad to be in the company of such affable fellows and not sitting cramped over the dusty pages of Ovid.

And so we proceeded.

Because I had not ruled out the possibility that John might find his comfort in the poorer sections of town, and because they believed these unsavory neighborhoods were safer before dark, my friends began our tour of the city there. Fine cobbled thorofares gave way to rutted muddy lanes where decaying two and three storey houses, each floor jutting out two feet farther over the street than the one below it, prohibited any sunlight to fall onto our heads. In deed all that came from above was garbage, offal, and excrement thrown out the windows of these humble residences. There were heaps of filth piled everywhere and squishing under our boots as well. To the general congestion of the poor citizens in the street was added a menagerie of fleabitten dogs, stray cats, pigs and even a small flock of geese which were the most dangerous to pedestrians, as they pecked viciously at the shins when crossed. The stench of it all was, in places, unbearable and amazing in its variety.

The first several of the ale houses were so wretched I doubted John would have travelled so far to entertain himself in such low conditions. So a head poked in the door of the poorest houses sufficed. By ten in the morning each of the taverns was at least half full and by noon to the drinking was added — despite law forbidding it — all manner of gaming. Dice, card playing, shuffleboard.

"But drinking," Lanky Hair intoned with the voice of a great philosopher as he downed in one long swallow a cup of beer — as he and his friends had done in each of the establishments we had visited — "aye, drinking is the major sport in England." From what I had seen I had no cause to doubt him.

There was at all times during our tour a colorful and running commentary from my boon companions on all the sights, but particularly on the people that we observed. A sweetfaced young woman was "the queen of curds and cream," in other words a simple country girl just in for the market. A rolypoly churchwarden with porcine nose and chubby pink cheeks, hurrying by with a big ledger tucked under his arm, was said to have violated every young boy in the congregation. A little lad not six years old was the citys most proficient cutpurse.

I think I was shown every one of the Maidstone brothels, "houses of good fellowship" as Broken Tooth liked to call them, and I wondered if John were to be found inside. But I felt it unwise to add such places to my itinerary, knowing anyhow I would not be admitted with no money. At each bawdy house the most notorious common queen was pointed out, she generally standing in the doorway waiting for her sporting gents. Sometimes lewd commentary on her particular skills was provided by my friends, with knowing winks and nods tween them.

Some time after midday when most folk stopped for their dinner we sat down on the town green, a pretty place lined on three sides with rich homes and on the fourth with an ancient Cathedral, the one whose spire could be seen from miles away. There was much picnicking on the grass, and all manner of manly sport — cudgel throwing, bowling, shuttle cock, wrestling. Several young ladies indulged in archery. We watched as a too rowdy game of football which had spilt into a busy street was broken up by the burly town killjoy. We contemplated this pathetic creature, wondering why a man would ever assume so hated an occupation. Sturdy proclaimed he once knew a killjoy whose misery in his job and the odium it provoked had driven him to hang himself. Then Sturdy stuffed the better part of his earlier purchased meat pie in his gob and chewed largely.

We saw Market Street next, and though the farmers had begun packing up their wares for the trip home, the streets here were crowded still. On Carver Street was the Angel Inn, a fine place with rooms upstairs boasting canvas sheets which the proprietor, standing arms akimbo at his front door, claimed loudly were washed after every customer, tho no one in their right mind did believe him. And nearby were several well appointed publick houses, but my brother was nowhere to be found. I asked for him at all of them, but how could the keepers help me find, in such a large place as this, a stranger of unremarkable description named John? What had possessed me to think I could?

By late in the afternoon we had visited more than half the inns and ale houses in the city, now filled with men three sheets to the wind, valiant pot knights and workingmen lately come from their labors to spend their wages making merry. My companions, having downed a cup of ale in almost every establishment we had visited, were themselves a sight more than merry. They were now steering me towards the west end of town where they promised the greatest concentration of fine inns in which we might continue our search.

As we headed down a broad cobbled street there came a commotion. A large crowd, with more than its share of clergymen in and amongst them, preceded a horse drawing a rough cart. As they drew near we pressed our selves against the shop walls to let them pass. And tho I knew what I saw — a scene of publick penance — I did not know the wherefore of it. The faces in the crowd were somber and some angry. Tied and forced to walk behind the cart were a man and a woman all dressed in white, tho the man was stript to the waist, and both carried white rods in their hands. A churchwarden followed them, whipping their backs, perhaps more ceremoniously than painfully, tho by the penitents faces I could see the humiliation was extreme.

"What have they done?" I whispered to my friends.

"Only the worst of the venereal sins," said Sturdy, himself looking soundly chastened.

"Incest?" I asked.

"Naa," came Broken Tooths reply. "This man and woman are convicted not once but twice of begetting bastards."

I was struck speechless, but my mind was instantly spinning the story of these two passionate souls trapt in a sin worse than buggery, worse than bestiality. For a family to have its bloodline tainted, its continuity questioned, in deed threatened the most sacred law of primogeniture.

"Come on then," cried Lanky Hair, yanking me away from the scene. "The night is before us, and some serious quaffing as well."

As the darkness gathered citizens one by one lit candle lanterns outside their doors making a pretty glow down the lanes. Ahead of us the road ended with no outlet at a huge white building, the Crown Inn, which stood alone, its great painted sign creaking in a breeze which had lately blown up. Twas a busy night at the Crown with men, women, even children streaming in its front door. None of my friends wished to stay outside minding Charger with so much excitement going on inside, so they drew straws and Broken Tooth was the loser.

The rest of us entered to find this was a courtyard style inn. Within the courtyard a stage had been erected. Some men in exotic costumes were working on it, hammering down planks and such. I knew these to be stage players, as I had seen an itinerant troop of the same come through Enfield once, but I had never seen such an elaborate stage as this. To think that added to all the wonders of the day would be a performance by stage players in the courtyard of a fine inn! Alice would be exceeding jealous, I thought smiling to my self.

But the performance was, by the look of it, some time off, and my soused companions were claiming a great thirst. So into the crowded tap room we made our way. Twas then I saw him, my brother John with a buxom bawd on his lap, her arms round his neck, her breasts entirely bared. And one of her nipples was planted firmly tween his lips. His eyes were closed and it was a good thing too, for the lass was neither young nor pretty, her lewd smile revealing a row of crooked yellow choppers.

I was at first paralytic with indecision, not being versed in the proper manners for a brother extracting a prostitute from the amorous grip of his elder and effecting his return home. I knew well that to cause him embarrassment might get me a pair of properly boxed ears, if not worse. But I had not come all this way to lose him again if he perchance left this inn for a brothel or another drinking establishment.

My mates were suddenly at my side with a glass of ale in hand, and one for me as well. Trying to appear unperturbed, I pointed out my brother who was now deliriously attached to the whores other nipple.

"Oi, tis Phoebe has got him in her clutches!" cried Sturdy, his eyes fairly leaping out of his head at the sight of the womans loose breasts. This led me to believe these boys, despite their knowing airs, had little more experience with the opposite sex than I.

"I hope he knows how to keep hold of his purse while she has hold of his cock, for she is famous for diving into gentlemens pockets and picking them clean," said Lanky Hair.

"By the look of him he seems not to care if she does," I said. "I fear he is so attached to the strumpet I shall not get a word in edgeways."

"No problem in it," said Sturdy. "Phoebe!" he shouted over the din.

But the whore was too intent to be pulled away from the matter at hand. As I watched, her fingers snaked down tween John's legs, and the other hand sought his pocket, this under the guise of passionate caresses.

"Phoebe!" my friend tried again. "You had best come at once, your house is afire!"

The whore was disengaged from my brothers embrace, stuffing her great bosoms back in her bodice, and out the door in the blink of an eye. I lost no time presenting my self to him, but what with the shock of his recent loss, his ale soaked brain and my altogether out of place appearance, he did not immediately recognize me.

"John," I said. "Tis me, Arthur. Your brother."

"Arthur," he replied, squinting at me with a puzzled look.

"And here are some friends," I said, indicating Lanky Hair coming up behind with Sturdy. It occurred to me only then that I did not know their names, aside from the epithets I had given them.

"Pull up some stools," I told them, "and you can celebrate our family reunion with us."

We found out we had saved John from very little at Phoebes hands. His pockets were already cleared out, for he had drunk and wenched and gambled every shilling away since Sunday night last. Had I never come for him, he said, in any case he would have been home on the morrow. But we did spend a pleasant evening dancing drunken jigs to a hornpipe and squeaky fiddle, and later the play was announced to begin.

We took our places on benches in the courtyard below the stage with all manner of folk — city merchants and their families, publick servants, plain citizens and apprentices. The covered seats in the permanent galleries were reserved for gentlemen with money, but we were never the less content with our arrangements. Twas well known that all the players were men, and boys pretended the female roles. But when the manager took the stage to apologize for a delay in the start of the show as "the Queen was shaving," it produced such howls of laughter and merriment which continued unabated that the piece, a high drama of history called "King John", could not be performed past five minutes, as the audience had never managed to contain themselves. But the players, wishing to proceed in some fashion, devised to perform instead a bawdy comedy called "A Sack Full of News" which was more to the taste of the audience. So silly a thing was it that we laughed till we cried and fell off our benches clutching our bellies.

Later John bade me go home with promises that he would return the next day, for he was in no condition to travel and had already paid for a bed at the Crown that night. He would have asked me to stay but he hoped for one more night of carnal pleasures, tho I doubted he would find much with an empty purse. So I took my leave of him with Martin and Paul, whose names I had lately discovered.

Only as we were leaving the place did my stomach heave at a terrible thought. In all the excitement we had forgot about Harry — that was Broken Tooth — who was left to tend Charger. And in deed when we found him he was fast asleep and snoring like a ripsaw in wood. Charger was nowhere to be seen.

We roused him with a good shake and a lot of shouting, demanding to know where my horse had gone. He was much chagrinned, claiming when he grew sleepy he had tied the rein round his ankle so any movement the beast made would wake him. In deed the end of the rein was still tied firmly round his leg, its cut end a testimony to the young mans stupidity or drunkenness, perhaps both.

We spread out and frantically queried everyone who might have seen the crime, but those citizens who loitered outside the Crown were loath to speak, even if they had seen it, for horse theft was a crime as heinous as murder and punished by branding or hanging. We were therefore reduced to scouring the streets our selves, each of us harboring the secret fear that when we found the horse he might be in the hands of not one or two lousy beggars, but a band of dangerous rogues and cutthroats. In truth my companions might have taken the opportunity to take their leave of me — they could have fled and I never would have found them again. But tho they were poor and rough and not quite sober, they had honorable hearts after all and vowed to stay with me till the horse be found.

Our first bit of luck came with the sight of a town constable roving the late night streets with halberd and lantern. We queried him and he said he had seen three men on three horses not long before, and they were only remarkable in that two of the mounts were calm and tractable, and one was unruly. Its rider was forced to beat it, as the horse liked to bolt in the opposite direction from which they were headed.

My heart leapt and pity surged thro me. Someone was beating Charger for his desire to return to my self. Which way was it they were travelling, I demanded to know of the constable, and at what speed and how long past? Toward the city gates, an easy amble, and not ten minutes past, he replied. I shouted out our thanks as we took off racing hell bent down the cobbled thorofare. As I ran I felt a winged Mercury, leaving my friends far behind, for twas a piece of my heart stolen, and for want of my own common sense that he was gone. I prayed as I ran that I would catch them before they reached the town gate, for once in the countryside they might take up a faster pace, and Charger would be lost for ever.

Then I saw them. Three full grown men, the one on Chargers back a great hulking thing, nearing the gate. In deed my horse was restless, needing the whip to keep him straight and steady, for I kept the softest bit in his mouth, and it must have been hard for even so brutish a man as this to handle him. Never missing a step as I ran, I stole a glance behind to see my friends running apace but clearly winded. They would be no good in a fight, I thought, even if they caught up in time. I looked up to find the sentries on the gate towers, but what I saw made my heart sink — the silhouette on either tower was slumped and sleeping at his post. I thought to shout and wake them, but worried that the horsemen, hearing me, would gallop off and leave me in the dust.

In a lightning sprint I came up their rear, they never hearing my footfall over the clattering of a dozen hooves on cobblestone. Thirty yards, twenty. I closed the gap and when I could see the white whorl at the base of Chargers tail I cried out loudly, "Ho, Charger!"

He wheeled round so violently at the sound of my voice that the fat riders neck got a good whipping. At sight of me the horse thief with all his weight and strength and spiked spurs tried to bring

Charger about and ride him away. The two ruffians with him were not ready to let a mere boy unhorse their companion who was struggling with his unruly mount, beating him unmercifully. They came at me, the Devil in their eyes and cudgels flailing. I warded off their blows as best I could, but one landed right on my left cheek, and I felt a gush of warm blood run down my face. Then I saw round about me my three comrades and it was, all at once, a proper melee with great shouts and grunts and pummelling, then a scream as Sturdy sank his teeth into a rogues thigh. Now the gate guards were roused and were shouting too. I knew I had to unhorse the fat one, and so I screamed above the fracas, "Charger, levade, hup, hup!"

My horse, God bless his soul, instantly obeyed the command rearing high on his haunches, flinging his forehands into the air and neighed loud and defiant for good measure. The thief, taken utterly by surprise and unbalanced, was flung backwards, his feet wrenched from the stirrups and thrown to the ground. He landed hard on his back, his head receiving a good crack on the cobbles.

I leapt onto Chargers back and called out to my friends, "Martin, Paul, Harry, fall back, fall back!" And like a well trained squadron heeding their commander they went clear of the three horses. And then mustering all of my wits, and with the strength gained from the reunion with my best and most trusted friend, I hove into action. I had no weapon but Charger, but we were in deed formidable. With a spirited series of rears and quick voltes, using his hooved forehands as pummels, and sharp yerks to the rear we unhorsed one more ruffian and disabled the other in no time at all. The fat man still lay unconscious and by the time the gate guards had raced down the stairs to assist us, the skirmish was over, the enemies fallen and nursing their wounds. With one look at their faces the sentries plied their locks and chains, for these were men wanted for thievery of every sort, and certainly bound for the city gaol.

With thanks to us and especial accolades to my gallant horse, the guards bade us good night and led the rogues to their deserved fate. Twas time for us to head home, so I said my goodbyes to my companions whose day of fun and adventure had been as fine as my own. Tho I could not promise that we would ever meet again, I said sincerely that I should never forget their kind assistance locating my brother, good fellowship and brave action in battle. They returned the compliments claiming that I was the most toward gentleman they ever knew, acting not too grand for the likes of them, that I enjoyed a good laugh, and especially was an excellent horseman. With much cherishing and stroking they told Charger what a great-hearted beast he was, and so as I trotted on my high horse out the gates of Maidstone my spirit was as light as an angels, and I felt more a man than I had ever before been. Fourteen, and my life stretched out before me like a highway. I welcomed it with wide open arms.

I was but two hours from home and my mood was still high despite the gash on my cheek, now throbbing painfully. I thought how lucky I had been not to have my eye put out, but instead be left with a fine manly scar, a testament to my bravery. We had on the journey passed a good many riders on horseback, peasants in wagons and on foot.

But now ahead I saw a well made cart drawn by two horses, and a lone lady at the reins. I was struck first by the smallness of her waist, her erect carriage as she took the bumps and ruts of the pitted road with a kind of grace. I could not see the color nor the style of her hair, for it was all tucked under a cap. My mind sprung instantly into imagination, painting the portrait of her face. She was young and sweet, the daughter of a rich merchant who had stolen her Fathers cart to run away, for he was cruel and beat her unmercifully. She was determined never to feel his lash again. A young lady unaccompanied on these roads was an invitation to scoundrels and rapists, but dying was preferable to her Fathers house, she would claim.

By the time I had conjured her name to be Annabelle, and her destination a kind elder sisters house in London, Charger had come alongside her cart. She turned to look at me and my heart seemed to stop beating altogether. When it began again it thumped double time, for this girl was not sweet faced at all. She was nothing less than exquisite. She was in deed young, perhaps my age or a year older, and her skin still wore the freshness of childhood, but the clear hazel eyes bore a knowing beyond her years. In sideways fashion she held my gaze steadily, and as I did not attempt to pass but continued to ride alongside, that shared gaze grew very long in deed.

"Good day," I finally blurted out. Her pink bowed lips curled into a smile that did not reveal her teeth. A brief thought, like a slippery frog escaping my grip, made the teeth behind the pretty smile all black and rotten, a joke on me. But when she replied "good day,"

her face turned full to me, I saw the teeth were perfectly shaped and white as the wing of a swan. I knew not where to go from there, but knew with certainty that twas not far from this girls side.

"You have a bad cut, Sir. Have you had a fall . . . or have you been brawling?" she asked with a frankness uncommon to a stranger.

"Brawling," I announced with equal directness, pleased in the extreme that it was no lie. She smiled again and this time twas not my heart that reacted violently, but a bodily organ situated somewhat lower. "A man stole my horse in Maidstone this morning and I was forced to retrieve him by measures more martial than peaceable, tho I am," I added quickly not wishing her to think me a ruffian, "a usually peaceable fellow."

"I do hope you were not wounded in any other way," she said.

I found that each word as it left her perfect mouth caused a small pulse in my cock, stiffening and enlarging it with each beat. I moved my hands holding the reins to cover my growing member.

"You say you are come all the way from Maidstone this morning?" she asked with an incredulous look which left me with the distinctly pleasant impression that my condition and the exploits of the previous night might prove interesting and exciting to this girl . . . mayhaps even arousing. That I even had such a thought was a shock to me, but I quickly recovered my senses, and asking if I might have permission to ride with her, began to weave my story.

I delighted her with descriptions of every sight and smell and taste I could recall. Some of my companions clever turns of phrase I made my own, and I even embellished several of the flights of imagination I had conjured, turning them into fact. It made for good telling, this day of mine. When I came to the part where I found my brother at the Crown Inn, the bawd in his lap, I included every lurid detail knowing that should I overstep my bounds she would fix me with an indignant glare, slap the reins and ride away with a haughty chin in the air. This never did happen. Contrariwise, when I said how John had his lips planted round Phoebes nipple like a suckling babe, I saw the young ladys mouth drop open slightly and her own doe soft chest begin to rise and fall a little faster. But twas when I told of Chargers theft and the battle in which I had apprehended him, sending three wanted criminals to gaol, that she turned to me with a look of such enamourment and awe that I swear if I had not striven to keep the horse tween my legs I would have fallen out of the saddle.

"What a brave man you are," she said with all sincerity.

A man, she called me a man, I thought, my heart racing. Did she not see I was only fourteen? I knew that I was tall amongst boys my age, and fairly muscular for all my martial exertions. And in deed I had recently engaged in numerous manly pursuits. What would it serve to tell her I was in truth only a lad?

"Who are you, and where from?" she asked suddenly. "I know your entire story and yet know neither your name nor your station."

"Arthur Southern of Enfield," I replied. "My Father is Keeper of the Chase there."

"Why, I have been there as a young girl! My own Father took me hunting once in that forest. I have never forgotten it."

"Then we must surely have met before, as I am my Fathers apprentice. I may have helped you into your saddle, or led your family thro the wood." I saw her smiling broadly now, clearly pleased that we were perhaps not strangers after all. "And what is your name?" I asked, finally remembering my manners.

"Mary Willis." She turned her face away suddenly and stared straight ahead down the road. "Lady Willis."

If she had said she was Lucifers daughter I could not have been more taken aback. She was a married woman! For a too long moment I was speechless, where before I had been a veritable fountain of words. She could not fail to notice my consternation and suddenly reined her horses to a stop. I pulled Charger up too, and we stayed unmoving and silent for what seemed an endless moment. When finally she spoke her voice was lacking its previous boldness.

"I am only just married to Sir Howard Willis a year now."

God, I thought to myself, my heart sinking with pity, an ancient codger for a husband — like Meg.

"He owns a large property and a fine manor house. His children are all grown . . . all of them older than me."

"How is it he lets you ride out by your self?" I asked.

"I was visiting my maiden aunt in Oxted for a week, but the manservant who accompanied me there broke his leg yesterday, and my aunt had no servants to spare. She pleaded with me to wait, but my husband gets very cross if I am away too long, so I took this with me." She lifted up a cloth beside her on the seat and I saw a pistol wrapped in it. "Had you behaved dishonorably back there I would have blown a great hole in your head." She smiled that utterly flirtatious smile again.

I thought with chagrin that this girls true story was a sight more exciting than the one I had conjured. "How long before you are home?" I asked, not knowing what else to say. She had quite taken the wind from my sails.

"I am home," she announced surprising me again. "This is the edge of my husbands land. The manor is but a few miles further." I was still tonguetied in the extreme. "Arthur Southern," she said suddenly. "Would you like to see my favorite spot in the world? Tis not far from here."

A voice in my head was shouting "danger, danger!" urging me to decline and ride away with a polite "good day." But an equally vibrant voice which was not speaking words so much as humming a sweet romantic melody — "Greensleeves" perhaps — intruded, drowning out the sensible one.

"Come see it," she urged. "No one goes there but me." Her hazel eyes were glinting in the sun, the upturned bow of her lips an unrefusable invitation.

I do not remember saying yes, that I would go. I only remember following her as she pulled the wagon into a copse of trees which hid it from the road. She had jumped down so quickly I had no time to dismount to help her, but she came immediately to Chargers side, gave me her hand, and I pulled her up behind me in the saddle. With her arms wrapt round my waist, I felt her breasts bumping on my back, her warm breath on my neck. At her direction we rode into a thick wood of ancient oaks with gnarled branches and no distinct paths. But Mary knew the way and before long I heard the sound of running water, too loud for a mere stream.

In deed her secret place was a mossy green forest glade suited perfectly, I thought, for fairies and nymphs, with a rushing rock waterfall and sweetwater pond below it. I helped her down and while Charger drank she looked round her and began to breathe deeply, as tho inhaling the beauty into her body. I thought I saw upon her face the same kind of pleasure I felt after a hard ride on Charger. Then she reached up and removed her cap revealing her tawny hair, which fell thickly round her shoulders and back. With her hair thus freed her face seemed even more lovely to me than before, and I could hardly tear my eyes away from her.

"Let me see to that cut," she said and without waiting for my reply dipped the hem of her skit in the clear water. "Come, Arthur, I shall not bite you." I came closer and found I towered over her tiny

frame. "Here, bend your head a little." She washed the gash thoroughly then, tho I do not remember the pain of it. I only recall that when she was done her arms came up, twining round my neck, and my lips found hers. They were the softest thing I had ever known, and her mouth the sweetest flavor. At one moment I do remember the taste of salt mingling with the sweet, but if I recognized it as her tears I did not stop kissing her. The feel of a woman close in my arms was as pure and wholesome as the rhythm of a galloping horse beneath me. I wished to slowly, tenderly plumb the many mysteries of Mary Willis — the skin of her tiny, perfect breasts and woman scented thighs so soft, the shadowy pits neath her arms, the small sacred darkness of her navel, the cleft tween her buttocks, the downy hair of her neck. But I was impossibly aroused, and so was led by that hard part of my self to rush, leaving behind tenderness, and cleave her body with my own. This I did, giving as full rein to my mind as my body, a revelation of passion. Then explosion. Then peace.

On my return from adventuring I was greeted with much displeasure from my Parents, for they were alarmed by my sudden disappearance without prior permission. Worse, I returned in a dishevelled state, my clothing filthy and torn, with bruises and a great gash on my cheek to attest to my ruffian's behavior. Neither had I accomplished the goal which I used as my best excuse for going — bringing John home with me. He did not, in fact, return as promised until two more days and nights had passed.

I was disgraced, and punished by having all my riding privileges revoked for one month. I was forced, humiliatingly, to walk to school. No weekend sessions with Charger were allowed, and my Mother oversaw my daily routine, adding more prayer and Scriptural study, and even some womens work which kept me indoors all the day long. I felt a bloody fool.

When the profligate son returned he barely had his knuckles rapped, and after a mild scolding was made much of by my Mother who, as always, forgave him everything. My Father, tho, was right and truly disgusted with his dissipated son, at eighteen a drunkard and a lecher. My Father feared that when John inherited Enfield Chase it would fall to wrack and ruin under so uncaring a hand. He saw me — the perfect landlord of this cherished Paradise — turned away from it by law to make my own way in a cold world. If my Father had been more wealthy in his own right, he would have made provision for me, but as it was our wealth was illusory. We lived well in our manor, surrounded by Natures vast treasures, but there was no inheritance save the Chase and it was, irrevocably, for John.

I survived my punishment in better form than might be imagined, as I took more flights of fantasy than ever before. I relived and embellished the memories of my day and night in Maidstone, the victorious battle with the horse thieves, and mostly my secret tryst with Mary Willis.

This one memory was the greatest balm to my soul and masculine pride, tho I did feel an imposter, for she never learnt I was but fourteen. I had no opportunity to apply the lessons Alice had taught, of a woman finding repeated satisfaction in sexual congress. In truth I do not know if Mary had been satisfied even once. After my own explosion of pleasure she had fallen to weeping, and I held her gently in my arms whilst she told how her husband never touched her, how he had lost his virility entirely with age, and only wished a keeper for his household — a pretty face to stare at over dinner, not a wrinkled old wretch like himself. Mary was more miserable than she ever thought possible before her wedding day, and these few hours with me, she said, had been a precious gift. We had parted sadly with no hope of laying eyes on one another again. But truly she was with me in my dreams and imaginings every day for many weeks after our meeting.

Therefore twas a great shock when some months hence on a stormy afternoon a strange rider came galloping hell bent thro the gates and up to the door of Enfield Manor. I was coming across the yard from the stables and saw the mud splattered messenger hand my Mother a sealed letter, then heard the man utter the words "Sir Howard Willis." He hurriedly watered his horse and excusing his haste — for he wished to be returned home by dark — galloped away.

I came indoors where I stood staring at the letter lying on the table unopened, till my Mother came and screamed at me that I was dripping on her floor. One by one I took the stairs feeling a sense of doom overtaking me. I knew my Father was away in the village at a church meeting and would not read the letter for some hours. But I also knew that when he did my life at Enfield Chase would come to a crashing end. For I had certainly impregnated Mary Willis, and her husband would know the child was not his own. She must have broken under his cruel interrogation — I shuddered at the thought of him causing her pain — and revealed the true paternity of her child.

This was an idea which for months had crept stealthily round the perimeter of my mind, but one which I had assiduously denied entrance therein. I had no need for my fantasies now. Mary and I would be tried by ecclesiastic court for the crime of bastardy and I knew, from my memory of that terrible procession in the streets of Maidstone, what fate and punishment lay ahead for us. Her husband might, it occurred to me, find further justice in having the cuckolder killed.

As calmly as I was able I weighed and measured my choices. I could stay and pay the piper, but I saw what retribution had been meted out for my absence without permission from home for two days. I knew also that my happy position at Enfield Chase was limited to the years remaining in my Fathers life, after which I might be allowed by my brother to stay, but would be at best a guest in his household, an employee in his service. Tho I had learnt and learnt well the profession of chase keeping, I knew in my deepest heart this was neither my love nor my calling. I was a soldier, a horse soldier, and I might as well begin now in that profession as later. If I waited, I reasoned, Howard Willis might kill or maim me and end my fine dreams for ever.

I chose instead to live.

I wasted little time, packed a few things — foremost my copy of Xenophon — and wrote a letter of explanation to my Father. I told him my plans, tho not my destination, and begged his forgiveness for my cowardly act of running away, and for the shame and scandal which would surely rain down upon our family. But as I believed he wanted me alive more than dead I thought my plan prudent, and would write from the battlefield. I did not know then which battlefield or which war it might be. I would, I supposed, have to settle for the life of a mercenary soldier, England having no enemies at present.

Alice was desolate when I came to her room and in whispers told her I was leaving. She had no allies but my self and would be forced to fight her battle alone. When she asked me how I would pay for my journeying I answered her with a blank stare, for I had no money of my own, and nothing of value except my horse which I could not, of course, sell. She went to a box she kept hidden neath her bed and drew from it a ring, a garnet set in gold.

"Part of my dowry," she said. "Mayhaps if I have less to make me worthy, no husband will want me. Here, take it."

I did not argue for I had no choice. I told her I loved her dearly, kissed her and with my cloth saddle pack slung over my arm, descended the front stairs. With a final glance at the letter from Willis which had sealed my fate, I walked out the door. My course was set.

Within half an hour Charger and I were on the road and riding to our destination — a village in southern Wales on the edge of the great Western Sea, a place that was home to a cavalry training school. As we flew down the highway towards a sunset dulled by rain I was warmed by thoughts of the place. Twas said there were parade grounds and an indoor riding school. The men learnt weaponry and equitation, with especial practice in jumping over walls and ditches. All the skills, I thought smiling, at which I was already adept. I imagined presenting my self to the school commander, enlarging my age to match my size, and then begging permission to demonstrate my skills as a horseman. I would mount Charger and within moments the commander would not only grant me entrance to the school, but raise me to instructor.

The miles and the days flew by. The land changed from flat marshes and pastures to rolling hills with villages called Swindon and Stroud, till finally I passed into Wales with its high mountains, and town with names like Caerdydd and Merthyr Tydfil. I slept where I could — in barns or stables or, if I chanced to make a kind acquaintance on the road, in a bed. My gentlemans manners and clothing, and such a fine horse as Charger gave me entrance into some grand homes as well. I never had fear of starving, always believing I would make my destination.

And so I did. Six days after leaving Enfield I reached the outskirts of the village of Milford Haven. As I drew closer I smelt a strange fragrance which was, in deed, more than an odor but a heavy freshness in the air. Twas the sea I was smelling, and I urged Charger on, my heart pounding with anticipation as upon entering the gates of Maidstone. We climbed a small rise and as my gaze filled with the sight of the grey and churning Western Sea, the breath left my body in awe and suddenly I wished, nay longed to be on the very edge of it.

Charger felt it too, for he needed no urging but just a loosening of the reins, and plunged galloping down a road made as much of sand as clay earth. Suddenly the sound of clattering hooves muted and the ride softened, for it was all sand beneath his feet, and every-

thing at once was the sea. Mountains of white topped water roiled and swelled, then crashed down upon the shore of a sweeping bay. Soaring gulls wheeled and shrieked above me. One, then another and another, laid back its wings and like an arrow falling from heaven, sliced down thro the chop and was gone.

I sucked pungent air into my chest in great gulps and felt the salted wind sting my cheeks. I was at the edge of the world and each thundering wave which crashed at Chargers feet seemed a message, a calling from far away, that I was meant to leave the shores of England, see other lands beyond the sea.

I climbed down from the saddle and led Charger south along the waters edge. In the distance a figure sat stooped in the sand facing the ocean. As we came closer I saw he was an old man, a fisherman bent over a net which covered his lap like a hempen apron. He was mending it with fingers as gnarled as an oak branch, no longer nimble but sure at their task. We were very close when he looked up to see us, and he nodded without smiling, but the eyes in his well weathered face twinkled, so I thought him sociable and sat down near to him.

He did not speak for many minutes and I remained quite as silent, contented to be gazing out over my destiny. When he spoke therefore, it startled me.

"Tis a fine beach, this," he pronounced solemnly.

"Tis my first," said I, "and I think it more than fine."

"More than fine, is it? Why, what see ye?"

"Beauty, for one," I answered quickly.

"Aye, that's plain. What else?"

I scanned the horizon. "The greatest force that I have ever known. More even than the fiercest thunder and lightning strikes."

He laughed. "Well then, ye should see this ocean in storm. It strikes terror into the hearts of the bravest of men."

"When I look out there," I ventured, "I see my future."

"Yer future?" His fingers never ceased their delicate work. "Tis the young who come to this place and see their future. Mayhaps tis only the old who care at all for its past."

"Past?" My ears suddenly pricked at the thought of an old man weaving a tall tale. I had many of my own making, but this was a gift not looked for. "Has this place a story?"

I hoped I had not been too eager, for I knew some men were stingy with their tale spinning and parcelled it out at their own will.

But this was not such a man, I learnt. Perhaps twas his only story, beloved but with scant opportunity to speak it, for when he began, the words tumbled and soared and at times exploded like the waves.

"Ten years short of a hundred year ago, Henry Tudor landed with his rebel troops upon this very beach of Milford Haven, intent on lifting the crown off the head of King Richard the Third. Look there." He pointed with a twisted finger to the north shore of the bay. "Three thousand men, some Norman French, others scum out of gaols who wished more to fight than hang, and some of Henrys own retainers long in exile with him. Those were his troops. Once on land he swelled his ranks with his Welsh countrymen, two thousand strong, and then Henry . . ." The old man gazed out to sea and said with trembling voice, ". . . without power, without reputation and without right, marched to Bosworth and took England for his own."

I saw the landing then. Saw the massed ships rocking in the violent surf, men and horses scrambling for the flat unruffled stretch of sand, gathering their forces into marching companies. I saw Henry Tudor himself come ashore in a dinghy, the fire of victory burning in his eyes and then, mounted, taking lead of his men. I saw how the march had left behind naught but the waves crashing on the sand, now trodden and trampled by the footfall of invaders, soon to be masters of the land.

"I was not yet born when the Welshman made himself the seventh King Henry of England. But I did see his son rule. Aye, Great Harry we called him. Married a Spaniard, then an English whore. The whores daughter sits on the throne of England now."

I was rocked by the anger of the mans words. Elizabeth, my own beloved sovereign, vilified by a rough fisherman. "She refuses to act decently and marry. She rules — a woman!" He spat the word. "When she dies childless, all that Henry Tudor fought for and won will be lost to God knows what successor. Tis a crime against the realm. Treason, I say!"

I had to speak. "I know the Queen!" I blurted suddenly.

"Know her?" The old man fixed me with those glittering eyes.

"Aye, I rode next to her and Lord Leicester on a hunt at my Fathers chase. She is . . ." I knew not what to offer in her defense. ". . . beautiful. And good. She loves England and is no traitor as you say. She may yet marry." I had heard my Father and Mother argue this very subject. "She is young enough still to bear children."

"Sure, as her sister Mary was 'young enough.' She married a Spaniard too, then bloated with pregnancy and gave birth to a black tumor in her womb, and died of it. Naa, this Queen of ours means to rule as a man. And a man without issue at that. I curse the day she was born."

I had never before heard such venom leveled at our Queen. I supposed he could not be the only man who thought this way. But before I could defend Elizabeth further, I felt a curious vibration neath me where I sat. Twas not the shaking of the earth from the power of the waves breaking before me. It came from behind. In the moment before I turned I recognized it as many hoofbeats, but was never the less startled to see a patrol of armed soldiers bearing down upon us.

I stood to face them as they came. I thought perhaps, magically, the cavalry school had found me before I them. For what else could these smartly uniformed soldiers want with one old fisherman and a boy?

"Arthur Southern?" said the captain of the guard.

I must be dreaming. This was all a dream. The beach, the diving seabirds, the fisherman who stared up at the horsemen with surprise and at me with wonder, for I knew he never believed I had known the Queen.

"Are you Arthur Southern?" the officer repeated.

If this was a dream I could very well speak, as we often speak in dreams, and so I did. "I am he whom you seek. What do you want with me?"

"We have orders to bring you home to your Fathers house," he replied with official blandness. "Mount up and come with us."

"Whose orders are these?" I cried entirely baffled. "I may be young but I am no fool, Sir, and I will not go willingly till you tell me where you come from."

"London. We are guards of the Privy Council. Now come along, lad, or we shall take you by force."

My mind whirled, flying like leaves blown about in a circular wind. Somehow my fantasies had receded and fact had taken the fore, becoming more strange and awesome than my dreams. Like a sleepwalker I moved to Charger and mounted him. The soldiers surrounded us, and thus prisoners of the Privy Council — why I could never fathom — we were escorted home to Enfield and my Fathers custody.

*   *   *

The memory blurs some. I do recall that the letter from Sir Howard Willis was naught but a request for a days hunt at Enfield Chase with his wife and children, and that when they did come Mary Willis and I passed many longing looks tween us that no one noticed. But we never did find time to talk privately of our passionate meeting before she rode out of my life for ever.

My punishment for running away to join the cavalry was less severe than for riding to Maidstone to bring John home, and all my queries of how the Privy Council could know of my flight or care, were met with stony silence. Finally the importance of the answer faded away as I returned to my life at Enfield Chase and waited for the day when I should ride off to my great destiny.

Eighteen

"So, my lords, are you suggesting that I execute my own cousin Mary Stuart in cold blood?"

Elizabeth glared piercingly at William Cecil, now Baron Burleigh, at Francis Walsingham, recently appointed head of her secret service, and at Robert Dudley, Earl of Leicester, who had in the past several years distinguished himself as a constant and trusted Privy Councillor no less than as a faithful lover. This triumvirate of her closest and most worthy advisors dared this time to glare back at the Queen.

"In her deviousness and scheming, Queen Mary would have had you murdered, England invaded by an army of bloodthirsty Spanish soldiers, and herself placed upon your throne," answered Cecil, his eyes cold as the midwinter morning.

"She has already fomented one Catholic rebellion in her name on English soil. Would you give her leave to begin another?" demanded Walsingham.

"I would not mind," replied Elizabeth evenly, "if the second revolt failed as miserably as the first. My prisoner could find no supporters to rally round her despite all of her legendary beauty and charm and two of England's highest nobles plotting with her."

Elizabeth turned her gaze on Robert Dudley, who stroked his bearded chin with all the gravity of an ancient scholar. "I wish to know your opinion, Lord Leicester, of what should be done with her closest accomplice. Do you agree with your colleagues that the Duke of Norfolk should have his head hacked off as well?" Her voice was particularly scathing, and she could not deny that she gained some satisfaction from the harshness with which she addressed the man she loved. She knew Robin would never — considering his past machinations regarding

Norfolk — answer the question cleanly or easily, and she wished at this moment to see him squirm as these three advisors were now causing her to do.

"Clearly there is no easy solution to this dilemma," said Robin soothingly. "How could we ever have guessed what an untenable position Mary would place herself in?"

"I suppose you blame me for allowing young Darnley to travel to Scotland, knowing how wickedly Lady Lennox schemed for her son's marriage to Mary."

"We do not blame you, Your Majesty," said Walsingham. "There was no way of foreseeing how desperately your cousin would fall in love with the boy."

"I suppose there *is* something irresistibly romantic about nursing a young man through a case of measles," said Elizabeth with unmistakable sarcasm.

Walsingham and Cecil chuckled but Leicester was stony-faced. He was no doubt, thought Elizabeth, still brooding about her scheme to marry himself off to the Scots queen, a plan she had never seriously intended to carry out, but one that had accomplished several political objectives at the time.

"I do understand obsessive love, my lords," said Elizabeth. "I saw my wise and levelheaded stepmother Catharine Parr lose her senses completely over Lord High Admiral Seymour. But her punishment was relatively swift and painless. She died in childbed. Mary's punishment has been a protracted agony. She marries Darnley impetuously and names him king of Scotland and within months he has become a syphilitic drunkard who whores with women highborn and low and openly plots to steal her crown. Seven months pregnant, she is forced to watch as her dear friend and secretary Riccio is beaten and stabbed into a bleeding corpse by the barbaric ruffians who are her highest nobles. Then Darnley himself is strangled in his bed by perhaps the same men."

Elizabeth felt herself wince, wondering if the reason was the horrors she was describing or the painful pang of jealousy she experienced every time she thought of the son Mary had birthed. James. A further threat to her throne, and a reminder of the child she had lost.

"My spies in Edinburgh," said Walsingham, "tell me Lord Bothwell was almost certainly the ringleader in Darnley's murder."

"Is he as hideously ugly as they say, Walsingham?" asked Elizabeth, her curiosity sincerely piqued. "I've heard him called 'an ape in purple.'"

"I have never met the man, Your Majesty, but there must be something which attracted your cousin to him. I do know he is not a large man, but very strong."

"I shudder when I think of Mary abducted by him." She looked away from her councillors. "Raped by him." Elizabeth found herself rushing to her cousin's defense. "She had no honorable choice after the ravishment but to marry him."

"But remember, Majesty," interjected Leicester, "she then protected Bothwell, supported him against his detractors. She'd clearly lost her reason."

"Indeed! They say she lost her mind completely. And who would not under such circumstances? A high queen of France, a queen of Scotland, reduced to a helpless prisoner on an island fortress in the middle of a lake! She did after all rally herself, my young cousin, and find a way to escape her prison, lead a rebellion."

"Sadly, by that time the love of her people and the loyalty of her nobles were altogether lost," said Cecil.

"What kind of people are the Scots?" demanded Elizabeth in a fury. "They murder their king, and prefer putting an infant on the throne over their rightful queen!"

"They are beastly lot, Your Majesty," said Walsingham. "A far cry from Englishmen. You have shown extraordinary kindness to your cousin."

"Kindness? You call imprisoning Mary in a bleak house in the far north of England kindness!" Elizabeth remembered the day the messenger had arrived breathless with the news that Mary, escaped from her failed rebellion, had landed on English shores wearing clothes borrowed from her maid, her once beautiful red hair shaven to disguise her.

"You had no choice," insisted Leicester. "How could you in good conscience bring to London the woman who still claimed to be the rightful queen of England?"

"He's right, Your Majesty," agreed Walsingham. "Mary was the fiercest competitor for your throne, and England is yet a country divided by religion. You know that your religious settlement is considered so lenient that both Catholics and Protestants are neither of them happy."

"And now that you have been excommunicated by the Pope . . ." added Cecil.

"Enough!" cried Elizabeth.

"No," said Leicester. "We are not finished. We have yet to decide what is to be done with this Catholic spider who has passed her whole confinement in England weaving webs of deceit and plots to have you murdered!"

Elizabeth had to admit it was true. Walsingham's secret service had intercepted dozens of Mary's dispatches attempting to raise support from beyond her shores. It had in the end, however, been Elizabeth's own Duke of Norfolk, and his Machiavellian scheming with the Scots queen and the Italian banker Ridolfi, that had irrevocably tightened Mary's chains of captivity. Elizabeth wished to be merciful of her cousin's cause but . . .

"Your Majesty," interjected Leicester, "I think Norfolk has shown his true colors — the colors of a traitor. And he must pay for it properly."

"I do not dispute Norfolk's complicity in the Ridolfi plot," she conceded, "but I am not convinced of Mary's."

"What more do you need to convince you?" demanded Walsingham. "The letters written by Mary to Ridolfi contained incriminating instructions and promise of financial commission to him. The woman planned to bring King Philip's most murderous troops across the channel from the Netherlands to invade England and depose you!"

"Your Majesty," said Robin, pleading with her sincerely, "we three are your most loyal advisors and believe truly that England is best served by Mary's execution, better now than later, for we have no way of knowing what harm she may do you in the future."

Elizabeth sighed heavily and raised her eyes heavenward. "My cousin Mary, the daughter of debate . . ."

She now faced her Privy Councillors squarely. "I will not have her executed. She is my kinswoman and a sovereign princess. If I strike out against her, this clearly gives others leave to strike out against me." Elizabeth thought, but did not say, how entirely repugnant was the idea of doing violence to her own family in the same way her father had done to two of his wives. Most people believed Elizabeth to be her father's daughter in temperament, but she could not, she *would not,* follow in his bloodied footsteps.

"Mary must of course be punished," continued the Queen, struggling to remain composed. But she was angry, very angry — with these men, with Mary, with the Fates. For Elizabeth had harbored a great wish, despite her ministers' cautions against it, to defy the familial strain of jealous cruelty and, on her own death, bestow St. Edward's Crown upon Mary Stuart. But the Scots queen had burnt Elizabeth's fine wish to ashes, and the great storm of controversy and hatred amongst her English subjects had scattered those ashes to the four corners of the world. "So," she continued with the official tone of pronouncement, "Mary Queen of Scotland is therefore forever barred from succession to my throne. Now leave me. All of you!"

The men wordlessly gathered up their papers and left the Privy Chamber. Elizabeth was alone. If her stays had allowed it she would have slumped against the highbacked chair, but the corset and stomacher kept her stiff as a washboard. Ah, she was weary. At times like this she felt most keenly the loss of her beloved Kat. When death had claimed her old companion Elizabeth had cried unabashedly for weeks before she was able to go on with the business of government. Never again would she have a friend who loved her basest flaws as much as her greatest strength. Now without Kat or sweet Mary Sidney at her side, Elizabeth seemed adrift in a sea of strangers who dutifully and impersonally ministered to her most intimate needs. They were all young and beautiful, and their very presence made her exceedingly cross.

She was weary of the eternal weight of government which lay like a heavy mantle upon her shoulders, one she knew would never in her life be removed. She loved England. Loved being queen with all the glory that surrounded her person, growing more splendid with each passing year. But wrapped as she was in this awesome cloak of responsibility, she could less and less easily fly unencumbered into the warmth of Robin Dudley's bed, lie naked in his arms, speak the tender, intimate words of love. With each passing year she felt somehow less human, less womanly, less a being of flesh and bone and blood, and more a frozen icon who might, like brittle ice, crack in extreme anger, or melt if emotion overtook her too forcefully.

She loved Robin Dudley more profoundly than ever. He had become something deeper than her friend, her amour, her favorite. He had become, as she herself had, a cog in the machine that was England's government. And though she missed what they had once shared so freely and frequently, this faithful presence as councillor at her side would simply have to suffice.

Robert Dudley, Earl of Leicester, had resisted slamming the Privy Chamber door hard behind him and tried to keep a benign look on his face as he strode down the broad corridors and up the stairs to his apartments. He was forced to pass many courtiers and ladies and wished to give them no cause to gossip, jeer at him, pity him, find pleasure in his displeasure. For Leicester knew he was still the most despised man at court, more so than previously, now that he held true power, was one of the most prominent men of government.

Today's meeting of the council had left him feeling frustrated, thwarted. True, imminent threat from that damnable Scots queen and her fanatic Catholic supporters had been temporarily averted. But if Elizabeth actually believed that a mere pronouncement denying Mary the succession would halt her cousin's attempts to steal England's throne, she was sorely mistaken. One thing and one thing alone would stop Mary's murderous plotting — the woman's death.

Leicester knew Elizabeth well, could see the lines of pain crisscrossing her forehead as they had spoken of executing her kinswoman. He knew how she resisted the bloodthirsty image of her Tudor relations, how fervently she longed to reign not only as a kind and beneficent ruler but as England's most glorious prince. Perhaps, mused Leicester, this was the reason his recent marriage proposals to Elizabeth had been met with such chilliness. He had felt the Queen distancing herself from him within their intimate relationship, craving their sexual union less and less frequently, if at the same time growing ever more dependent upon him as her political advisor. He was, increasingly, her Eyes, keeping Elizabeth cognizant of major and minor intrigues at the court, even as Walsingham expanded his network of spies on the Continent and kept her in intelligence of foreign affairs.

Leicester had watched the Queen's appetite for shrewd political maneuvering and the workings of everyday government grow into a kind of gluttony, and realized that if he wished to remain close and important to her life, he would be forced to share those concerns. And so he had. He was proud that, despite Cecil's continuing disdain for himself, they were the only two Privy Councillors who never failed to attend a meeting. And in recent years the Earl of Leicester had taken up the Protestant religion of his childhood with a new fervor, becoming the leader of the Puritan Party.

But it was not enough. His dream of marrying Elizabeth and reigning by her side as king was too long-standing and persistent to be abandoned now. He knew that Elizabeth, despite the infrequency of their ardent embraces, still loved him. And despite the ongoing marriage negotiations with myriad foreign princes, and irritating flirtations with English courtiers like that nuisance Christopher Hatton, he knew without question that in her woman's heart Elizabeth desired him above all men.

So lost in his thoughts was Leicester that he suddenly found himself at the Queen's apartments which adjoined his own, nearly colliding with the palace apothecary, a tall thin man named Treadwell who smelt rather unpleasantly of his laboratory. Each backed away with a courteous bow. As Leicester turned to continue toward his door, he saw Treadwell being admitted to the Queen's apartments by her lady of the bedchamber, Clarice Hartly.

Was the Queen ill? Why had he not been told? But he had just been in her presence. She looked well enough. A moment later the apothecary left the royal apartments and walked briskly past Leicester with a nod, wafting the scents of henbane and motherwort.

Robin entered his own chambers to find Tamworth with every pair of his master's boots lined up before him, polishing with uncommon vigor. "Good afternoon, my lord," he said and spit on a burnished leather toe before continuing his rubbing. "Will you be wanting to change your costume for this evening?" I'll just finish this -_"

"No hurry, Tamworth, go on with your work," said Leicester as he pulled off the boots he was wearing. In his stocking feet he moved to the far end of the bedchamber to a fall of curtains and, quietly pulling them back, revealed the private door leading to Elizabeth's chamber. Ignoring Tamworth's questioning look, Leicester opened it and tiptoed along the dark passageway. Very carefully he pushed open the door into Elizabeth's bedchamber and stood motionless behind the hanging that hid it. He could not see the ladies Hartly and Wingfield, but from the soft rustling that accompanied their voices he guessed they were working at the Queen's wardrobe, perhaps folding undergarments or laying out her gown for the evening's entertainments. They were also, as he had fervently hoped, gossiping about the package the apothecary had just delivered.

"She needs the potion less and less, it seems to me," said Clarice.

"She needed it not at all when she became queen, for then she did not bleed like other women."

"I never knew that."

"Indeed. We all thought her barren stock. And she played so carelessly with Robin Dudley when first she came to the throne, she must have thought so too."

"Do you truly think Master Treadwell's herbs can bring about an abortion, then?"

The words, so casually spoken, struck Robin with the force of a jousting lance. He had always cherished the hope that there would be another child, that the next time Elizabeth would be forced to acknowledge . . .

"There's no doubt in my mind," answered Lady Wingfield. "Lucy Clark — you know, the youngest silkwoman — and Lady Simms both used the potion, and 'twas a quick end to *their* troubles."

"I still say the Queen has little to worry about, bleeding properly or not. Leicester shares her bed hardly at all."

"Mayhaps young Lord Hatton will be taking the Earl's place between her fine sheets."

As the two ladies giggled Leicester backed into the dark passageway and quietly pulled the door shut behind him. Yet he did not immediately return to his rooms. He leaned against the wall trembling with humiliation. He and the Queen had, from the beginning of her reign, been the butt of lewd gossip, but the talk had always celebrated his manliness and virility. Now the Queen secretly schemed against him to murder his children, and every court gossip knew the infrequency of their bedding together.

The passageway was dark and stuffy, but for Leicester it held a reassuring privacy. Here he could think, plan, rearrange his thoughts far from prying eyes. He knew Elizabeth better than anyone else alive. And she loved him still. When he fell ill she nursed him with her own hands. Their lovemaking, though rare in recent months, still held at moments an incandescent passion. They shared between them the pain of a lost child, and he knew as surely as he lived that they were bound to each other for all the days that lay ahead of them. But how could he move her from her present mind, which cast him as a trusted advisor and occasional lover, to be her husband and king? How, he asked himself, is a mind so moved?

Suddenly he knew. There was an answer — in fact, the only answer. 'Twas a gamble and a dangerous one at that, but its power was enormous and altogether absolute. Jealousy. The Earl of Leicester would take another lover.

Nineteen

The King of Spain, sitting quite alone at the long council table, studied the document before him with astonishment and a fulminating rage. The margins of the Netherlands field report from the Duke of Alva had been blackened by copious notations in Philip's scratchy hand. It was his habit — some considered it an obsession, which he admitted gave him almost a physical pleasure — to take each paragraph, each sentence, of the hundreds of documents forwarded to him each week from every corner of his vast realm and government, and comment or question it in the minutest of detail. Equally, he enjoyed writing letters of enormous length, seething with complex instructions and opinion, to his ministers and generals and family.

But the contents of this communique were so disturbing, so infuriating, that the King found it difficult to go on reading, indeed to take a complete breath. Prince William of Orange had taken up arms against him in the Low Countries. The childhood friend, the young man upon whom his father, the Holy Roman Emperor Charles, had literally leaned during his abdication ceremony, had now dared to defy the King of Spain. Philip, a man ever comforted by his self-imposed tyranny of manners and morals, knew certainly that men betrayed other men. He had not been unaware, even in youth, of William's dangerous strengths — ones that threatened Philip's own weaknesses. But that the Prince of Orange chose to defy him in the realm of faith was almost too much to bear.

Philip, with one exception only, was devoted exclusively to the preservation of the True Religion. He was, of course, king of Spain and the Italian provinces and ruler of the Low Countries, overseeing their government with an exactitude that defied imagination. But even before these duties, he believed in his soul's core, he must obey God who had entrusted him and him alone with preserving his people in the True Faith, and use any means to accomplish it. He would, he had recently announced to his council, prefer to reign not at all than to reign over heretics.

And now William of Orange, prince of the Netherlands territory owned by Spain, gathering about him the despicable hordes of Satan-inspired serpents called Calvinists, had challenged him to war for the right of choosing one's own faith. William professed to believe that religion lived in the heart, and that every man must worship as his heart prompted. He had demanded that Philip's Inquisition in the Low Countries be halted, and that heretics no longer be persecuted — burnt in the cleansing fires of the Auto da Fé. Ridiculous! thought Philip indignantly. William himself was a Catholic. Had he forgotten the exhortation of Saint John? "If a man abide not in me, he is cast forth as a branch and withered; and men gather them and cast them into the fire and they are burnt."

And now the seventeen provinces of the Netherlands, always annoyingly independent, were demanding to rule themselves. Certainly they were rich, with their magnificent cities of Antwerp and Brussels, their booming textile industry and lively sea trade. But they were *his,* Philip's, inherited under God's law. William knew it. The other high lords who rebelled at his side knew it. Perhaps the King should heed the "Iron Duke" of Alva's suggestion, an exacting but well-deserved punishment for the aristocratic rebels — to chop off their heads. End this idiocy, this criminal waste of the precious gold being shipped into Spain from the New World. His best soldiers were being sent to quell an uprising in his own lands!

Philip's large pendulous lower lip quivered with feeling as he regarded Alva's report — the Low Country Calvinists invading his churches and monasteries, smashing and defiling sacred pictures, statues, and altars. Some of the Netherlands nobles had banded together, donned outrageous costumes of grey frieze with wallets and begging bowls, armed twenty-four vessels, and transformed themselves into pirates who had already done serious damage to Philip's revenues from commerce. The Sea Beggars were the terror of the oceans, and the King had no good way to stop them. And Elizabeth of England had given safe haven in her ports to these criminals, encouraging them further.

At least William, thought the King, claimed no identity with these hideous creatures. But he and his ragtag land armies had appealed to the hearts and minds of Low Country people of all classes, and become their rebel hero. Ambition and ambition alone, mused Philip, guided the betrayer William of Orange, for the man could never in his heart believe that his pitiful cause was a just one.

Philip sighed morosely, feeling the weight of the entire Catholic world lying heavy upon his frail shoulders. Huguenots challenged the True Religion in France, and now threatened to aid the Low Country Protestants in their fight. Europe's most Catholic queen, Mary of Scots, had been the heretic Elizabeth's prisoner now for several years. Had everyone gone mad?

A light tapping at the door, almost inaudible, caused Philip to smile. It was at best a faint upward curving of his lips, but he instantly laid down his quill and unconsciously began straightening his vest, sitting more erect. He wished, as he always did at these moments, that he were handsomer and taller, and did not own the Hapsburg deformity — a lower jaw and bulbous lip that jutted considerably beyond the upper. Still, Isabella seemed to look upon him with favor . . . with love. And aside from love of God and the True Faith, there was no one to whom he was, or had ever been, more devoted. He had never dreamed, when in order to cement the peace accord of Cateau-Cambrésis he had married the princess of his ancient enemy, France, that the sweet-natured child would bring him so much pleasure. His two previous dynastic marriages had been as hollow and chilly as a tomb, his wives' untimely deaths inspiring in him the merest trace of grief.

"Enter, my dear," he called.

The doors to Philip's council chamber were swung open to admit his young wife. In a fluster of tears, rustling skirts, and wringing hands she sought the immediate comfort of his arms and began to sob.

"Isabella, tell me, what has happened?"

It took her several moments to compose herself. She wiped the tears from her flushed cheeks and looked up into Philip's watery blue eyes. As slight a man as he was, Isabella was even more petite than he, making him feel more manly and protective than ever before.

"Don Carlos . . ." she began, but could go no further, for the tears again overwhelmed her.

Philip felt his own body shrink with the mention of his eldest son's name. What atrocity had he this time committed? What heinous and unthinkable acts would be added to the ever growing litany of indecent violations? The only offspring of his marriage to Maria of Portugal, Carlos had, fittingly, begun his life by taking his own mother's — a bloody death in childbed. He had grown into a huge-headed, unnaturally short young man with one shoulder higher than the other. The King, himself blessed with little physical beauty, would nevertheless have found something in his son to love and cherish had Don Carlos shown an iota of virtue. But his mind, it became apparent, was as deformed as his body.

When he was eighteen he had fallen down a flight of stone stairs while chasing a woman he meant to abuse, and cracked open his head. His brain had swollen and the surgeon had had to open the skull to relieve the pressure. Philip had gone to great trouble to save his son's life, having the corpse of a saintly monk disinterred to lie in bed with Don Carlos during his recuperation. The boy had lived, but from that day forward his insanity and perversion had blossomed like the branches of a putrescent flowering tree. Was this, wondered Philip for perhaps the thousandth time, a legacy from his *own* blood? The terrible familial strain of melancholia had held his grandmother Joanna in its grip for nearly forty years before she had gone to meet God. Philip prayed that he had himself been spared, and that in his old age the madness would not, like some firebreathing horse from hell, overtake him.

Now, however, he was forced to confront again the truth that Don Carlos had become a monster with a murderous heart. He had killed and tortured and raped citizens, royal councillors, highborn ladies, scullery maids, and animals. He delighted in the cruelest of acts and regularly flew into wild, uncontrollable rages, terrorizing the Court. The heir to the throne of Spain was entirely unfitted for inheriting it. Philip could not fathom the injustice of it all. Why had heaven bestowed upon him such an abomination for a son? He had prayed daily for more than twenty years, begged for guidance, peace of mind, and forgiveness — anything with which to understand so vengeful a punishment from the God he so devoutly served.

"What has he done, Isabella? You must calm yourself and tell me. Tell me now," Philip commanded his wife.

She refused to meet his eye, instead gazing out the window to the courtyard below. "I was in my little chapel praying, and he came in and knelt beside me. I thought that we might pray together, ask forgiveness for our many sins. I had lit some candles when he suddenly fell at my feet and swore he loved me . . . as a woman."

Philip's face twisted with revulsion. He knew there was more to Isabella's story and that it would be far worse than these first words had conveyed. He wished to hear no more, but she continued.

"He said things, Philip, terrible things that he might do to me, to my naked body —"

"Stop, Isabella. Tell me no more."

"I cannot stop, for you must know. Your son stood then and grabbed me, touched me. I tried to scream but he pushed me down on the altar and covered my mouth with his own stinking . . ."

"Enough! Go to your rooms, my dear. I will have the guards escort you. You will be safe from Don Carlos from this day forward."

Isabella did not move from her place, as though she were paralyzed, or perhaps did not believe her husband's promise.

"Did he rape you?"

"No, but I am nevertheless befouled, defiled by him," she said. "How could he . . . in God's house?"

"Look at me, Isabella." She forced herself finally to meet his eye. "Have your ladies draw you a bath. I shall have Father Miguel bring a sprinkling of holy water to anoint you."

"Yes," she said, relief flooding back into her shaken soul with her husband's wise suggestion. "I shall bathe."

"And I will see to Don Carlos," said Philip.

The King bent to kiss his wife's mouth, but she turned her face away in shame and moved to the double doors. When they swung open, Philip motioned almost imperceptibly and the two guards at their post fell in beside the Queen, escorting her away. Two more guards instantly replaced them.

The King, so small and insignificant in the doorway of the large and splendid chamber, stood for a long moment, very still, breathing in short shallow gasps. Then he ordered one of the guards to fetch his captain. Presently that officer appeared and followed the King into the council chamber. He remained silent, eyes downcast, awaiting his orders.

"Captain, it is my will . . ." Philip found himself moving his lips, forming the terrible words he had wished fervently never to say. "It is my will that my son be held under lock and key in his rooms."

The captain of the guard saluted and, never meeting his sovereign's eyes, marched, sword clanking, out the doors. Philip moved dreamlike to the council table and stared down at the field report that had, an hour before, shattered his peace of mind. But the import of William's pathetic revolt in the Netherlands receded like a light horseman galloping swiftly from sight, as the dead weight of the order he had just given crashed down around his head.

His world would never hereafter be the same. His son, heir to the throne, would never reign. And God's will, despite the pain and displeasure of the King of Spain, would be done.

Twenty

Robin Dudley was stretched out naked, gazing down at the woman asleep beside him. She was surely the most heavenly creature he'd ever lain with. He carefully pulled away the fine lawn sheet that covered her, and the glow of the late afternoon sun turned her limbs and torso into polished ivory. Everything about Douglas Sheffield, mused Dudley as he stared at her body, was ripe and rounded — from the perfect spheres of her rosy-nippled breasts to the small plump buttocks, the luxuriant sweep of firm soft skin over her tiny waist, her full and shapely calves. The exquisite face was also a study in curves, the lush-lipped mouth now slightly parted. . . . He felt a quickening between his own legs, a not unwelcome hardening as he continued gazing at her. The graceful slope of the nose, dimpled cheeks flushed with satisfaction. There was not a hard angle anywhere on her. Not a sharp bone pushing out against straining flesh . . .

Elizabeth! he thought with sudden pang. I am comparing her with Elizabeth.

He was saved, however, from the wave of guilt threatening to swamp his rising passion as Douglas Sheffield opened her eyes, large and languid, the color of dark honey.

"Mmmmm," was all she could manage at first. She gazed up into Robin Dudley's face lazily. "How lovely . . . I fell asleep." She reached out, ran her hand over the hard muscles of his chest and down his belly, still taut and rippling. She gazed unabashedly at his sex and smiled.

"I see I still please you after all these months, my lord," she said.

"How could you not please me, Douglas? You're the most beautiful woman I've ever known."

"More beautiful than the Queen?" she asked with what he perceived as a coquettish pout. But did not coquettes, though Dudley with irritation, have more sense than to demand an answer to such a dangerous question? Still, he did not wish to offend his mistress, featherheaded though she might be. What he wished more than anything at this moment was to plunge deep into her softness once again, feel the rich flesh alive under his touch. He cupped a hand over her breast, then followed the curves of her torso down over her belly as she had done to him.

"Tell me I'm more beautiful than the Queen, Robert."

He knew he should not betray Elizabeth in such a way, but he had fallen under the spell of this woman whose spirit was as yielding as her body, who was sweet seduction personified. Who accepted him fully and wanted him desperately. Also, she was married and therefore a safe liaison. For a man who had endured the Queen's refusals and embarrassing rejections for so long, a woman like Douglas Sheffield was irresistible.

He leaned down and circled one rosy nipple with his tongue, then whispered, "You are the most beautiful woman I have ever known . . . bar none."

"Lady Sheffield!" The knocking on the bedroom door was frantic and insistent. "Lady Sheffield!" It was her maid's voice and now Douglas sat up in bed, alarmed.

"What is it, Millie?" she called.

"Lord Sheffield, milady. He's coming down the road." There was a pause. "He's through the gate. You must get up!"

Robin began throwing on his clothes.

"I don't understand. He's not due back for days yet," exclaimed Douglas. "Millie, come in!"

The maid threw open the door and bustled in, ignoring the half-clad Dudley struggling with the buttons on his breeches.

"You should have some time, madame," said the maid as she threw Douglas's underkirtle over her lady's head and reached for the stiff corset. "He generally fiddles about downstairs awhile before coming to your rooms. Sir . . ." She turned to Robin. "Down the hall toward the back of the house are the servants' stairs. You can get to the stables without crossing the courtyard."

Dudley frowned. It was unseemly and ridiculous to be forced to escape from his lover's bed like some character out of a bawdy tale. But he had, it seemed, no choice. With jacket in one hand, boots in the other, he turned to Douglas.

"I'll write."

But as he spoke the door flew open and slammed back against the wall, sending a looking glass crashing to the floor. Everyone froze at the sight of Lord Sheffield, livid-faced and panting, his large and bulky shape filling the doorway. He had wasted no time below, but come straight and purposefully to his wife's bedchamber. In one hand was clutched a letter. "Write?" he said querulously. "It seems to me you've already written quite enough, Lord Leicester."

Dudley could see that the missive in John Sheffield's grasp was one he had written to Douglas in the first throes of lustful abandon. But how the devil had it gotten into Sheffield's hands? Dudley shot a searing glance at his lover, who looked back at him with the eyes of a cornered doe.

"I lost the letter at John's sister's house," she said. "I tried desperately to find it. She must have —"

"You explain yourself to *him!*" Sheffield thundered. He pushed past Dudley and toward his wife. "What about me! Do I not deserve an explanation!"

"You're never at home," she sniffed petulantly. "I've been lonely." Then, more defiantly, "And I do not love you."

Sheffield stared at his wife with a look of total astonishment, and then began to laugh. It was, thought Robin Dudley, a sincere laugh. Cruel and sarcastic, but truly amused as well. Finally Sheffield composed himself and said, "You forget yourself, Douglas. You are my wife. Love has nothing at all to do with it." Then he turned to Dudley. "And you, my lord, have strayed perilously far from the royal couch."

He looked back at Douglas with a neutral gaze. All the fury had gone from him and only bitterness remained. "We part beds tonight, madame. Tomorrow I'll ride for London and find us a divorce."

Douglas had recovered her dignity. "Good," she said in her chilliest voice. "Have a safe journey. Now do leave my room."

John Sheffield wheeled round and marched out the door, slamming it hard behind him. The maid Millie, who during the encounter had flattened herself against a wall and all but disappeared, now heaved a great sigh of relief.

Robin Dudley turned to Douglas, half dressed and looking quite dazed. He himself felt dazed, for his once safe liaison had just become a complicated affair indeed.

Twenty-one

This passage is one I wished never to write. That I feared writing. There is no easy way to remember violent death. But remember it I must, for my story cannot further unfold without its retelling. In deaths aftermath was my lesson in embracing hatred and sadness, and moving onward thro my life.

I was sixteen, no longer a boy and not yet a man. Perhaps full grown in body, but with a soul as tender and green as spring grass. My Mother had become a zealot and lived in abject fear of the Devil. He stalked her, she said, stalked her incessantly and her only protection against his evil was Scripture. We were all made to endure not only our usual morning and evening prayers, but several more every day, she deciding the precise hour for each using a sundial, the Book of Numbers, and a divinely inspired numerical logic which only she understood.

Her Bible had become an appendage as much as an arm or a leg. She would scurry thro the manor and the yard, and many times a day to the garden sundial, the book clutched in her white knuckled hand, muttering numbers and snatches of psalms, a litany of heavenly and fallen Angels, and exhortations for the Devil to be gone from the place she was going.

My Father, sister Alice and I tolerated her mania, for it seemed harmless enough. Twas, after all, the word of God and besides, we were able to slip away after several moments of her ministry, Maud reading from the book transfixed and rapturous, blind to the world around her. My Father had made some strange peace with her, and tho they shared a bed still, I do not think they took their pleasure in it.

That autumn, soon after the days shortened and the first bout of cold gloom descended on the Chase, the pitch and frenzy of her religious fervor grew frightening. She carried a flat iron pan in whichever hand she was not carrying the Bible, proclaiming that only with these two weapons would she be safe from Beelzebub and his minions. And she began to regard me with a suspicious eye, watching and listening carefully to see whether I uttered every syllable of every prayer. Forcing me to stand still while she checked my scalp and body for marks of the Devil. And she would not let me touch her with my six fingered hand.

By All Hallows Eve day her fears had grown so wild that my Father sought to keep her locked safe in the manor, before the hearth with her family round to guard her. She began reading from Genesis at sundown, and as evening waxed full, she droned on and on and on. My eyes grew heavy, and before I closed them I saw that my Father was already dozing. Alice was attending her needlework and seemed bored but never the less alert.

Twas Barlington shouting that awoke us, for even Alice had finally succumbed. Looking round groggily we all at once saw Maud was gone, her Bible with her. But most alarming was Barlingtons call.

"Fire! Fire in the stables!"

We all scrambled out the door and across the yard to a scene of chaos. Smoke billowing from the doorway of the long building along with soot covered stableboys emerging with panicked horses. A bucket relay had formed, but we could see at once it was a lost cause. The thatched roof was already ablaze. My Father grabbed a boy leading two horses from the conflagration.

"Where is my wife!" he cried.

"In there, Sir!" he shouted, nodding over his shoulder to the stables. "She rushed in with no warning, Sir, waving her Bible and screaming that Arthurs horse was the Devil himself and should burn in Hell. I saw her grab a lantern and make for Chargers stall down the end, but halfway there the lamp caught on a nail and the lighted oil spilt on some hay. It caught so quick, the straw and the wooden stalls . . ."

We three looked at each other, the horror rising in us all. Alice covered her face with her hands. My Father and I both moved at once, running for the doorway. Barlington came running alongside us carrying two pistols. I moaned inwardly with the sudden understanding of their use.

Now we were inside and thro the thick smoke could see that in deed the middle section of the stone walled stable was entirely engulfed, flames leaping from floor to roof. And whilst the horses from the front had all been rescued — their stalls on either side of the long aisle blessedly empty — the fire was racing towards the far end of the stable. Horses trapped in their stalls were shrieking in terror and pain, throwing them selves against the walls, some stalls ominously still, only fire rising where once living animals had stood.

And now thro the flames and the smoke we could see my Mother, far down the aisle near Charger in his stall. The fire had not yet reached them, she shrieking at the horse in a terrible voice, an exorcist to a possessed creature, and he kicking crazily with his rear hooves at the stall door, again and again and again . . .

A loud report at my ear. Barlington had put one tortured horse out of its misery and was taking aim at another.

"Maud, Maud!" my Father screamed helplessly and then, as in a dream, we saw her turn at the sound of his voice. There was a look of surprise on her face when she saw the wall of flames that separated her husband and son from her, as tho she was altogether unaware of the holocaust she had recently invented.

"He must be gone!" she called to us, thrusting her Bible in Chargers direction. "Do you not see, Robert, the Devil must burn in the fires of Hell!"

"Charger!" I screamed. I do not know if he heard my voice above the din, but it seemed as if his kicking of the stall door became more frenzied, and suddenly wood splintered.

"Charger, Charger, kick it down, boy, kick it down!!"

More splintering. Another shot as Barlington found a second merciful mark, and my Father clutching me, crying "Maud, Maud, Maud . . ."

And then with a roaring sound more terrible than I care to remember a great slab of thatch tumbled from the roof beams in an almost graceful descent, blanketing the length of the aisle with fire. The whoosh of furnacelike heat and smoke blew my Father and Barlington and me backwards as far as the stable door. And then I saw a sight that with mingling joy and horror I will revisit in my dreams for ever. Twas Charger exploding from the billowing smoke and flames, galloping, nay flying as though the Devil himself was at his heels. His mane and tail were afire, his eyes wild with fear and he would not stop, just thundered out the stable door into the night. I followed, crying his name again and again. Leapt upon a rescued horse and raced after him.

He had not gotten far when I found him standing still as a statue in the moonlight. I slowed, jumped from my mount and moved carefully to him. I could hear the unnatural breathing of scorched lungs, smell the foul stench of burnt hair and flesh, see the whites of his terrified eyes. As I reached him he suddenly sank onto his forehands, and I saw again the glorious day when he had knelt just so at the Queens feet and received her blessings. And now my proud and beautiful horse was dying. He fell heavily on his side and his breathing became more tortured. I laid my hands on his face, leaned close and whispered — I know not what I whispered, some meaningless comfortable words that I was there with him, and loved him, and he was not alone. And then my Father was at my side with a pistol in his hand and he gently lifted me away and wasted no time in releasing my friend from his agony. Then we clung together, my Father and I, and wept like children until there were no more tears to cry.

Twenty-two

Even as his barge scraped to a halt on the wooden dock, the Earl of Leicester could feel the ghastly pall hanging heavy over Greenwich Castle. He was, fittingly, all in black as were the lords and ladies of the Court, the guards, stablemen, laundresses. Though the autumn sun was shining 'twas a bleak day, and no one as he passed dared a smile, but only greeted him with somber nods. For death draped round about them in great bloody swaths. On St. Bartholomew's Eve last, six thousand Protestant brethren in Paris had been dragged from their beds and slaughtered by their Catholic neighbors like so many head of cattle. The butchery, fired more by the will of the queen mother de Médicis than her weak-livered son Charles, had spread across France in the following weeks, and the toll of Huguenot dead had reached staggering numbers. All talk of marriage between Elizabeth and de Médicis's youngest son were instantly suspended as the English Court descended into the deepest state of mourning. It was reported that Philip of Spain, on hearing of the outrage, had begun to laugh, for all worry about Huguenot assistance to the Netherlands rebels had been extinguished with the lives of the Protestants.

Leicester's once soft religiosity had, with news of the St. Bartholomew's Eve Massacre, finally congealed into a fervor of righteousness. Some felt his sudden Puritan devoutness sat strangely on a man so ambitious, so apparently insincere, and so fond of the splendors of courtly life. But in his heart, and surprising even unto himself, Leicester had found that earnest conversation with religious gentlemen and ladies was oddly exhilarating, and at the same time comforting. As Spain continued to persecute its Calvinists and France its Huguenots, the Earl had metamorphosed into a war hawk in defense of his newfound faith. The other advantage to these leanings, he thought as he climbed the palace steps, was that he now found himself, finally, on the same side of principle as William Cecil. A grudging respect for the once detested upstart had taken hold of the older man.

God, mused Leicester, had placed before the adherents of the New Religion a mighty challenge and Elizabeth, who resisted taking sides against Spain at all costs — for she still fervently believed the ultimate cost of a war would be her people's love — must be gently but firmly moved to support the Protestants abroad. He would speak to her today in the quiet of their rooms. He knew that she was as dismayed by the Dutch Protestants daring to revolt against their sovereign king, as by their persecution at the hands of Philip's Duke of Alva. Elizabeth and Leicester's recent separation while he'd been seeing to extensive construction at Kenilworth Castle, and now his return, he thought with a satisfied smile, would no doubt soften her mood in the matter of religion.

But as he approached their adjoining apartments Leicester noticed, with increasing alarm, a total absence of activity, as if the hand of death had somehow swept along this corridor. There were no courtiers or ladies in waiting fluttering about on their various errands, no petitioners — not even, most astonishingly, royal guards posted at the Queen's door.

As he reached for the door leading into the nest of royal apartments, he realized he had never before opened it with his own hand, the small service invariably performed by a liveried doorman. He stepped into the Privy Chamber and, still observing not a soul, walked through into the Withdrawing Chamber. No one. Now he stood before Elizabeth's bedchamber door. The eerie silence so unnerved him that for a moment he considered turning, leaving. Surely the Queen could not be in her room thus flagrantly unattended. But the mystery compelled him forward.

She was sitting bolt upright in her highbacked carven seat which had been placed squarely in the center of the room facing the door. Encased in a silken armor of mourning black Elizabeth was pale as a wraith, eyes smoldering with a cold fire, her long fingers curled clawlike round the ends of the chair arms. She was staring at Robin Dudley with so frightening an intensity that he found himself paralyzed. A hoarse breath escaped his lips and finally he composed himself enough to utter, "Your Majesty."

When Elizabeth did not answer with either word or gesture or the slightest flicker of her eyes he moved forward, feeling his joints wooden like those of a puppet. He knelt before her, a common suppliant and not her lover of many years. His alarm increased when she failed even to offer her hand to be kissed. This icy anger, this rage, was directed not at de Médicis or Philip of Spain, not at Alva for his atrocities in the Netherlands, not even at God for allowing such outrages to be committed in his name. He himself was the object of this terrifying fury. Elizabeth, he realized suddenly, had cleared her chambers so that no one should be privy to the coming storm.

Robin Dudley, always a man of unremitting bravado and ready eloquence, found that he was trembling and altogether devoid of speech. The silence between them — the first of their long, intimate friendship — was shattering, and he knew that it devastated them equally.

"Why?"

The syllable hung resonating between them like the pluck of a harpstring. 'Twas only one word, but no more was necessary for Leicester's understanding. All of the calculated answers he had prepared for this inevitable moment, all of his reasoning and arguments, he knew at once to be fatuous and wrongheaded.

"She means nothing to me," he finally uttered, but his voice cracked midsentence as a callow boy's might do.

"If that is true, Robin," said Elizabeth as if treading carefully on a brittle crust of snow, "then you have ripped the still beating heart from my chest . . . for nothing." She brought her hands together in her lap, laying one atop the other. They were very still and white. "Douglas Sheffield," she said evenly, "is a woman of rare beauty with the brains of a hedgehog . . ."

"Elizabeth . . ."

The Queen skewered him into immediate silence and he sensed that if he interrupted her again she would slice him open with the blade of her anger. He found he could not tear his eyes away from her pale, motionless hands.

"When Lady Sheffield's husband discovered that he had been cuckolded by you," she began again, "he flew into a rage and started out for London seeking a divorce. Is that correct?"

"Quite so," replied Dudley, his tone and posture taking on the sullenness of a child being disciplined.

"But Lord Sheffield did never arrive in London," continued Elizabeth. "He took ill and died suddenly, under mysterious circumstances. Many of his friends believe he was poisoned."

Finally she allowed a space for Leicester to answer.

He felt some of his senses returning to him. He stood, and answered her question with a question of his own.

"Why would I — for I assume you are impugning my innocence — murder the man unless I wished to marry his widow? And why would I — still believed by many to be the murderer of my own wife — put myself in the very same position a second time? I may be arrogant and vainglorious, Elizabeth, but do you really suppose me to be so unrelentingly stupid?"

"So you do not mean to marry Lady Sheffield?" asked the Queen, choosing to address his first question.

"I do not."

"What then will become of the child she is carrying? It is your child, is it not?"

'Twas the Queen's voice that was now breaking and, to Leicester's ear, was heartrendingly vincible. He had never meant his affair with Douglas, begun only to provoke jealousy, to continue as long as it had. Lady Sheffield was indeed a dazzling creature and had been an easy purchase, but as he basked in the warmth and unqualified devotion with which she blanketed him, he had grown sincerely fond of her.

With sudden annoyance Dudley realized that Douglas Sheffield had as much pursued him as he had her — the prey laying a trap for the hunter. She had snared herself a great prize, never once considering the consequences of stealing the Queen's lover. From this day forward, Douglas would find her life at Court was finished. Leicester had never, however reckless he had become, wished for a child with her. Finding that she was pregnant, Lady Sheffield had demanded that Leicester marry her, claiming rightly that she had rejected many offers of marriage and wanted only him. It even occurred to him that it was she who had had her husband poisoned, leaving the way clear for Dudley to marry her.

The Earl felt his mouth quiver with all that was unspoken. Elizabeth could not help but notice his agitation.

"Speak your mind, Lord Leicester," she said, her crimson lips a thin, cruel line dividing her face, "for it may be your last chance to do so."

"And how is that, Elizabeth?" he said tersely. He had finally found his voice and the words spilled out freely, filling the room with a rage equal to the Queen's. "Have you plans to banish me? Execute me! Has it taken you so completely by surprise that I could no longer live with your rude refusals? Did you believe that I had no feelings? That my masculinity could suffer your bloodless rejections forever!"

"I have never rejected you!" she shouted.

"You have indeed, Madame. I have begged you endlessly to marry me and you have turned your back on me again and again. You have, without my consent, offered me up to your cousin Mary like roast meat on a platter! I am a laughingstock, Elizabeth, I am your concubine!"

"Ah, I have not respected you." Her sarcasm bit like a January wind off the Thames. "And you have not happily and greedily accepted all the fame and wealth and honor and title this crown has generously bestowed upon you." She sat back in her chair satisfied, as though she had perfectly driven home her point.

"I have loved you, Elizabeth," Robin Dudley said simply. "I have loved you."

With that the entire magnificent countenance of the Queen seemed suddenly to crumble. Her rigid features sagged, leaving fine cracks in the whitened mask of her face, and her chin dropped to her chest in defeat, for she had no way to deny his words.

"We had a son, you and I," continued Leicester, "and God in His unfathomable wisdom saw fit to take him from us. But then, whilst you never sent me from your bed, you and your apothecary made certain that you would never again bear my children." Elizabeth flinched at this, but had no argument. "Am I not a man like any other, Elizabeth? Should I not desire a true wife and a legitimate son to carry on my family's bloodline? You know my brother and his wife are barren. If I die childless the Dudleys are finished."

At this last, Elizabeth slowly raised he head.

"A legitimate son, this is what you desire from me above all else?"

Dudley felt the ground giving way beneath him. He suddenly realized that he had spoken of the one matter that, unfailingly, drove Elizabeth into spasms of rage. Her father, with such a desire taken to excess, had executed her mother. But Leicester could not now retreat.

"Marry me, Elizabeth," he said with steady calm.

"Make you king of England?" she responded sneeringly.

"Marry me, Elizabeth!"

"Lay open to you my power, my country, my soul?"

He grabbed her shoulders and pinioned her hard against the chair back, forcing her to meet and hold his commanding eye.

"Marry me," he whispered fiercely.

He saw Elizabeth's eyes glistening, softening, her mouth trembling.

Finally she spoke, each word a dagger finding its mark in the softness of Dudley's heart. "Get out of my sight."

A long breath, a sigh, escaped him. Then Robert Dudley, Earl of Leicester, bowed, not stiffly or awkwardly as a man dismissed and disgraced might do, but with the grace of a proud cavalier paying high homage to his beloved sovereign.

"As you will, Your Majesty," he said, and never taking his eyes from the Queen's mournful face, backed slowly from her chamber.

Twenty-three

Slate grey skies oversaw the winter afternoon. Bitter wind whipped down through the Sierra de Guadarrama onto the desolate plain below. It was a day to mirror exactly the soul of the world's greatest king. Shrouded in black, cloak flapping round his wind-bitten face, Philip of Spain sat alone, perched like a raven upon a throne hewn from rock and set into the hillside. Spread out before him was the work of his lifetime — construction of a sprawling stone monastery which when completed would serve as his palace and home. Ten years had the builders been building, with ten more before they would finish the edifice he had created. Called El Escorial, the massive greenish granite monument was shaped like a gridiron — the instrument of torture upon which the King's patron, St. Lawrence the Martyr, had been put to death. But the forbidding building was more than a mere palace or monastery. Like some aging Egyptian pharaoh, Philip was overseeing the construction of his own tomb. Indeed, it was to be not only his own place of burial, but one in which he would gather the mortal remains of his entire family, and lay them to final rest. Now he became morbid thinking about their deaths.

His father the emperor, the most magnificent ruler the world had ever known, had ended his life in a spartan cell in the monastery of Yuste. He had died broken in spirit, failed in his quest to unite the world in Christianity. Philip had adored his father, his teacher, his inspiration — and at the same time hated this giant whose legendary greatness Philip could never hope to equal.

As for Don Carlos, Philip's prisoner, he had descended ever deeper into madness. He had starved himself into a living skeleton, then slept naked on a bed of ice in the scorching heat of summer. The King's only son had died violent, raving, and unrepentant. He would be laid to rest in peace beside Philip's beloved little wife Isabella, who had followed Don Carlos to the grave within months.

If, Philip thought morosely, he had not such important work to carry out — God's work — he would wish for the peace of an early death himself. Death in which he would be reunited with his family. But for now, the King of Spain would have to console himself with bringing them all here to face eternity.

Though the chill of the rock seeped through his wool tunic, Philip did not move to tuck the cape beneath him, for he felt that the pain of cold was his due. Fitting punishment for the sinner that, despite his many prayers and sacrifices and mortifications of the flesh, he knew he would remain till he died. Yes, he was a sinner — but not as great a one as the scarlet whore of England, Elizabeth.

When she, twenty-three and still beautiful, had come to his English wife Mary's laying-in, Philip had paid court to his sister-in-law. Mary was worn and old, too old to be birthing her first child. She might die, he had reasoned, and the Spanish-English alliance would of course need to be preserved. If Mary died he would marry Elizabeth, he had decided all those years ago. Elizabeth. She had been so beautiful. No one knew how he had desired her.

Now as Philip sat on his frigid rock throne as he shuddered with the very thought of it. For the heretic queen — his vilest enemy on earth, worse even than the misguided William of Orange — was the spawn of Satan and cursed enemy of the True Religion. He, Philip, had been chosen by the Almighty to visit His punishment upon the English infidels. When he died and flew to heaven, he thought, a thin smile finally animating his dour features, he would find his reward seated at the right hand of God.

Twenty-four

The man riding hell bent before me, I knew with certainty to be a poacher, for I had surprised him in the heart of the forest and some of his filched game had fallen from his mount when the chase had begun. My Father, in pain and sore winded, had dropt back, leaving the pursuit to me. The poacher was either an excellent horseman or exceeding desperate, I thought. He had perhaps poached on these trails before, for he seemed to know the twists and turns of Enfield Chase well enough to stay ahead of me.

I saw before the man a wooded fork and prayed he would veer to the left, for I knew in that direction lay a lately downed oak which blocked the path entirely. Yes! He rode into the left fork and within moments I heard a terrified neighing and a surprised shriek. I came upon a scene of confusion — the man thrown headlong off his horse into the tangle of fallen branches, his mount stamping nervously but unhurt. A brace of quail hung from the saddle next to a bow and quiver of arrows, and a hare bulged half out of a cloth game bag.

I jumped from Beauty and stood by as the poacher, a mass of angry scratches, a purple bruise beginning to bloom on his forehead, disengaged twisted tree limbs from his own. I leveled my pistol at him.

"Stand where you are," I said aware of the absurdity of the command as the man had nowhere to run, trapped already in an oak branch prison. "You are arrested for the crime of poaching in the Queens forest. Tell me your name." I was no stranger to such procedures for I had, since my fifteenth year, assisted my Father with the most consequential and most hated of all the duties of a Royal Chasekeeper — enforcement of the poaching laws.

The man was of middle age and poorly dressed, clearly no gentleman poacher as we oftentimes had cause to arrest. His face, aside from his current injuries, was lined with the worry and fear of poverty. He stared at me with sad, red rimmed eyes and wheezed with exertion. He was utterly hopeless as he spoke his name.

"Do you know the law?" I asked him.

"Aye," he answered. His eyes fell then on the stolen game hanging from his saddle and his expression seemed to say, "Christ in Heaven, I have lost my life for a brace of quail and a rabbit."

Twas then I should have taken custody of the criminal and escorted him to the Sheriff, but I suddenly felt my self unable, somehow unwilling to move in the direction of this poor mans destruction.

"Why have you done this," I said, "when you know as all men do what punishment lies ahead for it?"

He stood in his cage of branches and stared at me. "Why ask me such a question, Sir, when you already know the answer? Do not all lowborn poachers when caught redhanded cry poverty, claim a sick mother or starving children, and beg for mercy which is never given?"

I felt a sudden rush of shame and pity. "Have you a sick Mother?" I asked.

"It does not matter, Sir," he said, his arms hanging limply at his side. "Believe me, it does not matter."

I lowered my pistol then, and the weight of it dragged at my own arm. Then I turned and moved to his horse. I stuffed the hare, neatly pierced at the base of its skull, into his pack, walked to Beauty and mounted her.

"Go back to the fork," I directed the man, never meeting his eye, "and bear to the right of the bridge. Leave the forest thro the marsh. And never let me catch you here again or you will pay for breaking the Queens law." Tapping Beautys flank with my heel we turned and trotted away. I heard only the mans grunts as he scrambled to extricate himself from his oaken prison.

By the time I returned to the manor my Father was installed exhausted and snoring before the fire, his legs raised on a footstool. His muddy boots had never been removed and they begrimed the cushion embroidered dutifully by Alice the year before she married. Her husband — a man she did not love — was, tho neither old nor odoriferous like Megs husband, so exceeding stiff and pious that youth was entirely wasted on him. Alice had found no joy in their union but for the three children she had borne him in quick succession.

The fiery nightmare of All Hallows Eve had taken its toll of us all. We children mourned our Mothers passing, but I confess now I did not truly grieve for her. In fact I found my self for more than a year consumed with unceasing rage towards, if not her, then the madness which had held her in its deathly grip and made a horrible end of my Truest Friend.

With the girls gone, my Father and brother and I fell into the rough home life of men living without women. John stayed home rarely, his dissolute habits growing with every year. My Father did depend upon me for all his daily joy which was scarce in deed, and the burden of occupying that position more and more stifled my soul. My childhood habit of fantasy had died a slow but steady death after my arrest at Milford Haven. For a time I had dreamt that the Queen her self, after our meeting when I was eight, had secretly conceived of an important position within her Secret Service for me, and was keeping close watch over my growth into manhood, sending her Guard when it seemed I had gone too far astray. But that dream faded when in several years time her summer Progress came near to Enfield but she did not choose to visit the Chase . . . or her young agent Arthur Southern. Nor did the Privy Council ever again come to rescue me from any trouble. So by my eighteenth year the pull of a mans life outside of Enfield had become unbearably strong, the ties to my Father and the Chase stretched taut to breaking.

Horses still reigned supreme in my small country existence. I had died more than a little when Charger passed out of this life. I believed that no other four legged beast would ever take that brave stallions place. The black mare I now rode, given me by my Father, was smart as she was handsome as she was strong. They say black horses lack a good mouth — and that was true of Beauty — but of the spookiness and treachery attributed to them, I had never seen evidence. I know that she did never perform for me out of love but from duty and good habit instead.

With my Father slow and weak as he was becoming, and with my brother almost entirely absent, I was happily left the task of backing and training all new mounts which came into the stable. Not a man in the parish agreed or approved of my strange method — eschewing torture, and managing a horse into compliance with my wishes by means of a gentle dance I had created twixt the untamed beast and myself, a dance of posture and attitude, of bold concert eye to eye. To my neighbors chagrin all horses under my care learnt the dance and were quickly backed tho never — would I allow it to be said — broken.

My Father stirred in his chair and woke, clearing his throat and chest, and asked had the poacher been caught and properly dealt with. I lied so handily, claiming he had managed somehow to evade me, that I felt a pang of conscience for it, wondering if God would punish me on two accounts. For failing my duty to the Queen, as well as the blatant untruth I had uttered. My Father seemed, however, less concerned with my failure than I supposed he would be. He just stared at me, his eyes softening as tho the very sight of me completed him. I saw suddenly and clearly that the cause of his disinterest in the fate of the poacher was a deep weariness, the slow uncoiling of his soul. I pulled off his boots and kneaded his stockinged feet tween my hands. He groaned with pleasure.

"You are a good boy, Arthur," he said and smiled weakly. "A good boy. My son."

That evening I rode to the village ale house, as had lately become my custom. The Sows Belly was small and stank of piss and stale beer, and was dark as a witches cunt. But it was in the heart of Enfield Towne and was as lively a place as could be found for many miles round. I knew I would find my brother there, eyes bloodshot and bleary, lolling drunkenly cross a table, too far gone even for gaming and gambling.

I had lately come to love dice, and my friends were already there squatting in a corner, whooping and shouting as the bones clicked and clattered against the wall. They were all sons of farmers, all young men I had met at the shire muster the year I had become liable for military service. Side by side on the village green, outfitted in armor brought from home, we had practiced firing clumsy arquebuses and learnt to march in good order, trying hard not to laugh aloud at the Muster Master. He was a spindly, spectacled Justice of the Peace other times, but for that week of the year he was commissioned by the Crown to whip the county men from sixteen to sixty into a fighting force.

We lads came away from the muster with a friendly bond and a shared love of the dice. We therefore conspired to meet at the Sows Belly, as often as our chores would allow. Whilst we drank, as all med did, we were moderate in our habits and refrained from loutish behavior, tho if a general ruckus did break out we did not shirk from the pleasure of a little brawling.

This night I had played and lost most consistently and so broke from my friends to swig a cup of ale in a solitary corner. Shortly thereafter into the publick house strode two strangers. All eyes fell on them suspiciously, till stepping up to the bar they ordered their drinks and showed us clearly they were not foreigners but English.

Visitors were rare in Enfield and I could see questions brewing in all the local patrons eyes. Who were these two? Were they brothers or simply travelling companions? Were they gentlemen or of lesser rank? I saw Harold Morton peer out the window to examine the horseflesh they had ridden in on. Where were they from? Why were they passing thro this village, how long did they intend to stay? And where were they headed?

I sat up straighter as I realized to my surprise that the strangers, cups in hand, were heading for my bench and table. They smiled in a friendly way and so I smiled back and with a gesture bade them sit. They were I soon found — for they were as talkative and good natured as men could be — bound for soldiering in the Netherlands.

I sat enraptured listening to their tales, most especially Hirst who had been to war once already as a volunteer, had been injured, sent home and was now returning to serve with his good friend Partridge. This man was well named, for he was tubby and soft featured, and his round birdlike eyes seemed never to blink.

"Aye tis hard, the life of a soldier," proclaimed Hirst, a tall rangy man with craggy cheeks and a thick head of hair within which were crawling a large company of tiny creatures. He downed his ale in a long gulp. "And harder still in the Low Countries, for tis bloody cold and raw in winter. The watch and ward is deadly tedious, and the food so wretched when you do get it, it heaves your stomach."

I could see Partridges big eyes growing even bigger with Hirsts description of their future life. Was he wondering, as I was, why if soldiering was so brutal, Hirst was speaking with such zeal?

"We travail and toil over hills and woods and vast flatlands — for the Netherlanders have claimed much of their land from the sea. We wade across icy rivers, lie in fields in rain and wind and frost and snow. But adventuring against the enemy, aye lads, there be the

point of it. The best of it. The worst of it. The hacked limbs, the lost lives, making our bodies a fence and a bulwark to ward off the shot of cannon. The noise and the stench of the battlefield. The fine exhausted sleep after a skirmish is won."

As he spoke I was seeing that fight, hearing it, feeling it, smelling it. I leaned forward clutching my cup. Hirst could not fail to see the effect he was having on my soul.

"I took a Spanish bullet in my thigh, so high up it was, I have not stopped thanking God for my manhood to this day. Well, it festered, so they sent me home to heal."

"And now you are going back?" I asked incredulously. "For more of the same?"

"Aye, but this time taking me friend Partridge here, to share the joy of it." They laughed heartily and I joined in with them.

"More brew at this table!" called Hirst. I cannot recall that anyone came to refill our cups, so bound up in the conversation was I. But somehow by the wee hours I had become roaring drunk along with my new companions.

We argued fiercely the relative merits of longbow versus firearms. Hirst propounded to my dismay that the day of heavily armed cavalry was past. Guns, he said, were the very cause of it. We all bemoaned the loss of that shining regiment of knights, the sheer beauty and brave form of an armored man on an armored horse. But modern pellets pierced armor handily, and heavy coats of metal slowed mounts when speed was more necessary than ever. All that was left of the cavalry, said Hirst, were the demilancers and light horsemen. That was enough for me, I thought relieved.

"How came you to be conscripted?" I asked Hirst, my tongue thick with more drink than I had ever before consumed.

"He was a cattle thief, due to be hanged," answered Partridge for him. Hirst glared at his friend who was too drunk to notice. "The judge in our town recruited all the rogues from his prison. Said he could kill two birds with one stone, ridding his streets of riff raff — the sleeveless scum, he called it — and helping fill the muster at that."

Hirst had quickly got over his irritation at Partridge for revealing his tainted past. "In prison I knew a good many men who took up a life of crime just so they would be levied. Twas a safer haven in the army than roguing their way across England."

"Now I . . ." announced Partridge with drunken pride, "I am

joining the Queens army of my own free will . . ." He leveled an absurd smirk at Hirst. "Answering the call of the fife and drum . . ."

A clout on the head from Hirst silenced Partridge. He slumped into a brief slumber whilst Hirst and I continued.

"I take you for a gentleman of sorts," he said to me.

"Of sorts," I replied amused.

"Of course none but nobles can be generals," Hirst continued. "Tis unthinkable for a common man to command. But gentlemen volunteers do sometimes rise to captain."

"They do?" I asked, my heavy lidded eyes opening wide.

Now Hirst leaned across the table and whispered conspiratorially, tho I do not know why he whispered, for surely no one left in the Sows Belly in that wee hour cared a whit what he said.

"I know of gentlemen who served abroad, and by ability and experience came to the notice of the Privy Council — tis them as gives commissions. On merit alone these fine fellas got as near to the top as men of their station could dream of. They were given commands of their own," he added with awe.

I was breathless, for I knew I had it in me to be a leader of men.

"I tell you," he went on, "those men are a sight better commanders than most bloody noblemen who cannot tell their arquebus from their arsehole."

We laughed so uproariously at that we woke Partridge. We stumbled out together into the moonless night. I remember seeing their horses tethered outside the publick house next to Beauty, and wondering were they stolen or legally procured, but I do not remember more than that.

When I woke at first light, groggy and looking for a near place to retch, we were all three sprawled on the village green. I roused my companions who cursed me roundly but came away with me willingly, alarmed by my report of a vicious town constable who enjoyed hauling ruffians and vagabonds off to gaol and throwing away the key. For Hirst and Partridge much feared any interruption of their journey. They were bound for glory on the battlefield and I, with scant urging to accompany them, mounted my horse and without a backward glance rode out of Enfield into the wide world to seek my fortune and find adventure.

Hirst and Partridge and my self travelled overland to the training camp where the latest regiment of English volunteers were being readied to make the passage abroad and serve against Spain. Twas a vast sea of tents peppered with firepits, crawling with young soldiers, trampled fields made marching grounds and artillery ranges all round it. The first sight of the place made my blood run warmer but caused Partridge to cry out, "Oi, tis enough for me, I shall be off, mates!" and wheel his horse round to go. Hirst caught him and gave him a friendly pummelling, then together we rode into camp.

We found a hearty welcome, the Lord Lieutenant greedy for men to meet his muster. We were given beds, equipment and a random array of uniforms which was, carped Hirst, anything but uniform. The Queen had no standing army, and truly there was at that time no real allegiance to England, the days not so long past when men served only feudal lords in foreign wars.

So we banded together, a rabble of raw and poor rascals, each of whom Hirst enjoyed describing as we toiled thro our drill and training. Cockburn was "a man with legs like pins, so thin the enemy might as well shoot at the edge of a penknife." And Masters was "as brave as an angry dove." We learnt to shoot with weapons as small as a robinet and as mighty as a cannon, how to present our piece, take our level and give volley at the same moment as our comrades. We were taught the importance of well rammed wadding and shot down a barrel, lest the gun explode, and when and how to give the push of a pike.

We learnt to march to the beat of the drum, observing our rank and file, and such commands as "advance your pikes!" and "triple your ranks by both flanks!" We learnt the S and the D formations, the squares, the wedges and the sheers. Twas hard work and we slept like dead men till the sun rose, and began again.

Our horses proved a boon to our enlistment. We were offered a choice on our arrival — sell the mounts to the army for a goodly sum which is what Hirst and Partridge did do, or join the cavalry which I did do. I found my company commander a good horseman tho not great, and he scoffed at Beautys training in manège, saying there was not time for "anticks" in a melee.

Hirst, wielding his rough charm like a cudgel, befriended the Master of Ordnance, a bumptious fellow with bulbous eyes and rotten teeth, convincing him to give us free gunpowder, for which we would otherwise have had to pay out of our meager wages. Partridge meanwhile acquired a passion for the art of encypherment, imagining himself a future spy in the Queens service tho, his low rank and lazy mind made such an occupation nigh inconceivable. At odd moments in our exhausting routine he would sit and ponder a pamphlet he had filched from the camp intelligence tent, all filled with strange symbols and cyphers. He gazed at them so asquint that I thought he could hardly have learnt their meanings. Still, as we had scant pleasures in that training camp, we did not dissuade him from his fantasy.

For my self, I was in glory. This was all I wanted for my life. There was no fear, no worry. Only anticipation. When I lay abed in my camp cot at night I saw my self a great soldier, ever victorious in battle and a man of great merit. How fortunately bound in ignorance are the young, for there never would be raised an army if all callow boys knew the truth of war.

Finally when time came for the levy we were ready as we were ever to be — that is to say not so ready at all. With our coat and conduct money then in hand we set out for the port of embarkation. There is not much to tell of Harwich. Only that the men who did not pocket their travelling wages and desert the Queens service were met with further privations in that town, as the Master of Merchant Vessels met with one obstacle after another in setting us upon the water for our journey to the Netherlands.

The weather had grown foul, the wind shifting direction from one hour to the next. The draftsman who made the horse slings had not yet arrived in Harwich with his necessary cargo, and local merchants refused the mean offers made for their goods to stock our ship. Delay piled upon delay and then dysentery struck the troops. Tempers frayed like the rags of a beggar. Fistfights and riots broke out. Desertion rivaled disease for the thinning of our once robust ranks. Townsfolk cried out in anger and fear against the foul conditions brought to their home, and we were finally forced to embark, despite the wicked weather.

The sea all round me was a terrible thing to behold. Great roaring waves like moving mountains rose suddenly, towering above the highest mast, then vanished only to be replaced by another, and another. The Channel was a living thing — a sea monster — and we in our tiny vessel were a parasite on its undulating hide.

Our crossing, which in good conditions might have taken six hours, now straggled into its fourth perilous day. Hirst and Partridge had shipped on another vessel within an hour of mine, but we had lost sight of them in the storm and could only pray to God for their safe deliverance, as we prayed for our own.

Never before had I been at sea and the long close confinement below decks with my fellow soldiers proved so unspeakable I thought I would brave the weather. As I stood on the ladder I could not at first budge the cabin door and thought it jammed. But finally it flew open, nay, was sucked open by the force of the gale as it changed direction, and a mighty slosh of seawater instantly drenched me to the skin. Whether twas the sight of those moving grey mountains or the sound of Gods fury in the shrieking wind I did not know. But I was filled suddenly with such a low dread that I could no longer stay, and so pulled the door closed, then clung shaking to the wall of the stair. I had seen Death out there and it was more terrifying an end than the agonizing throes of dysentery which had claimed several soldiers lives already, or the thought of the battlefield and its gory punishments. This death — to be swallowed whole by the monster and drown alone in its cold dark bowels — sickened me. All prayers fled my mind. My body could not stop its shuddering. I had seen Death rising behemothlike all round the ship, and if I never again stepped my foot outside that door, Death never the less would be there waiting for me.

I thought suddenly of Beauty down in the hold, trussed up in ropes and a canvas sling like the dozens of other cavalry horses swinging all round her. Sympathy shot thro me. Twould be excruciating, suspended as they all were for safety on the crossing, with their feet never meeting the floor, the cries of their companions confusion and terror. I was a coward. I could not bear to visit her, try to comfort her. And I could neither stand out on the deck to confront my own death. With only the stinking general quarters and the galley — now congested with a company of seasick soldiers — to repair to, I thought I might in deed spend the rest of the crossing where I stood on the stair.

How had I come to this place? Was it punishment for leaving my Father, abandoning him to a lonely ending in his hollow house? What kind of wretched son was I, I thought, to abscond without warning and only a shameful letter of explanation sent when I was halfway to the coast?

But no. There was nothing to be done now, I reasoned, and no cause for guilt. I was a grown man without a future at Enfield Chase. There had been no choice but to go abroad and seek a life for my self. Even with my gentlemans education I would flounder. In England rank and money were all, and I had neither. Perhaps, as Hirst had suggested that night in the Sows Belly, I might elevate my lot within the military.

Then a gruff sailor bumped past me with a low curse, threw open the cabin door with nary a care and plunged headlong into the shrieking abyss. When the door banged closed I found my self moving — down past the packed galley, down into the quarters, which were dark except for small candle lanterns hung in several berths. I heard the sounds of two men talking, someone moaning, another retching. I sought my bed — if you could call a few boards and a pallet of flea infested straw a bed — and lay down facing the wall.

As I lay in my berth cursing the army who had brought me to this vile moment, as miserable a state as I had ever been in, I felt a strange lightness come over me. I was suddenly and forcefully illuminated by reason. This ship could not possibly sink, for if it did I would surely die. And I could not die now, for I had not yet lived. My future, which I had seen stretched out before me on the beach at Milford Haven — to cross the sea and explore the world — was just beginning. I felt at once safe and snug in my berth, all fear subsiding like an outgoing tide. Slowly I rolled over and lay full on my back. I inhaled deeply. But the rank air and close darkness of the quarters, still rolling violently in a chorus of creaking planks which heretofore had filled me with dread, seemed only one side of the coin with which I had gambled my whole life. Sunlight, sweet wine and balmy afternoons wrapt in the arms of a beautiful woman were the other. I would have them all. Both sides of the coin. And thus encouraged by this great illumination I opened my arms and embraced my destiny.

Book Two

Twenty-five

My dream of youth had been fulfilled — I had crossed the water to a new land and become a cavalry soldier, tho ensconced behind the walled city of Haarlem in my garrison several months had gone by and I had not seen battle. Since my arrival in the Netherlands I had been dismayed to learn that most warfare in this day and age was a matter of siege — the Duke of Alva's Spanish troops surrounding a fortified city, and that citys residents and garrisoned soldiers valiantly resisting in isolation for months, sometimes more than a year. Haarlem, in one of the northernmost provinces, had not yet come under the gun.

Combat in the field was scarce and much less exciting than the magnificent battles of boyhood fantasies — thousands of trained soldiers in huge formations, colorful banners flying, great cavalry charges with kings and generals overwatching from a high hill. All we could hope for were skirmishes or sudden raids, ambushes which occasionally might grow into a fuller engagement.

By the time our volunteer army landed at Flushing after that wretched crossing, many horses had died at sea and others in poor condition were forced into an extended march almost at once, with no time to rest or have their terrors eased. Beauty was a champion amongst them, perhaps because of her excellent health and care previous to the journey. Her quick recovery and reunion with myself gave me a large advantage to begin my life as a soldier. Too, my knowledge of husbandry and study of Xenophons methods of care for horses in wartime held me in good stead with my cavalry commanders, most of whom were highborn but green, and none of whom knew more than me. On the march from the coast to our garrison I was soon singled out as a dispatch rider, carrying messages from commander to commander.

Partridge and Hirst and I had been reunited on landing, but they were infantrymen and so we were separated in different companies. We were never the less to stay good friends who, in stolen moments, gambled and drank and whored together. They were all the family I had in this strange land.

And strange it did seem to me at first. Unlike England with its solid ground of hills and forests and pastures bordered so rigidly by cliffs and beaches, Flanders seemed all rivers, bogs and marshlands, tho we did pass some forests of heather, pine and birch. And I had never before seen dunes, majestic mountains of sand sometimes two hundred feet high held together by grass and reed which stretched along the Channel coast from a string of northern islands, south to Calais.

Stranger still were the dikes — structures of granite, wood, sod and earth, built by Julius Caesars Roman troops and early Hollanders to protect them against their enemy the sea.

Haarlem, where our march ended, was collected behind old walls and crumbling towers, tho twas an otherwise fine and prosperous town. Edged by dunes of the North Sea to the west, there lay a beech forest to the south. To the east was a huge lake — which the townsfolk called a sea — on the other side of which in the distance lay the city of Amsterdam.

We learnt quickly why we English were there in the Low Countries, and twas not so much in those days to defend our longtime partners in trade from the cruel Spanish hordes, but to protect our own commerce. Never the less the Hollanders welcomed us, and we were free to come and go in their city as long as we obeyed the rules of our garrison which carried heavy penalties for drunkenness, gaming or swearing, or for quarreling or fisticuffs. Abusing women with children, old people, young virgins or babes was strictly forbidden. For the crime of leaving the watch, punishment was the loss of both ears and banishment, and for stealing weapons or desertion or mutiny, death. We were each and every soldier obliged to pray in church twice daily and were allowed no women except wives, tho all the men I knew found ways round that one rule.

Twas a sad fact, we learnt, that our captains were men of corrupted virtue. They were the link tween the company and the higher command in arming, feeding and clothing their men. They received their money "by the man" and so the more men, the more money. And these captains found many ways to make it seem they had mustered more men than really they had. They might dismiss a man in order to pocket his pay. Worse, they might send a man they disliked into dangerous and hopeless missions, knowing he would not return. This practice we called "dead pay," but we had no recourse, no choice but to obey orders.

Dutch folk I found to be as industrious and untiring as any I had ever known. Twas strange to see the women carrying goods on their heads and backs, and stranger still to see them with their wooden shoulder yokes hauling loads an English man *would shy away from. They were sober and sensible people, maybe too much so for my taste, as they frowned upon the theatre which I did love. But their stern nature made for a safe and orderly town on whose streets a man or woman could walk alone day or night without fearing for life or limb.*

One fine spring Sunday after church service I could not wrest Partridge and Hirst from their idea of wenching, and decided to take my self on a proper haunt of the city of Haarlem. My companys garrison lay along the seaward wall of town and so I set off towards the Great Church whose pinnacle led me to the city centre. It seemed to me that all was water and red brick, with as many canals as avenues, wide and narrow ones and many broad, low arched bridges. The bridges were red brick like the street paving, and the houses too. The canals on that Sunday were quieter than in the week, which saw them filled with fishing smacks and barges with their goods, the most colorful ones filled with tulips. The Dutch were so mad for their tulips that sometimes one bulb of a rare color might fetch the price of a house, or a rich girls dowry.

I headed into the city square which bustled with prosperous healthy humanity. Twas hard to believe that a war raged not far from here. Of all the fine buildings only the City Hall and the Great Church, with its steeple top shaped like a tulip bulb, were open. Services were long over, so I entered the church to find it as white and bare as our English cathedrals were ornamented, with a ceiling of faintly fragrant cedar wood, and a stair that took me up the steeple tower.

Looking down from there I saw the whole towne of Haarlem from the square. Gazing round I saw the billowing North Sea from which I had barely escaped with my life, the great forest, and the lake across which in the distance I could see the steeples of Amsterdam.

Back down in the square I wandered past fine shops all closed on this Sunday but, to my curiosity, each boasting a sprig of green leaves suspended from the doorbeams. I had hardly stopped to ponder this odd decoration when I heard a commotion from down the avenue and saw a procession coming towards me. I was reminded of that adulterers procession in Maidstone and hoped this was not such a solemn progress to dampen the happy day.

To my pleasure it was not, tho it did strike so strange a chord that I laughed aloud when I saw its nature. Twas a parade of marchers and musicians surrounding a fancy coach drawn by six horses, filled to its windows with herring! A large bough of the same green leaves in the shop doorways decorated the top of the fish coach. As it headed back for the square I followed along.

Two young people amongst this crowd caught my eye, for they were identical in form and feature. The same eyes matching the serene lightness of blue sky, the same rosy cheeks, small noses and wide pleasant mouths. The same flaxen hair. Yet one was a boy and one was a girl, maybe fifteen. I spoke to them in Dutch, those words I had learnt since my arrival in Holland, and the girl giggled at my pronunciation. Her brother, to my surprise, answered me in English — quite good English at that. They were Dirk and Jacqueline Hoogendorp, residents of Haarlem. They were as pleased to make my acquaintance as I was theirs, and proceeded to explain that the procession in which we were all now a part — as well as the leaves decorating shop doorways — honored the seasons first catch of precious herring, now being delivered with great pomp and ceremony to the City Hall.

They were more than friendly, these two. Besides plying me with intelligence about their town and the importance of herring to their culture — Hollanders are passionate about this fish whether green, white or red, smoked, dried, kippered, soused or boiled — they invited me to their home for Sunday dinner, and I instantly accepted.

The uniformity of the residential streets, the sameness of the rows of narrow red brick houses, three storeyed with three windows to each floor, filled me with wonder at how they could ever distinguish their own home from amongst them. And the city was clean, so clean I marvelled at it, the housewives even on the Sabbath sweeping their well scrubbed stoops with neat pairs of wooden clogs lined up near the door.

Gabbling all the way Dirk and Jacqueline finally brought me to 24 Blancken Stadt in a serene row of houses across from a tree lined canal. We removed our shoes and tramped up a dark narrow stair to find ourselves in the bright front room of a comfortable but plain Dutch home, beautiful smells of cooking food wafting up from the kitchen. I was enjoined to sit, and in a moment Jacqueline returned holding the hand of an aproned matron, all suffused in a cloud of pastry flour, very plump with those same sky blue eyes as her children, and a jolly laugh. This was the twins Moeder. She welcomed me heartily in Dutch, and Jacqueline translated, saying it was good to have another young man at her table, as three of her other sons were gone off to the war, all that was left being Dirk who was too young.

The dining room behind the front room was dim, and even in the day lit by candles, since the only windows in the long narrow house were frontwise. Already seated at the head of the trestle was Jan Hoogendorp, a tall wiry man with sleeves rolled up over well muscled arms, possessing the broad mouth his twins bore. With all of us seated the table was still only half filled, which I could easily imagine overflowing with his strapping sons. I was invited to sit, and my mouth watered as Moeder and Jacqueline brought out plates of herring and cabbage and pale steaming dumplings.

Jan was, I came to learn, a fisherman, owner of several boats which worked the waters of the North Sea. That intelligence alone caused me to look upon the otherwise unimposing man with awe. To think that someone would go again and again <u>by choice</u> into the belly of that terrible beast made me shudder. I admitted to Jan my fear of the sea and my loathing of it.

"Here in Holland the water is our element," he said in good English — he had learnt it for his business, selling hundreds of barrels of salt fish abroad. "We live by it, die by it. But most of all we have learnt to rule it. This land you see all round you, we took from the sea."

Dirk interrupted. "Here we say, 'God made the sea, men of the Netherlands the shore.'"

"Ja," his Father went on. "It is an artificial country made by Hollanders who by their will alone preserve it. But like herring, it is not to everyones taste." He took a whole fried fish and filled his mouth with it.

"King Philip calls the Netherlands the country nearest to Hell," Dirk told me seriously.

"And he should know," added Jacqueline, "for he is the Devil himself."

"Philip," said Moeder incensed, the very name sounding a blasphemy. She had finally taken her place at the table and begun heaping her own plate with food. Tho she spoke no English she knew our subject and was eager to expound upon it in Dutch, her pink face turning a violent shade of red as she spoke.

Jacqueline translated her Mothers words for me. "He was trouble from the day of his good Fathers abdication. Philip hated the Low Countries. Came here but twice in his life and wanted to make us all into Spaniards. And when we said no to him, to his stinking Inquisition and his Auto da Fé, he sent his monstrous Duke and murderous army to destroy us. He executed twelve thousand of our citizens and two of our highest Counts! All we wish is to rule our selves and pray in our own way. If you ask me he is a haughty, fat lipped little worm who does not even like food! I tell you," said Moeder, spearing a dumpling, "you should never trust a person who does not enjoy eating."

Truly, I was finding a new education at this dinner table. "So Philip rules the Netherlands from Spain?" I asked.

"His aunt, Margaret of Parma, is the Governor General of the Low Countries, but she acts wholly at the bidding of the King," answered Jan.

I saw the twins tittering between themselves and demanded to know what was so funny.

"Margaret of Parma has a mustache," giggled Jacqueline in answer.

"And a shaggy beard," added Dirk, stroking his chin.

"But what is <u>not</u> funny," proclaimed Jan, "is what the King has done to the man who would save us all from this persecution. William of Orange was once a prosperous Prince and beloved by all. Now, because he defies Philip he is a fugitive, penniless, having sold his lands and possessions to sustain our rebellion."

Moeder was nodding vehemently, having heard Williams name. "Fadder uff de Fadderland," she managed to sputter, and everyone applauded her efforts at English. Then she lapsed into Dutch.

"This poor man who has given all for freedom of his countrymen has suffered so badly," translated Jacqueline. "His first wife was a terrible shrew, and a drunkard as well who ran off with another

man. This is the Gods truth! And then the Duke of Alva, the Devil's spawn, kidnapped Williams only son and sent him as a prisoner to Spain where he still lives today. Imagine, he may never see his boy again. Ach, he has suffered so! When his army was beaten the first time and he was outlawed in his own land, William travelled around on a sorry old nag and was forced to write his Mother to find a pair of his discarded hose so he could be presentable when he went to foreign courts begging money for the cause. Poor man! At least he has joy of his new wife. Lady Charlotte, her name is. Did you know she was once the abbess of a Catholic nunnery who ran away with him and renounced the faith to become a Calvinist? She is very beautiful, so tis said. And they have three little girls. Would you like more dumplings, Arthur?"

Well, I had more dumplings and more herring and more beer until I thought I would burst. All the afternoon long listening to Moeder storytelling and Jacqueline translating, I began to hear and know the Holland tongue in a new way, and learnt a good many words and their meanings. Mister Jarrett had been correct. I did have an ear for language. Twas a gift, and I vowed silently to make use of it.

Then Jacqueline suddenly blurted, "Why do you wear only one glove, Arthur?"

"It covers a deformed hand," I replied. Without thinking, I had for the first time not used the lie about the scars from a bad burn.

"May I see it?" she asked guilelessly.

"Jacqueline!" exclaimed Jan sternly.

But I was comfortable with this family, and all at once the deformity seemed trivial, and I knew I would not be judged for it. I slipped off the gauntlet and laid my hand on the table. Jacqueline gasped in delight. "An extra finger!" she exclaimed.

"Tis hardly a finger," argued her brother, "just a bit of flesh." To me he said, "Why do you cover it with a glove, Arthur?"

I did not immediately answer. I had never thought upon it, had always simply worn the glove. But I knew now it was for shame. My Mothers shame. "Is it not unsightly to you?" I asked.

"Not at all, not at all!" Dirk exclaimed. His twin vehemently agreed.

"Then I shall wear the glove no longer," I announced, surprising even myself.

"May I have it then?" asked Jacqueline fingering the glove and this time horrifying her Mother.

With mock gravity I handed her the symbol of my childhood pain, and thought there would be no more perfect guardian for it than this sweet and openhearted young girl.

We had begun devouring a rich butter and honeyed pastry when Dirk appealed to his Father for permission to join with the resistance. But the sight of Moeders jovial face collapsing into a teary puddle, and Jan saying "And who then would I have to help me on the boats?" quelled all discussion, tho I thought I saw a strange glint in his sisters eye when Dirk spoke his passionate plea. It seemed almost Jacqueline her self wished to fight the Spaniards, tho of course that was quite impossible, for she was a woman. No one beside my self had seen that spark and I dismissed it, thinking it only a reflection of the candlelight in a pretty blue eye.

When I took my leave of the Hoogendorps I was made to promise to return as often as I was able, and to think of their home as my home since I was far away from my own in a strange land. I swear I never knew the real meaning of hospitality till that day or what motherly love should feel like. I was at once warmed and saddened, for my own Mother had shown me little more than the back of her hand all my life.

Soon I had no time to brood. Alva was on the move again.

One of his more recent targets had been the town of Leyden. The siege had lasted six months, with the citizens desperate and starving, the Spanish surrounding them on land in forts they had built, and the Dutch fleet anchored helplessly outside the dikes. William of Orange, with no other way to save them, had urged the townspeople to breach their dikes, to open their sluice gates so that the land should be inundated, allowing entrance of the Sea Beggars barges. The people had cried out that their rich polderlands would be ruined by saltwater, but William had persisted saying "Better a drowned land than a lost land." Finally desperation had won out and it had been done. The dike was dashed open and the sea had rushed in, the Hollander ships passing thro the breach. Tis said these sailors were a fearsome sight in deed, outlaws of the ocean dancing wildly on the decks, snarling, soot blackened faces, cutlasses clenched in their teeth, and their war cries of "Better Turks than Papists!" echoing over the face of the newmade sea.

The final clash had come in the midst of a terrible storm at midnight, some Spanish ships sailing out to meet the Zeelanders whose flat bottomed ships fared better in the shallow water. They say the battle was fought by the brilliant glow of cannon blast and great bolts of lightning, all amongst the tops of trees and roofs of submerged houses, Dutch sailors leaping into the shallows and pushing their boats onward by human fury alone. The Spaniards, who had seen nothing like it, were terror struck, their ships boarded and burnt, and fortresses seized by shrieking pirates who dispatched them with grappling irons and bloody swords, and threw them headlong into the ocean. Alvas troops were thus routed from Leyden and a victory won. But this was one amongst many more losses, and the Spaniards again were moving north.

At the height of summer a dispatch was sent to our commanders at Haarlem that the Spanish had built a fort near Gouda, five days travel south of our garrison. A decision was made to attack, and to the dismay of the burghers of Haarlem, all but a few of the English ranks there were to take part. Together we were fifteen hundred strong, infantry and cavalry combined — or that is what the muster said and the High Command was told, tho really we were no more than twelve hundred, if that. The discrepancy, result of corruption and dead pay abuses, seemed of little import as we departed in fine fettle and formation, uniforms crisp, boots spit and polished, artillery wagons rumbling importantly down the red brick avenues of Haarlem and out the ancient gates.

Moving south we passed the great bleaching grounds with miles of "hollands" — fine white linen — spread like a stark white sea under the blazing sun. Then we traversed a thick beech forest which charged me with my first pangs of homesickness, for the broad paths and lush verdant canopy of trees, the smell of damp earth, moss and mushroom, the sound of birdsong all evoked Enfield Chase and my bittersweet childhood. Now I was in the company of men marching to war, and as we finally passed out of the familiar forest into the Hollander landscape that was so alien to my senses, I felt something in me dying, tho the death was neither painful nor terrifying. Seated on my high horse I looked back once and saw behind me the wood from which we had emerged, and slithering from it like a long snake the army of which I was a part. In that instant I was reborn a soldier.

We were two days out when the full natural stupidity of our

Captain, young Lord Holcomb, made itself known. Midday he halted our company and announced that we would now practice formations. His men, standing at attention under a scorching sun waiting for further word, watched as the nearsighted nobleman — elegant in his starched doublet of fustian faced with blue taffeta — squinted through his brass rimmed spectacles at a small volume I recognized as Leonard and Thomas Digges military textbook "Stratioticos." I had often seen Holcomb poring over this treatise which calculated various marching and battle formations by algebra and arithmetic, and wondered if his lack of practical experience, together with the mystified expression on his face as he contemplated the passage in Digges, would spell trouble for our company.

"All right then," he called in his most authoritative voice which still squeaked with nervousness. "We shall execute the Ring Maneuver." Thus with one eye at his book he led us marching in single file round and round in a series of ever diminishing circles in whose centre, to his dismay and the stifled amusement of his men, he suddenly found himself entrapt. "Back, back I say! Give me light to see my book!" he cried with irritation. Then utterly flustered he elbowed his way from the spiral of humanity and bleated petulantly, "Fall in, shoulder your arms and march on!"

But that was not the end to our troubles. Countryfolk had left their polders, taking with them their cows and stores of grain so we were soon running out of rations — an eventuality our inept Master of Victuallers had never envisaged. Our horses were better fed than we were, and the sounds of grumbling men and growling bellies was everywhere heard.

On the morning of the fourth day I was called before Lord Holcomb. His tent was very fine, laid with silver plate and hung with heavy rugs to keep out the morning chill, furs on his broad cot. An adjutant sat polishing the Captains sword as Holcomb and two other company leaders, Billings and Medford — both older and I hoped wiser — stood gazing down at a map of the Netherlands. Holcomb did his best to appear commanding, though I thought he looked not unlike the flustered captive of his own circular drill formation.

"Sir," said I snapping to attention.

"We have need of a swift rider and a sound horse," he said avoiding my eye to admire his fingernails which were far cleaner than my own.

"I am that, Sir, and my horse is very fit," I replied.

"Our companies will proceed towards Gouda, and General Morely has promised reinforcements from the Amsterdam garrison. You will locate the rebel headquarters which we believe to be somewhere in this area." He flicked his fingers over a section of the map which in England would comprise an entire Parish, tho I knew better than to question him further, for if he <u>had</u> known the location of the Dutch resistance he would have told me of it. The other two captains, for their benefit of years, proved no more knowledgeable or interested than this green lad, and so I waited.

"You will find William Prince of Orange," he said.

"Sir?" I said, unable to contain my excitement.

He continued in what seemed a tone of boredom. "You will inform him of our movements and our proposed besiegement of the Spanish fort near Gouda, and of the reinforcements from Amsterdam."

"And what message would you have back from him, Sir?"

"We have no need of an answer, Private Southern. If he wishes to lend the support of his 'army'" — Holcomb exchanged disdainful looks with his fellow officers — "he is most welcome."

It suddenly occurred to me that these older men, though rumored to have had good field experience, stood lower in civil rank than Holcomb, and had not yet gathered the courage of their military equality with so highborn a man, and thus let him lead.

"Do bring us news of his position when you have found it," Holcomb went on, "and demand to know his movements in the next months."

"Begging your pardon, Sir . . . may I <u>demand</u> such information from a Prince?"

Holcomb answered me with a withering glare. "Leave immediately and do not return until you have found him. Is that clear?"

"It is, Sir," said I, and turning smartly on my boot heels pushed out the tent flap into the soggy morning.

I packed lightly for my self to make room for Beautys extra food, and strapped to the sides of my saddle the two pistols issued cavalrymen. And I considered my apparel. The officers did not say, but I knew it was a dangerous mission, a lone English soldier riding thro open country — a sitting duck for Spanish guns. So whilst I proposed to ride out wearing my companys canvas doublet and cassock, and metal helmet, I hid beneath them garb that a Dutch merchant might wear for a journey to Amsterdam.

Before I left I sought out Hirst and Partridge in their encampment. I found Hirst busy outfitting himself for the carrying of arms that day — a tedious business indeed.

"Where is our plump Partridge?" I inquired, jumping down from the saddle.

"Inside still. A bloody maniac he is, with his book of cyphers."

"Oh, a maniac, am I?" said our friend as he carried from the tent an arquebus and an armload of equipment, setting them down on the canvas where Hirst had nearly finished his preparations.

He turned to me and said, "Tis fascinating business, these cyphers. You have codes and symbols in place of letters of the alphabet. You have geometrical figures, like a square that means peace and a rectangle for war. Then a thing they call 'nonsignificants' which means a lot of nothing, but they get stuck in a dispatch to confound the enemy. And invisible writing with lemon juice is a fine device, you know. But tis not altogether safe, for anybody but a fool will know a blank piece of paper is a secret message. All you have to do is heat it over a flame and the words come . . ."

"Partridge," I interrupted, "I am altogether fascinated, but I have no time for the complete lecture just now. I'm off."

"Off?" said Hirst looking up. "You say it like this is somewhere other than where we are off to."

"That is what I am saying, lads."

"Where then?" demanded Partridge.

I punched him medium hard in the shoulder before mounting up again. "You should know better than to ask such a question, cypherer. But tis an adventure to be sure."

"Well, best not get yourself shot up just yet," said Hirst. "The war is just beginning."

"God speed," added Partridge, and I was off.

On first sight of the Dutch resistance headquarters my heart did sink. Twas pitifully small, maybe five hundred men altogether, the tents in tatters, the soldiers likewise, some with rags bound on their feet for boots. I could see the woeful dearth of heavy cannon. And the carts which carried them — wheels sunk to their axles in mud — might fall to pieces with the slightest jolt.

I was therefore unprepared for what I found within the dwelling of the Dutch commander. Twas a tent no better than the others, but guarded securely by half a dozen fierce faced men, three with muskets, three with halberds. From inside came a good deal of male laughter. I asked a guard to feed and water Beauty which he nodded with agreement to do. Then stepping thro the tent flaps I saw a plain soldiers place, no hangings, a dirt floor, wooden trestle and a basket filled with rolled parchment maps. A small fluffy dog lay sleeping on a narrow cot. Six men sat round the table drinking companionably but not heavily, and I could not at first make out the leader, for they seemed all equal in their good nature and dress and familiarity one with another. They did not mark my presence, and as I watched I soon came to know — thro their postures, the way they leaned in, their smiles turned all in one direction — which of them was William Prince of Orange. He seemed to me nothing less than a human magnet drawing in to him all his mens good will and loyalty.

Finally I was seen standing at the tent door, and the room quieted. I began to speak in the Holland tongue, but William stood and saluted me saying "I'll speak with you in English, which I seem to know better than you know Dutch."

He gestured for his men to make room for me at the table. This heedlessness of rank — allowing a mere messenger to sit at a table with a Prince and his Generals — so shocked me I was silent for some time, and I was sure my face must have given away my inner turmoil. Then a cup of beer and a plate of food were laid down before me and my confusion only grew, for I knew not whether to eat — I was ravenous, my own rations having given out the day before — or deliver my message. I began to speak, but the burly fairhaired officer next to me gestured for me to eat. So I did.

The conversation surged on round me all in the Holland tongue and there was some of it I did miss, but I could make out that they were speaking of an alliance they wished to make with England, and how Elizabeth had, in her own way, begun to assist their causes with less than direct measures. Already some years ago she had, in her most audacious fashion, seized four Genoese ships carrying £85,000 bound for the Duke of Alva to pay his troops, and kept the money for her self. Now her pirates regularly burnt Philips merchantmen, and intercepted his gold laden ships sailing from the New World back to Spain. Suddenly I heard the name Leicester and pricked up my ears, straining to understand all that I could. I gathered they wished his assistance in helping England to openly declare herself for the Netherlands, that his influence with the Queen was so great that he was in deed their best hope.

Several times when I chanced to look up from my plate I found the Princes eyes upon me. I chanced looks at him as well and saw a handsome, hard muscled man with a head that resembled a picture I had once seen — a statue of a Greek god. William had dark eyes and curly brown hair now streaked with silver. His manner was at once regal and altogether friendly. He was completely alert and engaged, and leaned forward into the group. He seemed to much enjoy this long earnest conversation. I wondered at these men together with their leader in this tent. One was a high Prince, perhaps the others noble too, but they were so marvellously plain . . . I had never in the English army seen this kind of purpose, strength in unity. They seemed to me a force of Nature as great as any whirlwind, any storm at sea.

When he saw I had finished my meal William wasted no more time. First he paid me compliment for finding their encampment at all, with hopes that the Spaniards had no scouts as adept as my self. His English was good with only a trace of an accent. The timbre of his voice was warm, steady and reassuring, and I thought it perhaps his greatest strength. Then he asked for the message I had brought. When it was given and William had translated for his officers, there was silence all round, and several men scratched their head. Someone made a remark in Dutch which I did not understand and everyone laughed, all but William who was serious now. He seemed to be trying to form his thoughts before he spoke.

"Private Southern," he said. "Tell me, how many troops have been left to defend the city of Haarlem?"

"Not many, Sir. One hundred infantry, fifty cavalry."

All laughter ceased now.

"And should Haarlem be besieged while the English army is unnecessarily besieging the Spanish fort . . . ?"

"Unnecessarily?" I asked.

One of the other officers spoke up in rough English. "Your leaders are bored in der garrison. Dey haf no vish to sit quiet vaiting for battle, but demselfs go seeking it."

I swallowed and felt myself flush with embarrassment, knowing what this man said was all too correct. Here were true soldiers who knew the meaning of war, and not some trio of effete buffoons in their starched taffeta.

"Dey put demselfs in needless danger, you see," continued the officer. "Dis fort near Gouda is vell armed and provisioned, and English losses are sure to be great."

"I must go back with your message and warn them!" I said.

William shook his head. "You do not understand. It makes no difference what I say. They will do what they will. You have said already they do not wish our assistance. And we have other pressing concerns."

"Sir," I stammered, "my orders are to learn your future movements and report them back to my commander."

William was silent for a long moment in which he considered my request. He never took his eyes from my own, seeming to search for my souls understanding in them. Then he answered my question with a question.

"Tell me, son, why do you think we in Holland are fighting this war?"

"Well, I believe it is that you wish to be a Protestant country, as England is."

"Did you know," he went on, "that I was raised a Catholic?"

"Sir?" I said my jaw dropping open. "I do not understand. I thought . . ."

"Do you know that here in the Low Countries, Calvinists have persecuted their Catholic countrymen as cruelly as the Spaniards have persecuted the Calvinists? Do you think a Catholic heretic dying over the coals of a slow fire suffers any less agony than a Protestant? Do you understand that the idea of tolerance embraces both sides of an issue equally?"

I did not answer. Could not open my mouth to speak, but opened my ears and my mind, for I knew I was here learning the essence of something very great indeed.

"I always believed in the Divine Right of Kings," said William. "Throughout the first rebellion I supported the authority of Spain over the Netherlands Estates. I requested . . ." He smiled ironically. "Ja, 'requested' that Philip stop the Inquisition here. Told him that his interests required a peaceful, prosperous country which I hoped to deliver him. I believed my old friend would come to agree. Instead he called for Alva to bring him my head. Instructed him and his army of twenty-four thousand to rain terror and death down upon the Low Countries people."

William drank deeply from his cup and seemed to be recalling a painful memory. "I raised an army to resist — perhaps not the best, mercenaries you know — and some of my countrymen fought with us, but some broke under Spains strength. Some peasants worked for Alva and gave our positions away. Our money ran out and my soldiers, they struck for pay. Some went over to the other side, and we were forced to disband. I was banished from my homeland . . . but not beaten."

Suddenly the little dog jumped down from the Princes cot and leapt into its masters lap. William stroked it absently as he went on. "I went begging to other Protestant countries and raised yet another army. We were to be supported by a large contingent of French Huguenots, and we had crossed into the Netherlands once again, this time at the Rhine. We were gaining ground, taking back many cities from the Spaniards . . ." He stopped, looking pained. "And then came the Eve of Saint Bartholomew. Everything collapsed. We were routed from our camp headquarters. Many of my men died. The rest deserted. Two of my brothers were killed in a battle soon after. Nothing was left of my army but a few loyal officers . . ." He looked affectionately round the table, and I knew these were those men. "And of course my dog," he added, smiling a small smile. "Alva surged through, retook those towns we had claimed. Punished, brutally punished all those who had helped the resistance. Only the North, only Holland held fast to me and my cause."

William was quiet for a long time, but I remained respectfully silent and finally he spoke. "What we in the Low Countries know now is that it is not necessary to hope in order to undertake . . . nor to succeed in order to persevere. We are poor in resources, but we are strong, so strong in spirit. I have begun to call myself a Dutchman," he said, looking round the table at his men, "and I have become a Calvinist."

Finally I ventured, "This army, your third, is it made all of Netherlanders?"

"I shall always need to hire a few foreign soldiers, but all of the others are Dutch Protestants. I am very proud of my men, for they fight patiently and courageously for a cause they believe in. I have promised them that as long as I live there will be no religious persecution in Holland."

William must have seen the fire in my eyes lit by his passionate words.

"Englishman, comrade, I see you are listening closely, but I want you to fully comprehend — I will never ever die at the stake for any religion, but I would die gladly so that tolerance for all religions be forever observed. Do you understand?"

I nodded vigorously tho I felt utterly stupid in the presence of such a man. Banging his cup on the table he adjourned the meeting. His officers stood and with hearty goodnights disappeared from the tent. I too stood to go.

"What is your first name, son?"

As I answered him I searched his noble face and remembered what Moeder Hoogendorp had said about his eldest boy taken hostage by Alva, and living a prisoner in Spain. And, too, about the wife he had married for love.

"Arthur Southern," he said with what I imagined was some slight affection, "you will send my regards to your commander and give him our position." He pulled a map from the basket and unrolled it onto the table. "I will show you where we are going . . ." Then he looked into my eyes and smiled. "But your captain should know that the plans for our movements may at any time change."

"I understand, Sir," I said.

As he walked with me to my horse he continued in a most friendly manner, as though I were his peer. "I fear your pampered commanders do not understand the will and the passion of the Duke of Alva and his professional soldiers. Like their King they believe they are fighting for God Himself. They hate our civilian ways, our wealth, the wordliness of our churches. They do not understand that we are merchants, and merchants make no distinction in whom they sell to. A Protestant or Catholic makes an equally good customer, you see. But Alva is mistaken in thinking we are soft, that he can tax us however he pleases. Now that Spain has ousted Jews and Moors from its lands and conquered the Turks, it feels it is invincible. Alva claims to have tamed men of iron, and boasts that he can easily tame the Netherlanders. 'Men of butter,' he calls us. Well, he will see . . ."

The Princes attention returned to me. "Get a few hours sleep before you set out again." He pierced me with those dark eyes as tho he could see something within me which was not apparent without. "Ride safe," he said and turned and repaired to his tent.

In that moment I knew there was nothing I would not have done for that man, that great Prince, who tho not my own by country was my own in heart and spirit. My education, which had truly begun at the urging of the Earl of Leicester, had taken a mighty turning at the table of William of Orange. I was grateful and vowed silently that this education would not be in vain.

Six hours later I was again on the road, having slept like a dead man on a borrowed cot in a ragged tent. I had dreamt of my Father and Enfield Chase, but in my dream he had sometimes had the face of Prince William and even once the poacher I had released from capture. I had woken stiff muscled but refreshed, with a feeling of sweetness in my soul. Twas strange, I thought as I pulled on my boots, to have so pleasant an experience in the midst of war and squalor. I remembered another such waking on the morning after my meeting with the Queen and the Earl of Leicester. The pain of my injuries had been extreme, but my mind was light and buoyant as a cork bobbing on the surface of a pond.

So we rode, Beauty strong and surefooted, I knowing my direction and destination, and having carried out my orders in all respects. I was feeling perhaps too confident, too full of myself for my senses to be at their clearest, for I quite suddenly found my nose twitching with a dangerous odor.

Twas the smell of an army marching before me.

Sure enough, the road was littered with fresh horse droppings. Faint but clear, the scent of human sweat and horse lather, the whiff of campfires which permeates every soldiers uniform. Now refuse — a bloodied bandage, a rind of cheese, even human waste where men had squatted quickly at the roadside and returned to their ranks.

I halted Beauty, pulled out my map and saw from their direction of travel that these could not possibly be the reinforcements from Amsterdam. These were Spanish troops and they were on the road. The road to Gouda. I was still five hours ride from the fortress and my company. I did not know the enemys numbers, but I did know movement of any army across the Low Countries terrain was slow, with carts rumbling along at walking pace. There were many rivers, bogs and streams to ford. Tho the cavalry could move faster than the infantry, the whole of the body crawled along at the rate of its slowest component.

I reckoned the rearmost troops could not be far ahead, no more than two miles, and counted my options, which were only two. I could avoid the army, making a great detour round them in which case I would lose time in getting to my destination. And the land on either side of the road was boggy and would provide very poor footing for Beauty. Else I could proceed on this road riding directly thro their midst, pretending to be a Dutchman friendly to their cause. This posed many obvious dangers, but its advantage was the straightest and quickest route to my company, giving them the most warning of the army which approached — and would in deed trap them tween their ambush and the fortress of Gouda.

I chose the latter and spurred Beauty onward to my first encounter with the enemy. I would have to be both clever and lucky to succeed, but I knew this one failure would cost many English lives, perhaps the lives of my friends. I straightened in my saddle, glad that I was meeting this moment of destiny on horseback where I felt most confident.

With the sound of a moving body of men growing louder and clearer, the rearmost regiment of the Spanish army came into view. I was surprised at the neatness of the final formation — a small unit of cavalry and a regiment of foot soldiers. There were no stragglers or laggards, which spoke of their high discipline, something I had heard much about. They were known to endure extreme hunger, thirst and heat. They were a proud lot even unto death. Cautious in combat. Skillful in skirmishes. Agile in climbing walls. Their infantry was more well thought of than their cavalry, but their horses were incomparable — 'Sons of the Wind' they were called. These were the men who in the Netherlands had swept all before them, and had twice smashed the armies of William of Orange.

As I approached, and so as not to startle them, I called out in my most cheerful and, I hoped, most authentic Hollander accent. "Goeden Morgen!" I cried, nodded and smiled as I came abreast of the horse soldiers who none the less regarded me suspiciously. They apparently spoke no Dutch, and my pretense convinced them well enough to let me pass. They knew I must, of course, overtake their superiors who would, if they so chose, stop and interrogate me.

To my dismay this was a long column, five companies strong of four hundred men each — cavalry with fresh, strong horses, an infantry of pikemen, arquebusiers, and musketeers. There were sixteen large cannon, gun carriages and trunions used to elevate guns, carts hauling small loads of metal cannonballs. This last told me the army had been out besieging, and might well have depleted stores of artillery. I saw pieces of a pontoon bridge carried on the backs of mules which could easily be fitted together to cross a moat, and a large contingent of priests who walked silently, hands folded within the sleeves of their robes. I counted carefully and committed to memory what I saw, for my report must be accurate and full.

As I passed by the endless train I worried that they were in deed the troops normally garrisoned at Gouda. If so, how many of them remained inside the fortress to defend it? The number could be small. In that case the English siege might be going well and a sense of confidence engendered — a false confidence, my commanders never knowing what was stalking their backs. I cursed Lord Holcomb for endangering his troops in his naivete and poor intelligence, and kept riding, eyes straight ahead, occasionally turning with a broad grin and greeting to the Spaniards.

By the great feathered helmets and bright colored finery up ahead, I could see I approached the commanders of this regiment, tho I did never know if this was the murderous Alva himself, or another of his armies. My mind raced with my story which I was prepared to deliver, part in Dutch, part in halting Spanish, hoping to convince my interrogators that I was a Dutch merchant on my way home to Woerden, several miles closer than Gouda, and that I wished them well. I prayed their scouts had not yet reached Gouda to find the English attack in progress, which would make my claim of being an innocent a short lived joke, and my life as a spy similarly abbreviated.

But luck was with me. As I came abreast of the two commanders I found them involved in so heated an exchange that they did not remark me, and those men who did see me must have assumed I had been granted leave to pass from those behind them. Such was the ignorance and inefficiency of all great bodies of men, and I was overjoyed to use it thus to my advantage.

Before long I had passed the forwardmost troops, but I kept my pace leisurely till I was well out of sight. I even left enough distance so that the dust cloud I raised as I spurred my horse to a gallop would have settled, and therefore not make them suspect my true occupation. But finally I was riding at full speed, Beauty needing no urging to fly, my great and serious purpose flowing wordlessly from my body into hers. Farms, canals and windmills were a blur to my eye. A bridge out, we pounded thro a shallow stream, the cool water splashing up high as my head. I felt light and free and endlessly heroic on this savior's journey — and then it ended suddenly.

Beauty was undeniably favoring her right front leg. I halted her and examined the foot. She had thrown a shoe. Damn, damn myself! She had lost it, I suspected, in the stony stream bed some miles back. Twas my own arrogance and stupidity, my lack of careful preparation for the ride that had caused it. I should have checked her back in the Dutch camp, but I had been too eager to depart, too caught up in my glory and my sweet dreams . . . What a fool I was!

I walked Beauty slowly into the next village, thankfully but a mile off. When I arrived I found the blacksmith had just left for his midday meal and, his apprentice assured me, the man was never known to rush. I had no choice but to wait, all the time knowing the Spanish army approached. To pass the time I tried speaking with the apprentice lad, but he was very dim and anyway more interested in his noon day meat pie than in me. So, angry with myself still, I roamed the village.

Finally I saw the smith returning to his shop. He was by the look of him indeed a man who enjoyed his food, carrying it in a great wattle of fat at his neck, and a band of it round his middle. I rushed in behind him to see the apprentice fanning the fire with the bellows. He must have told his master of my plight, as the man was already taking a horseshoe down from a peg with a great set of pincers. We quickly struck our deal. He made measurement of Beautys hoof and set to work. As I watched him hammering the white hot shoe into its form I saw that despite his bodys soft borders, this was a mighty man with arms strong as the metal he worked.

I heard a child shouting and knew that the Spanish army approached. The smith was only half done with his job, holding the shoe to Beautys foot and finding the places for adjustment. He plunged the shoe back in the fire. The sounds of the troops clattering into the village grew very loud. I prayed they would not stop, but doubted my prayers would be answered. A moment later several Spanish cavalry soldiers entered, needing the blacksmiths services, and he gestured politely that he would help them, but they would have to wait.

They eyed me and I nodded to them. Then one spoke to me in Spanish. "We saw you on the road, did we not?"

I hesitated a moment, then replied in poor halting Spanish that

I supposed a common Dutchman might speak, that they had indeed passed me and that my horse had thrown a shoe. Then I looked at them helplessly with a comical grin as if to say I wished I could speak their language better. But the one soldier persisted.

"Where are you headed?" he asked.

Twas such a common query, I could not, even in that language, pretend incomprehension. "To Woerden," I replied.

"And what is it you do when you go to this town?" the other asked, his eyes narrowing. I sensed danger but now the blacksmith, oblivious to my discomfort, was pulling the cooled shoe from the tub of water and taking it outside to begin nailing it onto Beautys foot. I needed time. I kept grinning and pretended, using what passed for my Dutch, not to understand the question he asked in Spanish. I noticed the apprentice looking at me oddly, for I had probably blundered in his tongue. Was he a friend or a foe of the English? I could not tell, but he was looking round at the soldiers, at myself, and out the door of the shop to the fat smith just now finishing up his job.

"William Prince of Orange!" I blurted.

The two soldiers were suddenly upon me grabbing my arms roughly. The apprentice, entirely alarmed, flattened himself against the wall.

"What do you know of this villain?" they demanded.

I forced myself to reply calmly in my most halting and pathetic Spanish, complete with hand gestures, that in my travels I had come across his encampment. I wondered if they had need of its location for I, I said smiling shyly, was a good Catholic and wished to see that heretic thrown out of Holland for ever.

They pressed me to know where had I seen him and when.

"Not ten days ago . . ." said I, and they both groaned and dropped my arms in disgust. The whereabouts of the Prince of Orange and his rebel army ten days before was as useless as a two legged table, for he moved about so frequently and clandestinely. He could be anywhere by now.

Just then the smith burst largely thro his door announcing my horse was shod. I paid him, tho not so quickly as to arouse further suspicion and ambled out, smiling at the soldiers and wishing them "Buen dia."

Happily back on my horse, I rode out through the troops who had stopped for a midday meal and a watering of their horses at the town well. I tipped my hat in a friendly fashion and some nodded back, for by now I was a familiar figure to them. Once out of sight I rode hell bent for Gouda thanking God for my heretofore undiscovered talent for deception, and the thickheadedness of some men.

My unbroken ride on to Gouda was uneventful. But within several miles of the fortress I was able to hear the boom of guns large and small, and see a cloud of smoke hanging above it, announcing that in deed our attack had begun. Then I passed a single rider galloping in the opposite direction as if the Devil were at his heels — a Spanish soldier, or a scout. He would, I reckoned by his speed, be giving word to his commanders in less than an hour. With their progress quickened by the news, the Army of God could arrive by sundown.

The 'trecht' which led to the wood and behind it the fortress at Gouda, was a steeply raised roadway flanked by canals running straight and narrow between two great fields of tulips, one red, one white.

The scene that awaited me as I emerged from the wood before Gouda was not at all what I had expected — towering fortress walls rising above a neat encampment, trench masters overseeing the pioneers in feats of digging, rows of soldiers firing their arms, culverins and cannon manned by teams of artillerymen, engineers busily constructing war engines and siege ladders. All of that, from the sounds I heard, was most certainly somewhere before me, but none of it could I see, for a pall of smoke so thick as to be impenetrable enshrouded everything beyond arms length. Together with the stench of burnt powder and the patchy red glow of fire, it seemed a very Hell. The stinking haze seared the nostrils, stung the eyes and left me entirely confounded, without direction. I heard the continuous roar of small shot, the thunder of cannon, the occasional scream, and low moans of agony.

An explosion very near caused Beauty to rear with terror, so I dismounted and with soft words of calming led her step by careful step thro the thick smoke. Several times I came within a hairs breadth of crossing a line of fire, or tumbling into a trench manned by cursing soldiers. All the men I met peered back at me with red rimmed eyes, noses running black. I found my cavalry unit unemployed in their tents, seeking respite from this stinking Hell, then tied up Beauty with the other horses and asked directions to Holcombs tent. I was admitted to find my Captain arguing petulantly with the captains Billings and Medford.

"If we continue our bombardment thus, the breach shall be ripe

for attack in several hours time," declared Holcomb. "We now have intelligence of the location and strength of their flanking walls. Remember this is no ancient bastion twelve feet thick. It has been hastily thrown up by the Spanish and will fall with persistence. You must trust me, gentlemen. I have studied the mathematics of it, and my engineers are confident of our success."

"Sir," I said with an urgent tone which was entirely unheeded.

"A moment, private." Holcomb returned to the other two whose faces assured me they had abandoned their wariness of offending the high but utterly ignorant nobleman. "Tho the Spanish defenses flanking the breach walls are strong," Holcomb went on, "my men are most eager for action and I believe it is near time to attack."

"Captain Holcomb," reproved Medford, the older of the two other commanders, "have you forgotten that the reinforcements from Amsterdam have yet to arrive? This engagement was planned with their numbers combined with our own in mind. We are fewer in muster even than we represented to them, as we have suffered substantial casualties. We have no business pursuing the offensive with such small numbers."

"Sirs!" I intruded insistently. "You must give me leave to speak!"

All eyes finally found me. I took a deep breath and began my report — the Spanish armys imminent approach, their numbers, the state of their guns and ordnance, the hour of their estimated arrival. I watched the officers faces change as I spoke, Lord Holcombs from calm assurance of his well laid plans for an easy victory, deteriorating into rigid fear of a bloody rout. The two others seemed to calm as Holcomb froze, as if they were fishes kept too long from the water, finally released back into the sea. They began ignoring Holcomb almost at once. Billings turned to me.

"The Spanish scout you saw — how long before he reaches the vanguard of the approaching army?"

"He was flying, Captain. An hour at best."

The two true soldiers put their heads together. Holcomb, I could see, was trying to recover ground. "We can quickly move the long can —" His voice cracked embarrassingly. ". . . cannon from the offensive positions to the . . ."

"We can move nothing quickly, my lord," said Medford. "The ground is very soft and the guns very heavy. But we must begin moving men posthaste to positions flanking the road to the fort." Then Holcomb was dismissed as a child would be from the dinner table,

as the elder captain turned with urgent purpose to Billings. "See to it that the numbers of men continuing the bombardment are not so depleted that the enemy senses our weakness."

"Very good," replied Billings. "I'll send Renfrew out to check the ground there, and deploy the cavalry."

Holcomb suddenly noticed me listening to the proceedings and to his casual dismissal by the two more experienced soldiers.

"Get out!" he shrieked at me, his voice cracking again.

"Yes Sir!" I said, then added, "Would you first like news of the Prince of —"

"Out!"

I turned sharply to go. Then heard a steady voice behind me.

"Private . . ." I turned. Medford regarded me with a respectful eye. "Well done," he said. "You may rejoin your company."

"Thank you, Sir," said I and strode out into the inferno.

A stiff breeze had cleared the air enough to reveal a scene so devastating I wished suddenly for the return of the smokey haze. There in deed stood the fortress, rude outer wall of stone and wood well battered by our concentrated assault, from whose ramparts and hornworks emanated puffs of smoke and large explosions of fire directed back at the English. Our soldiers squatted in a network of hastily dug trenches firing their small guns. I saw one man, fatigued beyond knowing, firing mechanically, reloading and recocking, unperturbed by the body of his comrade, half his head blown away and slumped not three feet from him in the trench. I passed other soldiers who seemed to be hoping for safety behind their larger cannon which belched yellow fire and steel balls. Those manning the catapult with its complicated weights and counterweights were now loading its cup with a pile of sharp edged rocks and several dozen dead rats, those for the hopeful spread of disease within the walls of the fort.

I stopped short at a large hole in the ground with a man inside hauling from it bucket after bucket of wet dirt. This, I comprehended, was the opening of a tunnel to the base of the fortress thro which would be transported explosives to undermine its wall. I cringed to think of the men underground passing along those buckets of muddy earth, the danger of the tunnel collapsing and the horror of being buried alive. I thanked God I was a cavalryman.

"Southern!" I heard my name called in a friendly voice, looked round and saw Hirst resting his back up against the wall of the

trench ramming home his shot. Had he not signalled me I think I never would have recognized this bandaged and begrimed soldier. I jumped down and squatted at his side.

"You're hurt," said I, staring at the bloody rag wrapt round his left shoulder, "tho I see it is stopping you not at all."

"Aye, I believe I do be safer out here than in the infirmary tent. They cauterized the wound with hot oil and that was bad enough, I can tell you. But when the surgeon came at me with an ointment made of two whelps boiled alive, mixed with earthworms steeped in white wine, I said thank you very much and took my leave."

"Where is Partridge?"

"Down the line," replied Hirst. An explosion twenty yards from the lip of the trench propelled great clods of dirt onto us. "He was still alive an hour ago," he continued, brushing the dirt from his eyes. "We called out to each other and sang lines of a filthy ditty between blasts."

"We are in trouble, you know," I said. "A great company of Spanish troops are coming this way. We besiegers are about to be besieged."

"Trapped, are we?"

"Aye, but at least not ambushed. I saw the enemy on my way back in. Just made my report."

"How did our good Captain Holcomb like the news?"

"Very well indeed. He looked to have swallowed his tongue." I stood and vaulted out of the trench. "See you in the field then. Take care, Hirst."

"And you!" he called after me.

In the dark I could not see the English infantrymen who, in a single line, lay flattened against the steeply angled walls on both sides of the raised gravel roadway. Under cover of night they had each dug a small trench in which they could kneel, positioned to fire up at the army as it passed by, whilst trying not to slip back into the shallow canal. Billings and Medford had had very little to comfort them in their plan of attack, except that the Spanish believed themselves to be ambushing us entirely unawares. Our disadvantages were many. We were small in number, a great many of us were green in the ways of combat, and we were physically trapped between the Spanish stronghold and seasoned soldiers, a force perhaps twice our size.

Holcomb insisted that the reinforcements would appear in time to save us, and became paralyzed when the moment came to withdraw the bulk of his forces from the Gouda stronghold. The siege had been his grand design, and suddenly his dreams of glory had collapsed.

I and my fellow cavalrymen sat mounted and silent in the dark of the forest awaiting the order to charge. Billings and Medford had concluded that the Spaniards would, at first light or just before, preceded by the cavalry, do double time down the road and overcome, with their sheer force of numbers, any English guarding the forest entrance, then surge onto the field surrounding the fortress. If their spy was correct, they would assume, all of our guns would be directed to the fort, and they would easily overwhelm us.

Uncomfortable in their hip length armor, the men on either side of me fidgeted in their saddles, checked and rechecked their pistols, ammunition. Few spoke, even in whispers. I too found little to say, for I knew what lay abroad with the coming of the dawn. I prayed then for Billings and Medford, for their wisdom and strength, and for a miracle too, for the Spanish army was a fearsome force. I had seen it with my own eyes.

Inside my metal plate, heat and fear and longing rose from my shivering skin. I lay along the length of Beautys neck, my lips to her ear which flicked nervously. I whispered soft encouragement, stroked her, sniffed her scent for my own comfort.

A ripple down the line. They come, they come! Indeed the ground begins to rumble neath us. Thundering of Spanish cavalry hooves on the gravelly road. And the tromp of foot soldiers double time, the distant clank of their metal parts, closer and closer. The sun barely peeking over the eastern horizon. Pinkish grey light. A field of tulips revealing their scarlet heads.

We must wait. The men flattened against the angled road wall, too, have orders to wait. Wait till the trecht is filled from end to end with enemy troops to begin their assault. Everyone is still. All wait, hearts fluttering. The Spanish must believe their surprise complete so that our surprise may itself be complete.

I have never seen the sun rise so quickly, the sky go from pink to stark blue in the space of a breath. The tulip fields are entirely illuminated now. The one before me red, the one beyond the trecht bright white. The road has filled with men and horses. I see them coming. Beautiful Spanish horses thundering towards us.

Then it comes. Sound of the drum. The signal. And it begins.

All at once the men, each in his small trench along the road wall, stand and fire. I am reminded of the troops of Pharaoh driving their chariots onto the bed of the Red Sea, how Moses waited till the dry path was filled from end to end with the enemy before he lowered his staff and brought the great waters crashing down upon their heads. So many men and horses fall in that one blazing moment. Human shrieks and screams of horses shot from below at close range into soft underbellies. From a distance I see mens heads and chests explode. No one left standing on the trecht. A moment of triumph for the English — but short lived.

For now King Philips Army of God in its multitudes comes pouring from its source, rushing down the slopes on either side of the trecht, splashes thro the shallow canals and out into the tulip fields and with unimaginable precision and speed forms into Spanish Squares, one on either side. The inner square is a tight phalanx of five hundred pikemen, their tall spikes pointing heavenward, the outer border several men deep, armed with muskets and arquebuses, each corner fortified with more men still. The square moves like some terrifying geometrical monster.

Those of the square closest to the trecht exchange fire with our men backed up against the raised road. Tis the English who are slaughtered now, for our men are but a single line, and the Spanish are several deep. One line of the square aims, fires, then falls back allowing the next line to kneel and fire. I see tiny puffs of white smoke from hundreds of guns in rows like white tulips formed from thin air.

We cavalry are waiting still for the order to charge, our horses blowing and pawing the ground restlessly. Now we watch as the bulk of our infantry streams forth from the wood onto the field. From the road in the wood three gun carriages emerge — all that can fit on the narrow gravel pathway, for the fields are too soft for heavy cannon.

The English form squares too, in the fields of tulips, but they are smaller squares, fewer men. They form wedges, S's and D's taught in drills on easy ground in England. Protect the ensign bearer. All squares and wedges firing. Men falling. We are outnumbered two to one.

The sound comes for the cavalry to charge. A cold thrill shudders my tightly wound frame as suddenly horses all round me bolt from the greenwood into the scarlet field. I am unaware that I have spurred Beauty to action but she has none the less taken me, and we are running amongst them. We horsemen form, in four lines one behind the other, a great sweeping phalanx to harry the outer edge of the Spanish Square.

My thighs squeeze Beautys sides with all my might for I must sit tall, a tower of strength galloping full speed forward towards the mortal enemy. All of my life, all of my dreams have driven me towards this moment. And I am afire, fearless, entirely mindless whilst altogether conscious.

I am in the second of our four lines of cavalry. I slow to watch the first line approach for assault, discharge both pistols into the square. The man before me is knocked from his horse as if a great hand has dealt him a backhanded blow. His mount, confused, stops dead and is her self felled by enemy fire. That sight at close range — the horse dying so easily, even more than the man — is a lance to my belly. But wild blood now flows in my veins and no sight, neither pitiful nor infuriating, stays my course. Beauty and I charge ahead to take the position of the fallen rider. I have promised my self to never fire blindly in order to make a hasty retreat, so I halt for the space of a breath, silently thanking Beauty for her unearthly calm. Feel a pellet streak close by my ear. Steady. Find my target — a short Spaniard kneeling, aiming at me. I fire. He is knocked violently backwards and quickly replaced by another arquebusier who, kneeling, lowers his gun to aim. I fire again, wheel Beauty about and retreat to the rear line, never waiting to see the result of my second shot.

I lie low down on Beautys back whispering frantic assurances in her ear. I reload my pistols but never have time to remove to the front line, for now the enemy cavalry is upon us. A mounted Spaniard gallops at me, a madman, guns blazing. In the moment before I fire back, still lying low on Beautys neck, I see a side of the Spanish Square crumbling, the terrible pikemen released from their protective shield wall of artillery, spilling from the rupture onto the field. Two blasts from my guns. The Spaniard spins sideways and tumbles from his stallion which keeps coming, coming. So close I can reach out and touch him, but I do not. I force my mind from the fate of horses on the battlefield.

I see Captain Medford leading a wedge of infantrymen against the onrushing foot soldiers. I hastily reload. Catch from the corner of my eye the sight of a pikeman, weapon poised at myself, a perfect target on my high horse. He is running, shrieking an inhuman sound as he comes. I leap down from Beauty. Kneel below her belly. Fire. He falls. My horse bolts with the unexpected explosion under her. "Run for the trees!" I shout at her, but I know she can not hear.

For one blessed moment my body is not under immediate siege, tho all round me are pairs of men doing heinous battle, one with the other, hand to hand. The shroud of smoke has obscured the clear morning sky. Fallen men and fallen horses lie torn and gutted, bleeding their scarlet blood onto scarlet flowers. Most obscene butchery amidst Gods greatest beauty.

Another of the enemy rushes at me and I, this first day a soldier, find my self on foot, pistols useless, flung away. I raise my sword and as I charge the Spaniard I hear a loud bloodchilling cry — an animal cry — and only in the moment when metal clashes with bloody metal do I know the sound is in my own throat. Then I am lost entirely, have only vague memory of the melee, the anguished sounds of men dying, the numbers I have killed or maimed, how long I have danced that dreadful dance. I know only I am alive still when the fife sounds the retreat, hear that it comes not from the direction of the fortress but from the road away from Gouda. We are leaving the fort to its owners, and we attackers are fleeing. Roundly defeated, leaving our dead behind.

I am numb, can barely whistle for Beauty. I stumble round the field blinded by the thick smoke, tread with my boot upon the gutted body of an Englishman, his face strangely peaceful in death. I recoil. Then remember seeing Hirst die. He was kneeling, struggling to reload. A horseman racing up behind him, sword in hand. The blow. My friends blood spurting a terrible fountain.

I shout Beautys name unable to mask my growing desperation. Suddenly she appears through the grey mist. She is unhurt, entirely sound. I love that brave horse in that moment all that I ever loved my faithful Charger. Mount her and she gallops off, trampling with her hooves a path amidst the red Dutch tulips on the way to our shameful retreat.

Twenty-six

Even as a young soldier I knew that the close companion of victory was defeat, but I did never imagine how bitter losing could be when the cause was stupidity and the outcome unnecessary. In the Battle of the Tulips, as the soldiers came to call it, together with the losses of the siege, we lost almost three quarters of our force. A thousand men dead and three hundred horses. Medford and Billings both mortally wounded, dying on the road during the days of our ignoble retreat. Hirst was gone, tho Partridge had survived.

Our return to the city with our vastly diminished force, tails tween our legs, alarmed the Hollanders. One day soon after our return I saw a group of solemn and dignified burghers going to meet with Holcomb in his headquarters, no doubt to demand some intelligence of the engagement, wondering if England would be sending more troops to refortify the garrison. I saw the old men emerge even more grim than they had entered, and guessed Holcombs answer had not pleased them.

I wondered if my Captains corruption was so great that he would continue to receive dead pay on the thousand men he had lost in the Battle of the Tulips, or whether conscience would overtake him and he would confess the loss to his superiors. But it was not till we had been back in Haarlem a week that I understood the danger this mans shameful conduct posed to myself. With Billings and Medford dead, only one young private knew how great a folly was the siege of the fort at Gouda in the first place.

Holcomb shortly began sending me on every dangerous mission he could conceive. Spanish troops were in the countryside round Haarlem — I was sent out alone in full uniform to scout their positions. A deadly epidemic of dysentery broke out in the English garrison at Amsterdam — I was sent to deliver a shipment of homing pigeons to them and stay there, no good reason given, for a fortnight. An ancient tunnel was discovered under Haarlems south wall — I was to lead the team assigned to fill in the dangerously crumbling passage, so the Spanish could never make use of it in an attack. I somehow managed to avert death and confound Holcomb at every turn. Each time I returned from a deadly mission unscathed the Captain fumed more vehemently, and it became a joke within the ranks that I was unkillable.

Partridge meanwhile had profited from the defeat at Gouda. Tho he had lost his longtime friend Hirst, with the severe reduction of troop levels — encypherers amongst them — he put him self forward as an expert in that field and was taken at his word. Whilst I remained a mere private, he was raised to lieutenant and found himself working in the relative luxury of headquarters. What skills he did not possess when he began his assignment he quickly learnt on the job, and I found much to commend in him for sheer audacity and inventiveness.

Whenever I could I slipt away to visit the Hoogendorps, but all was not well in their family. Two of the sons fighting with the resistance had been killed, and Moeder's jolly laughter was silenced, the rosy cheeks now lustreless. Spanish ships off the coast were harrying the Dutch fishing boats and diminishing the catches.

Jacqueline, that fresh faced youngster, had in the space of a year become a woman. She alarmed her mother by the company she kept, tho twas not some man who her Mother feared might deflower her daughter. Twas a band of girls who fancied themselves soldiers, led by a strange widow woman and shipwright named Kanau Hasselaeer. To everyones dismay and not a little derision, they trained for battle in armor Hasselaeer had paid for herself — with guns, old fashioned bows and arrows, kitchen knives and sharpened broomhandles. Captain Holcomb especially condemned them as freaks of nature, and forbade them to continue. Unperturbed, they simply ignored him and became as defiant a band of warriors as any I had ever known.

Jacqueline spoke to me of her soldiering, and I found her much changed by it. She was hardened, no longer the flirtatious young girl I had first encountered on the day of the herring parade. Kanau, she told me, had herself been made a grieving mother by Alvas troops.

She inflamed her followers with stories of the Amazon women of ancient Scythia. Tho she did not suggest the Dutch girls should lop off their right breasts as the Amazons had — to make shooting arrows easier — she did demand obedience and a fierceness of spirit from her troops. Every one of them, said Jacqueline, would gladly die for their leader and the cause of Dutch Freedom.

And all too soon the call came. The Spaniards, led by Alvas son Don Frederick, marched that winter up from the south to attack the city of Haarlem. It began with a bombardment which went on for days, spewing death and destruction far into the city. One cannonball flew as far as the centre of the town, lodging in the wall of the Great Church, but the ancient city bastion held firm against the assault. The townspeople — tho all together with the English garrison could count no more than four thousand armed defenders — did rally together for the defence. They took to the battlements, fired torrents of bullets, threw rocks, poured vats of boiling pitch and oil onto the Spanish invaders. After several more days both sides resigned themselves to the inevitability of a long siege. Twas in that time, six months in all, that I learnt the true valor and mettle of the Dutch.

After weeks of fighting we were much cheered by the sight of countryfolk who appeared thro the mists, gliding on the ice covered canals in sledges, delivering food and ammunition to their city brethren. But Prince Williams first battalion of three thousand soldiers, sent to rout the Spanish besiegers, were themselves demolished by Don Fredericks superior numbers. Those who were not killed outright were taken prisoner and hanged en masse in front of the city gate for all to see. But the people would not despair. William began sending messages by carrier pigeons, promising further troops, but even more important a message of hope and courage, that our fight was just and that all of Holland was rallying to our aid.

Weeks, then months passed in waiting for that help, and food and firewood ran short. Partridge reported to me that a dispirited Lord Holcomb had retreated into seclusion, leaving the business of the English defence of Haarlem to several of his officers. He himself spent the days composing long letters to the Privy Council begging for withdrawal of his troops from the Netherlands. Partridge was charged with encyphering the letters. But the only means to get them out of the city were the homing pigeons — and these when thrown into the air were promptly shot dead by Spanish marksmen who knew that any other kind of bird in the entire city had already been eaten by the hungry citizens.

Prince William kept his word, sending more troops to fight the besiegers, but we in the city were forced to watch helplessly from the walls whilst the tiny Dutch force was decimated. Soon after the battle had begun, the Spanish catapults sent flying into the city a gruesome cargo — severed heads, arms and legs, halves of torsos, male sexual organs of the defeated resistance fighters. This horror at first did much to dishearten the Haarlem townsfolk who wept openly for their countrymen lost in the defence of their own city. But as the people came together to gather that terrible harvest, and dug the impossibly frozen ground to bury the dead decently, I saw come over their faces so fierce a hatred and as grim a determination to punish those who punished them, that I was not surprised when another delegation of burghers went marching into the English garrison — their purpose to propose bolder measures than had yet been attempted.

As the missions were dangerous I, of course, was called upon by Captain Holcomb to lead or participate in several of them. But now in the defence of Haarlem I gladly went. One moonless night a band of English, Dutch and a dozen well trained horses snuck out the city gate, and with the most extreme stealth and much stumbling about — for even a small candle would have given us away — we planted mines round the tents on the perimeter of the Spanish encampment, set our fuses and crept away. When the explosion came, flames and chaos enveloping the camp, we quickly hooked our horses to six gun carriages and dragged back in thro the gate six good sized cannon, without a single casualty amongst us.

There was so much rejoicing at our conquest, small tho it was — for we had no proper ordnance for the cannon — that men, women and children danced in the streets and sang songs of victory. They screamed the name of William of Orange and carried the attackers on their shoulders to the city square. Some climbed the walls and shouted down at the Spaniards that they were pigs, and hurled garbage into the burning camp with catapults borrowed from the English garrison.

On the heels of that victory came another, again small but one which gave the Haarlemers more hope still. A group of perhaps a dozen of the youngest and "prettiest" of the men — I was chosen from the garrison, and Dirk Hoogendorp from the town — were tarted up as painted whores, complete with falls of hair cut from the heads of city matrons. The girls who shaved us and dressed us did so with the greatest of hilarity, pulling the corset strings tight so, they claimed, we should know the pains they suffered just to put on their clothes in the morning. We were perfumed, our lips and cheeks rouged, bonnets tied under our chins with pretty bows, and then in full daylight, accompanied by only one real woman — twas one of Kanau Hasselaeers girls — we opened the gate and sauntered out in sight of the Spanish army.

The girl, Margriet, called out in her most alluring voice that we were starving prostitutes and were sick of the siege. As we were Netherlanders, she continued, we were good business people and would not mind taking money from Spanish customers, as men in the city could no longer afford our services anyway. Then we sat down on a low wall and waited. Three soldiers approached, but warily, until Margriet moved to the fore, puckered her lips and scooped her pretty white breasts right out of her bodice! The men fairly ran the rest of the way into our circle — and were dead, stabbed a dozen times each, a moment later. All in a piece we turned our backs to the Spanish camp who we had no doubt were watching, hiked up our petticoats, bent over and jiggled our hairy balls and arses at the enemy. Then we hied back in thro the gate, carrying the dead soldiers with us. Later the burghers of Haarlem chopped off their offensive heads, and the townsfolk gleefully catapulted them over the wall into Don Fredericks camp.

But our victories were short lived. Supplies of food from the country had dwindled and we in the city had well and truly begun to starve. All stores of dried herring and flour were gone. People had begun eating the spring grasses and flowers, and even killing dogs and cats for meat. The once prosperous folk of the jewel of Holland had gaunt faces and too bright eyes bulging from dark sockets. Clothes hung on skinny frames. Tempers flared, and people whose children were nearly dead of hunger began to argue about surrendering to the Spanish.

I went to see the Hoogendorps but I did not at first recognize the person who opened the door. I thought I had perhaps gone to the wrong house, as they all looked the same. But indeed it was Moeder. Gone was the plump maternal woman who had plied me, her family and herself with mountains of dumplings and fishes and cakes. There stood a bag of bones with great folds of skin hanging like obscene flesh draperies from face and neck and arms. Her clothing she had not bothered to tailor to her new shape, and that too hung limp on her sad frame. She smiled a brief but sincere smile on seeing me and invited me in, but I could tell she was ashamed, unable as she was to provide her former hospitality. I tried to make light of it, launching into a story of how I had left the garrison bearing her a box of succulent mice to make into a stew, but before I could finish the tale she began to cry — great, round tears which coursed down her hollow-cheeked face. Through her sobs she admitted that she had actually stooped to catching rats and mice, and cooking them. All the housewives were doing the same, and now there was not a rodent to be found in all the city.

In the height of summer a carrier pigeon from Prince William made it through to Haarlem, its message that a huge force of Dutch soldiers was coming to liberate the city. Weak tho we were we allowed ourselves to hope, and soon we heard the booming of cannon from what seemed like all directions. I ran through the deserted boulevards to the Great Church and breathless — my own strength at low ebb from starvation — climbed the steeple stair. From that high vantage point looking east, I could see the vessels of the notorious Sea Beggars doing battle with Spanish galleons on Haarlem Lake. Turning south I saw the armed encampment outside the city walls now thrown into disarray by William's infantry and cavalry. I stared in disbelief, for there looked to be as many as five thousand Dutchmen! Twas a great battle, and as I gazed out over that field of action, I wished fervently to be fighting the enemy as a true soldier and not as I was — a trapped, helpless and starving animal in a walled prison. In that moment I knew, too, I longed to be fighting at the side of the good Prince of Orange, having more allegiance to him than even the Queen of England.

Then I watched with growing alarm as the battle on land and sea turned in favor of the Spanish, and hope died. As I descended the tower I saw congregated a crowd of city folk, quiet and still, awaiting my report. At first sight of me a great moan went up, for I was unable to hide from their eyes the truth of our terrible defeat. Later that day we heard loud pounding and crying at the city gate. Guards opened it to find Williams most senior officer, alive and walking, but with nose and both ears slashed from his head, come to bring evil tiding from Don Frederick.

Now naught was left but desperate measures. Every citizen

turned out to watch by torchlight as Kanau Hasselaeer and her army of three hundred women said their goodbyes to family and friends. I saw Moeder Hoogendorp gripping Jacqueline to her skeletal self with such tender ferocity I could not stanch my own tears. We all watched as those brave Dutchwomen marched out to do battle under a full moon with the Spanish fiends. We did never expect a one to return alive, but many times that terrible night as we stood on the city wall staring out at the Spanish camp, it was whispered in hushed and reverent tones that there were fewer screams of pain and dying than on a similar field of warring men. And we did never mention what fate we knew awaited those not killed but captured.

By the morning light, the unequalled courage of those women had fomented such a common mind of general rebellion that it was decided by citizens, one and all, that they would form a great legion — very compact, with women and children in the centre, armed men surrounding them. This mass of humanity would rush out the gate all at once, trying to force their way thro the enemy camp. Lord Holcomb, in all his foolish puffery, forbade them to go. No one, of course, listened.

But then, from Spanish camp a message arrived tied to a scrawny dog — for they knew with all that had taken place, any Spaniard come knocking at the gate would be instantly and horribly dispatched. Twas a full pardon for the inhabitants of Haarlem from Don Frederick, and it would be honored if the town surrendered without delay. Lord Holcomb spoke up quickly and passionately. This, he cried, fairly tearing at his shirt, was the citys only hope of saving itself. Haarlem must be given over to the Spanish. The survivors would at least have their lives, if not their freedom. Some muttered that Don Frederick could not be trusted, that he would betray them in the end, but everyone was already half dead with starvation and disease. After a final meeting and a prayer together, twas resolved to surrender. The council adjured the townsfolk to go to their houses, saying that by morning supplies would be coming into the city, and the horror of these six months past would be ended.

But when the gates were swung open and the vanquishing army marched thro, twas not with food that their arms were loaded, but muskets and unsheathed swords. They rained down upon the good citizens of Haarlem who had trusted them, the most horrible punishment and death. They swarmed the residential streets and smashed down doors, dragging people from their homes. The first thousand men, women and children they found they beheaded. Two hundred others they tied together in pairs and threw into Haarlem Lake and drowned.

A subsequent attack on the garrison had every Englishman fighting for his life. I and twenty soldiers defended the armory in a blazing firefight. Men were felled all round me. I too would have died there, had it not been for Dirk Hoogendorp who had made his way thro back alleys to find me. His eyes were wild. Moeder was dead, his Father battling somewhere a losing battle. But he and his friends knew a way out of the city thro the sewers. They intended to escape and find their way to the Dutch army of resistance and fight with William of Orange to the death or to freedom. Did I wish to join them? My answer was a resounding "Ja!" I said I wished only to find my friend Partridge, if he were still alive, and bring him with us.

Making from the armory to headquarters, we dodged a hail of bullets and defied death by a hairs breadth again and again. We climbed in thro the back window. The Spaniards had already come and gone, leaving a scene of carnage. Piles of English corpses, thick gore under our boots. Twas still and quiet as only death can be. I scanned the place, but Dirk was tugging at my arm.

"Arthur, come! Your friend is dead. We have no time, we must go now."

"Arthur?"

Twas barely audible, literally a voice from the dead. Dirk and I fell on the gruesome pile, digging like madmen, Partridges muffled calls leading us to him. We pulled three bodies off his. He was covered head to foot in blood. Suddenly he sat bolt upright, altogether intact.

"Ughh!" he cried. "The blood is not mine. I played dead. Come, get me up!"

We did, and started out the back window. Suddenly Partridge grabbed my arm and I turned to see his face, the whites of his eyes clear and yet perplexed amidst the clotted red features.

"You came back for me," he said.

"As you would have done for me," said I.

"Quickly, if you are coming!" cried Dirk, already half out the window.

We followed, and with that I began the second phase of my life as a soldier.

Twenty-seven

Elizabeth had meant to surprise Robin as he took the waters at Buxton Spa, and to her delight she had succeeded. In the midst of her summer progress in Derbyshire she had found herself missing the company of her favorite, who had been sent by his physicians to bathe and drink the healing waters of St. Ann's Spring. Ensconced with her Court not far from that place, this morning she had set her household atwitter, suddenly ordering the smallest of retinues to accompany her on a journey — two ladies, her dwarf fool Mrs. Tomison, and four royal guards. She had ridden out with little pomp on her new chestnut gelding, arriving in Buxton in the late afternoon, and now gazed out over the buildings Lord Shrewsbury had cleverly erected round the spring. There was the bath house itself, all of warm pink marble, after the Roman style with columns and walkways and hanging gardens, and a row of houses that Shrewsbury rented to lodgers come for the bathing. One of these had been hastily vacated for the Queen, and now she was allowing her women to slowly unbutton and uncorset her.

Mrs. Tomison, more elegant and well spoken than a lady three feet tall had a right to be, sat on a pillow at Elizabeth's feet. She was certainly improved by the gowns she wore, the Queen's castoffs cut down to fit her diminutive proportions, but she had also managed her own education, so that her conversation was at once erudite and bitingly witty. "A droll troll" is what she would call herself. Elizabeth had, after reading in her mother's diary of Anne's beloved fool Niniane, sought out a woman jester for her own pleasure. She felt she could keep one of her own sex nearer her more of the time, and as the years wore on the Queen found a bawdy tale or a raucous laugh an ever more frequent necessity.

Her women helped Elizabeth into a red brocaded robe lined with many layers of fine lawn, and she made her way alone down the marble walkway to the columned building. All other bathers had very quietly been summoned from the pool and, when they emerged, been told that the Queen had recently arrived and wished for privacy. Lord Leicester was therefore, when she entered, the solitary bather in the mist-filled bath house, sitting neck deep and eyes closed in the tiled pool, his loose lawn shirt floating bubblelike about him.

Making no sound above the lapping water and hissing air, Elizabeth removed her bath robe and, clad only in a thin sleeveless shift, slipped into the warm water. She glided slowly across the pool toward Robin, challenging herself to keep such silence and stealth that she would be face to face with him before he could open his eyes. The feel of the water on her skin was delicious, with fine bubbles which tickled her throat and the soft underpart of her arms. The sensual delight was almost unbearable. A gleam of vapor coalesced on Elizabeth's face, which had been cleansed by her ladies of all cosmetics. She felt young again and perfect.

Robin's face became clearer as she floated closer. He was beginning to show his age, but he was still beautiful, she thought. Red-brown hair and beard were streaked with grey, the wide-set eyes radiated fine wrinkles from each side, and the slightly arched nose was a bit sharper than in youth. Still, there was no man she desired more, who knew better how to please her, soothe her fears, make her smile. No one was more devoted and tender. And no one, she thought with a shiver of excitement, was as dangerous. There lurked an animal beneath the fair skin, a ravening beast of ambition, and she knew she could never take her eyes off him for long — never *completely* trust him. In some perverse way this made her love him more.

Elizabeth was pleased. Robin's eyes were shut, he still unaware of her presence. She made her movements so subtle that he never stirred, and for a moment she wondered if he were dozing. Now she was inches from him, crouched between his parted knees, so close she could feel his slow breath on her face. He licked his lips. He was not asleep.

"Lord Leicester," she whispered in her softest and most comfortable voice. So comfortable indeed that he did not even open his eyes.

"I am not ready to come out. I have only just come in. Leave me be."

"I cannot leave you be," she said, almost crooning. "I have never been able to leave you be."

His eyes fluttered open. Though there was no perceptible start in his body, she felt his whole person, his very soul, illuminated suddenly with the sight of her. He did not smile but fixed her with a familiar, penetrating gaze. She wondered if he would reach out for her, pull her the last few inches toward him. But he did not. And she was not surprised.

According to her wishes, Elizabeth and Leicester were no longer lovers in the most intimate sense, had not been for more than a year. She was too proud to share him in that way with another woman. With Douglas Sheffield.

Something changed in his eyes. "Why are you here, Elizabeth? You're not ill." He said this more as a command than a question.

"No, not ill. My cheek is still slightly sore to the touch with neuralgia, but the ulcer on my shin has healed. No, I have come asking after yourself, my lord. I understand the malaria has gripped you again, and it worries me." She put her hand to his face. "You do look feverish."

Now he smiled slowly and, with an amused look, took her hand to his lips and kissed it. "'Tis no wonder, Elizabeth. This is a hot pool. Believe me, I am already much improved after two days here. But if you are come offering to nurse me, I shall gladly become ill again."

The intimacy of his words made Elizabeth suddenly uneasy. She pushed her back against the water, then turned and sat side by side with him on the tile ledge so she would not have to meet his eye.

"How does your son?" she asked evenly. It took all of her strength and composure to speak to him on this most sensitive of all topics.

"Well. I've taken him from his mother to be brought up in my uncle's house."

His son with another woman, thought Elizabeth bitterly. Their beautiful son, lying dead between them.

They shared this painful image in silence as Leicester sought words to soothe her aching heart.

"Lady Sheffield still presses me for marriage" — his tone foretold his next words — "but I continue to explain that I cannot. Can never marry her."

Elizabeth could not suppress a wry smile. "My lovely cousin Douglas. Is she very angry?"

"You should not gloat, Elizabeth. It ill becomes a Queen. If I were less a gentleman, I would harry you about Christopher Hatton. He seems to please you a little too well these days, on *and* off the dance floor."

"'Tis not my young Mutton who should be troubling you, my lord . . . ," teased Elizabeth.

"And who should, Your Majesty?"

"I have had recent correspondence from de Médicis. She has asked if I could fantasy a marriage with her youngest son, the Duc d'Alençon."

Dudley laughed aloud. "Alençon! I think he would please you not at all, Elizabeth. He is twenty years your junior, barely a man. He's puny and pitted with the pox and wears a large swollen nose on his face. 'Ugly' is the word that's commonly used to describe him."

"A marriage with him would solidify the Treaty of Blois," she insisted.

"You know very well France will keep that treaty without any marriage. You just pretend to consider Alençon to annoy me."

Now it was Elizabeth's turn to laugh. The sound echoed over the water and through the steam-shrouded bath house. Leicester was right, of course, though he and all the world should never know it. She alone knew that she would never marry the French prince. Still, in the coming years she must pretend to take this proposal seriously. Very seriously indeed. The matter was not yet clear in Elizabeth's mind, but the alliance with France — even if it were an illusion only — would prove to be of some great import in the political maneuverings with Spain, and the Netherlands war. But she did not wish to think of that now, the ghastly stories of mayhem and slaughter leaking from Flanders like an unstanchable wound. Nor did she wish to contemplate her Scottish cousin Mary, still locked away in the north of England, and her endless plots to steal Elizabeth's throne. No, she was here for her Robin, to soothe him, prove that their love and friendship still flourished despite that one intimacy lost. She would speak of cheerful matters.

"One of your Oxford boys was in Greenwich before I left, taking advantage of your lodgings at Court. With or without you there, it has become a great place of meeting for men of letters, poets, students, players. Philip Sidney's literary circle, too. They all speak of you with such fondness — the Great Patron. There is talk that you take your chancellorship at Oxford overseriously, but they forgive you that as well."

He was amused. "I've decided that receiving the love of artists and thinkers is sufficient balm for the hatred of politicians and princes, which I continue to incessantly attract." He smiled. "Lady Shrewsbury showed me the letter you wrote her about my prudent diet that you wish me to follow. No more than two ounces of meat, and the twentieth part of a pint of wine at dinner?"

Elizabeth chuckled. "And as much of St. Ann's sacred water as you wish to drink."

"But on festival days," he said, quoting the letter, "I might have the shoulder of a wren, and for supper a leg of the same."

"That is *besides* your ordinary ounces, my love."

"Oh, thank you, Your Majesty."

"This is for your own good, Robin, and mine too. When we stand together we should not want others to whisper behind our backs, 'Ah, there they go, Fat and Skinny.' We should become a laughingstock."

"Ah . . ." Leicester suddenly leaned his head back and closed his eyes. His forehead wrinkled in pain.

Elizabeth grew alarmed. "Robin, love. You did not eat before you came to bathe?"

"I am fine, Elizabeth," he said weakly.

She placed a hand on his forehead. "You're burning, Robin!"

She called out and two female attendants hurried in at once.

"Take Lord Leicester to his house and call my physician."

The attendants began pulling him, weak-kneed, out of the pool.

"Gentle with him!" she commanded, her panic rising. "I'll join you presently."

She watched as they bundled him into his robe and helped him away. Left alone, she allowed herself only a moment to consider the world without this man. Then she rose from the water and, unattended, pulled on her own robe.

She would let nothing in the world happen to her Robin, she vowed silently. Nothing. Nothing.

Twenty-eight

More than four years had I been a soldier when one summers night, a bright starstrewn sky our only cover, I lay naked in the softness of the dunes with Marje Bleiden cupped within the warm crescent of my body. We had been lovers for many months, and I had happily learnt under her expert tutelage the sweet dark secrets of female flesh. My sister Alice would have been proud, I thought as I grazed Marjes nipple with the lightest touch of my outstretched fingers, causing her to push her curved buttocks back against me. For I had finally become accomplished in the art of pleasing a woman several times over before I myself experienced release.

I nuzzled her neck with my face more playfully than passionately. We were both entirely satiated, but wished the closeness to continue a few moments more. She turned on her back then, and I propped my self on one elbow. Her full breasts spread pendulous at her sides. Marje was no longer a young woman, and even in the moonlight I could see the deepening lines of her careworn tho still pretty face.

"Why do we fight?" she asked suddenly. "Tell me the reason men are constantly at war."

I had never known the woman to be self pitying, but she was deeply saddened by the hand the Fates had dealt to her and the man with whom she was in love. She was not my woman, you see, but the long time companion of an officer of Prince Williams army — a general named Roost. Most of this brave soldiers male parts had been blown away in battle, and he had no longer been able to properly please her. Whilst she was not his wife, merely a camp follower and nurse, they had grown too fond of one another to part after his injury. He insisted, however, she find satisfaction elsewhere. In this she had complied, but she vowed to remain his woman in heart and spirit until one or the other of them died. All of our fellow soldiers knew that I was the one she bedded with, even Roost, and I wondered at his courage, and the courtesy which he ever extended to my self. I decided to oblige Marje by answering her question if it might soothe her mind.

"There are soldiers who fight for money. You yourself know how full most armies are of mercenaries. Tis never a fine living, but a better one than many can find in their home parishes. I know that some come to the military believing they will find advancement in their station. Perhaps here in Holland a mans efforts on the battlefield are rewarded, but in England tis only a dream. Nobility rules above all," I said, unable to keep the bitterness from my voice. I had never forgotten the waste of mens lives — at the whim of highborn Lord Holcomb.

Marje was still restless, her eyes seeming to search the heavens for answers.

"I have fought with men who simply like to kill. They are few and far between, those men," I said, wishing I believed my own words. I had meant to soothe Marje, but this subject excited an unhealthy passion in her. So I continued. "There are men like myself who enter the military service seeking a manly life. A life of excitement and adventure." I laughed ruefully. "I have certainly had my fill of both."

Now she turned to me, propping herself likewise on an elbow. She ran her hand over my face and I saw such kindness and caring in her eyes. "Why then do you stay? This is not your war, sweet boy."

I thought for a long time before I answered, remembering the siege of Haarlem, the friends I had lost there. Soon after my escape and my coming to Williams army, the Spanish troops had turned mutinous for lack of pay, and in a frenzy the likes of which had never been seen before — even on the Eve of St. Bartholomew — had set a course of pillage, rape and slaughter in Europes most fabulous city, Antwerp. At least the infamous butchery in Paris had been driven by a cause held meaningful by its butchers — purging the city of Protestant heretics. But in Antwerp, what was now called the Spanish Fury had been a most senseless mayhem. No political or religious pretext had been invoked, for the city itself was in the south, and therefore loyal to Philip.

The soldiers had come intent on finding payment — if not from the king's bankrupt treasury, then from the towns richest merchants. And certainly there was enough wealth for the taking to satisfy every marauder who had come. But something unholy had happened as the intruders passed thro the city gates. Some kind of madness descended upon them, and their intent to simply plunder turned to wanton, mindless destruction. They set fire to magnificent homes whose possessions they might have stolen. They threw priceless tapestries into canals, smashed bottles of costly wine, trampled gem encrusted jewelry underfoot. Houses were ransacked and furniture smashed into useless piles of rubble. But in those three days of rage much, much worse was the cost in human lives.

The tales shocked even the most hardened of veterans. Men hacked into tiny pieces. Women — young girls and grandmothers alike — ravished by gangs of drunken soldiers. Homes broke into, children tortured in front of parents eyes. Twas said the marauders had found in one home a wedding in progress. The groom was stabbed a hundred times, the brides gown and underclothes stripped from her body before she was thrown naked into the street. All the guests were locked in the cellar as the soldiers partook of the wedding feast, and when they were gorged and wild with wine, the familys most precious belongings in hand, the intruders had departed, setting fire to the house and burning to death all those who remained trapped in its cellar. All told, eight thousand citizens — Catholic and Protestant alike — had died in three days time.

For all its horror the Spanish Fury had birthed one shared sentiment in the hearts and minds of all Netherlanders — north or south, previously loyal to Philip or not. They had finally come to see his army in their land as farmers would view a plague of locusts. All seventeen provinces had united, and in the city of Ghent an agreement to expel the Spaniards from their land had been signed. The right to choose ones own religion had been promised, and William of Orange had known some joy that all his countrymen now stood behind him as their leader.

"I myself continue to fight," I said to Marje finally, almost shyly, "for the last of all the reasons. To be the kind of soldier I have

met only in Prince Williams army. The man who is fighting for freedom."

Marje looked away then, for she could not meet my eyes, so filled were they with the truth and the pain of my words. Twas the reason Roost fought, why all her countrymen fought despite the great and terrible punishment King Philip continued to rain down on them year after bloody year.

The war fought in Holland by the Dutch had made a man of me. No base or mercenary instincts moved these soldiers hearts as they did the English, German or Swiss. Twas a long hard fight on poor ground for fighting. There were skirmishes amidst the bogs, dikes and flood marshes covered in thick grey fog, air so moist our guns refused to fire. We were a poor army and so became, of necessity, an army of ingenuity — mobile, swift of movement and masters of surprise. We found every way to harass our enemy. We struck when they were on the march or fell into disorganization — perhaps whilst they crossed a river. We cut Spanish lines of communication, stole into their camps at night and drove iron spikes into the touch holes of their guns, so the powder could not be ignited. We cut bridges, sowed the roads with sharp thorns, and poisoned enemy wells. To gain advantage our infantry might wade many miles thro water lapping their armpits, knowing full well a high tide could drown us. The city garrisons, now manned by well trained and fervent burgher guards, repulsed even the most vicious of sieges. But only "Mad Margaret," a cannon eighteen foot long with a bore of thirty three inches, struck real fear into the hearts of the Spanish army.

For myself, I rode with the Dutch cavalry, men of such courage and soldierly grace that I felt I had found another family. Tho she still held back the real aid we needed, my Queen had sent to us a thousand English horses, and from that number I found many fine animals. Several died under me and I mourned their brave and beautiful souls, every one.

But Holland was no suitable place for cavalry maneuvers and we struggled valiantly for small reward. Once outside of Brill, our infantry locked in bloody battle with an enemy regiment on the dunes, we sallied forth to attack a long line of Spanish cavalry disposed along the coastal road. Hooves flying, pistols blazing we shattered thro their line at two points, throwing them into utter disarray. We drove them off and when their battered remnants fled, we charged across the dunes with high and terrible cries, coming to aid our embattled comrades on foot. That ambush routed the Spanish infantry and cut them off from all retreat.

Victory was ours that day and sweet, tho these moments were few. But we fought on, for our leader Prince William was a faithful beacon to the cause. He believed that God would not forsake us, even if all our Protestant neighbors did, and his words became our anthem — "Tho we be utterly destroyed, it will cost the Spanish half of Spain in money and men before they have made an end to us!"

Marje seemed finally to have calmed. She began dressing, and I watched her as I put on my worn breeches and shirt. I had perhaps grown too fond of this woman who was not mine to love, tho if I were altogether honest I would admit she stirred no longing in my soul. Now it was I who grew pensive, musing upon the illusive dream of romantic love. I had rarely seen it expressed, tho it was reputed that the Queen and the Earl of Leicester shared a great and longstanding passion. Prince William and his wife Charlotte, too, were said to have married for love. Did a woman live, I wondered, who would burn my soul and imagination as fiercely as she did my loins? She must. As I had once looked out over the waves at Milford Haven and seen my future abroad, I now felt sure such a woman must exist.

As Marje and I, arms entwined companionably, tramped back across the dunes to the flickering lights of camp, I threw my head back, gazing at the heavens and knew with a sudden surge of joy that those stars which ruled my fate this night, shined down upon my true love, wherever in the world she lived and breathed. Perhaps, I thought with a smile, she is right now staring up at the same stars dreaming of me.

Twenty-nine

It seemed to King Philip, as he made the day's fifth solitary journey from chapel to Council Chamber, that he was little more than a mass of aches and pains and creaking joints. He was aging very badly. When he'd been a younger man his black clothing had contrasted handsomely with his fair hair and blue eyes. Now the hair was turning a dull grey, and the skin of his face had a sickly pallor that almost matched it. Because of the stern black he now wore exclusively, he seemed as he moved through the palace courtyard more a dark shadow than a man.

A sudden catch under his right lower rib was the unpleasant signal that another gall bladder attack was imminent. His physicians would no doubt begin pestering him about his diet. "Your piles," they would exclaim like a bunch of dithering women, "will never improve eating all that meat, Your Majesty!" Damn the doctors, Philip thought with irritation, if I wish to eat meat and meat alone, meat is what I shall have. The King of Spain had partaken of neither bread nor fruit nor vegetable for many years and, he concluded with finality, he had no intention of beginning now. Besides, his gall bladder and his asthma, even the occasional bout of malaria, were nothing compared to the troubles now doing battle inside his skull.

Philip paused briefly to stare into a cage along the cloister walk which housed some long-limbed monkeys from the New World — his Great Empire, which had expanded to encompass more than fifty million subjects. The strangely human beasts behind the bars were squabbling over some food, poking and grabbing with those spindly arms, baring their teeth, howling and posturing ferociously. Finally the largest of the monkeys wrested the coveted morsel from the others and retreated to a far corner of the cage to consume it greedily. Philip felt uneasiness overtake him and he turned away quickly, telling himself it was the mess and filth of the cage that repulsed him. Perhaps the royal zoo he'd had built for the children had been a bad idea. His fourth wife, Anne of Austria, had persuaded him that the girls and young Prince Philip would enjoy the caged oddities. Now he could see that such animals so close in their midst might cause disease. He must write an order to have them removed.

When he arrived at the Council Chamber three members of the foreign policy *junta* were already waiting. This committee was more casual than his fourteen formal councils, with their endless reams of *consultas* which Philip annotated in his spindly scrawl before sending them back. These assembled councillors, with bearings and countenances as grave as their king's, all bowed stiffly as he took his chair behind the table and gave them leave to sit. Each face, observed Philip, looked more grim than the one before. Philip much preferred reading the *consultas* his committees sent him, and writing his replies to them, to these face-to-face meetings in which he was required to listen and speak and, worse, make hasty decisions. Philip sensed that today's *junta* would prove particularly detestable. Well, he had best begin it so it should be finished the more quickly.

"Give me news of the Netherlands," he commanded, then sighed morosely.

"Your Majesty," began his most trusted councillor, Ruy Gómez, "the uniting of the seventeen provinces has proven most troublesome. Its treaty, which the people call" — Gómez sneered — "the Pacification of Ghent, aligns even those previously Catholic Estates which had been loyal to you, in a concerted effort to entirely oust the Spanish presence from the Low Countries."

"What, in your estimation," asked Philip of Antonio Pérez, "has caused so violent and sudden a reaction?"

"Your Majesty . . ." Pérez paused, unsure how to phrase his answer. He did not wish to speak to the King as a teacher to a child. "We all agree that the massacre at Antwerp is its primary cause. Catholics and Protestants alike were slaughtered indiscriminately."

"But did the citizens not understand these were not soldiers under the command of a Spanish general, but mutineers? That there were as many Germans in their ranks as Spaniards?"

Philip's finance minister Iñigo Ibéñez was similarly tongue-tied as he tried to explain to his king that a person watching his wife torn apart by a mob of Philip's soldiers might be unable to make such distinctions.

"I have recalled the Duke of Alva from his duties in the Low Countries. Was that not enough to satisfy the Dutch?" The King's voice was growing shrill. It irritated him to know that Alva's presence had had the opposite effect on the rebellion than that for which Philip had sent him in the first place. "His successor General Requeséns," the King went on, "was far more reasonable in his campaign to suppress the revolt, and my half brother Don Juan, God rest his soul, was in his short tenure positively lenient. I allowed him to offer pardon to all those who had taken up arms against me. I promised to cease the war, restore taxing power to the Estates . . ."

"You refused them pardon of the one thing they wished for above all, Your Majesty. Heresy," said Cardinal Granvelle.

"And the Prince of Orange, though he continues to refuse the Netherlands crown, has become . . . you might call him a national hero," said Ruy Gómez. "As Spaniards celebrate Don Juan for defeating the infidel at Lepanto, the Dutch celebrate William in much the same way. And what he is telling this unified people is that there will be no peace until the Spanish are driven entirely and irrevocably from the Netherlands."

"Preposterous!" Philip shouted and pounded the council table with the flat of his hand. Instantly he regretted his outburst. He could not afford to show weakness to his underlings. It was unbecoming in so great a king. "What plans has William for the crown if he does not wish it for himself?" asked Philip, attempting to bring a chill back into his voice. "Does he expect to entice the heretic Queen to wear it?"

"It seems more likely the Duke of Alençon will take the bait, Your Majesty," offered Antonio Pérez.

"Is the little gnome not still courting Elizabeth?" asked the King.

"The two have yet to meet," answered Pérez, "but the marriage plans are proceeding through proxies. The usual . . ."

Philip let his mind wander as his councillor related the vaguely irritating information sent back from England by court spies regarding the courtship dance between Elizabeth and the youngest son of de Médicis. The French. So long Spain's enemy. And yet so beautiful a gift had come from there — his beloved Isabella. At least the House of Valois was no longer sending subsidies to the Netherlands Calvinists. The French internal struggles and the weakmindedness of the royal family had finally given Philip a formidable advantage. But France allied with England — that could indeed pose a problem.

". . . bankruptcy." The word spoken by Iñigo Ibéñez brought Philip instantly out of his reverie. "If we do not quell this rebellion quickly we face yet a second bankruptcy. This year alone your total debts and liabilities stand at seventy-four million ducats, Your Majesty — a sum equal to fourteen times the Crown's annual revenue."

Philip felt his head begin to spin. The world's richest man was hopeless with finances, had never entirely understood the business of loans and interest. All he knew was that his ships were still sailing into his ports from the New World laden with gold. How under heaven could this be happening? But even as the question formed in his head the answer became clear. William of Orange had taken his place beside the whore Elizabeth as Spain's greatest enemy. And he had to be stopped.

"We must nullify the Prince of Orange," announced Philip suddenly. "He must be knocked forcibly from the field of play, do you understand me? Like a piece taken in a brilliant move from a chessboard." All the old hatred for his father's favorite came rushing to the fore. William was a scoundrel, a traitor, a heretic. Philip felt his pale face flush red with rage. "I wish him dead!" he hissed.

There was silence amongst the King's councillors. Then Cardinal Granvelle spoke up in the calmest of voices. "We could name him an outlaw, Your Majesty. Put a price on his head."

"Yes, an outlaw, a public plague, a murderer of Catholics," agreed Philip. He was warming to this plan, and the words rolled off his tongue effortlessly. "All my subjects shall be forbidden in every country, territory, and estate I rule to live, speak, or in any way communicate with him. They may not give him food or drink or shelter on pain of death."

"What shall be the price placed on him, Your Majesty?" asked Antonio Pérez.

"Twenty-five thousand crowns in gold," replied Philip evenly. Someone gasped. Even the King himself was astonished at the sureness and swiftness of his decision — and the enormous amount of the bounty.

Granvelle had been scribbling on a blank sheet of parchment. "Shall we 'give leave to any one of our subjects,'" he now read, "'sufficiently loyal to his King to rid us of this evil man, delivering him to us dead or alive'?"

Ruy Gómez added, "If that subject succeeded, we could ennoble him as well. And if he had committed any crime, he would be pardoned."

Philip nodded slowly. He was enjoying this fantasy of William's assassination immensely. "I think that if this loyal subject should die in the act, having succeeded in the Prince's execution, his family should receive the money and honors in his stead. Do you agree?"

As his councillors enthusiastically nodded their assent, Philip smiled a small but a distinctly pleasant smile.

"Compose the edict in your own words, Cardinal Granvelle, and I will sign it immediately. Thank you, gentlemen. You may all go."

Their spirits raised considerably, the men bowed and backed out the Council Chamber door.

Philip straightened in his chair. He felt a lightness, almost a buoyancy in his body. Several minutes after his councillors had departed he found that he was still smiling. And the pain under his right lower rib had completely disappeared.

Thirty

The Earl of Leicester stood perfectly erect in the cool morning sunlight staring at his reflection in the tall gilt-framed looking glass. He had always been a vain man, admired by men and women alike for his rugged handsomeness and startlingly masculine vigor. But the image that gazed back at him, he realized, was no longer one to inspire admiration from without, or vainglory within. Now forty-five years old, he had long ago lost the fresh vibrancy of youth. He looked weary, and the eyes wore round them a pained mask of wrinkles. His jowled cheeks above the grey beard glowed with an unhealthy floridity. And with his gout preventing the constant strenuous riding he had known his entire life, Robin Dudley was slowly going to fat.

The rich garments, he thought, turning slightly to one side, the folds and slashes of brocade and satin, the ruffs and ribbons, did hide a multitude of sins. And the calves under the fine silk hose were still firm and well turned. He sighed. This morning as he stood in the peach and silver opulence of Wanstead House, he was dressed for a bridegroom, but the bride waiting below in the chapel was not the one he had dreamed for so long of marrying.

He did love Lettice Knollys. Even after giving birth to three children, Lady Essex was very simply a gorgeous woman, utterly sensual, and she matched him stroke for stroke in rampant, unquenchable ambition and scheming. When they had taken up together he had come nearly undone with wanting her. Had gone to extreme lengths to have her husband, Lord Essex, sent far from England into the wilds of Ireland so they could carry on with their exorbitant passions unhindered. When, providentially, Essex had died of a fever, Leicester had still been so firmly clutched in the arms of desire that he had sloughed off all rumors that had him — for the third time — murderer of an unwanted spouse. He had even offered his previous lover, Douglas Sheffield, a generous settlement. Indignant, she had refused and, finally accepting that Leicester would never be hers, begun entertaining other marriage proposals. It looked as though she would accept one from Sir Edward Stafford, ambassador to France.

Leicester had managed, unbelievably, to keep news of the affair with Lettice from her cousin the Queen for more than two years. Lady Essex had, like himself, always traveled within the highest of Court circles. Perhaps, mused Leicester, Elizabeth believed he was still sleeping with Douglas Sheffield. Despite the child he'd fathered on Douglas and her unceasing demands for matrimony, he had promised Elizabeth he would never marry that lady. Perhaps the Queen had been lulled into a kind of passive acceptance of his unfaithfulness. Perhaps she had been overwhelmed with affairs of State, or obsessed with pangs of guilt for sending insufficient aid to the blood-soaked Netherlands. Or perhaps the courtship with the Duke of Alençon, and all the proxies sent to woo her, were more serious than Leicester wished to believe.

Sometimes it had seemed unreal, the sheer deceit and contrivance of this affair with Lettice — both women together under one roof, Lady Essex at times playing hostess to the Queen. Last summer he had thrown a lavish two-week water party for the Queen at Kenilworth Castle. It had been an extravagant fairy tale of fireworks and musical masques, rustic diversions, exquisite open-air pageants. People from miles round had come, to view their beloved Queen as much as the entertainments. And Elizabeth had been altogether enchanted with the wonders he had created within and without the palace — a pleasure garden of marble fountains rippling with colored water, strange sculpted beasts, walkways bursting with flowers and fruit-bearing trees, beds of sweet strawberries there for the picking. Amongst the small party of guests was his sister, Mary Sidney, Elizabeth's most beloved and sorely missed companion. Ignoring Mary's pox-ravaged face they had strolled together like young girls, heads touching, arms round each other's waist. Lady Essex, like some voluptuous serpent in the Garden of Eden, had watched silently from the shadows, smug with her secret. Leicester had spent the fortnight consumed with guilt and fear of exposure, but he was foremost a showman — the Queen's Master of the Revels — and in the end Elizabeth was never the wiser.

He had been surprised that the scandal machine of Court life had somehow failed to manufacture even one scintilla of gossip about its most despised member, to discredit him with the Queen. True, she had once confessed to another of her favorites, Christopher Hatton, that she'd had a bad dream — something about a marriage that would do her harm. But her suspicions, to Leicester's great relief, had fallen on Hatton. He had had to swear to her that it was not *his* marriage of which she'd dreamt, and all was soon forgotten.

Leicester turned from the mirror and stared out at the grounds of Wanstead, a once run-down house Elizabeth had given him, now beautifully restored. He could see the chapel from the window. In a few moments he would enter there and marry the woman who was seven months gone with his child. If Lettice had not become pregnant, he wondered, would he still have wished to wed her? Yes, he thought suddenly. He did in some part of him wish to marry Lettice. He longed for legitimate children. Brothers and sisters as playmates for each other, like he had enjoyed in his own family. *An heir.* He could admit to himself that he longed for an heir, though the word spoken aloud to Elizabeth was like invoking the Devil himself. Suddenly Leicester felt a flush of warmth creeping from chest to neck to face, and pushed open the mullioned window. Pray Jesus it is not the malarial fever again, he thought, sucking in great gulps of the cool morning air.

When had he finally come to know that marriage to the Queen was an impossibility? That his greatest of all desires — to be husband of Elizabeth and king of England — had been pulled forever from his reach? She had forgiven him Douglas Sheffield, and he had afterwards moved even higher in her trust and favor than before. Then Elizabeth had taken up with the French prince in a way that defied reason, and Lady Essex had begun to nag him.

"The Queen will never marry you," Lettice had said. "She would have done it by now, had she meant to. Do you not wish to be like normal men with wife and family, and not some pathetic, eternally groveling creature of an aging, ridiculous royal hag?"

Leicester had, in fact, waited until the last moment to make this marriage with Lady Essex. Some perverse idea, perhaps some maudlin memory of his childhood friendship with Elizabeth, or the fullblown passion of their long affair, had caused him to hope against hope that she would come about, like a great sailing ship in an unpredictable wind — shift direction and admit that she would die if she could not marry him. But of course this had not happened, and with each passing month Lettice had grown more ponderous with her pregnancy.

Oh, why had he not simply told Elizabeth the truth? Asked for her blessings on the marriage? She had scorned his proposals repeatedly for twenty years. Could she be so unreasonable as to assume he should stay a bachelor for the rest of his life?

At once the answer to his question came to him in the form of an image in his mind's eye — an image of Elizabeth as she had sat, a pale and furious wraith, waiting to condemn him for mere infidelity with Douglas Sheffield. No, he realized, if he had begged for her royal approval of a marriage with Lettice, Elizabeth would have denied it. Forbidden it. And she would have punished him. Rescinded all of the astonishing gifts of influence, power, prestige, and riches she had bestowed upon him with her loving and generous hand. One day, Leicester knew, the truth of this marriage would come to the Queen's ear. Perhaps by then he might have found a way to pacify her, make her see reason in it. And perhaps not.

Oh, how had it come to this! Leicester had always believed in the Machiavellian principle of *virtù*. That a great man could, by bold endeavor, control some part of his future not ruled by the Fates. Early on, he had concluded that he was indeed destined to be Elizabeth's husband and king. But if he were somehow wrong and it was not, in fact, written in the stars, then instead all of his patience and hard work and brilliant scheming must finally lay the same prize at his feet. He had believed that once.

But there was nothing to be done now. He must celebrate his marriage with joy, and look forward to the birth of his child. With any luck it would be a boy, and at least the Dudley blood and name would be passed down into future lineage as it was meant to do. The ceremony would be brief, only three or four witnesses — all family — and a discreet local chaplain presiding. He would not allow himself to think of the Queen's planned visit to Wanstead in two days time. No trace of the wedding would remain. He would send Lettice away, and in months to come move her up and down the countryside to keep her out of the Queen's sight. Return to Court as though nothing at all had happened. The audacious deceit of it, thought Leicester, the lies . . . Was everything his enemies had said of him throughout the years, he wondered, true? Was he the selfish, arrogant, avaricious scoundrel of his reputation, or rather the good, caring friend and kind patron that he insisted to himself every day he was?

Leicester turned for one more look into the gilt mirror. He tugged at the buckram-stuffed doublet and sucked in his softening belly. He had done all a man could humanly do to calculate his future and defy the Fates. Now he must accept defeat. Slowly he screwed his face into a semblance of a smile, and strode through his bedchamber door and down the great stairs of Wanstead House to marry with Lettice Knollys.

Thirty-one

Elizabeth, enthroned, looked slowly about the Presence Chamber and declared herself content. Half a dozen of her councillors stood round in small self-composed groups discussing, she presumed, her great and minor affairs and divers matters of state. Her waiting ladies, loitering nearby at their ease and tittering with gossip, were very pretty in their gowns of the newly fashionable black and white. Amongst them all there was not a jot of color anywhere, except for pink of cheek or vermillion of lip. She herself had become partial to the fashion, and she gazed down with pleasure at her overskirt with its embroidered jet silk pattern stitched into the stark satin background. Black pearls on her white wrists. White pearls in her black periwig. I am still attractive, she thought, her mouth tilting into a subtle smile, even at my age.

Elizabeth was pleased with good reason. She had managed somehow to navigate shoal after treacherous political shoal, pacify warring factions within her government, control her own rampant emotions, and emerge into the clear light of her people's love. Independent of her own efforts, an adoring cult had actually sprung up to worship their Virgin Queen. All the past scandals naming her and Robin lovers, with hordes of illegitimate children, had vanished.

Of course the Puritans were a nuisance, and a potentially dangerous one at that. She surveyed the room once more and spotted their numbers amongst her councillors instantly. The men were strange with their wild, shoulder-length hair. They wore all black, not as a fashion but as a sober vestment, morbid and rigid as their faces. But this was an illusion, thought Elizabeth, for Puritans were cloaked in the violence of their speech — their apoplectic sermons damning every fathomable vice, frantic prayer meetings and prophesyings, and condemnation of iniquitous and foolish women. They even gave their children ridiculous names such as Reformation, Tribulation, Repent, and Be Thankful. Oh, they were horrid, these Puritans, chasing players from quiet villages and forbidding Morris dancers from dancing. They had even the audacity to rail hysterically from their pulpits against herself and her "inadequate" efforts to reform the church. Sometimes she wished they would all disappear.

Leicester, once again absent from Court, was a Puritan but a reasonably one. But Walsingham, in all other ways prudent, sophisticated, and broadly cultured, was a fanatical Puritan who stubbornly insisted on putting Religion before State. If it were up to him, thought Elizabeth with irritation, she would be at war with every Catholic power in Europe, and her cousin Mary would be a headless, rotting corpse. Walsingham had announced — to her extreme annoyance, though of course there was nothing to be done about it — that he "wished first to God's glory and next the Queen's safety."

Well, despite him, despite them all, she would prevail. Her mind's Great Plan would bear the fruit her womb would never do.

Her Great Plan.

She had taken no one, not one soul, into her confidence. She thought again of her mother, the diary Anne had kept for so long, all her own. And she thought of the lesson within that journal. *Trust no man completely, for all men are ambitious or scheming or weak.* Even her devoted Cecil — the man who shared most exactly her political aims and fears — was aging. These days he more enjoyed bouncing his grandchildren on his knee, and riding a little donkey round the garden paths at Theobalds, than strategizing with her on matters of foreign policy. And dear Robin was a problem. His fervent opposition to the Duke of Alençon's marriage proposals and his vehement demands for official military intervention in the Netherlands threatened the perfection of her Plan.

For months she had spent every waking hour thinking on this puzzle. She had dreamed dreams of it. Seen in her mind's eye great maps of the world — Europe, the East, the West Indies. She had considered her allies, her enemies. She had consulted the stars, had had John Dee cast horoscopes for all the monarchs of the Continent. She had control of Parliament, and she had surrounded herself with councillors wise each in his way but none, in singularity or conjunction with others, stronger than herself. She had planted herself on this throne and for twenty years waited patiently as the great taproots of her power and authority bored slow and deep into the heart of England. No one knew better than she what was Britain's future course, for no one loved nor understood it more.

She was the architect of the Plan and, with God's help, the arbiter of its outcome.

'Twas so simple, Elizabeth thought, leaning against the down cushions at her back. It all rested on her urge for peace being as zealous as King Philip's desire for war, and the understanding that *France* and not Spain was the greatest danger to England. Why could no one else see what she so clearly saw? Perhaps in France's weakened condition it appeared as no threat, but the ancient enmity ran deep, and the country was bigger and more populous than Spain. But worse, for the first time in history it controlled the entire southern coast of the Channel. Threat of invasion from France's fleet was eminently more plausible than from Spain's Armada.

The balance of power, as it stood now with France caught between Spain in the south and the Spanish-controlled Netherlands to the north, had allowed England's profitable trade with Flanders to flourish for generations. If England destroyed Spain, and the Low Countries came under the protection — or even the domination — of France, all would be lost. The European coast from southern France all the way to the northernmost parts of the Netherlands would be controlled by the French, and England's intercourse with the Continent entirely compromised. Worse, the cost of keeping the whole of the south and east of England on permanent military alert would devastate her economy. Without financial stability she would lose her capacity to expand her influence in Europe, and in the unexplored lands of the New World.

There was a way, Elizabeth had decided, a brilliant solution to the puzzle. It hinged on the intricacies of diplomacy, not on barbaric aggression, and it lay within the complicated tangle of her marriage dance with Alençon. Let all, especially the Duke himself, believe she was serious in her intentions to wed him. Ignore all of her subjects' howls of rage that she should consider marrying a Catholic, and a filthy Frog at that.

The French prince had already visited her once for twelve days, preceded by his representative Simier, a darkly handsome and elegant courtier adept at the games of love. And whilst Alençon had been as ugly as his reputation made him — uglier even — there was something wonderful about him. A sophistication unknown to Englishmen, and a wicked charm. "Small but mighty," he would brag of himself. So despite his appearance — Lord Cecil had actually contacted a specialist reputed to be expert at removing the scars of smallpox — Elizabeth found the flirtation bearable, sometimes even enjoyable. She had gritted her teeth and allowed her Court physicians to examine her and pronounce her fit for childbearing, for another seven years at least. Elizabeth smiled. Perhaps she had missed her calling. Perhaps she should have been an actor on the stage, for there was not one amongst her councillors, even Leicester and Hatton, who did not believe her ploy. And they were beside themselves with worry.

The Plan would be complete when Alençon, encouraged and subsidized by herself, and acting as an independent potentate — independent from his brother the King of France — moved into an alliance with the Dutch. He would become a hero, a defender of their liberty against Spanish tyranny. This would strengthen the Netherlands against Spain without the risk of France's usurping the Low Countries — and without England's all-out war with Philip. It would require her moment-to-moment oversight of the military situation on the Continent, a quickstep of minimal intervention when seriously threatened, balanced by the drawing in of her horns when the threat diminished. There would be countless envoys sent to Flanders, and many mediations with Spain. She would, this way, postpone any truly bellicose tactics indefinitely, possibly until the danger passed altogether. Elizabeth knew very well she would, with this method, continue to drive her councillors mad with exasperation. But her deepest instincts cried out against confrontation with Philip, and she was as determined as she had ever been in her life to win this battle through compromise alone.

"Sir Philip Sidney!" shouted the crier as the Presence Chamber doors opened and a courtier, thin and beardless, eyes flashing with intelligence, strode in and dropped to one knee in front of the Queen.

Elizabeth adored this young man, only son of her dearest friends, Mary and Henry Sidney. She had known him since birth and watched him grow to a superb manhood. Even at his age, Philip Sidney was idol of the most forward circle of young intellectuals, poets, and playwrights in England, and was universally beloved by all generations, having no apparent enemies. Today, however, the Queen had summoned him here for a scolding. Sidney, alarmed by her proposed marriage with Alençon, had written her a long letter of protest, decrying the treachery of the French and begging her to reconsider the match. Now Elizabeth gave him her hand to kiss, and she felt the fervidness of his devotion to her as he pressed her fingers to his lips. With a single gesture she waved all courtiers, councillors, and waiting ladies out of earshot, and then spoke only in hushed tones.

"Come, Philip, sit close at my knee," she said, and the young man obeyed, staring up adoringly at his Queen. "I am very cross with you, Philip. You have no right to question my decisions or my motives."

"Begging your deepest pardon, Majesty, but I must continue to risk your displeasure and stand by my letter. Remember, I was there in Paris on Saint Bartholomew's Eve," he whispered fiercely. "I saw the butchery with my own two eyes! The family of the man you are planning to marry was behind that slaughter. They are avowed enemies to the Protestant cause. His mother is a very devil! The man himself is repulsive, the marrow of his bones eaten by debauchery. Do you not see how this marriage does offend your subjects, Your Majesty? Do you not care?"

Elizabeth did all she could not to wince at Philip Sidney's words, for she knew them to be the truth. But she could not afford to listen, to let them move her. Now she took up his hand and held it in her own. The skin was soft, pale, uncallused — the hand of a gentleman. She leaned down and spoke in an intimate tone.

"Do you trust me, Philip?"

She heard him swallow hard. "Of course I do, Your Majesty."

"Then when I tell you I love my people, and I will do nothing, ever, to harm them, will you believe me?"

He struggled with his answer. What he believed he knew made assent impossible. But he did know the Queen, love her, and trust her very deeply. And there was a twinkle in her eye that suggested there was more that she was not telling him, perhaps wished to tell, but could not.

"I believe you, Your Majesty. Of course I do," he said, and laid his cheek upon the back of her white hand.

"Tell me," she said, adroitly changing the subject, "have you heard lately from your tutor Doctor Dee?"

Philip Sidney smiled. It always made him happy to speak of the good doctor. "I have had many letters from him from abroad. He is ever proud to be in your service, but he sometimes wishes to be closer to home, to Mortlake, to you."

"And I him," said Elizabeth. John Dee had become a vital member of her inner circle who, with his magic as well as his mathematics, helped her determine the fate and future of England. Walsingham, head of her secret service, had become close friends with Dee, and was even now using him as a spy on the Continent.

The Queen smiled enigmatically. "Close your eyes, Philip." He did as he was told. "Now open your hands." When he had done this Elizabeth placed in them a new leather volume embossed in gold letters. Before he could open his eyes she said, "Do you know what it is?"

"Yes!" Sidney's eyes flew open and he quickly turned to the title page. "*Perfect Art of Navigation* by John Dee. Oh, Your Majesty, thank you!" He thumbed through and found the dedication. "'To Christopher Hatton.'"

He looked up at Elizabeth. "I've heard Lord Hatton's investment in the voyage of the *Golden Hind* was the largest share by far."

"Indeed," said Elizabeth, again suppressing a smile. She had largely helped finance Francis Drake's circumnavigation of the globe. But it was of course an unofficial investment, since Drake's legendary piracy, with Spanish ships and ports his primary victims, could not look as though it were sanctioned by the Queen of England herself. It did, however, give Elizabeth perverse pleasure to revenge herself upon the King of Spain this way. It did enormous damage to his credit, and siphoned untold riches from his coffers that he might otherwise use to inflict harm on England or the Netherlands.

"I am told it is a most exciting voyage," said young Sidney. "That Drake himself has trod upon the western coast of the New World above the thirtieth parallel."

"I will tell you a secret, Philip. Your Doctor Dee foresees the English Empire expanding onto those very shores."

"The *western* shores of America?" he asked incredulously.

"That is correct. But do not tell my lord Cecil, or I'm afraid he will fall into a fit of apoplexy. So, no one will know of our conversation on this subject, Philip, not even my petticoat!"

Philip Sidney laughed delightedly and the Queen joined him. At that moment the Presence Chamber doors flew open and the Frenchman Simier burst in unannounced. He was red-faced and very, very angry, and he was shaking off a royal guard from either arm. Ladies gasped at the sight. Noblemen all instinctively moved — some protectively round the Queen, others to impede Simier's forward motion. But Elizabeth could see he was unarmed and waved everyone off him.

He moved to the throne and fell on both knees before her. She could hear his ragged breathing and feel the heat coming off his body in great waves. He rose without her leave and she could see that his handsome face was contorted with rage.

"Someone has tried to murder me, Your Majesty."

The murmur in the Presence Chamber grew loud and unruly.

"Silence," commanded Elizabeth. She turned sympathetically to Simier. "Tell me what has happened."

"I had left my apartments and was coming across the north courtyard when a bullet . . ." He stopped, as though reliving his near brush with death. " . . . a bullet flew past several inches from my head. There was but one shot, and I ran to the place of its origin, where I found no one except a small contingent of Privy Council guards."

Another flurry of talk all round.

"Silence!" shouted Elizabeth. Her own heart had begun to pound. "Did you question them, Simier? Had they seen the culprit, any suspicious activity?"

"Culprit, Your Majesty? There was no culprit except some murderous fiend amongst the guard themselves."

As the outraged mutterings grew, Elizabeth acted quickly.

"Leave us. Everyone!" she cried, and the Presence Chamber began quickly to be vacated. Several of her high councillors looked at her pleadingly for permission to remain.

The Earl of Suffolk spoke up. "How can we leave you alone with a man in so agitated a state, Your Majesty?"

"Thank you for your concern, my lord. I assure you, Monsieur Simier is no danger to me. Do stay close, however. I may have need of you."

Suffolk and the councillors followed the others out and closed the Presence Chamber doors behind them. Elizabeth, in the space of a breath, considered the personal approach, using her feminine wiles to defuse Simier's anger, calling the Frenchman by the affectionate name she used for him in private — her Monkey. No, she thought quickly. He was far too agitated for that, might consider her manner condescending. She would take her most dignified and queenly posture.

"Now, Monsieur Simier," she said in an unhurried and stately voice, "have you calmed sufficiently so that we may talk about this rationally?"

"Oh yes, Your Majesty," he said with a decidedly bitter tone. "We may speak rationally, and I will tell you the truth of it."

"Good," she replied. "We have always been truthful with one another." Elizabeth strove to keep her features even and her eyes unreadable, for her words were clearly lies. All of the marriage negotiations between Simier and herself had been an intricately woven fabric of deceit.

"I do not know which of the Privy Guards tried to assassinate me," he said, "but I do know very well who was behind the attempt."

"Tell me who."

"The Earl of Leicester, Your Majesty." Simier's normally handsome face had grown ugly with naked hatred.

Elizabeth was silent as she composed her thoughts and her reply. Simier's accusation did not entirely surprise her. Twas no secret that Leicester was the member of her Privy Council most vehemently opposed to her marriage with Alençon. Robin spoke openly of his loathing for the French prince as well as for his proxy Simier. Elizabeth had, in her deepest heart, been touched by Dudley's position, and believed at the bottom of it all was simply jealousy. She had enjoyed that thought very much indeed. But she knew the Earl's mind. He was far too astute to have perpetrated an assassination attempt on Simier. It would serve no purpose and it was not his way.

"Monsieur," she went on. "You know that I hold you and the Prince in the very highest esteem, and that I will investigate this heinous attack on your person until the culprit is discovered and dealt with severely. But as for your accusation against Lord Leicester, I can simply imagine no motive. *Au contraire,* whilst he clearly opposes the alliance between our countries, he would never jeopardize with violence the future peace which such a marriage would guarantee. Besides, Leicester is my oldest and dearest friend in all the world. And my most trusted advisor."

"Trusted?" repeated Simier. "Lord Leicester your most *trusted* advisor?" His voice dripped with sarcasm.

Elizabeth quite suddenly felt as though the blood had cooled in her veins, and an eerie premonition of disaster came upon her.

"I think if that is true, Your Majesty," Simier went on, "England is in very great danger indeed. For this man has deceived you so treacherously and for so long, that if he is your dearest friend, then you have no further need of enemies."

"Tell me what you are saying, Simier. Explain these accusations at once and, I caution you, they had better be founded in provable fact or there will be hell to pay."

"The Earl of Leicester . . ." he said, holding Elizabeth with a hard and steady gaze, "*is a married man.* He has been so for six months. Your cousin Lady Essex is his wife."

In that moment Elizabeth felt as if her body rocked precariously on the throne. She was speechless. Entirely speechless. Is this what a mute must feel, she found herself thinking, with words spinning in one's head but no way to utter them? She struggled to recover her voice so that she could argue with Simier. Then she understood that he would never have made such serious accusations if they had not been altogether true.

Robin was married. Robin had betrayed her.

"And there is more, Your Majesty."

Elizabeth wished to cry, "No, stop. Say not another word!" But she continued in her paralysis, entirely unprotected as her mortal enemy prepared to fling yet another poisoned dagger into her beating heart.

"They have a child. A son. He was born a few short months after the marriage. I believe your dearest friend and advisor has not informed you of the changes in his . . . situation. Lord Leicester," Simier went on in Elizabeth's stunned silence, "is thought by all at Court except yourself, Majesty, to be a vile and dangerous man. A murderer three times over. He does whatever he wishes, to get whatever he wants. And he wants the Duc d'Alençon to disappear from your life. He is behind this attempt on my person and I demand —"

Elizabeth stood suddenly. She still had not found her voice but she could, she discovered, move. Her legs felt wooden and her face was a rigid mask as she walked silently past Simier. The closed doors were an obstacle, so she raised her fist and pounded once. They flew open instantly and she was confronted by the gaggle of councillors, their concerned faces upon her as she sliced through them, her eyes commanding them not to follow. The walk to her apartments seemed the longest of her life. She remembered waving everyone away, clearing her bedchamber of her ladies, and finally finding herself quite alone and very, very still.

Then like a great and terrible whirlwind Elizabeth began to move. Wildly. And like the wind she began to howl and shriek and moan. Her arms flung wide, she knocked all manner of objects from tables and boards, grasped curtains hung from bedposts, ripped them down. She sent benches flying, dashed mirrors from the walls, scattered myriad jewels, and trampled plate underfoot. She could not hear herself screaming, but the sound rocked the halls and corridors far beyond her door.

Her councillors who had followed the Queen to her apartments now congregated in the antechamber, exchanging looks of confusion and alarm. After Elizabeth had stormed from the Presence Chamber, Simier had confessed his revelations to them, and whilst they had all known the storm would inevitably one day break, they had not been prepared for the violence of Her Majesty's fury.

The almost inhuman cries, the shattering glass, the sounds of ripping fabric and crashing furniture, were unbearable for them to hear, and it was incumbent upon them, despite her command to leave her to this private grief, to attend to their Queen's safety. It was decided that the Earl of Suffolk should brave the tempest. Undoubtedly one of Leicester's greatest enemies, he was nevertheless a man who saw things clearly — indeed had, almost twenty years before, favored a marriage between Dudley and the Queen if that were the surest way to a royal heir. With a final look to his peers Suffolk tried the bedchamber door. It was unlocked, though he had to push firmly to open it.

Inside he found an overturned table blocking his way and set it upright before lifting his eyes with great trepidation. Elizabeth had become very still, the Queen who had wrought so much havoc about her chamber. She was dishevelled, locks of her black periwig askew and one sleeve of the black and white gown ripped and hanging down, exposing the bare skin of her arm. Her crimson lip color was smeared away from her mouth, and the eyes, thought Suffolk, the eyes were terrible, red-rimmed and altogether mad. He found himself trembling, for the sight of his beloved Queen was at once ghastly and unutterably sad. Then she spoke. Twas a low, hoarse whisper, and he could not make out her words.

"Your Majesty?" He dared moved a few steps closer, and then she repeated what she had said.

"I want him dead."

"Oh, Your Majesty, no . . ."

"Arrest him. Put him in the Tower." She was unnaturally calm. "Take him through the Traitor's Gate. He follows the footsteps of his father and his grandfather and his brother through that gate."

"Please, think, Madame," began Suffolk. "Let some time pass before you —"

"'Tis bad blood," she said almost matter-of-factly. "Not altogether his fault. Bad blood. Kat always said that about the Dudleys." Elizabeth looked up at Suffolk, and although she had been speaking to him, she appeared surprised that he was standing before her. "Go now. Go. Arrest him. I do want him dead. I do want him . . . dead."

With that the Queen's body heaved and she commenced weeping, her sobs so heartwrenching that Suffolk, forgetting all protocol, went to her and enfolded Elizabeth in his arms. She, no longer the Queen but merely a wronged and wretched woman, allowed herself to be held and comforted, though it was clear to them both that no comfort, no small fragment of solace was to be found on this black and terrible day.

Book Three

Thirty-two

As a captain in the Dutch cavalry I had been summoned to Delft to celebrate Prince Williams inauguration. He had for so long and so steadfastly refused the crown of the country whose destiny he had singlehandedly guided towards independence, that I hardly believed it was finally happening. Since the days of the Pacification of Ghent, events had unfolded in the confusing and complicated manner of all political maneuverings. The King of Spain had sent his most recent henchman, the Duke of Parma, and his highly disciplined troops to wrest from the Dutch their newfound liberation. As brilliant a diplomat as he was a soldier, Parma had won dozens of engagements where others had failed, simply by studying the Netherlands terrain. Even more impressive, he had cleverly laid promises of pardon and return of property at the gates of the southernmost provinces. In a trice they had relinquished their hardwon freedom and resubmitted to Spanish rule.

William, meanwhile, had done everything in his power to entice a foreign Protestant monarch to accept the Netherlands crown. All those Dutchmen who loved the Prince of Orange fervently wished him to become Stadthouder, but to their dismay he clung to the principle — as a barnacle clings to a dike wall — of the Divine Right of Kings, and swearing he had no such claim repeatedly refused. In his heart he knew the Low Countries could never, despite his almost superhuman will, and the bravery of the Hollanders and Zeelanders, stand alone against Philip. He therefore held out the golden plum of Regency to England, France and Germany.

I was sore disappointed in my Queen who hemmed and hawed, continued to send small contingents of English volunteers to

Holland, and financed a pathetic army to fight Parma. Prince William held out hope that Elizabeth would rouse her self from what he called "her long dream of peace" and accept sovereignty of the States, but all she did do was send fifteen ships across the Channel carrying her betrothed, the Duke of Alençon — a little brown oaf of a man with a head too large for his body. Welcomed with open arms, he was officially named Protector of the Netherlands. But the evil toad wasted no time, forsook his pledge, and began to plot with Philip of Spain to dissolve the Estates and reestablish Catholic supremacy.

Treacherous in the extreme, he actually sent his troops to invade Antwerp, but they were inept and ill prepared, and were soundly trounced by the burgher guard and citizens at once. The uprising Alençon wished to be remembered as the "French Fury" was better termed the "French Farce," and spineless creature that he was, he refused responsibility for the attack, claiming it had been a mere misunderstanding — the result of a quarrel between his bodyguard and a Dutch gatekeeper. Within the year the Duke had died, some said of poison, and tho many rejoiced, all hope of a French alliance died with him.

So finally and reluctantly William of Orange had acceded to his countrys pleadings, tho he agreed only to assume the office of Count, and answer to the will of the Estates General.

In the previous years I had made my way up thro the ranks of Williams army and found my self in the great mans presence several times. He had, astonishingly, remembered me from our first meeting — I a lowly private in the English army coming with news of my companys suicidal siege. Now he had personally requested my attendance at his coronation, and my pride knew no bounds.

I had ridden into the garrison at Delft and was delighted to meet up with my old friend Partridge. He had ascended thro the ranks as an expert in cyphers, and in deed had found a permanent place close at Williams side. My first night in the city we visited a popular tavern and sat quaffing good Dutch beer, and feasting on the herring and dumplings we had both, after many years in the Netherlands, come to consider delicacies. My plump Partridge had, without the exertions of the battlefield, become positively rotund, but he was glowing with vitality and his usual good nature.

Despite our continuing allegiance to William and the Dutch cause, we were never the less Englishmen in our hearts, and fell im-

mediately to talk of home. Whilst his family was diminishing — a spate of untimely deaths — mine was growing. I had nieces and nephews I had never laid eyes on, and my brother John had happily overcome his dissipation enough to marry and begin managing Enfield Chase with some semblance of order. My Father was aging and crippled in his legs, but wrote regularly and ever declared his love for me. He had long ago forgiven my desertion of him, saying he had never honestly expected me to stay, and felt sure I was destined for greatness. Those letters always made me smile — to know that a man could hold his second son in such high esteem. Well into our third plate of fish Partridge and I began loudly debating Prince Williams efforts to bring Lord Leicester to the Netherlands to administrate the country.

"Your dear friend the Earl," said Partridge — he had oftentimes heard the story of our meeting at Enfield Chase — "is far too busy dodging the Queens daggers to come here. I doubt she would give him such a high commission, the trouble he is in."

"I hear she has forgiven him," I said feeling like a gossipy old washerwoman — the English did enjoy their rumormongering. "He was under house arrest for only a week, and was never sent to the Tower, though Lady Leicester is allowed to come nowhere near the Court."

"Tell me," said Partridge gesturing to the innkeeper for what seemed like our twentieth round of beverage, "do you believe the Queen ever meant to marry the slimy little Frog, or not? Tis said she and Alençon exchanged rings before he left England with a pocket full of her money." Partridge stuffed a fat herring in his mouth and after chewing for a moment, stuck his fingers in after it and pulled out a bone.

"Well," said I, less than sober but not yet stinking, "she never did marry him, and they had courted for five years. I cannot believe she would consider Alençon for a husband. She is too fine." I smiled sentimentally then, remembering the Queens grace and beauty and strength, the sight of her on a high horse that day so many years before.

"Well, he is dead now, thank Christ. And may the Devil keep him."

I raised my glass to second that. "So, Partridge, will you come with me to the whores when we are done here? You can show me the best houses." I had been in the field for many months and longed for the soft touch of a woman. General Roost had moved on to another command, and his ever faithful Marje had gone with him.

Partridge never answered my question except with a loud belch. I looked up to see he had stopped eating and wore a very odd look on his face.

"What is it, Partridge? Are you ill?" I peered into his eyes. "Are you drunk?"

"I am legless," he admitted, "tho I am not ill." Then he hesitated, regarding me carefully before he spoke again. "But I do not go with women anymore."

His statement had the effect of stunning me, like a fish laying on the ships deck, clobbered with a large club.

"Tis all right, Arthur," he added with a lascivious grin. "I do not fancy men nearly as old as you are." Then he giggled like a silly boy, and despite my self I found it infectious. Even as we laughed I knew I should be repulsed or offended at such perversion, but perhaps the great quantities of beer consumed had blunted all judgments. Or perhaps I had been more deeply imbued with Prince Williams lessons of tolerance than I had ever imagined.

"Do you not miss the loveliness of a woman, the sweetness?" I asked feeling genuinely perplexed.

"Sometimes they dress as girls," he whispered drunkenly. "And you never know the difference till their petticoats are thrown up over their pretty painted faces." He leaned over the table conspiratorially. "Arthur, you would not believe what —"

"Say no more, Partridge! I fear I have heard all I need to know . . . and then some."

He leaned in closer. "Is my secret safe with you, then?"

"Altogether," I assured him.

"Ah, what a friend you are," he said, grabbing my hand across the table. We both looked down at our joined hands, then up at each other and roared with laughter once again. When we had finally quieted he drew a satisfied breath and said, "Will you come and join me when I visit Prince William tomorrow? Just after the noonday meal. His home. You have not yet met Louise."

I felt instantly sobered, as mention of the Princes new wife reminded me of the heartbreaking death of Charlotte, his true love. Twas a tragic loss, and all at the hands of King Philip, that tyrant whose real wickedness I had finally begun to understand. Several years back the Spanish monarch had placed a price of 25,000 gold crowns on his enemys head, and in the time since, five attempts had been made on Williams life. In one, the attacker had fired from such short range that Williams hair and beard had exploded into flame. In another, the aspiring assassin — a Dominican monk — had put a bullet thro an artery in the Princes neck just under the ear, a place which could not be properly bandaged without choking him. His life had been saved by Charlotte who — her self but weeks out of childbed — sat vigil by her husband day and night for a week, stanching the flow of blood with her very own fingers. Finally the wound had begun to heal, but the worry and exhaustion had taken a terrible toll. Within months the beautiful lady was dead. With a houseful of young and motherless children William had taken a companionable wife, daughter of the French Huguenot de Coligny, who he hoped would bring them all some comfort.

I was keen to be in Williams company again, especially under such pleasant circumstances as Partridge had proposed, and had never been admitted into the privacy of his home. I quickly accepted the invitation, hoping my friend would remember it the next day when he was sober.

Twas a fine summers afternoon as we strolled thro the streets of Delft towards the Prinsenhof. The whole city bustled with great and joyful preparations for Williams coronation, and a water procession had been planned. Already spotless streets were scrubbed and scrubbed again, houses along the parade route received new coats of paint, monuments were erected, stages for pageants built, and colorful banners hung. The canals were teeming with flower barges, and as we crossed a low bridge I chanced to see one filled with red tulips, thousands of them. I nudged Partridges arm and pointed. We stopped for a moment and stared as the barge floated past. Our minds — without a word spoken — both soared back across the years to that battlefield at Gouda. Partridge removed his hat and placed it on his breast.

"Poor Hirst," I whispered.

"God rest his soul."

We walked on in silence, I pondering how Death was a thief, one with an arbitrary eye. On that bloody day he had surveyed the red field like a robber who chooses one bauble that catches his fancy and leaves behind many others of equal value.

We arrived at the Prinsenhof, a refurbished nunnery, and were shown into the antechamber. Twas a large place, tho more plainly furnished than most would think suitable for a man of Williams station. I wondered if perhaps his years of privation as a soldier had curbed his appetite for grandeur. Suddenly we were fallen upon by two of the Princes pretty little daughters who ran circles round our legs and tugged at our jackets until their new stepmother, Louise, came out from the downstairs dining room, and with kind but firm remonstrances sent them off to the nursery to play. She begged us to wait just a moment more, for her husband was nearly finished with his dinner. Just then the dining room doors opened and Prince William emerged with his sister Countess Schwartzburg and a city burgher whose proportions and demeanor were uncannily akin to Partridges. Louise began the presentations but then William, a grin brightening his tired face, and with an arm round both of the large men said, "My dear, no need to make these two acquainted. They are father and son!" We all laughed at the small jest. The Prince beamed with delight to see me again and thanked me humbly for coming to Delft for his coronation. He was such a warm and kindly man, and I felt cheered to see him so carefree and happy.

The burgher bid us farewell and departed. Then, still smiling, William asked us to join him in his study which was on the second floor. What happened next I have regretted every day of my life since, and no amount of comforting from friends who say I could have done nothing to prevent it, calms my mind or eases my aching heart.

With no warning a small, pimply faced young man emerged from the shadows under the stairwell. I had barely time to think "What an odd place for a servant to be standing" when he drew back his cloak, produced a pistol and fired point blank into Williams chest. Even with my soldiers instincts I was unprepared for so violent an act in so serene a setting, and was struck witless. By the time I lunged for the man he had dashed out a side door. I gave chase. He threw down into my path a large pile of crates he had perchance stacked there for that very purpose and I stumbled, cursing my self soundly. As I pursued him past the stables and down the narrow lane I prayed with all my might for the Princes life . . . but knew surely he could never survive such a wound as he had received. My hatred for this cowardly assassin grew with every step closer I came to him, and I thought "I shall tear him apart with my own two hands. Gouge out his eyes. Rip out his heart . . ." He had jumped upon a canal wall and seemed to be blowing frantically into a pair of ox bladders. I sprang. He tried to leap into the water with what I now realized were floats for his escape by canal, but I wrenched him back and flung him to the ground. By then Partridge and some housemen had arrived to help subdue him. But there was nothing to subdue. He lay still, smiling serenely up at us, that ecstatic abomination of a face, repeating over and over again, "My high and holy mission fulfilled, my high and holy mission . . ." Partridge had to stay my hand from throttling him.

Balthazar Gérard. Fanatic Burgundian Catholic. Since the age of twelve he had believed it his sacred destiny to take the life of the Prince of Orange. In an ironic twist of fate, twas not even for Philips 25,000 crowns he had killed the Father of the Fatherland, but for Gods grace. <u>Gods grace</u>.

As tho in a dream, forcing one foot before the other, I returned to the Prinsenhof to find William laid upon a dining room couch. Bloodied and grey faced, he clung to life, Louise clutching his hand to her heart. Everyone was weeping — women, children, men — for all loved this man so passionately, he who had loved his country unto death. When he felt the last breath of life slipping away, good William Prince of Orange summoned his voice and cried, "God have pity on my soul, have pity on my poor people!" then closed his eyes and died.

His people were inconsolable, for he was while he lived — as his epitaph was later writ — the guiding star of a whole brave nation, and when he died little children cried in the streets. I mourned him longer and more deeply than any man or woman I had ever known. Suddenly, with the loss of a single person, a whole country was neither a comfortable nor happy place for me to reside. I never the less went back to the cavalry, for the only love left in my life was for horses. Besides, I was a soldier and this was the only war that mattered. My heart had been broken, but I continued still to fight.

For more than a year I watched forlornly as Williams good works in the Netherlands, bereft of his leadership, began to come undone. Parma and his army were, city by great city, devouring the Low Countries, and all but the northern provinces had fallen. For the first time, I found my self questioning the Fates, but had for so long believed in the strength of my destiny that I knew no other way to proceed. Twas in this condition of mind that I received word from my sister Alice that our Father lay dying. I resigned my commission in the Dutch army and took passage back to England.

Thirty-three

Enfield Chase. From the small rise I could see in the golden light of late afternoon the whole of the greenwood, the foggy south marshes and in the distance, smoke from the manors several chimneys. I was finally home.

This time the Channel crossing had been a swift one and had left me more queasy than terrified, but I none the less came away with a desire to travel those waters never again. I had ridden directly from Harwich, stopping only to feed and water the poor broken nag I now rode, he being the only mount I had been able to purchase on such short notice. He needed frequent rests without which I feared he would collapse entirely. I fought to keep my temper with him, knowing the fault was not his, but I was desperate to reach my destination. Alices letter had been clear. Father was failing and had begun to suffer. He was holding on to the slim thread of life until he could see me once more. I had a horror of any creature suffering, especially on my account, but I sore desired to see my beloved Fathers face again, and the closer I came to Enfield, the sharper that pang of longing became.

Grateful to be on the downslope, and perhaps sensing my anticipation — or at least the smell of the stables — the old horse picked up his speed to a full canter. I rode thro the gates into the courtyard. All was quiet and well nigh deserted. The stables, usually bustling with men and beasts, were silent, the great doors already shut for the evening. But Enfield Manor seemed entirely unchanged, as tho time had stopped. Twas no larger nor smaller than I remembered, no more shabby nor tidy. The ivy trellis under the nursery window was still thick and sturdy enough to hold the weight of an eight year old boy climbing to his escape. I knew that inside was my whole family, into whose bosom I was soon to be welcomed. Yet as I dismounted I felt a stranger. I tried to recall my leaving, and what good reasons would have kept me from my home and kin for so long. But there was no time to ponder.

Quietly I let my self in the front door. Some youngsters — my nieces and nephews I supposed — were congregated in the Great Hall trying their best to be sedate, tho as I slipped past them I heard one childish laugh and several other giggling voices hushing it. I took the stairs two at a time and came up behind a clutch of relatives at my Fathers bedchamber door. Alice saw me first and burst into tears as she rushed into my embrace. The others surrounded us and in that close pressed circle, I found the sweetest outpourings of love, familiar faces — older and wearier, tho no less lovely to my sight.

"Thank God you are come!" cried Meg clasping both arms round my waist. "All he does is call for you. I will tell him you are here," she said and went quickly into the room muttering, "Thank God, thank God."

"Arthur, meet your sister in law, Kate," said John whose eyes were red rimmed from crying. He stepped aside and his wife, a tiny creature with inquisitive almond eyes stepped forward. Even with me bending down to kiss Kate she was forced to stand on tippy toes to reach me.

"What think you on coming home after so long, Arthur?" she asked quite impulsively. "Tell us your first impression?"

I thought for a moment. "Tis strange to be in a country not at war. Suddenly I am a soldier amidst peace." I turned to John and Alice. "What think you on seeing me amongst you again?"

"Only that you have grown," said John, breaking into a warm smile. "My God, you stand a full head taller than anyone in our family!"

Alice as waiting to give her answer. "How right it feels that you are home with us, Brother. That you are where you should be."

Meg emerged from the bedchamber, beaming. She stepped aside to let me enter. The sight of my Father was less terrible than I had imagined. His face and body were withered and weak, but he was sitting propped in his bed against the pillows, and at first sight of me his eyes shone with happiness, and not with pain as I had expected. He suddenly flung open his arms and in the space of those several steps into them, my own eyes filled with tears. He clutched me fiercely and I kissed him — his cheeks, his head, his hands. I, his chiefest joy, had kept my self from his sight all these years past.

"Arthur . . ." His voice was feeble.

"Oh Father, thank you for waiting." I could hardly speak for my weeping. "If you had gone before I came I could never have lived with my self."

Then to my surprise he laughed, not largely but a laugh all the same. I sniffed back my tears and regarded him closely. He was smiling a crooked smile.

"I had to wait, you see. If I had died before you came," he said, "I would surely have gone to Hell."

"What a thing to say!" I exclaimed. "What do you mean? You of all people, Father, going to Hell."

"Arthur, I have very little strength left, and there is something I must tell you. Tis why I have managed to cheat Death for so long. Why I have waited."

"What is it, Father?" I saw him gazing at me steadily. "What can be so important? You must tell me!"

One last hesitation, then, "You are not my son."

I stared at him stupidly. Could think of nothing to say.

"Neither was Maud your Mother."

"I was . . . adopted?"

"When you were only a few weeks old." His eyes stared past me. He seemed to be remembering. "A tiny little boy with a pair of lungs like bellows." Now he took my hand in his and grasped it with what little strength he had left. "I loved that babe from the first moment I set eyes on him."

"It matters naught who I was born to," I insisted fiercely. "When you took me in I became your son!"

"Yes, you did become my son. But I am dying, Arthur. And I want you to know you are not orphaned. Your parents . . ." He hesitated. ". . . are alive."

"I have no wish to know them! They gave me up. They never cared for me, schooled me, showed me how to live. They have never loved me!"

Father looked away then, unable to look in my eyes. He said gently, "They do not know you are alive."

A strange premonition of momentousness suddenly enveloped me — as tho my true destiny could be glimpsed again. Not clearly, but laying just beyond a thick wall of mist.

Then in a voice quavering with feeling, my Father told me the names of my parents and the full circumstances of my birth. I was still as stone as he spoke and I remember wishing desperately that he would not leave me, could somehow go on living. And also hoping with all my might that what he was saying was untrue, merely the delusions of a dying mind. For suddenly all that I knew, my whole past, had become a lie, and my future a quagmire. I was not my self. I was something more. Something less.

"Forgive me, Arthur," I heard him saying. "Can you forgive me?"

"There is naught to forgive, Father. But what shall I do?" I felt a young child again, helpless, a stranger in my own life. His eyes had closed and he was suddenly very still lying against the pillow. "Father!"

I saw his mouth move, but no sounds emerged from them. Frantic, I placed my ear at his lips and heard a terrible rattle called Death rising from his throat. Then, amidst these sounds of dying I heard the words, so weak as to be barely discernible. "Go to them. Go to them."

"Alice, Meg, John, come quickly!" I cried. The door flew open and they were there crowding round the bed, each finding a place on our Fathers body to tenderly grasp as his soul rose out of him. Then he was gone.

We laid my Father out on a simple bier in the Great Hall and in the following days, all the family friends and neighbors streamed thro to pay their respects. I was meanwhile introduced to my young nieces and nephews, each of whom I saw as thro a gauze curtain, for I knew they were — like their parents — tho dear to me, not my own flesh and blood. I strove to be strong, to celebrate my Fathers long Godly life and peaceful death, but my heart and mind raged with dreadful turmoil.

Go to them.

Lord Leicester my true Father. The Queen of England my Mother. Twas unbelievable, unthinkable.

We buried Robert Southern in the heart of the greenwood, and as the final shovelfull of earth was packt upon his grave, I broke. Tears blinded me. I somehow found my mount, leapt into the saddle and rode off at a gallop. Happy to lose my self in the deepest part of the forest I thundered along the narrow trails, branches whipping my face. I had ridden so many times in this wood on a hunt, but to-day I had no heart to kill any living thing. I had seen too much killing. Too much blood. Had lost the lust for soldiering. Lost two Fathers — William, Robert. Lost a familiar world. What was I to do?

Go to them.

How could I do such a thing? Face Elizabeth and Leicester, convince them I was their child? How could I convince my self? Finally I reined in my mount. Climbed down, sat, my back against a tree and tried to think clearly, devise a plan. My mind grew muddled at once. She was the Virgin Queen. Beloved. Revered. I tried to remember their visit to Enfield Chase. I was too young to understand such things really. Yet they had been known as lovers. There had always been rumors of bastard children. But surely they had been false rumors, and people had been punished for gossipmongering.

For a moment I tried to fit the idea on to my self, as I would a new boot. I was illegitimate, a bastard. The Queens bastard. Royal blood ran in my veins. The blood of Henry Tudor who had taken the crown from King Richard. The blood of the great and terrible Henry VIII. I was his grandson.

No. Impossible. Quite impossible.

I remembered my Fathers deathbed confession. The story of my birth on a stormy night, the switching of a dead child for my self. Kat Ashley. William Cecil. I held my left hand out in front of my face, stared down at the sixth finger. Anne Boleyn had had six fingers on her left hand. Elizabeths Mother. My Grandmother.

Go to them.

I had been a soldier, faced my enemies, proven my strength and mettle on the battlefield. Now suddenly I cowered at the thought of speaking to the two people who had given me life. I rose, mounted my horse and rode for Enfield Manor. I would say goodbye to my family once again and ride to London to confront Elizabeth and Leicester. There was nothing else to be done.

Thirty-four

London. My first sight of it from a small wooden rowboat on the Thames was its pointed church steeples spiking up thro a thick haze of river fog. So many of them, I thought. If there were so many churches, how many thousands of people must reside there? As the oarsmen had rowed upriver, farm and pasture land had given way to village clusters growing closer and closer together, till now the shore was a solid mass of buildings and quays. The traffic of large sailing vessels, wherries and skiffs had multiplied, till now all round us was water commerce in every shape and form.

A sun browned ferryman who sat facing me, his rowing arms the size of tree limbs, jerked his chin in my direction. "First time going in to the City, Sir?"

"Am I so obviously green?" I said, feeling a flush rise from neck to cheeks.

"Can always tell by the eyes," he answered. "The bigger they are on first sight of the place, the fewer the times they have seen it. Yours are the size of saucers." He smiled in a friendly way.

I told him I had been abroad fighting in the Netherlands.

"Well," he said, "more may soon be going, for the Queen is mustering an army, she is. Oi, look there." He pointed, again with his chin, to the south bank of the river, showing me the two greatest places of amusement in London, the bearbaiting theatre and the playhouse — which, he added, were much the same in his mind.

Thankfully the fog was burning away in the morning sun so I could see the sprawl of the city — almost unimaginable — and the lights sparkling so bright on the water I could pretend not to see the brown filth of its surface.

"The Tower?" I inquired of a massive stone fortress at the waters edge.

"Aye, and a place I hope never to see the inside of, my self," he offered. "They say the ghost of Henrys whore still walks inside its halls."

The ghost of Henrys whore. The most infamous inhabitant of that infamous tower. My Grandmother. How many others of my family had colored the yard with their traitorous blood? I wrenched my self from such thoughts, for I knew if I allowed my self to dwell too long on such things I should never ever go thro with my plan.

"Now out in front of you," announced the boatman, never turning round to see it himself, "is the glory of London. That there is surely one of the great wonders of the world."

I stared goggle eyed as a huge wall spanning the river loomed before me. Twas like no bridge I had ever seen. Not simply enormous, of great stone blocks, thick piers and narrow arches, but built from end to end with high houses, and only a single drawbridge at the centre to let pass the tall masted ships. My first thought on sight of London Bridge was the stuff of childhood nightmares — the severed heads and quartered bodies said to be stuck up on poles on either end of it. And I was not disappointed, tho I could barely see the gruesome parts for the masses of blackbirds feasting and fighting over them.

"You had best be hanging on, Sir," said the ferryman. "The current is a bit rough underneath the arches."

For the next moments my talkative friend and the other oarsman were silent and concentrating hard as we approached the bridge. Then suddenly our boat was sucked into the swift waters below the dark and moldy arches. The craft rocked and lurched dangerously, the oarsmens oaths and grunting nearly drowned out by the echoing crash and churn beneath us. As I clutched the seat white knuckled I remembered my fear of the water and cursed my self for not riding on horseback into London. Then, just as suddenly as we had entered the rapids we were back out in the sunlight, the river placid once again. My friendly guide pointed out Fishmongers Hall and its wide dock on which were sold all manner of wet fish, but once past the bridge my eyes were caught and held by one sight alone, and I stopped the boatman in his chatter to ask him of the massive edifice some distance back from the north shore.

"Aye, Saint Pauls. If you want to be learning the lay of the land in this city — all manner of business, legal or otherwise — tis there you will be heading, Sir."

Landing at Three Cranes I was finally on dry ground again, and altogether thankful for it. I began my first walk — no doubt looking saucer eyed and stupid — thro the most amazing place in all of the wide world. I thought how like night and day were London and the cities of the Netherlands. Streets and lanes filthy, dark, winding where the Dutch ones were spotless, orderly and fresh. Here, on both sides of me were endless shops and company halls. There was a constant racket of clattering horses and carts. Citizens bawled their greetings to each other, bold merchants cried out their divers wares, and others simply called to anyone who passed, "What do you lack!" There were numerous tobacco shops — something I had not seen in Holland. Here smoke was the rage, tho the leaf was dear — five shillings an ounce. I had shared a common pipe of it at a tavern the night before and liked the rich taste very well, but I did not stop, for I wished to make Saint Pauls before the day was spent.

Twas a sight, this Cathedral. It towered over the city like a great stone behemoth and all round it, and streaming in and out thro its mighty portals, were all meet and measure of humanity — high lords and lowly beggars. Men, women, children. Clerics in their sober garb. Prostitutes with their bare breasts exposed. I saw a dozen shapes of beards, and mens hair crimped and curled as often as womens.

I entered the cavernous hall to behold a scene I could never in my wildest dreams have imagined. Here in Gods house was nothing less than a street fair. Whilst a preacher stood in the pulpit trying to shout above the din, hundreds of people congregated in pews and naves and aisles, conducting business of every sort. There were gaggles of ladies gossiping, lovers trysting. I passed lawyers advising clients, gentlemens valets touting their services to prospective masters, and merchants using the tombs of ancient Kings as counters over which they sold beer and bread and cheese.

Outside in the churchyard were still more crowds. There were stalls selling books, oysters, marzipan and marrow on toast. I even saw horses being bought and sold!

I stopped a moment and forced my mind to quiet. I was there for a purpose, and I must not be getting waylaid by the hubbub. I stepped back inside the Cathedral and my eyes fell on a group of young men who, by their posture and manner and fancy dress of velvets and ruffs and lace, I took to be courtiers. I moved to their clutch and insinuated my self quietly amongst them, becoming all ears.

There was some talk of the plot recently discovered by Secretary Walsingham made against our Queen by the Scots Queen and an Englishman named Throckmorton. How Elizabeth had, in a rage, sent the Spanish ambassador Mendoza — himself involved in the plot — packing for home, and had authorized the hanging and quartering of several guilty priests, most probably those I had seen on Tower Bridge. But these gentlemen found more interest in, and steered their conversation to, the prospect of our official engagement in the Netherlands War. Antwerp had, since my return to England, fallen to Parma — a great disaster for the Protestant cause.

"He is a brilliant soldier, Parma," pronounced a gentleman with a starched ruff as big as a cheese wheel, and every man in the group nodded in grave agreement.

"If you ask me, he is part sorcerer," offered a man with a pointy waxed beard, "the way he persuades his enemies to hand over their cities with nary a fight."

I wished to object, to defend the honor of the courageous Dutch and their numerous fights to the death. To cry out that I had never seen nor heard tell of any band of English women turned warriors to defend their beloved city. But I held my tongue, knowing these gentlemen would speak more forthrightly without my bumpkinly intrusion.

"Parma may be a sorcerer, but King Philip is the Devil himself. Only the northern Netherlands is left to conquer, and after that we all know who is next."

"Thank Christ the Queen has finally moved against him." Starched Ruff referred to a force of 6,000 troops, 2,000 of which had already sailed for Brill and Flushing — a true English army, no longer volunteers.

"About time too, tho I hear our Bess rages at the very thought of our being drawn into the fight with Spain. She still avers a peace can be negotiated."

They all laughed uproariously, as tho such a thought were utterly ridiculous. Some of these young dandies bragged of their own commissions and seemed, in their naivete, to seek war as an amuse-

ment, a diversion from their otherwise tame existence. I thought, but did not say, how hard and bloody would be their future.

Then I heard the name of Lord Leicester spoke. That he had been chosen by Elizabeth to lead the army into Holland! My heart fairly leapt from my chest, part in joy, part in fear. Joy, for I knew how fervently the Dutch — Prince William particularly — had prayed for Leicesters helping hand. Fear that he had already set sail, and I had missed him.

My mind wandering, I was brought up short by renewed shouts of raucous laughter. When I put my ear to the conversation I found a derisive limerick was in the process of being devised in honor of my Fathers wife. The men were having trouble with the second line which rhymed with "There once was a Lady named Leicester," tho they had already written the final three which went, "She was known as a cunt, and fucked Christopher Blount, and for that Queen Elizabeth blessed her."

As several of the gentlemen continued their poetic anticks, I skirted behind the group to hear several others discussing Lord and Lady Leicester more seriously. I learnt that he had been made a cuckold by his wife and young Lord Blount, a man half her age. I learnt too that Leicesters only son by that marriage — the four year old Lord Denbigh — had recently died. What shocked me most profoundly, and for which I was entirely unprepared, was the hatred and contempt in which all of these gentlemen seemed to hold my Father. I had known him only as a hero. The greatest lord of the land. A horseman of great renown. Loyal friend of the Crown and lover of the Queen. Here now was a far uglier portrait. A greedy, selfish man consumed with ambition — one who fully deserved his horrible shrew of a wife, his cuckolding, and the death of his son. Apparently a pamphlet was circulating London, vicious and satirical, purporting the "truth" about Lord Leicester. That he was a voluptuary who needed Italian potions and salves to keep him erect, that he had embezzled money from the Queen and harassed her night and day. Worse, that he was not truly of noble blood, and worse still, that he was a murderer many times over. The pamphlet even claimed that Leicester had poisoned his own son because the boy had the falling sickness and one leg shorter than the other, and that the Earl could not brook a crippled child.

I was staggered on my feet, not solely to hear the slanderous words about the man I would soon claim as my Father, but to know that these gentlemen, every one, clearly believed them to be true. Suddenly I found the air too thick to breathe — a rich brew of human sweat, perfume, food odors, beer and piss. I backed away from the group, pushed thro the crowded aisle and stumbled out the doors.

As I gulped in the cool air I determined to gather my good spirits and wits, and dispel any doubts cast on Lord Leicester by a pack of jealous courtiers. I knew the man my self. He had been kind and concerned for me, and had set my mind towards education — an unequalled blessing. God blast what others thought! Her Majesty Queen Elizabeth and Robert Dudley and I were joined in our destiny. I was not a religious man, but now perceived God as the dealer of this mystical hand. We were a Queen of Diamonds and two Jacks. To my mind only one card was lacking — my own Queen of Hearts.

Robin Dudley's belly was paining him. As he moved round the royal stables on his regular inspection he found himself attempting to mask the cramps and rumbling gut with a veneer of brusqueness. He knew the stablehands would be unperturbed by his manner. They knew him well and he always dealt fairly with them, but he did hope to be spared the indignity of a headlong rush to the jakes.

He'd not been right since God had taken his son. The poor, sweet child. As he brought to mind the face of little Lord Denbigh another pain, sharp as a dagger, threatened to breach his composure. Twas harder and harder every day, thought Leicester miserably, to refrain from the habit of self-pity, for it seemed the world was falling down around his ears. His only heir, a gorgeous boy who had adored him and whom he had loved to distraction, was a dead and moldering corpse. So were his dear sister Mary Sidney and her husband Henry. *So much death, so much death . . .*

Having finally relinquished any hope of marrying Elizabeth, he had, perhaps unable to give up all pretensions to royal connections, attempted to arrange a marriage between his wife's daughter and the King of Scotland himself. When Elizabeth had discovered it she was livid, calling Lettice a "she wolf" and claiming she would rather see King James dead than married to Lady Leicester's bitch. The plan had of course come to naught.

His great enemy, Lord Sussex, had died, but the nobleman's deathbed utterance about Leicester to the Queen — "Beware of the Gypsy. He will be too hard on you all" — had soured any rejoicing Dudley might have felt to be rid of him.

And though he had long ago lost any real love for Lettice, the careless publicity with which she was conducting her affair with the young upstart Blount galled him. Too, there was the matter of the libelous pamphlet about him, calling him a murderer. . . . Even the great enjoyment of riding had, with the excruciating ache in his joints, become little more than a chore. Still, these were only domestic problems and somehow manageable.

But Mary Queen of Scots and her damnable plots continued to bedevil the Privy Council. The nephew of Elizabeth's trusted ambassador, Throckmorton, had been executed for his part in a Scottish-Spanish-Jesuit plot to overthrow Elizabeth. And with known assassins afoot she stubbornly scoffed at Leicester's concerns for her safety and continued to ride about in crowds or stride through Richmond Park on foot. Many a night he wakened in the cold sweat of a nightmare — the Queen murdered as he stood by watching helplessly.

But there was worse still. Elizabeth, with all the anguish of a prisoner having her fingernails ripped out by the roots, had finally consented to sending aid to the Netherlands, and had named him commander of the entire expedition. It was perhaps the greatest honor she had ever bestowed upon him, a vote of confidence in his talents, and a sign that she had forgiven him for marrying Lettice. But his joy was short-lived, for the moment the first two thousand troops had sailed for the Low Countries, the Queen had been seized by remorse and indecision. She was sure she would, by her actions, bring the full fury of Spain down upon England's head. She would make paupers of all her subjects and they would come to hate her. And she suddenly could not bear the thought of sending her Robin so far away from herself.

She had forbidden him to go.

Mercifully, only a handful of her councillors and his few friends — Walsingham, Hatton, Clinton, and Shrewsbury — knew that Elizabeth had called off the mustering of the remaining four thousand troops. Appearances had been maintained that all was going ahead as scheduled. But no amount of reasoning, cajoling, or badgering had yet moved Elizabeth to reconsider. Though Leicester had, over the years, acquired a thick hide, he felt — and his aching belly was the visceral proof — that he could simply not endure the humiliation of having this splendid commission rescinded.

* * *

To my mind the Royal Stables at Hampton Court were nothing less than Heaven on Earth — a place where the finest horses in the world were bred, trained and cherished. Twas well known how the Queen loved these animals and said that even now, well past fifty years old, she still rode vigorously every day the weather allowed. The previous day, my Dutch officers uniform and my confident and commanding demeanor — perhaps my greatest feat of playacting ever — had gained me entrance to the stable environs. I was escorted by a young stablehand thro the long stone stalls that housed two hundred mounts, the training grounds and the equipment hall. This last was filled to the rafters with elegant equestrian accoutrements and ceremonial finery — high plumed helmets, colorful banners, fringed saddles of cloth of gold, solid silver bits and bridles.

I had learned from the stablehand that Lord Leicester — still Master of the Queens Horse after all these years — would make his inspection the following day — today. I felt my palms sweating under white leather gloves purchased especially for this meeting. My uniform was worn but it was as clean as I could make it. I had wished to wear something new for this occasion, something to celebrate my new life. I had paid far too much for the soft kid gloves, but was glad I was wearing them now.

As I passed the training grounds where a half dozen horses were learning the basics of manège, I felt my body trembling. Twas fear. Fear that the presentation of my claim to the Earl would be clumsy and humiliating, that words would fail me, that I would begin and be unable to finish. Or worse, that once spoken — even eloquently — my claim would be denied. After all, what reason had I to hope? Why should such a high man believe the story of a common soldier?

I commanded my self to stop, cease all ideas of defeat at once. Truth. Courage. Destiny. Only those thoughts should be allowed. I spotted the young stablehand from the previous day and strode to greet him. The boy was once again friendly and told me that I was in luck, for Lord Leicester had arrived and could be found in the stalls. I thanked him and allowing my self no further hesitation, hiked my self high, squared my shoulders and made for the long stone building.

Inside I felt my body relax at once. The dim light, the musky odors, the sight of the animals in all their strength and beauty, comforted me with their familiarity. Just ahead I could see Lord Leicester conferring with a pinchfaced officer of the Royal Guard. Whilst I knew certainly that the older of the two men must be the Earl, I found myself daunted by the cruel toll the years had taken on my boyhood idol. Tho still tall, the grace with which Lord Leicester had once moved was gone, replaced by stiff, painful jerks at his joints. A bloated face and belly marred the outline of his once spare and muscular form. But as I moved closer I could yet, despite the unhealthily florid cheeks, sagging jowls and full silver beard, recognize this man as the one I had met some fifteen years before. Then the pinchfaced officer departed, leaving Leicester alone, one hand resting on his distended belly, staring in at a stately piebald of sixteen hands.

"Lord Leicester," I said. "Begging your pardon, Sir."

Robin Dudley had been contemplating a visit to the stool when he heard a deep, melodious male voice addressing him. He turned to face a striking young man. Square jawed. Young, he thought, but too weathered to be green. Tall, even taller than himself, and solidly built. There was a depth to the eyes, black eyes that contrasted strangely with the pale skin and reddish-gold hair clipped short. He wore the distinctive uniform of a Dutch officer but he was, from the sound of his voice, clearly an Englishman.

Leicester felt his stomach seize again. The man looked vaguely familiar. Could he be an assassin? He had more than his share of enemies.

"Who are you? What do you want?" he fairly barked.

The young man stood his ground without flinching. He has seen battle, this one, thought Leicester suddenly — known worse than a rude reception by an ill tempered old fart in a stable.

"My name is Arthur Southern, Sir. Lately a captain in Prince William's cavalry."

Leicester regarded the man more closely. 'Twas a strange thing to say. William of Orange had been dead for more than a year. Arthur Southern sensed the silent question.

"It will always be his army, Sir."

Leicester had met with William once, knew of his grace and magnetic power over men. Briefly he wondered whether he himself would ever engender such love and loyalty from his troops . . . if ever he was given an army.

“ ’Tis excellent news you are going to the Netherlands, my lord,” offered Arthur Southern. “The Dutch people dearly wish for your presence. ’Tis what the Prince himself wished for.”

“You knew him?”

“I did.” Arthur’s black eyes turned suddenly liquid. “I was with him when he died, Sir.”

“Why do you look familiar to me?” demanded the Earl with a touch of irritation.

Surprisingly the young man’s face exploded into a broad smile. A smile, thought Leicester, which was itself familiar.

“We have met, my lord. Many years ago the Queen and yourself—the entire Court came through my father’s estate on summer progress. Enfield Chase in Surrey.”

Leicester searched his memory. “Enfield . . . ha! A wild goose chase in a lovely greenwood. Yes, I remember.” A smile began to grow on his tired face. “A young boy performed for us on his horse that day.” He stared into Arthur’s face. “ ’Twas you!”

“It was, Sir.” They were both smiling delightedly. “You gave me a book, do you remember?”

Leicester searched his mind, shook his head.

“Xenophon’s *The Art of Horsemanship.* It changed my life.”

Finally remembering, “You learned to read Greek, then?”

“I did indeed.” Now they laughed.

It was all coming back to Dudley. “So, have you come to take me up on my offer? A position with the guard?”

“No, Sir, I have not.” Arthur had grown suddenly serious. “I have come . . . I . . . wish to tell you . . .”

Now courage failed him. Truth seemed a thousand miles away from this place. And destiny seemed nothing more than a boyhood fantasy. Leicester was staring at him expectantly, but the words simply would not come.

“Augh!” Without warning Leicester clutched at the stall door and his red cheeks paled alarmingly.

“Sir?”

The Earl’s breath was coming in short gasps. “My rooms. Help me to my rooms.”

“Lean on me,” said Arthur.

“No!” Leicester straightened, struggling to preserve his dignity. “Just walk with me. Stay close.”

“Yes, Sir. ’Tis my honor, Sir.”

* * *

The Earl's lodgings were several large and comfortable rooms on the second floor of Hampton Court's west wing. When he and Arthur entered they found the rooms excessively occupied by young men — an odd mixture of them, students poring over their books, sensitive-faced youths bent double over sheets of parchment, quill in hand, a daydreamer dreaming in a windowseat, several men browsing amongst an impressive collection of books. Around a table a group of courtiers loudly argued the merits of one of Philips Sidney's poems versus one by another young poet, Edmund Spenser, who lived under the Earl's roof at his famous London mansion Leicester House.

Leicester dismissed them all and cleared the room within moments, motioning only for Arthur to stay. Then he rushed behind a wicker screen to his closed stool and loosed his poisonous bowels, moaning all the while in agony and relief. When he had finished, he reappeared to find that young Southern looked surprisingly more distressed than disgusted, and quickly rang for a servant. As the valet scurried in and removed the covered pot, Leicester swallowed a mouthful of liquid from a blue glass flask. The valet returned almost immediately and smoked the room with puffs of incense and pungent herbs.

Finally they were alone.

"Are you ill, my lord?" Arthur inquired.

Leicester was moved by the apparent depth and sincerity of the young man's caring, and just as baffled. It suddenly occurred to him that he had, a moment ago, allowed a complete stranger to be witness to a most personal and incommodious display. There was something about him . . . a kind of comfort. Leicester suddenly recalled that the little boy who so many years ago had astonished them with his masterful performance of manège had recently been beaten bloody. The Earl had been a witness to *his* private disgrace. Was this then the tie?

"I would have to say . . . I am not myself," Leicester finally answered, realizing as he did that his head was spinning. "The potion is an opiate, good for the pain, but dizzy-making. Perhaps I should lie down for a moment."

Arthur sprang instantly to help the older man and gently eased him down on the magnificent canopied bed, boots and all. Dudley felt his leaden eyelids slowly closing, though he did not sleep. He was subtly aware of Arthur Southern's sentrylike presence, and finally he felt the pains in his miserable body begin to abate.

He heard the knock on his door as in a dream. Then Arthur Southern was whispering in his ear. "My lord, 'tis a message from the Queen."

Leicester forced open his eyes. The young man held out a folded parchment with Elizabeth's seal affixed to it. He rallied himself, rose on an elbow, and ripped open the letter. "Oh, thank Christ!" he cried.

Arthur was beaming with shared pleasure, though he would never presume to inquire of the message's nature.

"'Tis good news, Arthur, very good news indeed." Leicester sat up in bed, blinking back tears of relief. He suddenly felt altogether well and wondered briefly if it were the opiate potion working its magic in his veins, or the news that Elizabeth had finally relented and given him leave to depart for the Netherlands at the head of her army. God be praised!

"We shall have a drink," announced Leicester, almost leaping off his bed. He moved to a table and poured claret into two fine Venetian goblets. He handed one to Arthur. "To victory in the Netherlands," he said, raising his glass.

"And to Prince William's dream," added Arthur, touching glasses with Leicester. They drank. The Earl offered his guest a seat next to his and, pulling out a carven wood pipe, filled it with tobacco. The afternoon spent itself at a slow and languorous pace, the two men smoking and drinking and laughing as if they were companions of a lifetime.

By the time the valet had come and lit the candles, set a blazing fire in the hearth, and laid a simple supper on the board, Robin Dudley and Arthur Southern were well and truly drunk.

"Do you not wonder, my lord Leicester," began Arthur, having swallowed an enormous mouthful of red wine, "why I have come to see you today?"

"'Tis not for a post, you told me that. 'Tis not to murder me, for you would have done that long ago. Methinks you have come . . . though I do not know why . . . to *befriend* me."

Arthur wiped his mouth with the back of his hand. "No, my lord, I have not come as your friend." Leicester sat back in his chair and stared. "I have come . . . as your son."

Leicester regarded the younger man stupidly. "My son? No, no, my son is dead." His eyes suddenly filled with tears. "My little boy. Only four. He limped, you know. One leg shorter than the other. I had him made a tiny suit of armor. He would put it on for me and pretend" — two large tears rolled down Leicester's ruddy cheeks — "pretend he was Saint George . . . slaying the dragon to protect me. He wanted to protect *me.*"

Arthur listened, thinking of little Lord Denbigh, the Earl of Leicester, Robert Southern . . . himself. And suddenly, despite the copious amount of wine he had consumed, he felt as sober and clearheaded as a Puritan preacher.

"I was born, Sir, in August of 1561. In Fulham Castle. 'Twas the night of a terrible storm."

The Earl of Leicester was struggling to clear his muddled mind. He found he could not take his eyes from the face of the young man sitting across from him. He was speaking of things he had no business knowing, saying words he had no business saying, stirring long forgotten memories from the depths where they had been laboriously buried. *That terrible night. Another dead child.*

He lunged suddenly at Arthur Southern, falling on him and throttling him. "Who are you!" he shouted.

Arthur's answer was barely audible, a harsh whisper choked from his throat, but he neither fought back nor even struggled. "Mistress Katherine Ashley . . . the lord William Cecil . . . secreted me away that night." The force of Leicester's grasp lessened, and he stared owl-eyed at the man beneath him. "A dead infant was shown to yourself . . . and the Queen."

Leicester suddenly unhanded Arthur Southern as if he were made of hot metal, then sat heavily on the floor near the young man's feet, staring into the fire. He was utterly silent as Arthur related what he had been told of his own circumstances by Robert Southern.

"Have you proof?" Leicester asked woodenly, still staring into the fire and never meeting Arthur's eyes.

"What did you name that stillborn babe, Sir?" asked Arthur.

Leicester was silent.

"Did you not name him Arthur?"

"It means nothing," Leicester shot back.

"Look at me, my lord." But Leicester was still as stone, refusing stubbornly to move. "Look at me and tell me you do not see yourself . . . see my mother in me!"

"You have red hair, pale skin. So do a full quarter of the people in England."

"I have your height. Elizabeth is tall. My grandfather Henry was —"

"Shut your mouth!" shrieked Leicester, finally turning on Arthur in a fearsome rage. "You have no right to use their names in such a way. No right to trick me! Get out, get out or I swear I will murder you with my two bare hands!"

Arthur remained calm. "Perhaps, before I leave, you should look closely at *my* two hands." He unbuttoned his white kid gloves and removed them.

Leicester found himself unable to continue his attack. He simply stared at the square, callused, soldier-scarred hands, their strong fingers spread out before him. Slowly Arthur swiveled his whole left arm, thumb pointing down to the floor. Leicester blinked. Was the firelight playing tricks on his eyes, or was there in fact, protruding from the outer side of Arthur Southern's hand, a nub of flesh and within it a bit of nail? A sixth finger?

Slowly he looked up into the young man's eyes. All at once he knew where he had seen those infamous black and beguiling eyes before. In portraits of Elizabeth's mother . . . Anne Boleyn.

"Dear God," said Leicester quietly as he stared into the face of Elizabeth's son. His son.

When he began to tremble uncontrollably, the young man slowly enfolded in his strong, muscled arms the body of the man who had given him life. Together they began to weep, first in anger for the many years wasted, the love lost . . . and finally in joy for the love found, and the great miracle that God, in His infinite mercy, had finally seen fit to bestow.

We never slept that night, my true Father and I, and before the sun rose into the misty morning he had given me his name. I was Arthur Dudley, and for that I was most proud. Tho my courage had only been achieved thro the use of strong drink I had never the less revealed the truth, and laid my foot down upon the path of my new destiny.

But more valuable than his name, this man had given me his heart — that faithful organ long battered by disappointment and scarred by the years of hatred and jealousy it had had to endure. Despite this, his was not a bitter heart, and it overflowed with love for my self.

Once he had come to accept my true birth, Lord Leicester opened himself to me — and I to him — and we spent the too short night pouring forth like two fountainheads into a common pool the stories of our lives — our loves, enemies, trials, hopes and mysteries. He spoke at length of his attempts to marry my Mother the Queen. How all had believed he pursued her solely for the advantages to his position. He owned forthrightly his ambitious nature, but swore —

and I believed him — that he had loved Elizabeth passionately from the time they were young children and adored her still. He wept many times that night, but none more bitterly than when he spoke of the moment he had understood she would never be his, that the dream of marrying the woman he loved must finally and irrevocably be laid to rest. He told how hard it had been to watch Elizabeth carrying on with her publick life, knowing in some deep part of her soul she wished desperately to be tied intimately with himself. And how extraordinary a person my Mother was — singular and entirely enchanting. He quoted a poet who described her thus — "She fishes for mens souls with so sweet a bait that no man can escape her net." Then he laughed ruefully, calling himself the biggest salmon in her sea.

He spoke of her beauty, especially in youth. Of her velvet white complexion before it had been marred by the smallpox and harsh cosmetics which ate into the flesh like deadly acid. How her long curly hair had been the color of a late afternoon sun. And how the majestic grace of her movements was itself a kind of loveliness.

He spoke, too, of the other beauty my Mother had possessed, and possessed still. The beauty of her mind. My Father confided this was the best part of her. Not simply her intellect — product of a steely mental constitution and magnificent education — but her wit, sometimes biting as a baited dog, other times sweetly rollicking, and others as raw and bawdy as a street whore.

Despite his own disappointments in matters of the heart he urged me to ever follow mine and to faithfully seek the woman I admitted I had been dreaming about since the age of fourteen. He hoped that she would possess, as my Mother did, that rare combination of beauty and strength of mind for, he cautioned, even the most delicious of cunts grows old and withered, but a great mind, like a fine wine, grows all the richer with age.

As the sun rose higher into the soggy sky we stood staring out the window towards the Thames and began talk of a more solid nature. Lord Leicester was leaving immediately for the Netherlands, so all arrangements with regard to my self would, of necessity, take place immediately. He said he had, during the past evening, considered the vagaries of our situation.

"Ah son, tis more complicated than even you can imagine. Your Mother — you know she is now forced to wage war against Spain in the Netherlands."

"I do. And this distresses her."

My Father laughed mirthlessly. "She is in a state of such appalling upheaval and fragility that I fear the sudden shock of your existence might kill her." His voice grew gentle. "Your Mother cannot at present be told you are alive." As we watched the vessels large and small coursing along the great water artery to the citys heart, Leicester put his arm round my shoulder. "You are like a frigate under full sail, Arthur. Pretty . . . but dangerous. I hope you understand why we shall have to wait for a more opportune moment to tell her."

I would be a liar if I said I was not disappointed, but I saw his logic and knew that he shared with the Queen an indisputably honorable quality — the love of his country and the ability to put its needs before his own personal desires. And more important, I had at least claimed his *love and acceptance. Patience, I knew, was a virtue I would have to learn.*

"I understand, I do," I replied, "but I wish so dearly to serve England, my lord!"

He smiled and said, "Father. I wish you to call me Father."

We embraced and I whispered the word in his ear, mightily thankful there was still a man I could call by that name.

"Let me think on your future awhile," he said, "for I can tell you this. If any harm should come to you on my account, when your Mother finds out, she will have me beheaded!"

We laughed and I assured him no one, himself included, could keep me long from harms way, for I lived for action, even danger, and I craved new sights and adventure in the way a drunkard craves his spirits.

"Perhaps you should come to the Netherlands, serve as my right hand," he suggested.

"No, Father, I am no diplomat. I am a soldier, and one who has lost the taste for fighting — at least in the way the Dutch and the Spanish still fight. The siege . . ." I could hardly go on. "The siege holds only horrible memories for me. I somehow feel I have given all I can give in the Low Countries."

He stroked his jowly chin and regarded me carefully. Then he questioned me as a schoolmaster might — but the subject was my self. What were my skills, besides the obvious? What were my loves, my hates? I said I had several languages besides English.

"Hmph. Your Mothers son in that. Elizabeth has a brilliant ear and speaks eight languages fluently."

I smiled, shyly delighted to be compared to the Queen, for tho I was fast becoming comfortable with the thought of Leicester as my Father, Elizabeth as my Mother was as exotic as a tribe of New World savages.

I told him I enjoyed disguising my self and taking on alien roles, and related my experiences on the road to Gouda pretending to be a Dutch merchant, and of dressing up as a Haarlem prostitute to lure the Spanish soldiers to their death.

"What think you," he said slowly, as if forming the thought only as he spoke, "of a career as a spy for England?"

I fairly whooped with joy.

"Walsingham has his men," Leicester explained. "Some on the Continent. Others in Spain itself. But I could use my own 'eyes and ears' abroad. Someone I could trust implicitly."

I thought my heart would burst with pride and excitement. We began making our plans at once.

My Fathers secretary, Mister Fludd, was assigned to deliver me to Francis Walsingham and request that he issue me a passport. Fludd had been told, and was to tell the man, I was an especial friend of the Earls, and to make haste in concluding this business.

We arrived at Secretary Walsinghams house on the Strand in the early evening amidst a great downpour. When he saw Fludd Walsingham graciously bid us enter, for he was a good friend of my Father and was eager to help him in any way he could. Fludd, however, must have been flustered by the suddenness of my appearance from nowhere, believing he knew all of my Fathers friends and acquaintances, and was perhaps wary of the urgency with which he had been directed to acquire this passport for me. So whilst he carried out his instructions correctly in every way, his manner of explaining my situation was so nervous and stuttering that Walsingham — head of the Queens Secret Service — became immediately suspicious. He said he would be glad to issue me the document but — he hoped I would forgive him — he would need to interrogate me fully. With England poised to make war against Philip of Spain, he explained, the security of the country was at stake, and he could not be too careful.

I, of course, agreed with him enthusiastically and said I would answer all his questions and provide him with all of my papers which were in my saddlebags. I excused my self saying I was going to retrieve them and walked out the front door. Taking my horse from the groom I mounted her and rode hastily away into the storm, never looking back, for I had promised my Father that no one should know my true birth until the time was right. He for his part would refrain even from confiding to William Cecil that he knew of my existence. I now feared that Walsingham, a talented interrogator, might learn more than I — just beginning this life of subterfuge — and my father wanted him to know.

I had said my goodbyes to Lord Leicester, who claimed to be cheered beyond measure by my appearance in his life, and promised to stay in close contact with me on my sojourn. But he himself was in frantic preparation for his journey to the Netherlands — expecting to remain there a year or more — and tho he fervently wished to spend more time with me, said it was impossible. He looked forward to the day when he, my Mother and my self would all come together, and prayed it would be at a time when England had been delivered from the threat of war, and our meeting would be not simply a personal one, but a celebration of the peace which Elizabeth sought so religiously.

Leicester had given me more than sufficient funds to begin my life as a spy, with assurance that money should never again be a worry for me. My first expenditure — as the bid for a passport had been a failure — became a generous bribe to a sailor who happily smuggled me aboard a vessel bound for Calais. Twas the easiest crossing I had yet made. It surprised me how little I regretted leaving England again, and so soon. As the ship weighed anchor with a stiff breeze filling the sails, I gazed briefly back at the sparkling cliffs of Dover, then turned my eyes towards the other shore. In four hours time I was in France, and my life of spying had begun.

Thirty-five

"He has done what! Say again, Mister Davison, for I fear my ears may be rebelling in my head, as my teeth are currently doing. Repeat what you have said of Lord Leicester carefully and slowly." Elizabeth sat this morning in council with Lord Cecil, Secretary Walsingham, and her new favorite, Walter Raleigh, staring incredulously at the envoy from the Netherlands.

"He has accepted the title pressed on him by the Estates, of Supreme Governor of the United Provinces, Your Majesty."

Elizabeth was seething, but managed to restrain herself in the presence of Leicester's adjutant, recently arrived at Court.

"To be fair, Your Majesty, they did press this honor on him very heartily, for they are so sorely in need of a leader since the death of the Prince of Orange."

"Oh indeed," sneered Elizabeth, "as sorely as they needed a way to ensnare England into an irrevocable gesture of hostility against Spain, a way that leaves me no choice but to commit all of my financial resources to win their war!" She turned to her advisors. "What think you of this contemptible treachery, gentlemen?"

Cecil and Walsingham were in silent but frantic contemplation of this entirely unexpected development. Leicester never failed to impress them with his self-seeking machinations, but this far exceeded any previous acts of insolence.

"I must say it surprises me, Madame," offered Cecil. "Leicester knew quite well that you yourself refused the very same title some months ago."

"And for good reason!" shouted Elizabeth. "'Tis an open proclamation of war against Spain!"

Walsingham squirmed in his seat. His friend had gone beyond the boundaries of good sense, and now the Secretary groped for a response that would not further anger the Queen, yet might offer a reasonable defense of Leicester's lunacy. Walsingham was doubly uneasy, knowing he must soon tell Her Majesty of a plot he had recently uncovered — once again devised by that evil spiderwoman Mary Queen of Scots, along with an Englishman named Babington — to overthrow Elizabeth, yea assassinate her. This time the Queen would have no choice but to try Mary for treason. Oh, how his head ached, but he forced himself to remain calm as he said, "Lord Leicester has shown tremendous organization and good sense in his garrisoning of your forces in Holland, Your Majesty. The troops are well behaved, they attend services regularly, and restrain themselves admirably in the retaking of the cities from the Spanish. There has been no looting or pillage or raping, and Leicester is credited with their most civil presence in a foreign land."

Elizabeth snorted, but Walsingham went on. "I have had reports from Lord North that Leicester is going about inspecting fortifications and having numerous trenches dug. North says he does not shrink from placing himself in danger of musket shot and is apparently respected by the army. Perhaps, under the circumstances, his way is the most reasonable course of action."

"*I* think he could not resist the temptation of such grandeur," interjected Raleigh, perhaps with too flippant a tone, though Elizabeth seemed not to notice. She was very, very angry at her old friend, and the darkly handsome Raleigh — arrayed like a peacock in his splendid new clothes and altogether magnetic charms — expressed perfectly her own thoughts on Leicester at this moment.

"If Robert Dudley was denied the crown of England," Raleigh persisted, "he would no doubt settle for the crown of Holland. He is an arrogant, avaricious man. How could he resist the welcome he received? They say 'twas fit for a king — bells chiming, cannons saluting, feasts and pageants in his honor, fireworks. Even a triumphal arch. And I can only imagine the glee with which Lady Leicester is even now preparing to join her 'sovereign' husband."

"Oh!" cried Elizabeth, flushing so angrily that pink glowed behind the thick white makeup she now wore. "I can just see the ostentatious display. Lettice already rides about Cheapside in a carriage drawn by four milk white horses, with four footmen and thirty mounted gentlemen before and behind her. God's death, there is but one Queen in England!"

Walsingham wished he could stuff his fist down Raleigh's throat to stifle his inflammatory remarks. Damage had been done and repair was in order, not further incitement.

"He will publicly renounce the title at once," said Elizabeth, rapping her knuckles sharply on the table.

"I think perhaps that is unwise, Majesty."

Walsingham turned in surprise at Lord Cecil's cool-tempered response. Perhaps age had indeed mellowed the old man's loathing for Leicester. Or, thought Walsingham, William Cecil was simply the most levelheaded councillor Elizabeth had had the good fortune ever to have serve her. Indeed, the Queen's agitation, though still palpable, appeared to be receding slightly.

"You are suggesting we let him keep the title, William?" she asked.

"I'm afraid we must. 'Twould be far more disastrous to remove so lovingly bestowed an honor. A slap in the Estates' face. And frankly, Your Majesty . . ." Cecil paused before continuing, as though the words he was about to speak were distasteful to him. "Though I have always shared your reluctance to openly engage with Spain, the die has unfortunately been cast. Philip, despite your protestations otherwise, cannot fail to see that you mean to protect the Netherlands against his invasion."

Elizabeth's face set itself into a stony grimace. She closed her eyes and breathed fiercely through flaring nostrils. "Oh, Robin, Robin, what have you done? What have you done?"

Thirty-six

No longer was I armed for a soldier, but for a spy. With my Fathers intelligence to guide me I sought to know all of Walsinghams secret agents abroad, there to learn the tricks of the trade, and also to improve my command of the languages which would become an important part of my disguise.

Leicester bade me present my self to the English Ambassador in France, one Edward Stafford, cautioning me on two counts to be ware. Firstly, Staffords wife was Douglas Sheffield, once my Fathers lover, and proof of my association with him would lend an unpleasant air to any relations I might attempt to promote with the couple. The libelous pamphlet about my Father had recently reached Paris and was causing no end of embarrassment to that lady, exposing all of the dirty linen of their affair and of the suspicious circumstances surrounding the death of her first husband.

Secondly, Leicester and Walsingham were convinced that Stafford was a double agent, a go-between for English and French Catholics in the pay of the Duke of Guise, and they suspected he also gave our secrets to Spain — both grossly treasonable acts which they explained away, quite cheerily, as a result of the Ambassador's poor financial condition. I found the attitude strange, but learnt that Walsingham had once served in the very same post in France and likewise suffered in his tenure from the Queens meanness in salary and grants. The temptation towards bribery was undeniable. But Walsingham, besides being a principled man and a patriot, had no demanding wife to support in a state of luxury, and so never succumbed to such treachery. Too, he reasoned that Stafford, having gained the trust of the Spaniards by handing over English secrets, was therefore as valuable a source of information in the opposite direction, and that the one outweighed the other. Stafford was therefore allowed to retain his position. Twas in the very fine English Embassy in Paris that I visited him and his wife.

I was eager in the extreme to meet them both, and I was not disappointed. The Embassy was exquisite, decorated in the French style which appeared to my eye — relatively untrained to luxury — more delicate, light and fanciful than the English. Lady Stafford, Mother of my half brother Robert, was still a beautiful woman with a great expanse of peach and cream bosom rising out of a low cut silken bodice. Twas easy to see how my Father could have fallen under her spell. Sir Edward was a staid fellow with a blunt, almost rude manner which I — somewhat unbalanced in my first undercover engagement — found slightly unnerving. Knowing I would be long gone from Paris before he could find out otherwise, I presented myself as Harold Morton, one of Walsinghams cadre of highborn students he used as agents.

As we supped in their dining room under a gold leaf ceiling, Lady Stafford openly made eyes at me, whilst her husbands face was in his soup, ranting about Walsinghams idiocy for bankrupting himself to keep his Secret Service afloat. Elizabeth apparently had not yet committed sufficient funds for the task at hand, still not believing the situation was as grim as he and her other war hawks did. During the capon and roast quail Sir Edward made mincemeat of the debauched French King Henry whom he disparaged for dressing like a woman, complete with makeup, hair done up in great ruffles, and a passel of tiny living dogs hung about his neck like a necklace.

But during the fish course Stafford began questioning me to determine both my credibility and my potential usefulness to himself. Having been briefed by my Father I had sufficient inside information to put the Ambassador at his ease, and so he admitted — with the first glimmer of any emotion save sourness that I had seen in him — that he had recently had intelligence from his Spanish sources. He had not yet passed along to Walsingham the information that within several months Elizabeth would be assailed in her own realm, and that a great Spanish army was preparing for it.

I had been in mid chew when he divulged this, and discovered my mouth hanging agape. Spain meant to attack England! Stafford went on to say that Philip and his agents had taken great pains to keep this information from Elizabeth, and that it should go a long way towards opening her eyes to the immediate danger Spain posed our country. I composed my self and — whilst chancing a flirtatious glance back at Lady Stafford, who seemed unable to tear her eyes from me — considered how clever was Francis Walsingham. Leaving the devious, bribable Stafford in his place had paid off handsomely, if only for this single brilliant piece of intelligence.

When the meal was done and all the civilities had been performed, Sir Edward excused himself for a meeting, and Lady Stafford showed me to the door. In retrospect I was less shocked than I thought I should be when she pressed her body next to mine and fondled my manhood which — somewhat embarrassingly — was unprepared for the assault. Douglas Stafford pulled away with a petulant frown. Knowing we would not soon meet again, and made bold by her boldness, I said in the pleasantest of tones, "How does your son, Robert Dudley?"

Her shock gave me a perverse sense of pleasure, but it had also taken her off guard, so she answered without questioning my curiosity, and perhaps more directly than she might have otherwise replied.

"He is in England and I rarely see him, but I understand he is well. He is almost thirteen now. They say he is tall and handsome . . . like his Father." This last word she uttered so scathingly that I had to steel my self from cringing. Then she looked at me again with such searching eyes I thought it best to remove my self from her sight lest she see who I really was. I turned to go. She caught my hand, placed it on her pale breast, moved it down inside her bodice so my fingers grazed her risen nipple and said, "Do come again, Harry. You are always welcome here."

I felt my self harden on the spot, but dared not linger a moment more. I went back to my rooms and composed in a rude cypher I had recently learnt, my first dispatch to Lord Leicester in Holland, informing him of Spains outrageous plan to invade England.

Having acquired knowledge of King Philips nefarious intentions I wished fervently to leave quickly for Spain to put my services to their best use. But Lord Leicester in his encyphered letters instructed me under no circumstances to leave Europe without first meeting up with his dear friend and tutor Doctor John Dee — a famous man to be sure, but one whose usefulness to the English cause was, to my mind, somewhat dubious. I never the less bowed to my

Fathers wishes and travelling overland to Bohemia and the capital city of Prague, arranged to call upon Dee at the Royal Palace of King Rudolph II.

As I rode in thro the city gates I was at first unimpressed with the town, it seeming no more or less grand or downtrodden than any other European city I had seen in my recent travels. But as I rode into the central environs where the Palace stood I became gradually aware of an odd atmosphere pervading the place. Not so much the buildings, for they were unremarkable, but the broad mixture of voices, languages and accents I overheard — German, Italian, Muscovy, French, English, Italian, Arabic. There were small groups of students and of older men, even women congregated, their heads bent together in an attitude of passionate discourse, or poring over an open book on a garden table. Twas entirely enchanting to know that here in Prague was a melting pot of cultures, ideas, education. It seemed all at once, despite its grey stone walls and dirty streets, nothing less than a city of light.

By the time I found Doctor Dee in the Palace courtyard — he was a long nosed, long bearded elder with the piercingest eyes I had ever seen — I was already in a state of wonder. All round were gardens planted in the most intricate of geometrical patterns, elaborate sundials, green grottos enlivened with statues of mythical gods, horned and winged creatures, and other worldly mechanical contraptions. Dee clearly enjoyed my rapturous appraisal of the Palace grounds, and after the briefest of introductions, he endeavored to give me a tour of the place.

He was clearly more than a visitor here. He was a close confidant of King Rudolph, and had been given complete freedom to roam the castle at will. As we explored Dee began a discourse in which he opened him self to me — a measure of his trust in the man who had brought us together, Lord Leicester.

"One would never guess King Rudolph is a Hapsburg," said Dee as we entered a small but impressively stocked library. "His nephew Philip of Spain finds him very queer indeed, his interest in the occult and the sciences nothing short of madness."

I kept silent, as I had also heard that Rudolph was altogether balmy and, too, that Dee himself was of questionable character.

"All who travel to this city are blessed for having such a safe haven for ideas of every nature," he continued. He looked away pensively, surveying the carven shelves laden with leatherbound

volumes. "My own library at Mortlake was recently looted by a mob of Puritan zealots. And of course Spains influence is not altogether absent here. My associate Edward Kelly and I were detained by the religious authorities — arrested in deed. They wished to send us to Rome for interrogation regarding our magickal practices, but Kelly is a good talker. He talked the papal nuncio out of all thoughts of persecution — for the time being at least." He fixed me with those piercing eyes. "One must always take care, Arthur, even in Prague."

Now he pointed out to my surprise that the books in this library — every one — were of a mystical nature. He pulled out an ancient volume and paged thro it almost tenderly.

"Your magickal practices," I asked. "Can you tell me more about them?"

"You must understand that there is a difference between malificarum, *black witchcraft of which I have been accused, and* magica, *the study of Natures hidden powers of which I am a devoted adherent. From Nature can be extracted all manner of science, and in science lies the future, yes!" His mood seemed suddenly to have been lifted by the subject, and his voice grew strong and passionate.*

"Knowledge of science — technologia *— must be learnt by everyone, artisans in particular. There is no limit to what can be done with such knowledge, none! I believe entire countries can be soundly defeated without the use of an army, yes!"*

So preposterous was that statement that my politely curious mien turned to one of utter shock, but before I could ask him how such a thing could be accomplished he had changed the subject, asking after Lord Leicester. As I related his news I could see how affectionately Dee felt towards my Father. Part of me wished to declare my parentage, for I knew the truth would be safe with him, but I had promised to tell no one, and so I remained silent.

As our tour of the Palace took us into one of Rudolphs wonder rooms — outfitted no doubt by the Doctor himself — I observed all manner of intrigue from the astrolabes, globes, retorts of the alchemical laboratory equipment, to a crystal showstone which purportedly revealed the future, to the charted horoscopes of every monarch on the Continent. By the time he suggested we retire to his home I was dizzied with the sights and sounds, and ideas, and readily accepted his invitation.

As we rode slowly through the town and out the city gates into the lush countryside, Dee inquired after another of his students very dear to him — Philip Sidney. I had learnt during that first night in my Fathers rooms that his now deceased sister Mary Sidney was the Mother — and therefore I the cousin — of the much loved poet, Philip. The young man, who had married Francis Walsinghams daughter Frances, had been given a commission in the Netherlands as Governor of Flushing. I could now add to that the knowledge, gleaned from my correspondence with Leicester, that Philip Sidney the soldier was engaging in open warfare with Parmas Spanish troops, and had distinguished him self with feats of courage and bravery in the field.

I saw Dees face grow dark and asked to know what troubled him.

"I do not like Philips stars," he said simply. "They bode very evil. And yet . . . what can be done?" He looked at me very closely then and I wondered if he saw my future in my eyes. Then I thought, no, he has not cast my horoscope, he has not consulted his dark crystal, he knows nothing about me except what I have told him.

We reached the magnificent estate of Trebona, where Dee and his associate Kelly had lived for more than a year as the guests of Villem Rozmbeck. I was shown to a lovely chamber overlooking a flower bedecked pond, and after some simple refreshment I found the Doctor most eager to continue our conversation. We left the main house and wandering thro some overgrown garden paths, finally came to a small cottage, the top half of its wooden door open, a skinny, middle aged man dressed simply in wool breeches and a linen shirt, bent over a table doing some manner of close work.

"Here is Kelly," said Dee. The man looked up. He had shaggy brown hair and a bright, open face with a large smile, marred by the loss of one tooth on the bottom and its mate on the top. "Meet Arthur Southern, Edward. A friend of Lord Robert."

I entered and within moments the three of us were engaged in the liveliest and most unusual conversation that I have ever experienced. Whereas I had believed, in my naivete, that the substance of Doctor Dee's philosophy had been explained to me at King Rudolphs castle, I now discerned he had barely scratched the surface of the brilliant crystal that was his mind. Here in the private and protected sanctity of his laboratory Dee began to speak of the real reason for his presence at Rudolphs Court. He was one of Walsinghams spies.

"I may be a magician, but above all I am a patriot," he explained to me, running his hand absently over the page of a large open volume, "and I have learnt a way of using the magick arts . . . as a tool of State policy. I began many years ago when I cast a horoscope for Princess Elizabeth to determine the most auspicious day for her coronation. Later I used my gazing crystal to discover the mode of transmission of treasonous correspondences between Mary Queen of Scots and her conspirators. Twas in the wine bottles," he added mischievously. "You see, my boy, I believe in an incomparable and unconquerable United British Empire with the Queen its Emperor, overruled by God, and armed with the invincible weapons of magica and technologia."

Kelly spoke up in a voice that was mellifluous and commanding, and touched with more than a bit of cynicism. The very timbre of it caused me to attend carefully, and I could see how he might easily sell a rag to a ragpicker. "The good Doctor contends that our Queen is a direct descendant of King Arthur of Camelot, and that the Tudor State is a restoration of his very kingdom."

I turned to look questioningly at Dee — for Kellys statement was stunning to me and I suddenly wondered at the name my Mother had given me. Was it merely coincidence? I found Dee staring intently at my self.

"Did my . . ." I was flustered, flushed red. Doctor Dee pierced me with those eyes. "Does the Queen know this theory of yours?"

He nodded slowly, never taking his eyes from me. I wished to ask for how long she had been aware, and if she concurred, but I dared not hold open my hand that wide for his scrutiny.

Kelly went on, the edge of sarcasm sharpened to a point. "I do believe my associate sees himself as Elizabeths own Merlin."

Dee was perturbed neither by this revelation nor the tone of Kellys voice. He said, "Kelly and I converse with the Angels, Arthur, in an attempt to bring Heaven and earth into Divine harmony. The Angels tell me that my work alone preserves England from Gods wrath and destruction."

In deed, I had heard tell of these "conversations" with angelic personages. Twas this, more than anything, which had soured Dees reputation in England and made him a laughingstock everywhere but in freewheeling Prague.

"Your work. What is your work, Doctor?" I demanded, surprised at my own audacity.

"Symbols," he answered simply. "The devising of our own secret cyphers, and the decyphering of the enemys."

I gawked at him, and suddenly all I could think of was Partridge poring over his first stolen book of cyphers.

Dee turned the pages of the book under his hand to its frontpiece. I could see the title was "Monas Hieroglyphia" and the author was himself. There was an odd symbol mid page, a looped cross surrounded by other equally esoteric figures and signs.

"You are a secret agent, Arthur, and you must therefore know that spying depends entirely upon the effectiveness of cyphers. For years we all — Walsingham, Leicester, Cecil, Elizabeth — used the Alberti manual. Then I discovered a long lost text by Trithemius. Twas called the 'Steganographia' and it was esoteric beyond measure, but from this book I learnt unimaginable secrets and techniques, in no time at all. Only then was I able to write my book. No one at the universities understands 'Monas'. Before, the world believed I was a black magician. Now they think me a lunatic." He stopped, smiled ironically. "Let them think it. We who must understand the book, do. The Queen supports me entirely."

"I wish to learn its use," I said with all the urgency of a starving man set before a trestle covered in savory foods.

"You have not the time, my boy," replied Dee. "You have important work to do elsewhere. Come."

He took me by the arm and led me out the back door of the cottage into a walled yard. There stood a rather undistinguished Greek statue standing in a tub of water. Twas stained, both arms and the nose broken off, and the yellow afternoon sun was just beginning to fall in angled light upon it. As it did I thought I heard a faint moaning sound emanating from the statue, but just then I felt Dee drape an arm round my shoulder.

"I have a son named Arthur," he said gently. I turned to him and saw his eyes were closed, the lids fluttering. Suddenly his grip tightened and I felt his body shuddering subtly. "Your Mother and Father . . ." he said slowly, "are very dear to me, you know."

Now <u>my</u> body began to tremble, and the droning sound became louder. I was torn, not knowing whether to keep my eyes on this strange man who had uttered so stunning a remark, or to turn my gaze on the singing statue. I turned. The angled light had crept farther onto the stone shape. The sound was clearly growing louder as *the light moved across its face. I forced my self to look back at Dee. His eyes had opened.*

"I was told you had died at birth," he said.

He knew who I was! "So were my parents told," I fairly croaked. "My Mother still has no idea I am alive."

"That is wise. Yes, very wise. Tell me, Arthur, do you know the date and time of your birth? I should like to cast the horoscope of another of King Arthurs descendants."

I was suddenly mute and motionless, my mind whirling. How had he known? Did I so resemble my Parents? Had his mere touch probed inside my very mind and extricated the truth? A descendant of the Great King. I stared at Doctor Dee stupidly, then back at the fully illuminated statue, now droning loudly and discordantly. Finally I found my voice.

"How is it done? You must tell me!" I cried, never knowing which of his strange experiments I was demanding he explain.

Dee smiled, his long teeth glowing ivory in the setting sun. "Magick, my boy. Tis simply magick."

Thirty-seven

"Sir."

Francis Walsingham turned to see the messenger standing before him. He had come seeking the Secretary in the Great Hall of his London house, now made into an elaborate cypher department. "A letter from Lord Leicester."

Walsingham took the sealed parchment and ripped it open. It was not in cypher, but in his friend's regular hand.

Walsingham moved to a window for some good light. But after reading the first several words he stopped, thinking that from this moment on there would indeed be less light in the world.

> My dear Francis,
>
> It is with the deepest sorrow that I write to you with grievous news of your much beloved son-in-law. This day Philip Sidney died of his wounds suffered in the battle of Zutphen. I appreciate your shock at this morbid change in events, as my last letter assured you that the bullet wound to his thigh was healing well, with no signs of blood poisoning. Your sweet daughter Frances, though six months gone with child, was nursing him assiduously. His appetite was good and he slept easy. We were all therefore unprepared when, ten days ago, Philip lifted the bedclothes and smelt the odor of putrefaction. Gangrene had set in. Everything possible was done, but it was, alas, hopeless, and whilst still in good mind he made his will. He spoke his last words to his brother Robert, saying, "Love my memory."
>
> Philip should have no worry on that account, for my nephew was as well loved a man as ever I have known. All here mourn bitterly, and there is a story of his selflessness that is circulating

amongst the troops that I know you would like to hear. After he was wounded and had ridden two miles to my camp with much blood lost, he was at last taken off his horse. He was desperately exhausted and thirsty and was about to take a drink of water when he saw another soldier — a dying man — being carried past on a litter. Philip hobbled over and put the flask to the man's lips and said, "Take this. Your need is greater than mine."

Oh Francis, this is an uncompassable tragedy, for young Sidney was not merely beloved to family and friends, but in his talent and greatheartedness was a national treasure more precious than diamonds and gold. I weep for your sorrowing daughter who has lost a husband and her unborn child a Father. For my own part I have lost, besides one of the main comforts of my life, a most priceless help in my service here in the Netherlands.

Lastly, I send you all of my strength for helping you to convince the Queen to pass a sentence of death upon her cousin Mary, lawfully convicted as an intriguer and compasser of Her Majesty's destruction. England will never be safe whilst that evil woman lives. Force the Queen's assent if need be, but have it done!

So I end with hope for your own good health, a reminder that poor Philip is at last with God in Heaven, and a prayer that our own efforts will bring England through the coming storm.

Yours in Christ and your faithful friend,
R. Leicester

Thirty-eight

I had spent some time in Italy, as it was the best listening post for Spain in all of the Continent. Countless ships from Spanish and Portuguese ports crisscrossed the astonishingly blue Mediterranean, anchoring in the many bustling seaport cities of the boot. Parma's reinforcements marching into the Low Countries travelled through Milan. Genoese money supported Philips war, and without Naples Spain would have been bereft of its greatest shipbuilders. The Vatican believed itself vastly powerful, but of course twas little more than a pawn of Spain. Philip was, after all, more pious than Pope Gregory himself, and victory over the English infidel would certainly land the Spanish King in Heaven before the Pope.

In Italy I learnt the language, hardly difficult with all my Latin. I made acquaintance of the local forgers who were some of the best in the world, and learnt the trade which I would claim for my own once in Spain — that of an Italian merchant, seller of the most exotic spices from the East.

During my stay I managed to gain regular entry to the Vatican, replacing one of the Swiss Guards. There I listened to all the palace gossip — of the Pope, Cardinals, Bishops and their households — and found it more lewd and perverse than any I have been privy to in any country before or since. And I watched and waited for the moment I might do some disservice to Gregory himself, a man who had urged upon all Catholics of the world the assassination of my good Mother, saying that whosoever dispatched "that guilty woman of England" not only did not sin, but gained merit in the eyes of God.

I learnt thro one of Walsingham's spies at Rome, Francesco Pucci, that the Pope was in possession of a letter from King Philip discussing Gregorys suggestions on the invasion of Ireland to build up a force preparatory to war against England. The missive lay in Gregorys private cabinet. It needed copying, but I had been assigned nowhere near the Popes inner chambers. I conceived of a plan which I executed with great care one Saturday evening.

My shift over, I marched up the great stairs looking properly official in my Swiss Guard uniform — one which I had come to hate, feeling more like an outlandish court jester than a soldier. At the Papal apartments I assailed Giorgio Odotto, one of the gentlemen of the bedchamber, with great good greetings and some bottles of claret. His master was out for the evening — whoring, said Odotto — so we sat in the Holy Fathers fine gilt chairs drinking into the night. When Odotto was drunk I administered an herb potion obtained from a local chemist to a fresh glass of wine, and once quaffed the gentleman fell deep asleep and snoring. I rifled thro the Popes numerous cabinets filled with official papers until I found the one I sought, and sat by candlelight copying it by hand painstakingly, word for word.

I had only just completed it when I heard a commotion outside the door. I extinguished the candle and fell into a heap next to Giorgio, pretending a drunken stupor. When the Pope arrived in the company of a most beautiful courtesan, he found his manservant and a Swiss Guardsman in an appalling condition. We were booted out instantly and poor Odotto, badly disgraced, lost his position, demoted to the Vatican laundry. I was thrown out on my ear altogether for my part in it, and I happily departed, translated letter in pocket.

My next stop was the Pucci villa. Francesco was extremely pleased with my efforts, for my success in this difficult but crucial assignment had fulfilled Walsinghams imperative to Pucci himself. Now all that was left was personal delivery to the next in line, and to my delight I learnt it was John Dee in Prague. He would take my copy, transpose it into his cyphers and send it along to England.

But now it was time to leave Italy and hie me to Spain. I chose to avoid yet another sea voyage, even the calm waters of the Mediterranean, and so travelled overland up the leg of Italy and into France, crossing into Spain over the jagged peaks of the Pyrenees. During this rugged journey in the icy rarefied air of the Alps, my horse suffered more than I, and I wondered if I would not have done better with a mule, as so many of my fellow travellers rode. We gratefully descended and crossed a dangerous torrent called the Bidassoa and I finally found my self in the country of my enemy.

Above all Spain was warm. When I arrived it was March and in England, or the Netherlands, this was the bitterest of months. Here it was spring, and the sun on my skin caressed me like the soft hand of a Mother. I was slowed, found my self taking thought of abandoning the past and all knowledge of my Family. I briefly imagined fleeing into the countryside. Living amongst horses. A beautiful woman. But like a pack of moonlit bandits, these thoughts took me by surprise, then vanished back into the black night. Of course I could never abandon my mission, service to my Country and my Parents. Blood was everything in England, and my blood was England.

At the border town of Irún I found no one but the agents of the Inquisition interested in my crossing into their country. They asked for no passport or documents, but interrogated me only to find out if I carried any heretical literature in my bags. They seemed to accept my claim to be an Italian spice merchant, and to be on the safe side I gave them cardamom and cloves to take home to their cooks, and the bribe worked very well.

Twas in Castile that I encountered my first customs house and here, too, there was little interest in who I was, but many customs officers who required me to register not simply my merchandise but every piece of clothing I owned and every penny I possessed . . . so they could tax it. Here they wished to see my passport, but solely so they could demand to examine my bags, hoping to discover some small article I had failed to declare and wring every last pistole out of me.

Finally on my way again, I wondered that King Philip was so lax at his borders, arming them with mere tax farmers and heretic hunters, and not agents of his government, there to ferret out spies like my self. But I blessed his greed and religious zeal, for it made my job that much easier.

My first night at a Spanish inn was a disaster. No one had explained to me that a traveller must bring his own victuals with him — oil, bread, eggs, meat procured from a local butcher — which he then handed over to the inn keeper for cooking. As no other customers were that night amenable to sharing, I went hungry. A filthy wretch looking like a beggar served me wine, not from a bottle but from a goatskin, and the beverage — otherwise reasonable in quality — stank of hide and pitch. I thought my self lucky to get one of the rooms with a bed — others had mere piles of straw — but I slept that night with so many fleas and bedbugs that when I awoke the next day I looked to have a bad case of measles. Wishing to be quickly gone I left just as the sun rose, only to find that my horse had dropped dead with exhaustion.

I noted that many people of quality in this country rode about in litters drawn by two mules — in deed there were more mules than horses. Tho I had no desire to travel on such an animal, I was forced to bargain with a muleteer for two of his beasts to carry my self and my load of spices until I could find a proper mount. I was unused to the dryness of the air and landscape, the stark sierras and the arid plains. The only vegetation I might see in a whole days travel was thyme, grazed upon by herds of sheep, and not a tree in sight.

Twas my mission, as it was for every other English spy in Spain, to report on the vessels in Philips fleet — their number, kind, tonnage, munitions and provisions brought aboard, and the number of soldiers and sailors and galley slaves mustered. So I headed west for Portugal — recently annexed to Spain by King Philip — with plans to survey the coastal towns, ports and dockyards for that vital intelligence.

My patience was running thin with the mules, but I had been having no luck at all finding a good horse. I did not wish just any horse, for this journey required excellence, nay perfection, and the right companion was essential to my success. Besides, Spain was renowned for its Arabs, and I was determined to find the horse of my dreams.

Still in Spain on the road leading into Pontevedra I chanced upon a sun wrinkled old but sweetfaced Spaniard who was training a still leggy young gelding in a field. I stopped and silently watched him for a long while. He noticed me right away but gave only the barest acknowledgment, a slight tilt of his head in my direction. I could see he treated the horse with a firm but gentle touch, and spoke almost constantly to him in an engaging and flattering tone. When the man was done he gathered in the rope and began to lead the horse away. I called "Señor!" and he indicated I might cross over onto his property and speak with him.

He was not too grand — a hidalgo perhaps, that is a Spanish gentleman of the lower order — and despite his stoop and rheumy eyes exuded that amazing pride of spirit that the Spanish possess, almost to extreme. Politely, and adhering to all the rules of etiquette I had previously learnt of these people, I told him of my plight and asked if he had any horses for sale. I said that his method of training animals was akin to my own and that I expected any horse he had raised up would be an extraordinary mount.

As he slowly led the gelding to the stable, allowing me to walk with them, he told me no, that sadly none of his horses were for sale. But he was lonely for company, and would I care to stay for a meal? Truly I was disappointed, but I valued the opportunity to sit with a Spaniard in his home and learn the local gossip. We ate outdoors under the one large tree on the whole of his property, served by an ancient hobbling maidservant. The food was simple and delicious, and he offered me, besides the roast lamb, all manner of fruits in their wholeness — pears, persimmons, apples, and sweet oranges which he peeled, pulling apart the sections and offering them to me.

The man, Juan, was a great talker and his favorite topic was horses. As a Spaniard, he told me, he of course hated the infidel Moors, but many hundreds of years ago they had brought Arab horses up out of the African continent into Spain, and that was an infinite blessing. He spoke of the perfection of the Arab horse, how it might go at speed for a whole day or more without eating or drinking, that it had, besides endurance, rare intelligence and oftentimes a heroic spirit. He spoke of Al Borah the Lightning, a white winged stallion ridden through the skies by the Arabian prophet Mohammed. And he related with great relish the famous story of El Cids final victorious ride in battle — a dead man propped up by armor and saddle on the back of his valiant Arab, Babieca the Booby.

My own tongue loosened by the sun and the wine, I repaid Juans stories with my own, changing only the details needed to maintain my imposture. I had been a mercenary in the Battle of the Tulips — for Spain. When I was fourteen, my horse had been stolen by ruffians in the city of Naples, and at age eight I had outsmarted my cruel mother to perform manège for the Duke and Duchess of Milan.

He laughed and clapped his hands in delight at my stories and finally as the sun began to set he said "Come with me" and I followed him to the stables. He had a boy lead a bridled but unsaddled horse from the stalls which, in the golden light, was a sight to behold. She was a beauty — a chestnut with one white foot and a crescent of stark white on her forehead. Her high arched tail and mane had been lovingly oiled and braided, and I suddenly had a vision of a lovely pampered woman in a harem. She was splendid in every point —

legs like steel, a fine shoulder, high withers. Her head was magnificent — long and handsome, jawbone clearly marked, nostrils lying flat in repose. Her eyes were large and liquid and the skin round about them was black and lustrous.

She seemed to be eyeing me even as I was her. I moved to her and she nickered mildly as I approached. I stroked the deep and lean cheek of her, and her ears flicked as tho I was of some interest to her. I looked back at Juan who was smiling, inviting me to have my way with his lady. I took no time in grasping her plaited mane and heaving my self onto her bare back.

"What is her name?" I asked.

"Mirage," he replied, which instantly conjured in my head a vision of the desert upon which her ancestors had once run.

"Come, Mirage," I whispered. "Show me who you are." And she did. I swear I never did give a full command, for the horse anticipated my every thought, every maneuver, and all with a grace and precision I had never before known in a beast — even my beloved Charger. Her gallop was marvellous strong and speedy, and I guessed from the pure joy with which she ran that she had too little of it. When we reluctantly returned, the light almost gone, old Juan was picking his teeth with a piece of straw. As I sat on her back contemplating every argument I could summon for why he must sell Mirage to me he said, "How much will you give me for her?"

I wanted to shout "Everything I own or will ever own!" but I remained calm, just leaned down and lay upon her warm damp neck feeling a sense of tender happiness that I had found a new friend, and guilt that the man who had so kindly brought her to me was in principle my mortal enemy. I made Juan a generous offer which he accepted with a sly smile saying that she was worth more, but that my stories had counted for something towards her purchase, and he was happy with the sale on all accounts.

I thought many times that the journey down the coast of Portugal was far too pleasant a one. After all, I was a secret agent gathering intelligence for my country, soon to be besieged by the enemy. But the spring weather was fine, I was joyful in the company of my new horse, and I found the Portuguese a sturdy people who bore no more love for King Philip — the usurper of their rightful Monarchs throne — than did the English.

Their harbors — Vigo, Oporto, Lisbon — were every day filling with the Kings ships from the world over, and with them came thousands and thousands of sailors and soldiers who, to the Portuguese, were foreigners trampling their shores, depleting their markets of food to provision the ships, and sending the price of goods to the heavens. And for what? King Philips desire to do battle in Gods name for <u>*Spain*</u>*? Everywhere I went, in every tavern I stopped I heard the people protesting that twas for Philips own political aggrandizement and not the Lords.*

It was also a matter of pride, I learnt, for the Portuguese seafaring tradition had much preceded and outshone Spains. They had founded the principles of navigation upon which seamen from every nation in the world now relied. Worse still, Philip had requisitioned their largest and finest galleons, calling them his own.

I would ride into a seaport town and hie me to the quays or dockside inns where I would open my cases and hawk my wares to the many ship captains who hoped someday to be released from Philips "Great Enterprise" to again ply the waters in trade. I learnt a great deal in my smooth dealings — which and how many foreign ships had been commandeered, impounded or chartered, how well the vessels were being provisioned with dried fish, salt beef, biscuit and wine. How much cordage and sail were taken aboard and most important, what were the stores of munitions. A new type of ship called a galleass was anchored in several ports. These were propelled not simply by galley slaves at the oars, but with oarsmen and sails together. These ships were thought to be the greatest strength of Philips new Armada.

There was no surprise that gun and ordnance were being amply provided for each vessel. More to my dismay was the news that much of the cannon, ball and shot was English made. What logic, I wondered, was there in supplying our enemy with fire power!

News of Captain Francis Drake flew all round me. Called El Draque, this English pirate was widely feared for the mischief he did to Spain on the high seas and its New World outposts. But he was respected, too, and more than once I saw gentlemen haggling over the price of a miniature of the captains portrait. I knew that of all the intelligence I sent back to my Father, some would surely be used in the service of this hero of England.

I continued south and round the corner of Portugal to Spain, heading east along the coast into Andulusia, a land of innumerable olive and orange and cypress trees which spread in great forests over the land. Here I saw slaves for the first time — Moors and Blackamoors, following after their mistresses and masters, sometimes arrayed à la Turque.

The ancient port of Cadiz was a strangely shaped island lying just off the coast of the mainland which, by its curving coast, formed a magnificent double harbor bisected by a small neck. At its mouth were two great forts armed with heavy guns. What alarmed me, however, was not the harbor itself but what I found within it — nearly one hundred ships, from small barques to great galleys to merchantmen, armed to the teeth — and they were, tho not altogether ready to sail, farther along towards dispatching than any fleet I had yet seen on my journey.

I sat on the point at Santa Katerina across from the fort and made my report to Leicester, complete with crude drawings, tho I had yet found no network of spies and couriers for England so far south as this, and therefore no easy way to convey this letter to the Earl, as I had from other cities. If need be I would ride back to Lisbon, for this intelligence I believed was vital to Englands defence. Finished, I replaced my correspondence and writing implements in my saddlepouch and set out to find respite from the afternoon sun.

Not far up the coast road from Santa Katerina point was the village of Santa Maria, and Mirage, sensing a rest and a feed for her self, made a brisk pace for the town. Twas not a large place, but this day was alive with celebration. I had found in my travels that in Spain almost anything was an excuse for rejoicing and festivals — Royal births and marriages, visiting Princes, every Catholic holiday, even the consecration of a shrine or the procession carrying a holy relic from one place to another would suffice.

I knew nothing of the cause of this days revels, only rode as part of the boisterous procession down the main avenida. The shimmering air vibrated with music of guitar and tambourine. People were singing, dancing, some in fancy costume, others dressed like animals. Monks rode on mules draped in blankets of flowers. Vendors hawked orange juice and strawberry water, and fine ladies in lace veils sipped cups of chocolate so thick they were forced to follow with equal cups of water. We passed a raised stage where dancers danced a frenzied chaconne. Ladies twirled and turned their high chinned heads, tossing their hair and snapping their fingers.

A sudden commotion. There is screaming. The crowd parts. Mirage and I are pushed back to the wall and trapt there as a fine carriage drawn by two horses thunders past — driverless — only the figures of two small children clutching the seat in terror. Some men grab for it but it speeds out of reach and on to the coast road. All — on foot, a few riding mules — are helpless.

I shout to those who pin me against the wall for Gods sake let me pass! I work Mirage thro the crowd, anxious not to trample anyone in the throng, more anxious still to catch the carriage. The crowd makes way.

The horses send up a cloud of dust on the packed earth road, showing me where to follow. Heading for Santa Katerina point where the road suddenly ends at a high palisade over the harbor. Mirage runs like the wind, closing the distance. I am not close enough to hear the children screaming. I can see the point approaching fast, the horses wild, slowing not at all. An unimaginable burst of speed, bless Mirage! Now three beasts galloping side by side. I dare not look at the children huddled on the seat, just fasten my gaze on the team. They are a hand higher than Mirage, making my leap to their backs difficult. Pounding hooves deafen me. Dust chokes my mouth and nostrils. I lift my self to a squat in the saddle to rise above the team. I know if I leap on a horses back between strides, he will surely fall. The carriage will crash, the children be catapulted into the air and they and both horses badly injured — or worse. I wait a beat. Hold my breath. Matching the rhythm of the stride, I leap upon the near horses back. Still, my weight throws off its gait. It stumbles, rights itself, but I lose its back, fall tween the pair. Desperately I clutch the wooden tongue. Searing pain! My thigh impaled, a hook on the tongue. I hear my self scream. Feel the horses slow with my weight on the tongue.

All is still and quiet now except the children whimpering, the horses panting, the carriage creaking even at rest. And the sound of water crashing on the shore below. I lift my self, agonized, off the hook, out from under the team. Blood soaks my breeches. I turn to see the children. So small, eyes still bulging in terror. I limp to them, lift them, one in each arm, from the carriage. Hold them as they weep . . .

Mirage comes then, cantering gracefully as tho nothing at all has occurred. She is followed by several men from town on horseback, another carriage, a friar on a mule. All gather round us, and a woman in a wine colored gown, her veil pushed back from her tearstained face, gathers the children to her. The men examine the carriage and thro a haze of pain I hear them exclaim their surprise that both horses are sound, only the tongue of the carriage broke. Suddenly they are all round me, staring at this stranger come to their town. The woman, her head buried in her childrens hair is crying "Gracias, Señor, Dios le Bendiga . . ." Then all before my eyes goes white and I am gone from this world altogether.

Thirty-nine

When I awoke, the daylight was fading and I found my self abed within a fresh and pretty chamber, its large windows and a door opening onto what appeared to be a Spanish courtyard, all of greenery and the sound of a trickling fountain. The furnishings were fine but lacked the splendor of the kind I had seen in my Fathers lodgings at Court. A crucifix hung on the wall, and below it was a small altar with an icon of the Virgin and several candles, all lit. No one was about, and I could take stock of my circumstances.

The pain in my leg was severe, and a look under the covers to my nakedness revealed a well made bandage so large as to cover my whole right thigh. I imagined that my temporary departure from the world had had to do with my loss of blood, and that some one of the townspeople had taken pity on me and brought me hence. Who that person was, was suddenly revealed as the door opened and the woman in the wine colored gown entered with a tray of bandages and instruments.

At once she saw me awake, and her serious mien transmuted into one of the sincerest joy. I was startled by the beauty of her, for on our first meeting she had been wracked with terrible emotion and copious tears, and I with blinding pain. But now I could see she was extraordinary. Her large dark eyes were wide set above high rounded cheeks curving downward to a delicately pointed chin, so that together with the deep widows peak in the lustrous black hair she wore pulled back in a silver comb, her face was a perfect heart.

"Señor," she said putting down the tray and taking up my hand in hers. She spoke in a rich throaty tone very soothing to the ear. "I

am so glad to see you awake now, tho it was a lucky thing you were dead to the world whilst the surgeon attended you."

The pain was still so severe that I hardly trusted my self to speak, knowing that I must needs keep up my charade as an Italian, albeit one who could speak to her in Spanish. My hesitation prompted her to continue. "I do not know if I can ever properly convey my gratitude to you for saving my children, Señor. They are my life."

I smiled, and the one she returned to me was as warm as the Andalusian sun. Then she retreated into a typically Spanish restraint.

"I am Federico Reggio," I finally managed, my voice akin to a croaking frog. "And I am grateful that God was so kind as to allow me the opportunity to help your children." In the past months I had become adept at the Latin formality of speech which was foreign to me, as well as the insertion of God into almost every aspect of conversation.

"I am Constanza Lorca de Estrada, and this is my Fathers house."

Without thinking, my eyes went to her hands and I saw that she wore a marriage ring. Her husband, I reckoned, was away in the Netherlands War. I remember feeling immediately saddened that she belonged to another man, but was at that moment gripped with so terrible a bolt of pain in my whole leg that I cried out involuntarily and broke instantly into a sweat. Constanzas face seemed to mirror my agony and I was ashamed of my unmanliness.

She became very brisk and professional. "You must forgive me, Señor Reggio, but I am your only nurse here, and I must check your wound and change the bandage. The surgeon fears infection. Your leg was torn very badly."

It occurred to me then that this injury might kill me, and I thought upon the irony of surviving five years of war only to die from an accident in civilian life. The door opened then and an older man I supposed to be Constanzas Father, and her two children entered.

"I see the patient is awake," he said. He seemed at first glance a crusty gentleman with a gruff voice, but his smile was kind, and he came to me and grasped my hand firmly. "I am Ramón Lorca. Constanza has, I know, thanked you, Señor. Let me add my gratitude to hers. And here are two others who have something to say to you."

The children rushed forward and commenced smothering me

with soft hugs and milky kisses which threatened to bring tears to my eyes. I chanced a look at Constanza who was having difficulty controlling her own tears. But in a moment she gently shooed them out, saying she needed to attend to her patient.

Don Ramón bowed formally and said before he closed the door behind him, "We are taking good care of your horse who is, like your self Señor, a hero in our house. What is her name?"

"Mirage," I answered, and smiled to think that someone shared my admiration for that extraordinary beast.

With Don Ramón and his grandchildren departed, Constanza lifted the blanket covering my injured leg. "I will be gentle as I am able, Señor. I have made a poultice of sage and garlic, tho the surgeon forbade me to use it."

She pulled the dressing off and her face screwed up in such pity at the sight of my wound, I was afraid to see it my self. But I knew I must. I lifted my self on an elbow and fairly gaped at the great tear in the flesh of the inner face of my thigh which was, tho stitched together with some skill, never the less angry purple, and swollen all round it. I fell rather than lowered my self back onto the pillow, exhausted from even that small exertion, and wondered, if in deed I survived this injury, would I be crippled for life? And more pressing than that, how would I send my intelligence report of Cadiz out of Spain? I had little time to ponder it, for in a moment I felt a coolness over the sore and saw Constanza taking several fingerfuls of a wet grey substance and applying it to the wound.

"What is that?" I asked her.

"My sage and garlic poultice," she answered.

I thought it odd for a woman to so blithely disobey a surgeon. Yet I felt comfortable with her ministrations, and trusted her altogether.

"It may fester no matter what I do, Señor. There were many splinters of wood from the carriage piece. I do not know if the surgeon . . ."

"Señora," I said subduing the urge to moan as another wave of pain spread like fire from foot to groin, "you are more than kind and are doing everything you can. My recovery is entirely in Gods hands."

"Where was God," she whispered fiercely, "when the horses ran off with my children?"

Again this woman had surprised me. Were not Spaniards, of all the worlds Catholics, the most fervent in their faith in Gods unfailing wisdom?

"Are you hungry?" she asked laying a new dressing over her poultice.

"No," I replied. "Tho I would be grateful for a sip of wine." As she wiped her hands on a pure white towel I was suddenly reminded of the bleaching fields of Haarlem, and wondered had her husband sent back the thing from the Netherlands. Then I felt Constanzas strong arm under my shoulders lifting me, and the cup at my lips. As I drank the cool spiced wine I drank in, too, her warm beauty and thought to myself that her presence alone might be enough to heal me.

I was wrong. Some time in that night the infection in my leg blossomed like a malevolent flower, spreading its poisons into my veins. I woke briefly, ablaze with pain and heat in all parts of my body. I was aware of Constanza sitting beside me, pressing iced cloths to my head and neck. But if I spoke it was senseless, and I remember seeing two of her and thinking, Ah, she has a twin sister, one for me. Then I was spinning and falling into darkness and oblivion . . .

I came back to the pretty room in the Spanish house with the feel of a soft wet cloth gently wiping the crust from my eyelids which I still had not the strength to open. I heard a womans voice saying "See how much easier he breathes. And his color is good."

Someone grasped my hand and laid his fingers on my wrist. "The pulses are much stronger, Señora Estrada. He is a lucky man, this Reggio. God has rewarded him for his good deed to your family."

When the doctor left I slowly forced open my eyes. Even this was a chore. I could feel keenly every part of my body, and whilst there was no pain save a dull ache in the injured leg, I was weaker than a babe, and in deed felt as tho I were limp and wrung out as a housemaids rag.

Then Constanza came into my vision. The look on her face was not so much happiness as quiet triumph, as tho she had single-handed vanquished a monster. I smiled up at her, acknowledging the conquest. Without speaking she sat next to me simply stroking my hand with a strange intimacy. Then I thought it was not so strange, in fact, for we had become entangled in the tenderest of bonds — I having saved the lives of her children, and she having saved mine. We stayed thus, silent and contemplative, our hands joined, for a very long time. Finally she smiled and said she wished to tell her Father that their honored guest had come back to the land of the living. I remember thinking as Constanza closed the door behind her that I already missed the sight of her, the sound and smell of her. And I was thrilled as I was terrified to know I had met the woman of my many dreams.

Twas not till Don Ramón returned with Constanza and I bade her prop me to sitting in order to receive them with some dignity, that I chanced to see my saddlebags hung over a stool in the corner of the room. My belly, thankfully empty, lurched violently but I quickly forced my eyes back to my hosts. I was further alarmed to note that Don Ramón was regarding me perhaps more coolly than he had in our first meeting, tho Constanza was unreservedly gracious. She was saying that I should consider their home my own until I had entirely recovered.

"Is there anyone you might wish us to write to in Italy, Señor Reggio, your family perhaps?" inquired Don Ramón in a tone I thought mild and at the same time pointed.

"Yes, my Mother," I responded quickly, providing them with a fictitious name and address in the city of Turin, knowing that by the time the letter had reached Italy and been returned to the Lorcas, I would be long gone from their house.

Suddenly that thought caused a sensation in my chest, an empty ache. To leave Constanza . . . No, I must get hold of my self! She was a married woman, a Spaniard, a Catholic. And I had no reason to suppose my love was in any way returned.

"When you are strong enough, you must come to the workshop," Constanza said mildly. "We are a family of saddlemakers, have been for many generations."

"When I am stronger I shall be delighted," I said glancing again at my saddlebags, wondering if they had been opened, if my letter to Lord Leicester with the map of Cadiz Harbor and its naval preparations had been found, if my true character as an English agent had been discovered. Searching their faces I suddenly thought not. Had I been found out they would have had sufficient time to summon the authorities to arrest me — a spy in their home, an enemy of Spain, a heretic. No, I argued silently, there was no need for pretense on their

part. They had in deed respected a gentlemans privacy. My suspicions of Don Ramón were entirely unfounded. I was safe for the moment.

Once it was confirmed that my life was out of danger, tho the hospitality of the Lorca household continued, I was sadly denied the tender nursing services of Constanza, and saw her rarely. Maids came with my meal trays, and an elderly manservant attended to my personal needs. Slowly I increased my time out of bed and exercised my hurt leg, knowing that sooner or later I must smuggle my document on the Armada at Cadiz to my patron.

Finally one morning after breakfast I ventured from my room, stiff legged but thankfully upright and moving. I descended the stairs into the garden courtyard round which the entire casa had been built. It was literally abuzz with bees and hummingbirds feasting on the nectar of a thousand blooming flowers, riots of color cascading down the whitewashed walls, all round the gushing fountain. My heart quickened at the sight of the garden, for I anticipated finding Constanza there, perhaps surrounded by her children, sewing or reading quietly. I imagined my self coming quietly up behind her, taking her by surprise. She would gasp, then smile to see me up and about, perhaps ask me to join her, and there we would stay — me paying court to the beautiful lady of the house, her contemplating cuckolding her husband with the Italian stranger whose life she had so lovingly saved.

But she was not in the courtyard, nor was she anywhere to be found in the large, handsomely appointed casa. I dared not ask her whereabouts of the servants, so I headed for the stables, thinking I would visit with Mirage. Inside I found a dozen horse stalls but no animals. A stablehand pointed out where the animals were grazing in a distant pasture, very green and, I thought, a splendid place for Mirage to be spending her morning.

Now denied the company of my two favorite ladies I was never the less feeling very well, with the morning sunshine warming my pallid skin, and my leg paining me less and less with every step. Before me was a large oblong building of one floor, plain and unadorned except for a flower bedecked statue of Saint Francis of Assisi near its front door. I heard coming from within the place myriad sounds — voices, pounding, scraping and sloshing — and knew this must be the saddlemaking shop. I had been invited to visit and never having seen such an operation, went inside.

As I passed thro the door I was at once assailed by the ghastly smell of hides simmering in vats of tanning broth, then saw the tanners, noses covered with masks which did not keep their eyes from watering, their brows permanently carved with wrinkles of disgust. I wondered how a man could work a lifetime at such a foul occupation, but then thought perhaps another man might wonder at the occupation of a soldier — killing other men for wages.

Thro an archway I passed into the next room to find men stretching and dying the hides, much of it black, and recognized the results — cordovan and barbary leather used for the finest Spanish saddles.

Yet deeper inside the factory I saw the saddles taking shape, some of the wooden trees heavily padded for soldiers — pommels and cantles high and sloped sharply from front to rear. Others were gentlemens saddles with stylishly low cantles and horns. I watched as a metalsmith formed winged cantles so large they would curve armorlike round a soldiers thighs. Some frames already bore their leather coverings, skirts and stirrups. Others were mere bony skeletons awaiting their skin.

This being southern Spain the stirrups were all short, as the horsemen rode "a la gineta." That is, short after the Turkey fashion, knees bent at a sharp angle, sometimes rising to stand in the stirrups to gallop. If this had been the north of Spain I would have seen longer stirrups for riding "a la brida," in the orthodox fashion favored by Europeans and the knights of old — legs straight, heels angled forward. I had learnt it was a matter of honor and high praise for a man to have it said of him that he rode well in both saddles.

Thro another arched door was a very Hell of heat and sound — the metal shop where sweating loriners wrought and cast from molten gold and silver, all manner of mountings fit for the saddles of gentlemen and Kings.

The final arched door revealed a chamber altogether different from the previous ones. A quiet haven, soft voices, the rich sweet fragrance of finished leather. Twas a place of artisans — men who sat happily hunched as they polished and inlaid, engraved and embossed in high relief the gold and silver bits, ornate scabbards and stirrups. Apprentice boys fashioned from velvety soft moroccan leather all manner of reins, bridles, martingales, straps. Velvet skirts were embroidered, tasseled and befringed by half a dozen spindle fingered grandmothers.

My eyes beheld the rich beauty of the art and I felt the passion of the artisans moving in quiet waves all round me. I saw a woman, her back to me, head bent over her work so intently that I became curious to see it. I moved closer, standing almost over her shoulder. With a tiny hammer tapping on the end of an awl she was creating a cut and raised design of astonishing intricacy in fine black leather — swirls and flowers, tongues of fire, a mythic whiptailed dragon doing battle with a bold knight on horseback — all on the flap of a saddlepack.

"It is magnificent," I murmured, quite unable to disguise my awe. The artist turned then, and I found myself confronted by Constanza Estrada.

"I am glad it pleases you, Señor Reggio." She held my eyes for what seemed an eternity, then continued her work. She did not, however, dismiss me. Instead she spoke in that sweet cultured voice while she tap, tap, tapped the detail into a curl of flame projecting from her dragons mouth. She asked after my health and in particular how my wound was mending. She apologized for her absence from my bedside in recent weeks, saying that her work had piled up while she nursed me and she had had to catch up with it. I found my self contented to listen to her speak, gaze down at the dark hair curling in soft tendrils at the nape of her neck, and watch her deft fingers position and angle and pound, just so. Now she was teasing me, telling me that I had set her back two good weeks and that her Father would take it out of her hide. Then she laughed at her own foolishness and I laughed with her.

"Señora Estrada, you must tell me. How is it that you work . . . in such a way?"

"Do you mean why do I work as a common laborer in my Fathers shop?"

"Not a laborer," I protested. "An artisan to be sure . . ."

"But still, it puzzles you, Señor."

"I have never seen a gentlewoman anywhere labor thus."

She smiled a mysterious smile then. "You must first understand how deeply this . . ." She ran her fingers caressingly over the carven leather. ". . . satisfies me."

I was horrified to feel my sex pulse and rise as she uttered those two final words.

"When I was a girl," she went on, unaware of the effect she was having on me, "I had taken to stealing scraps of leather and tools from the shop, and begun creating my own designs. I hid them of course, for tho embroidery was encouraged in a lady, for a woman to work in leather was unseemly, unheard of. Then when I was thirteen I chanced upon a pamphlet of my Fathers discussing the saddlers guild in England, how they had been the first to allow entry to women. I dreamt of becoming a proper saddlemaker, tho I knew that Spain was not England and that all my dreams would come to naught. But one evening when my Father was sad and missing his wife — my Mother died when I was young — I took my small creations and without speaking, laid them out in front of the fire. Of course he was curious and examined each of them closely." Constanza smiled then, a smile of remembering. "He was excited by the work, said he had never seen such finely wrought detail, said the artist had managed to bring the leather alive. Then he demanded to know where I had found the pieces, for he needed to speak with the artisan, persuade him to come to work for him. Suddenly my plan seemed to have worked too well. How could I tell my Father the artisan was my self? He would never believe me, might punish me for lying. He demanded once again to know the mans name. Finally I blurted out that it was me. That I had stolen the leather and the tools, and begged his forgiveness for tricking and humiliating him. Then he took my hands in his, held them up before his eyes and gazed at them saying 'These are the hands of an artisan . . . I have known all along it was you, Constanza. My carvers reported to me that you had made off with their tools, their discarded leather. I knew what you were doing.' He kissed both my hands. 'But I had no idea you possessed so profound a talent. Will you honor me by working in my shop?'"

I saw the color rise in Constanzas cheeks — the flush of her natural modesty embarrassed by the richness of her Fathers love.

"Of course there was a great outcry in the town, even letters from saddlers all over the realm protesting such an outrage. But in the end we were left alone, for my Fathers determination to employ me and his reputation for the finest saddlery anywhere proved greater than all the small minds and ridiculous uproar. I worked for five years . . . until I married. Come, Señor, I need some air. Let us walk."

As we strolled slowly round her Fathers compound Constanza continued to talk, and it seemed as tho twas the first telling of her life to another soul. All of her opened to me like a flower under the warm sun, revealing the delicate parts which, when closely observed, are so fantastical. So beautiful.

"My husband was a traditional man, and he demanded I stop my work when the children came. At first I objected." She smiled again. "Then I understood the little ones were my finest creations, and for several years I devoted my self to them. What longings I felt for my art I pushed aside. Besides, there was no one to whom I could talk of it, nothing to be done. I was a woman and that was the end of it."

We had walked to the field where the horses grazed, and she was quiet. There was so much I wanted to ask, but I could not bear to break the silence which seemed somehow sacred — the telling of her life a gift she was conferring in pieces, all in good time. Finally she spoke.

"My husband died very suddenly."

The statement took my breath away. Constanzas husband was not fighting for Spain in the Netherlands as I had assumed. She was a widow. I found it difficult to control my elation, forced my self to remember she was a Spaniard, mi enemiga.

"I had loved my husband, and together with the children we had been something very strong, very complete. I mourned, perhaps too deeply and for too long, refused to remarry. Grew very thin. Finally I lost the will to live. People were appalled — What kind of woman was I? Did I not still have my children? What more should I need? Ah, Señor Reggio, I was ashamed that motherhood alone could not lift me from my grief. Then my Father came to me one day last year and invited us to live in his house. He said he was lonely too, and we could assuage each others sadness. I agreed. When I walked for the first time into my bedchamber, there mounted on a block near the window was a raw leather saddle and a set of carving tools . . . I took one look and wept like a babe, then I sat down and began to work. Time disappeared like magick. I paused only to light the candles and never bothered to eat or sleep, feeling like a traveller too long in the desert, finally stumbling upon an oasis, taking the first cool drink. You see, the work was what I lacked. What I needed. My children, my Father, my art. I felt happy again."

Suddenly Constanza flushed a high pink. "Good God, I have told a complete stranger the story of my life!"

I reached out and in an impetuous gesture took her hand. "You know very well I am no stranger, Constanza," I said, regretting in my bones that I could never likewise share the true story of my life with her. Our eyes locked and held, and the smoldering gaze was broken only by Mirage insistently nudging my shoulder with her nose. Constanza and I laughed, and for my horse and me twas a sweet reunion, made sweeter by this lovely womans presence. Yet I was torn, for the Fates had played an unhappy trick on me, and for the first time in my life I began to question destiny.

In the days that followed, chaos ruled the kingdom of my mind. I had found my love, yet she was forbidden to me. I thought that she returned my passion, but she believed I was someone that I was not. I was under commission from my Father and England her self, and time was racing from me, the Cadiz intelligence lying undelivered in my saddlebags. But I was as yet unhealed of my injury, so that the mere fulfilling of my bounden duties might kill me. And if my efforts prevailed I would betray my kind hosts, to whom I owed my very life.

I hardly slept. My days were spent exercising my leg, then packing it in mud for the swelling. I worked patiently, translating the Cadiz information into cyphers as best as I could, and wished more than once to have Partridge here when I needed him. The cooler regions of my mind were occupied with my duty and loyalty to England. Other parts of myself knew only Constanza. I visited her daily in the shop, she never minding my company as she worked. Sometimes the children, Lolita and Marco, came in to see their Mother and we spent the time most pleasantly. Marco wished always to hear of my exploits on horseback and begged me to take him riding with me when I was well. Little Lolita was a black haired, black eyed Angel who gazed so adoringly at me we were finally moved to laughter. Don Ramón, too, was so warm and welcoming that each mealtime was a delightful confection of food, wine and lively conversation. He and Constanza were both historians of horse and saddle, and we would sit for endless hours exchanging stories.

I was awed at the extent of Constanzas education. She read Greek — and so knew Xenophon. She was even then studying the Arabic language, slowly translating pieces of the Koran. Don Ramón was a collector of antique horse accoutrements. He took great pleasure in pulling me aside to display the contents of his many domed chests — 13th century armor fashioned from scales sliced from horses hooves and sewn onto a tunic, a heavily armored glove used by a knights groom to lead an unpredictable stallion thro the battlefield, a pair of high widetopped boots he claimed belonged to a King, one boot of blue moroccan leather lined with green, the other of green leather lined with blue.

Constanza added bits of lore from the nomadic Huns who had lived on horseback, to my Great Grandfather King Henry VII, who would starve his horse before state occasions to promote its docility, as he was a poor rider.

There was little opportunity or time to be with Constanza alone. But even the briefest of walks from casa to shop after the afternoon siesta, or sitting up for hours at her table after Don Ramón had gone off to bed, seemed to my lovesick mind overbrimming with fully requited romance, made even more passionate by its restraint. Of course I was desperately torn, for the deeper in love I fell with Constanza, the harder it was to think of leaving her.

My good Mirage could not have made my first ride any gentler. Yet, even with the easiest of gaits, it felt as tho hot pincers had been applied to the leg, and the wounds very seams threatened to rupture. Constanza and her Father, concerned for my safety, devised a clever contraption of padding under and round the thigh, and a special stirrup which held the leg at a comfortable angle. This familys genuine sweetness and caring daily turned on its head my conception of the haughty Spanish character.

But in those days of my recuperation, too, I observed at the Lorca farm what I thought to be more than a saddle factorys share of comings and goings of urgent messengers. I wondered if Don Ramón was providing the King of Spain with saddles for the invasion, and thought perhaps I could use the services of one of these couriers — heavily bribed — for my own purposes. Twas risky to place the letter in a strangers hands, but here on a finca in the southernmost reaches of Spain, the intelligence was utterly wasted. I completed the encyphering of the information as best as I could and devised a seemingly innocent destination for it in Genoa, knowing that Walsinghams agent there would send it on to John Dee in Prague, and he to my Father, still commanding the troops in the Netherlands.

The messenger I chose to approach one afternoon as the family were withdrawing for their siesta, was a young man with the rudest saddle and most threadbare clothing of all the couriers I had observed. We had seen each other several times in the previous weeks, and I assumed he knew I was an honored guest of the Lorcas. As he saddled up to leave the compound I walked over, exaggerating my limp for sympathys sake. The boy — for he was hardly yet a man — was deformed by a hare lip, tho otherwise quite a handsome lad. He was shy as the afflicted often are, and I spoke to him kindly, admiring his horsemanship a la gineta. He was Enrique, he told me, and he fairly glowed with pride at the compliment. We spoke for a time about the mount he was riding — not his own. He was too poor to own his own horse. This belonged to his employer.

Judging that this might be my best and only chance, I let slip that I had an urgent letter needing delivery to Genoa and asked if Enrique knew of anyone who would be up to the job, sorry that he could not do it, as he was so closely employed by Don Ramón. His face lit up instantly, and he said that in fact he was just now off to Barcelona on the Mediterranean coast, and that numerous ships departed from that port to Italy every day. I shook my head, saying that the message must have one deliverer only, but that the payment, half on departure and half on return with the signature of Signor Bellini, would be five ducats — which I knew would be more than enough to buy a horse. I could see the boys eyes darting every which way as he conceived of a plan by which he could manage the job himself, at which time I bid him adios, wished him a good journey and turned to go.

"Senor, I can deliver the message! When I reach Barcelona I will take ship for Genoa and put the letter into Signor Bellini's very hands my self."

"Are you not expected back here by Don Ramón?" I inquired mildly.

"Oh, he has many couriers, Señor. I will claim illness and someone else will take my place until I return."

So with that the deal was struck. With a prayer to God that I was a good judge of character, and that the message would find its way only into friendly hands, I gave it into the boys safekeeping. He rode off and with the sun scorching in the cloudless sky, I retired to the casa, where everything in the household had ground to a halt, except for the maids sprinkling cool water on the flagstone floors.

On the balcony near my room I found myself face to face with Constanza just leaving the nursery, having put the children down for siesta. She glowed with a slight flush to the cheeks. Damp hair clung to her neck, flutters from her black lace fan cooling her not at all. She smiled when she saw me, an intimate smile, one which I believed in my heart was an invitation. I felt the last of my restraint slipping away and so without speaking took her into my arms and kissed her. Far from resisting she drank deeply from my mouth, our bodies melting together in the heat of the afternoon. Groping with my hand I opened my bedroom door and we sought its cool secret refuge with equal ardor.

Once inside I was startled by her passion which I never expected to equal mine. The bed seemed too far a distance to travel, so we stood clinging together back against a wall, she murmuring "mi amor, mi amor" as she lifted her skirts and helped guide me into the sweet warmth of her.

As the moment of her supreme satisfaction came upon her Constanza began to cry out and I covered her mouth with my own, but the violent pulsation at the core of her triggered my own explosive release and I buried my face in her shoulder to silence my ecstatic moaning.

Altogether spent and weak kneed, we could barely stand. I tried to lead her to the bed, but she shook her head, straightened her skirts and kissed me once before disappearing out my door. I laid my self down, disheveled but fully clothed and slept, adrift on a sea of unimaginably lovely dreams.

When I awoke it was nearly dark, and so I quickly dressed and descended to the dining room. The events of the day were crowding my mind — satisfaction that I had finally dispatched the Cadiz intelligence, worry that it would somehow go astray, or that with the delay caused by my illness the news would come too late to be of any use. And finally the thrill of having Constanza return not only my friendship but my passion. I was therefore lost in contemplation as I reached the closed doors of the dining room, and found myself confused by what I was hearing. Twas indeed Constanzas voice, but a language unknown to me. There was something ancient in its guttural and mysterious tones. I stood very still, listening. What I was hearing, I finally understood, was Hebrew. I remembered John Dee telling me that thro the sacred Hebrew language could be tapped supercelestial powers. Had I stumbled onto a family of Hermeticists?

"Baruch atah Adoni eluhainu melach haalum . . ."

I opened the door.

Constanza stood surrounded by her family, a short lace veil covering her head and face, lighting candles which, I thought with a shock, had to be Sabbath candles. It was a Friday night. They were Jews.

When she had finished the prayer Constanza exchanged kisses with her Father and children, then looked up and smiled at me entirely unalarmed. "Come in, Señor Reggio," said Don Ramón. "And you should close your mouth, Sir. You are gaping." I shut the door behind me and at once servants began serving the Sabbath meal. Entirely speechless, I took my place at the table as the Lorcas did the same. Only Don Ramón sat in a chair, with Constanza and the children lowering themselves onto high cushions after the Moorish fashion. I waited for them to speak, illuminate the strange circumstances, as I could not for the life of me conceive what to ask.

"Did you know," began Don Ramón, "that in the same year that our illustrious monarchs Ferdinand and Isabella backed the first expedition of Christopher Columbus to the New World, they forced exodus on every Jew in Spain? Our own ancestors were among those miserable refugees who could not fathom why such a fate had befallen them. They had, after all, been among the great conquerors and settlers of this land. Their culture, with that of the Moors and the original Iberians, had combined over the centuries into the delicious flavor that was Spain. The early Jews had been fierce warriors and extraordinary horsemen. Over the centuries they had counselled Kings, built mercantile empires, produced architects, artisans, intellectuals." He sighed heavily. "For this they were rewarded with the Inquisition. Hounded, tortured, burnt alive by the thousands. Many fled across the sea, or across the border to Portugal, our family amongst them. Other Spanish Jews converted to Christianity, preferring not to struggle against overwhelming adversity. These New Christians were called 'marranos' — swine. They were widely despised and regularly terrorized, tho many were, I think, strengthened by the knowledge that they were adhering to their principles. For amongst those who outwardly accepted Catholicism, a goodly number yet maintained the religion of their birth. These were secret Jews and their lot," he laughed mirthlessly, "their lot is the hardest by far. We are secret Jews, Señor, as I am sure you have by now guessed."

"But," I said, "I thought your family had moved to Portugal."

"They had, but they were ill contented there and soon the Lorcas masterfully embraced subterfuge and deceit along with the Catholic sacraments, for we longed to return to our homeland. We

have been covering our tracks for more than sixty years now, concealing the roots of our family tree. We are everywhere in Spain, involved in every trade and every level of government, and we keep in close contact thro a network of messengers. We have been extraordinarily successful, even if our religious practices have suffered. Without the luxury of praying together in a synagogue, some rituals have been lost or forgotten, others bastardized. But we do our best."

Don Ramón took a sip of wine and gently placed his hand on Constanzas arm. "But times are changing, Señor. King Philip has endowed the Inquisition with a frightening new intensity. He has no patience with heretics or infidels or Jews. He knows we exist in his country and he wishes us all to burn. He is a madman. An animal! Unworthy of the Spanish crown. He has whipped the Christians into a frenzy with this ridiculous notion of 'limpia sangre' — for no one in this land today can say they have truly pure blood. We are all of the same blood and it is mixed blood! And with the country on the verge of a second bankruptcy, citizens are starving, desperate for money, and paid informers are everywhere reporting their friends and neighbors as clandestine Jews. We have been lucky so far, and of course we are very, very careful, but I do not know how long we will be safe. For me, the agony of the flames would be nothing compared to the knowledge that my family might suffer."

I looked imploringly at Constanza then for some guidance, for despite her Fathers eloquent explanation, I was still at a complete loss. Why had they told me — a stranger — and, as far as they knew, a Catholic — such things?

She smiled then, indulgently, as a Mother would to a young child. "You are wondering, are you not Señor, why we have revealed such a dangerous secret to you?" These were the first words Constanza had spoken to me since that afternoons astonishing tryst. I thought her unbelievably calm. No one could have guessed at what had passed tween us hours before. "The truth is," she said, looking deep into my eyes, "we know quite well that you are not our enemy. You are a spy, Inglés, and wish for the downfall of the same enemy as ourselves."

"You know!" I blurted, feeling an utter fool.

"In your delirium you cried out in your native language," Constanza said unemotionally. "So I searched your saddlebags."

I laughed, horrified, outraged, amused. "You have known all along!"

Constanza and her Father exchanged a conspiratorial smile. Then she looked back at me. "My husband, in fact, was a Catholic, and he died never knowing that he had married a Jewess, nor that his children by their Mothers blood were both Jews. I know you will forgive us our deceit as we have forgiven you yours. We understand you must deceive to survive, and we are a family of survivors."

"What plans have you?" I asked, leaning across the table urgently. "How do you propose to protect yourselves?"

"As I have said," replied Don Ramón, "the net of our family is thrown very wide over Spain, and we are prosperous and respected. Whilst this has always been a strength, now it also means more opportunities for exposure. Each of our members must take especial care to anger no one, create no resentment nor jealousy, for if one of us falls, all of us will follow."

"We are looking to the possibility of emigrating to the New World," said Constanza. "Jews are flocking there in great numbers, you know. The King has recently granted an enormous tract of land in the northernmost territories to a hundred Jewish families. Whilst there is an Inquisition on the other side of the Atlantic as well, it is not so active as the one in Seville."

"You would leave Spain after all your struggles?"

"Not willingly," she went on, "but until times are better, what is important is simply carrying on, keeping our children alive. Little did you know, when you risked your life to stop a runaway carriage, that you were preserving the bloodline of Abraham."

I smiled, and Constanza made no attempt to conceal her love for me, tho I doubted her Father knew of that afternoons intimacy.

"You must tell us the true story of your life," she said. "But first, we have recently received a piece of intelligence you will surely appreciate knowing." Constanza then pulled from her lap the letter I had that afternoon given into the hands of the harelipped courier, along with the payment I had made him. I laughed at my own naivete, amused at how easily I had been fooled by a young messenger boy.

"The loyalty of our servants," said Don Ramón, "is precisely how we have sustained our selves over the generations. Now, there is something you must know. Your countryman Drake, with a force of more than twenty English vessels, has been sailing down the Portuguese coast doing mischief to the harbors and the ships being assembled in them. He is likely heading for Lisbon, and we thought you

would wish him to know of the fleet at Cadiz which has, in fact, come to a point of readiness to sail in the past week."

"Yes, he must know!" I cried. "Can you set me on the quickest overland route to Lisbon?"

"The arrangements have already been made," replied Constanza quietly. "You will ride at first light. Enrique will ride with you to see to your comfort."

I could detect pain in Constanzas eyes at the thought of my leaving, perhaps never to return, and worry about my barely healed injury on the long treacherous ride. She was forced to maintain a brave facade, however, as larger matters were at stake than our love for each other.

"Now, amigo," said Don Ramón sitting back in his chair, "let us hear all about your self. First, so we can call each other honestly, tell us your real name."

"My name," I said, vastly relieved to be finished with lying to these good people, my friends, "is Arthur Dudley."

Constanza and I had spent my final hours locked in each others arms. Her perfect body, rich in luxuriant curves, sweet, mysterious fragrances, the strength and unreserved passion of her embraces, forged for ever their memory on my soul. When the candles had burnt low, I knew finally that she must go from my bed, and I from this place. She fixed me with eyes which were overfilled, took my hand to place it over her breast and said simply, "This can never be broken, my love, not thro time, nor thro distance, nor thro death." Then she kissed me once more, rose and left my chamber.

I dressed, and in what was left of the night walked to the stables where Enrique had already saddled Mirage with the special saddle the Lorcas had fashioned for me. Hanging around the pommel I found a beautiful silk sash. I could see that besides an exquisitely embroidered horse, its legs lifted in a regal levade, some writing had been stitched in below it. Holding the sash up to the light of the lantern I read,

> When God created the horse He said to the magnificent creature: I have made thee as no other. All the treasures of the

earth shall lie between thy eyes. Thou shalt cast mine enemies between thy hooves, but thou shalt carry my friends upon thy back. Thy saddle shall be the seat of prayers to Me. And thou shalt fly without wings and conquer without sword. O Horse.

— The Koran

Even as the sun began to peek over the eastern horizon Enrique and I mounted up and rode out of the finca gates. I was glad of the remaining darkness, for he could not clearly see my forlorn face nor the silent unstanchable river of tears which flowed from my two eyes.

Forty

Three blows, thought Elizabeth, trying desperately to quell the sick churning in her gut as she sliced, a solitary blade, across the frosty ground of Greenwich Park — three blows from a clumsy axeman to sever the head of my cousin Mary. Had she lost consciousness with the first? Please Jesus that she had! Or had she experienced the full agony of being butchered alive? At least her dear mother had felt nothing, Elizabeth told herself. The swordsman from Calais that her father had hired had swept Anne's head cleanly from her slender neck in one swift blow. No no, she must stop thinking on the horror of it.

Returning from a hard ride the Queen had heard London's church-bells pealing merrily and asked a stableboy the cause. She'd been told that the Scots queen had finally met her end, with the added detail that the executioner, picking up the severed head for all to see, had come away with a red wig in his hand, the skull — its lips still moving in papist prayer — covered in a fuzz of thinning grey hair.

How had this happened? thought Elizabeth. Yes, she had signed the death warrant for the woman who had, year after year, attempted to usurp the English throne from her. Yes, she had signed the death warrant. She had even sent it with Secretary Davison to be passed under the Great Seal of England. But she had withheld the final order that the warrant be carried out, strictly forbidden her ministers — Leicester, Walsingham, Hatton, Cecil — to take that final irrevocable step. Forbidden them!

Or had she?

Suddenly Elizabeth could not remember, could not be entirely sure. God knows she had meant to be clear with them. But they had all nagged her unmercifully day after day for years. Argued that her subjects wished fervently — no, *demanded* — Mary's death. That if and when an invasion came, her Catholic subjects should never be afforded the choice of rising in defense of a Catholic monarch instead of a heretical Protestant one. That there should be one and only one living queen in England, and that queen must be herself. Elizabeth finally had given in and signed the warrant, but all the time knowing she could withhold the final signal for it to be carried out.

Instead her treacherous councillors had moved round her, defied her, taken the law into their own hands, laying her open to the full reprisals of the French and, worse, Philip. Oh, they would be punished! They would know her fury!

A gaggle of cheerful courtiers at the castle steps bowed low as she thundered past them. She restrained herself from lashing out, slapping the smile off a vacuous face, boxing the ears of a grinning idiot. How dare they smile? They were laughing at her, enjoying the hoodwinking of their queen at the hands of her loyal noblemen.

"God's blood!" Elizabeth shrieked as she pushed her way through a rustling flock of waiting ladies into her bedchamber, slamming the door behind her. "The head of a sovereign queen has rolled, and I swear by Christ there will be hell to pay!"

In that moment the Queen caught sight of herself in a looking glass. It was a terrible sight, tears streaking the caked white alum, red rouge dripping down to the creases of her downturned mouth. All I need are some snakes in my hair, thought Elizabeth bitterly, and my ugly, hateful countenance could turn a man to stone!

Suddenly a worse thought arose. Whilst outwardly she might resemble Medusa, in the very core of her soul she had finally become her father. Murderer of queens. She could rant and carry on in fits of hysteria, blaming everyone round her for Mary's death. She could cite national security, claim that she feared for her own life. And yet the fact remained. She alone ruled. If there was one lesson she had learned from Henry VIII and had indeed practiced from the beginning of her reign, it was the art of ruling with absolute authority. Let all others believe she vacillated, that she depended altogether upon the counsel of her advisors, that she was after all only a weak woman. Let them believe. But she was Queen of England, and she knew that every day for the rest of her life she would wash her snow white, long-fingered hands in the blood of Mary Stuart.

Elizabeth stared contemptuously at her own image, then picked up a small silver trinket box and flung it violently into the mirror, which shattered, with what was left of her peace of mind, into a hundred thousand pieces.

Forty-one

"Damn my eyes!" muttered Francis Englefield as he caught himself from stumbling, on the arm of his young secretary, Randall. Making their way down the endlessly long east corridor of El Escorial, Englefield cursed his dimming vision, not only because it had turned him into a clumsy fool, dependent on another for reading and writing, but because he was wholly unable to enjoy the wonders filling the monstrously large and magnificent palace, described by his employer King Philip as a dwelling for God on Earth. Here amidst eighty-four miles of corridors and halls, Englefield could make out only the vaguest forms in the bold El Greco masterpieces or the one-hundred-eighty-foot-long mural depicting the battle at Higueruela. Most frustrating, however, was Englefield's inability to enjoy the palace's extraordinary library, stocked with thousands of the world's greatest books, its high arched ceiling decorated with frescos depicting the seven Liberal Arts.

The pair of English pensioners moved into the Patio of Kings, which was thronged with masses of people — courtiers, students, friars, fine ladies, beggars, and caballeros on their horses. Randall — Englefield's eyes — kept up a running commentary the whole way.

"The Duchess of Osuna has gotten very fat."

"Perhaps she is pregnant," suggested Englefield.

"No. She has been drinking too much chocolate. My God, an entire army of artisans are erecting statues in front of the church. None of them look as if they've slept in a week."

The pair climbed the steps and entered the church to find the hubbub of the courtyard altogether absent. The awesome domed chapel of San Lorenzo was still and deserted except for a lonely black-clad figure kneeling at the High Altar under which, it was reputed, the entire royal family now lay entombed. Philip was thoroughly immersed in his devotions, one of four he practiced every day. The cavernous space echoed even the smallest of sounds, so Randall cupped his hand round Englefield's ear and quietly explained the scene. There they waited, fidgeting for three quarters of an hour until the King struggled to his feet. He turned, saw the Englishmen, and beckoned them to follow.

As they advanced toward Philip who was now hobbling through a door off the High Altar, Randall whispered, "His gouty old knees are the size of bloody melons. Imagine, kneeling like that on marble. The *pain* of it!"

They caught up with the King as he settled himself into a chair in the monklike austerity of his apartments. He had had his rooms designed, it was said, so that when he became too weak and feeble to attend the Mass in church, he could do it from his very bed. Englefield and Randall made their obeisance.

Philip, as always, spoke in Spanish — the only language he knew. "You have heard that the heretic queen has had her cousin Mary executed — unlawfully executed," he said.

"I have, Your Majesty," said Englefield. "A loathsome, cowardly act." An Englishman born, and once a servant to the royal family in Queen Mary Tudor's time, Francis had come to despise Elizabeth, not so much for her Protestant faith as for her continued refusal to release his legally inherited family properties and fortune to him. True, he was a sworn Catholic and had left England a disgruntled man, but she had consistently ignored his written pleas, driving him, penniless, to seek protection from the Spaniards. True, he had plotted with his fellow expatriate Throckmorton to dethrone Elizabeth and raise the Scots queen Mary in her place. The plot had unfortunately been uncovered and Throckmorton had lost his head. Then Elizabeth, unable to lay her hands on Englefield, had taken his properties from him once and forever, giving them to her beloved Lord Leicester. Now Francis was a common pensioner in Philip's court — his English secretary — and had very little in his life to enjoy. News of Mary's beheading had depressed him to the point of illness.

"She's probably better off dead," said the King offhandedly. This caused Englefield to gasp involuntarily and Randall, who was much younger and whose loyalties were far less formed, to laugh, though he stifled it quickly. "I did never trust the woman," Philip went on. "Catholic though she was, she nevertheless had her mother's French blood."

"Then you prefer her son James for the English throne?" asked Englefield.

"No, I trust him even less. He cares very little for religion but claims to be a Protestant. I cannot undertake a war in England merely to put a young heretic like James on the throne. What kind of son was he, anyway? He made it quite clear that his mother's execution should not damage his alliance with her murderess. And before she died, I persuaded Mary to disinherit James and bequeath the claim to me. I have heard of several species of animals whose mothers eat their young. Here, the offspring will just as easily devour its mother."

"Then you mean to take the English throne for yourself?"

"In the main, yes, though I shall let my daughter, the infanta Isabella, rule. I am far too busy myself."

"But, Your Majesty —"

"There will be no problem whatsoever. England is filled with Catholics who will embrace us, so says my ambassador Mendoza."

Englefield bit his tongue. Mendoza was perhaps the one man who hated Queen Elizabeth more than himself. He too had been caught conspiring against her, and had been humiliatingly tossed out of England on his ear. But Mendoza had, Englefield believed, led King Philip to think that the Protestant faction in England was a minority, which it sadly was not. Even if the King conquered the little island nation, he would surely find there a people who would die before they accepted Spanish rule. Dear God, worried Englefield, Philip would be forced to erect and support permanent garrisons, like those in the Netherlands, to subdue the vast majority of English who every year grew more patriotic and loyal to their beloved Gloriana. It was an expense in manpower and money the King could ill afford. None of this, however, did Francis Englefield dare to speak.

"What is your wish, Your Majesty?" he said instead.

"I wish you to compose a letter to the Catholic lords yet in Scotland. Offer them . . . I will fill in the amount . . . a great deal of money in return for the promise that upon my subduing England they will, however they see fit, 'release' young James from the Protestant lords who now control him, and return Scotland to Catholicism. Then he shall rule that country while Isabella and I rule England."

Philip rose laboriously and moved to a table on which were spread three documents, only the middle of which was in the King's spidery scrawl. He stood looking down on the documents with an expression which Francis Englefield could only describe as ecstatic, transcendent, glorified.

"The two pieces of my Great Enterprise against England," he announced with the smallest glimmer of a smile, "may have originated in the minds of my two greatest generals, but the idea of combining them was wholly inspired by God through the vessel of my own mind. God and I are one in this invasion and that, Englefield, is why we can never fail."

Francis found himself trembling with excitement. The King of Spain was about to reveal his plan for the Armada to himself, a lowly pensioner.

"Admiral Lord Santa Cruz several years ago devised a scheme for ridding my oceans of Elizabeth's pirates and invading England with an Armada sailing up the Channel." Philip tapped the document on the left of his desk. Santa Cruz's estimates of the force needed were far too high, but the plan was clever nonetheless. "My brother Don Juan, God rest his soul," said Philip, laying a hand on the parchment on the right of his table, "conceived a plan to invade England with our land troops from the Netherlands. The Duke of Parma has recast the plan — a surprise attack, a short hop across the Channel with an invading infantry. The Jesuit Father Parsons has pointed out to me that in England's history, attempts to invade the island have been made sixteen times. Fourteen were successful."

"And you — with God's inspiration — conceived of combining the plans?" asked Englefield.

"Precisely! Yet now all I hear from Santa Cruz is whining and complaining. 'We should not sail in the winter, Your Majesty. The gales in the Channel will blow us to Kingdom Come.' 'We are not yet provisioned. We need more time.' And from Parma in the Netherlands even worse. Silent disapproval and sulking. The two of them keep insisting upon war councils. Santa Cruz nags me incessantly to travel to Lisbon to view the fleet. But it is *unnecessary*, don't you see? Why must they meet with each other or with me when the Enterprise is inspired, overseen, and advised by God Himself!"

Englefield found that he was still trembling, but no longer with delight. He was no genius, but he saw now that two of the empire's greatest military minds had serious doubts about this plan into which the King had thrown the country's every last soldier and resource and ducat. If the invasion of England failed, thought Francis Englefield, Spain was most certainly doomed.

Forty-two

Elizabeth finished reading the decyphered dispatch from John Dee and laid it down on the silver-topped table to allow Mary Ashby to place several rings on the finger of her right hand. All round in her bedchamber, waiting ladies added final touches to her immaculate morning toilette and began restoring the room to order after the elaborate ritual of dressing the Queen. But she was blind to it. All she could see was the impact of the letter. England was finally, irrevocably on the brink of war with the richest and most powerful nation on earth. No longer could she evade or postpone it. She'd finally come to admit that the Duke of Parma's continuing peace negotiations with her Privy Council were a sham, meant only to pacify Elizabeth. The evidence pouring in from Walsingham's spies had become too overwhelming for her to ignore, or pray that she could somehow reverse.

Philip had built a terrifyingly large and well-provisioned Armada, the likes of which the world had never seen. Almost one year ago Francis Drake's waterborne raiding party at Cadiz harbor had destroyed a good portion of the fleet, setting the King's plans back substantially.

Captain Drake had returned to England buoyed by his rich spoils and convinced that the proper way to defeat the Armada was to never allow the ships to sail in the first place. He had urged Elizabeth to continue systematic attacks on Spain's home ports. Many agreed with him that England's defenses were too weak to withstand an attack on its own shores, and truly Elizabeth had been heartened by the Cadiz victory. But Cecil had unceasingly whispered in her ear what she wanted to believe — that peace negotiations could still save England from the horrors of war — and so she had denied Drake permission to sail again on his harrying missions.

In the year since, Philip had singlemindedly continued his subterfuge and preparations. Nine months ago John Dee had uncovered a heinous plot — by means she never questioned, for magic and spying were so deeply entwined in that man's character — to burn down the Forest of Dean, the largest source of wood for the building of the English navy. With information supplied by Dee, two enemy agents passing as woodcutters had been caught in the forest, preparing to put it to the torch.

Walsingham's spies on the Continent reported that Parma's troops in the Netherlands were involved with the invasion, and from Spain came word that Philip had recovered from his losses at Cadiz, rebuilding and reprovisioning his mighty Armada. Now it had become a simple matter of *when* they would strike.

'Twas strange, thought Elizabeth, how the threat of war, far from ruining her popularity with the people, only served to increase it. True, there was a kind of hysteria gripping the country, but it took the form of a fervent new patriotism and an evergrowing adoration of their Queen — Gloriana. So whilst Elizabeth found her heart gripped by terror of a war on her own soil, her soul was nourished daily by the great and growing love of her subjects.

Hysteria of a different nature reigned on the Continent and in Spain — another clever contrivance of her magus and master spy Dee. He had recently trotted out a hundred-year-old prophecy by the astrologer Regiomontanus that the year 1588 would bring upheaval and catastrophe, and that great empires would crumble. Dee added to that his own reading of the stars, claiming the year would see the fall of a mighty kingdom amidst freak and monstrous storms. But he had offered up this occult intelligence to a particular audience only. He had whispered it into the ear of King Rudolph in Bohemia who had, as expected, relayed it to the Pope, and he to King Philip. Dee's friend in the Dutch printing trade had likewise been informed, and his prophecies of doom blanketed the Continent in thousands of books and pamphlets, spreading terror and panic amongst the population there, undermining Spanish morale when it was most needed. Contrariwise, at Dee's urging, Elizabeth had seen to it that all such information was suppressed by English publishers so that her subjects would not become disheartened.

A brilliant strategy, thought the Queen, and a brilliant man. She picked up his latest correspondence. She could read between the lines Dee's aching to return home. He'd been gone for five years on his mission. His beautiful library had been looted. His wife had died. Still, Elizabeth could not afford to be sentimental at a time like this. She would call him home soon enough. Now she had to make sense of Dee's instructions contained within this dispatch. She picked it up and read again a paragraph near the bottom.

Most Gracious Majesty, whilst all conventional wisdom and consensus agree that England has not a chance under Heaven of winning a war with Spain, my own celestial consultations have shown otherwise. Be of good Faith, Majesty, for your glorious Empire expanding across the sea into New Atlantis is clearly foretold, and a crushing defeat by a tyrant such as Philip is simply nowhere to be found in your stars. Therefore proceed forcefully in this world — shipbuilding, armies, navies, provisioning and armaments (I highly commend your appointment of Lord Howard and Francis Drake to command the fleet), but begin as well the preparations which I have outlined below, those pertaining to the occult world. You may find such suggestions odd, even pagan in feeling and design, but do not doubt for a moment that for the purposes of winning this momentous battle, their efficacy is as great, and their results as real, as the mustering of men or the manufacturing of artillery."

Elizabeth suddenly noticed one of her ladies kneeling at her feet, and wondered vaguely how long the girl had been there. "What?" The Queen had lost most of her patience with the young ladies of her chamber. They were for the most part beautiful and well educated, but all but her fool Mrs. Tomison were terrified of speaking any kind of opinion in her presence . . . as well they should be, she supposed. Elizabeth had taken recently to boxing the ears of anyone, man or woman, who vexed her. Something in her had grown very cold, very brittle. Remorseless. She knew this, and it saddened her, but there was no remedy. For too long she had suppressed unsuppressible desires, suffered insufferable losses, forgiven unforgivable betrayals. Together with the gift — or was it the damnation? — of wielding limitless power, Elizabeth Tudor had, over the years, become a woman less of flesh and bone than of ether. She was composed, she sometimes mused, entirely of thoughts and ideas — the greatness of her little island nation, the fierce protectiveness of her beliefs, her loves and loathings. Her body seemed sometimes a wooden puppet doll, not actually alive but appearing alive owing to pulls on its strings and a voice projected by the puppeteer.

"What did you say!" snapped Elizabeth with more irritation than she had intended.

"I have just told you that Lord Leicester has arrived, Your Majesty," said the lady with downcast eyes.

"So you have," replied Elizabeth in a somewhat warmer tone. "I'm afraid in a few years your Queen will be deaf as a post. Take all the ladies out with you now, and send Lord Robert in to me."

"Yes, Your Majesty." As she spoke the girl dared to meet Elizabeth's eye. "You look lovely, Your Majesty," she said.

With her old lover about to be shown in, and her vanity still very much alive, Elizabeth chose to believe the girl's lie.

"I do admit I'm surprised at how well Drake has behaved," said Robin Dudley, "under the circumstances." He sat forward in the chair next to Elizabeth's highbacked one, and rearranged his swollen leg on the padded footstool she'd had brought in for him. "He wished for the appointment as High Admiral of the Fleet more than anything in his life. And in my opinion he deserved it."

"I agreed with you, Robin," she replied evenly.

Leicester observed the Queen observing him. Probably, he thought with annoyance, she is thinking to be mild with me because I look so ill.

"But Lord Howard is not only my cousin," she said, "he is the highest peer in the land with decent naval experience. Other ship commanders would never take orders from one of their own rank, even Drake. And frankly, Sir Francis has no one to blame for that state of affairs but himself. Was it not he who established the principle that a ship's captain, and not the highest ranking soldier on board, was its supreme authority? They all think of themselves as little demigods now, the captains. 'Twill take a man of the highest order to pull them together under one command."

"Indeed, I think your relative quite adept. He seems to have charmed our favorite pirate altogether. When last I saw him with Drake they were arm to shoulder, heads together and deeply immersed in nautical conversation."

"Tell me," she said, trying not to stare at the swollen ankle under his silk stocking, "do you think they are happy with their navy?"

"They like the new ships you have had built. They are sleek and sturdy and very fast. But I have heard both Drake and Howard complain about the provisioning of the fleet," said Leicester pointedly, "and I can attest personally to the great disservice it does to the men and the war effort in general." Leicester saw Elizabeth's eyes narrow. He could see that her mildness with him was about to end. He wondered if she meant to berate him one more time for accepting the post in the Netherlands, or his now infamous bad blood with the English officers there under his command.

"You have great nerve to take issue with my policy on provisioning, my lord. You are very fortunate I've not chosen to censure you —"

"Censure *me!* 'Twas I who struggled to feed and clothe and arm your troops in the Low Countries with too little money! And I who was chastised and ridiculed and nearly recalled from duty for my so-called poor accounting practices. *You* try keeping the records straight when the only way you can keep an army of six thousand men alive is to beg, borrow, and steal!"

"That's enough, Robin."

"I'm not finished." He saw her eyes snap open at his audacity. "I recommend that for once in your life you leave off crying poverty and throw every tuppence in your treasury behind the defense of this realm or I promise you, Madame, you will *have* no realm!"

"Are you through?"

"Yes."

Leicester was strangely calm. He had angered and defied and infuriated Elizabeth their whole lives together. She had shrieked and cursed, hurled abuse and punishment down on his head, and he had survived it. But he knew her heart and her mind. Knew that they were all for England, and that the advice he was giving her now was honest, and was for England too.

"I have been thinking about our land forces," she went on as though no harsh words had ever passed between them.

"And what have you been thinking?"

"That they are appallingly ill prepared. We have lived in peace so long in England we have neither the machinery nor the spirit for war. Our castle fortresses are falling down in disrepair. Our militias are inexperienced, and too hastily gathered, and our coastal towns are defended by farmers and fishermen who train together once a week. Robin" — she leaned forward and clutched his arm — "what will happen if our fleet cannot hold the Armada back? What will become of us if thirty thousand of Philip's rabid soldiers overrun our shores, sail up the Thames into London? Another Haarlem? Another Spanish Fury?" Naked fear shone in Elizabeth's eyes. Her thin vermillion lips were trembling.

Dudley's only answer was to place his reassuring hand over hers. He wished suddenly that he could gather Elizabeth into his arms, whisper soothingly, still the shaking core of her. He remembered the many times he had lain with her in her Bed of State and kissed away her terrors. Most of all he longed to tell Elizabeth about their son. That he lived. That he had grown into a fine man, tall and broad shouldered, a master horseman. That he had her skin and hair, and her mother's black eyes. Arthur . . .

But he could not. He had heard nothing from his son in more than six months. Dispatches had until then made their way to Leicester regularly. Arthur had traveled widely, quickly learned the art of spying, and sent valuable and necessary news to him from every part of the Continent. His intelligence regarding the fleet at Cadiz had made possible Drake's astonishing victory, buying England an additional year of preparation for the Spanish invasion. Leicester had received subsequent communications from Lisbon and the north of Spain, where Arthur had been surveying the progress of the Armada as Philip had begun rebuilding it. Then the flow of letters had ceased abruptly. Though Leicester could not bear to think it, his son might be dead. He could tell Elizabeth nothing until he knew. 'Twould be too cruel a twist of the knife to say now that their son had indeed lived, but might have died before she'd been able to know him. No, Leicester would say nothing to the Queen of Arthur Dudley. He would speak only to God in his prayers every day, and beg that their child's life be spared, that England somehow prevail in the coming war with Spain, that someday the three of them might stand face to face and rejoice in each other's company.

Robin Dudley was still a widely despised man, he knew, and possessed many qualities which deserved him of it. But he had been imbued with one excellent quality — an ever hopeful spirit. It had held him steady through dark times before and now he summoned that hope and clung to it with all the strength left in his bloated and feverish body. He would see his son again, and Elizabeth would know and embrace him as well.

"I must give command of the land forces to someone," said Elizabeth suddenly, shaking Leicester out of his reverie.

"Who is it you have in mind? Raleigh? Hatton? Northampton?"

"You, my lord."

Leicester was forced to turn away, to blink back sudden tears. He cleared his throat, but found he had no words.

"Robin," she said with a softness in her voice he thought never to hear again, "there is no one in the world I trust more than yourself. I trust you with my life . . . and my life is England." She ran her still beautiful ivory fingers in a gentle trail down his red-veined cheek. "I know you are not very well. That you are weary to the bone. But will you take command, my love? As a favor to me?"

He turned back and met her gaze, which was as clear and steady as it had been when she had conferred the post of Horsemaster upon him, moments after she had learned she was Queen of England.

"My honor, Your Majesty," replied Robin Dudley, taking Elizabeth's fingers to his lips. "It will be my honor."

Forty-three

My overland journey to Lisbon with Enrique had proven the most difficult ride of my life, but I had arrived some hours before Captain Drake again put out to sea, and delivered to his great gratification my intelligence of the fleet at Cadiz. I had afterwards finished my convalescence in Lisbon, making the acquaintance of Nicholas Ousley, reputed the bravest of Walsinghams agents inside of Spain. We two conspired to provide England with the latest news of the Armada, which began after Drake's devastation of Cadiz to rebuild with astonishing rapidity. Not only did we need to report the number of ships to the Queens spymaster, but each vessels tonnage, munitions, muster of sailors, soldiers and galley slaves, and of course provisions.

Ousley and I would sit of an evening on the balcony of his casa overlooking Lisbon Harbor, drinking sherry and conspiring against Spain. He was a jolly fellow with a broad face and large fat nose, whose imposture was as a Scottish Catholic wool merchant. His wife managed the largest wool shop in the city. He was reasonably safe, he always said, as the Portuguese hated the Spanish, all the more since Philips coup several years before.

We devised a plan whereby he would concern him self with the buildup in Lisbon, and I would establish my self in the northern ports of Corunna and Ferrol, assessing the concentration of the fleet and the fortifications there. There would be Breton captains to share gossip with, and I would ferret out Englishmen of doubtful loyalty who might be planning to give easy landing to the Spanish ships in the south of England, and agents of Philip making forays into En-

glish ports to spy on our fleets. Happily, the Kings intelligence gathering was inferior to Walsinghams, and tho they tried to search out English agents, they came up empty handed more times than not.

In the meanwhile Enrique had ridden back to Don Ramón with news of my safe arrival and success. The boy returned immediately under instructions to guide me into whichever city I should request and help establish me with the members of the Lorca family network in that place.

I took my leave of Ousley and rode north with what I supposed was my first manservant. Enrique was a great boon to me, very toward and likeable, and a fine horseman who looked upon me as his teacher as much as his master. When we reached Corunna there was great activity to be seen in the harbor. As shipbuilders and provisioners finished their work, vessels would depart, sailing down to Lisbon where the whole fleet was being assembled.

Enrique had delivered me to the home of Rodrigo Lorca, nephew of Don Ramón, a loriner by trade. His stirrups and bridles of worked silver were everywhere in Spain renowned. Rodrigo was a handsome fellow, impeccably attired and highly cultivated, short and swarthy with dark flashing eyes. He seemed to embody the spirit of the Spanish male so precisely that I sometimes had a hard time remembering he was not the devout Catholic he pretended to be, but a Jew. A highly skilled artisan, Rodrigo no longer plied his trade, and only oversaw the workers in his factory, this because of the Spanish tendency to regard manual labor of any sort as demeaning. In fact, like so many of his Spanish compatriots, despite an outwardly affable and courteous manner, he disdained anyone not Spanish, even countrymen not of his own region. For me he made an exception, he told me, for I was a friend of his uncle and was taking a bite out of King Philips despicable hide.

"Let me show you something," he suggested one evening after a meal I had shared with him and his wife, a rather unlovely woman with a simpering manner and syrupy voice. She was one female I believed was improved by the custom of heavy veils. He took me into his study and laid out on his desk what was clearly the Lorca family tree, beautifully lettered and decorated all round with painted and gilt figures.

"We call this the Green Book. Every family of honor has one." He pointed with his manicured fingers. "You see here, our lineage

can be traced back to the twelfth century. This is our proof of pedigree." He laughed humorlessly. "As you can see, we are old Christians with the purest of bloodlines."

"With a master forger in your employ," I added, smiling.

"We live so carefully," he said, smoothing his long waxed mustache. "The merest scandal would bring the Lorca family down like a house of cards in a high wind."

Rodrigo had been very kind, providing me with safe living quarters not far from his own casa. I was a frequent guest at his home, tho I used many disguises to come and go from there, to deter suspicion. I was sometimes a fat Italian silk merchant and other times a local beggar knocking at the servants entrance of the Lorca house. Each fortnight I would ride to Ferrol. The port was much smaller than Corunna, but enough shipbuilding was there to be of concern, so I added the intelligence to my regular dispatches to Lord Leicester.

Rodrigo was also my gracious conduit to Constanza who had written faithfully to me since my departure from Santa Maria. Her letters — always fascinating and articulate, warm and filled with news of the farm and factory, with encouragement from her Father and sweet kisses from the children — were a balm to my soul. My letters back to her were never as passionate as I wished them to be, but I had never written letters of love to a woman before, and I abhorred treacly words which could never begin to express what I actually felt in my heart for her. I prayed therefore, that she could read between the lines of my letters, and I knew that she could never misread nor forget what had passed twixt us the night before I had gone.

I used many other disguises to make my way round Corunna. I was often a meat pie vendor at the docks where I could easily count the soldiers and sailors coming and going from the ships. Twas here I learnt the true nature of Spanish military men which in deed caused me alarm. They were tough, disciplined and brilliantly trained, and strutted with a magnificent insolence that made them difficult to rule. Lowborn as many of them were, they were overbrimming with honor and dignity, for the profession of soldiering itself conferred a kind of nobility upon them.

They had no regular uniforms but dressed themselves with extravagant flair and richness — long cloaks, vividly hued doublets and hose, wide brimmed hats with swirling rainbow plumes. Their pride was unmatched, certainly by any English soldiers I had ever known, for they believed that they were fighting for the most righteous of all causes — God Himself.

One day when Enrique had begged to stay abed with a flux I dressed my self as a pilgrim with a wig of long wild hair. I carried a staff and begging bowl and fixed a badge of cowrie shells on my homespun cloak. I made my way from the arcaded city square out Silk Street, past its fine shops and porticoed great houses. Careful to keep my demeanor that of a humble penitent, I never the less observed all the variety of people in the street — for this was one of my great pleasures. Gentleladies veiled from head to foot on their way to church were followed by pages carrying velvet pillows which their mistresses would use to kneel and pray. I saw a man wearing a yellow hood and a long face, both penance for his confession of heresy before the Holy Office of the Inquisition, tho I thought him lucky to have escaped the flames. And there were countless beggars who, by law, held licenses issued by the church to beg alms for six leagues round.

I had nearly attained my destination on the outskirts of town — headquarters for the Royal Provisioners of the fleet — when I felt a rumble under my feet and knew that a company of horsemen were overtaking me. Head bowed humbly I stepped to the side of the road to let them pass when all at once they were upon me! Several soldiers jumped from their mounts and grabbed me roughly, arm and foot. I did not struggle, and spoke softly, hoping to convince them that they had made a mistake. But as they clamped a chain round my neck I heard their muttering. "It is he." "Inglés."

I lay in the stinking Court Prison of Madrid for a week with no idea how I had landed there. In the solitary silence of my cell I racked my mind for any understanding of my predicament. Who had betrayed me? Enrique, who had conveniently stayed at home that day claiming illness? Was it Ousley? He had told me many stories of English agents dealing treacherously with one another in the grip of jealousy and the greed for glory. Perhaps one of my countrymen coveted my post in Corunna for himself. Whatever the cause I was in terrible danger of my life. I knew nothing of my captors plans for me — if I would be interrogated, tried, allowed to rot in this place for months or years or the rest of my natural life. Would I be executed — shot, beheaded, or burnt at the stake for the heretic I was? And who in Gods name had betrayed me!

After one week in solitary confinement — or what I thought was a week, for there was no window to the tiny room — I was moved into the common chamber, a vast vaulted affair of dark dripping stone and crumbling masonry. I had never thought I would be grateful for a place amidst such squalor and dangerous company, but I found it an altogether better lot than the maddening isolation of my lonely cell.

When I first viewed the throng living together in conditions no better than a rats nest, my stomach heaved, for the stench was unbearable. I slowly moved across the crowded floor, perusing the inmates both male and female, allowing them to peruse me. There were ragged misfits, prostitutes, and rich gentlemen reduced to a living nightmare. Heretics waiting for the flames, picaros and cutpurses, cattle rustlers and church thieves. And whilst I saw two putas squabbling over a crust of moldy bread, and several miserable beggars fighting for a bigger piece of piss-soaked floor to stretch their legs on, I saw amongst them, too, glimpses of pure humanity. A woman tenderly ministering to a skeletal man, goodnatured camaraderie in a makeshift gaming area, a one eyed prisoner extracting the rotten tooth of a grandee wearing what remained of a fine suit. And of course the constant stream, day and night, of friends and relatives bringing provisions to their hopeless loved ones.

I had made my first round of the common chamber when the curfew bell was rung. Much to my surprise the prisoners did not begin to settle in for their nights sleep but all, in orderly fashion, assembled to face a raised stair upon which the one eyed man had climbed. Acting as a lay sacristan he bade them all kneel and each in their own way made a silent or muttered prayer. Finally the cyclops intoned, "Jesus Christ our Lord who shed thy precious blood for us, have pity on me, a great sinner." I was struck at that moment by the extreme religious fervor of even these pitifully confined Spaniards, and shuddered inwardly to think that we in England did have a grave battle before us.

I was thus thwarted that evening of any information gathering, and instead threw my self into a quiet game of knucklebones with a confraternity of "matones." These were men — the most dangerous in the prison — who murdered for money. They, with their leather doublet over coat of mail and broad brimmed hat with feathers, stayed to them selves — or perhaps others stayed away from them. My approaching them that night, and having them accept me into their game, earned me a measure of respect. So that night when it was time for sleep, a space was silently cleared for me, and a rolled jacket was placed as a pillow neath my head. But I slept very little that night, endlessly musing on the treachery which had landed me in such a hellhole.

I was surprised when I woke on the stone floor, stiff and aching, that I had even slept at all. I had dreamt for the first time of Constanza, bathing naked at the river, the voluptuous beauty of her, her thick wet hair curtaining her breasts. Then the morning routine of the common chamber began and banished all memory of pleasant dreams, replaced by a trio of ugly crones ladling out slops for our breakfast, long lines for the jakes which were beyond description, and the steady trickle of visitors growing into a roaring stream. Twas a social place if nothing else, this gaol, and I moved thro the crowded chamber searching for someone, something that I might use to my advantage — a way to send a message out to a friend, the scent of an escape plot being hatched. Anything!

Then I heard it. "Inglés!" My heart thudded hard in my chest. I stood on a high step and located the gaoler searching for me. I hesitated, knowing I could postpone his finding me almost indefinitely in this chaos, but concluded twas my only hope of learning anything about my condition.

"Inglés!" I called out over the din. He came at once and roughly took custody. He refused to answer any of my questions as he led me out of the common chamber and down a dreadful torchlit corridor. My heart sank as he opened a heavy door and I found myself on the brink of the prison torture chamber.

I have heard that the greatest extremes of pain and terror sometimes bring about a strange lapse in the mind. Memory of the excruciating moments simply disappears, leaving a blessed gap so that a person may continue in his life untormented. I wish that such had been the case with my self that morning in the chamber of horrors at the Madrid prison. But alack I remember it all — the torture engine in the shape of a ladder to which I was bound naked, limb and torso, with thin ropes. The sticks stuck twixt the cord and the flesh on my chest, lower arms and the scarred place on my thigh, which I guessed would be twisted garrot like to cause pain. The creak of wood as the ladder was slowly adjusted till my head lay slightly lower than my feet. I remember thinking then that no matter how terrible the pain twas preferable to betraying my country and my Fathers trust. I remember, too, the scabrous hands of the man who pried open my mouth and inserted a prong of iron which distended my jaws, the filthy strip of linen laid down the length of my tongue into my throat. I remember the first thrill of fear as bits of linen were stuffed into my nostrils, and the harsh sound as I began breathing through my cloth cluttered mouth. By this time I recognized the method of misery which my captors meant to employ — the water torture. Twas a favorite of the Holy Office, preferable I had heard, to the rack alone or the hoist or the roasting of the victims oiled feet over flames.

I now saw a cupboard opened, and inside lined neatly by the dozen were jars of brownish water. The chamber door opened and preceded by a cloying waft of jasmine perfume, in strode a Spanish official, elegantly clad in black and altogether puffed with the importance of his duty. Without waiting to question me he said to his assistant, "Begin."

The first jar of water was poured at a slow and steady rate down my throat. I tried at first to swallow the water but soon, with my lungs near to bursting, came the impulse to breathe. I could not, for my passages were yet filled! I gulped faster but the linen rag was soaked with water. I was seized by panic. I saw looming before me the monstrous black waves of the storm on my first Channel crossing. Which was worse, I wondered, the horror of drowning in mid ocean, or the horror of that same fate tied to a ladder in a Madrid prison? I gagged, spewing water, choked and began to suffocate. A blackness overtook me and blessedly I lost consciousness. The blessing, tho was short lived. I came alive from my asphyxiation with a bolt of fiery pain in my newly healed thigh as the stick twisted and tightened the rope tied round it. I shrieked with agony, yet remember thinking that this pain was bearable next to the cruelty of the water.

Now that I had been initiated, the official began his interrogation in a silken voice, demanding to know the details of my mission. He assumed I was one of Walsinghams men, and I did not disavow it. But after a time I understood to my horror that he had no real interest in anything I might divulge to him, for English spies had, every one of them, the same mission — to relay the movements of the Armada back to the Queen. What I knew had little importance. He had in his clutches one of his mortal enemies — God's enemy — and his purpose was simply to inflict upon my mind and body as much pain as he could contrive until I should die.

A plan was beginning to form in the chaos of my brain when another jar of water was taken down from the shelf, and the assistant brought the forked device in order to pry open my mouth again.

"I am not what I seem!" I managed to shout before the fork was clamped on my face.

"And what would that be then, Inglés?" said the official, only mildly interested. He had, of course, heard every excuse, explanation and lie conceivable from previously captured spies, including the one I was about to speak, tho I believed it would buy me the time I needed to organize my thoughts.

"I am a double agent, Señor."

With a tiny nod the direction was given to pry open my mouth. The official regarded me with a disdainful expression which said, You will have to divulge more than that, idiot.

"I work in concert with Sir Edward Stafford who, as you know, shares intelligence with Ambassador Mendoza in Paris."

This served to bring him up short, and now he gazed at me with much less indifference. There was no way of telling the extent of his knowledge of Spains network of spies, especially at so high a level.

"There is something more that you should know," I continued, planning my next words even as I spoke, for I knew that whatever was said in the next few moments would either save my life or end it. "I think you should know exactly whom you are interrogating, Señor. Whom you are preparing to torture to death."

Whether twas the words I had spoken or the conviction with which I had uttered them, the official waved his assistant away with a flick of his perfumed fingers.

And then I told him the truth. At least a part of it.

Forty-four

"The heretic queen's bastard, are you?" Francis Englefield quivered with sarcasm. He was furious, as well, for the miserable luck of being blind at such an interesting moment. If he could but see this young man. Well, not so very young. Randall had described him as twenty-five or thereabouts. Englefield had many times been in the presence of Queen Elizabeth at that very age, and even several times of Lord Leicester whom this person, this English spy, was claiming as his father. If only he could see the man himself — the reddish hair and dark eyes, the naturally pale skin, sun-burnt and weathered — surely he would know if there was the slightest chance that the story was true.

When the report from the prison had come to Englefield's attention, the secretary had at first scoffed at the suggestion. Certainly it was far-fetched. But then with a few calculations he had determined the vague possibility of its truth. Back in the first years of Elizabeth's reign, he remembered, rumors of illegitimate children gotten by her stud Robin Dudley were as thick as flies on a dungheap. So he had had the prisoner walk the thirty-odd miles from Madrid to El Escorial for interrogation. If only it were true, mused Englefield, a natural successor to the English throne in *his* power. He might persuade the King to abandon his suicidal plan to rule England himself. . . . No, he must not suffer any delusions. The man was surely an impostor. He must settle for amusing himself with the prisoner, listen and appreciate the story — the details and convolutions that a mind's imagination could invent in order to keep its body from the flames of the Auto da Fé.

"I am that indeed," answered the man who called himself Arthur Dudley. An interesting choice of a Christian name, thought Englefield. The name of Elizabeth's paternal uncle, first heir of the Tudor dynasty, who never lived to see himself crowned and whose untimely death put Henry VIII on the English throne. Yes, and the Tudor fascination with the Arthurian legend. . . .

"However, my mother as yet has no knowledge of me. She believes I was stillborn. Only my father knows I'm still alive."

Englefield was sure he detected a note of anger in the man's last response. Oh, this might prove to be a roaring good tale! "Are you getting all this, Randall?"

"Every word, Sir Francis. Have no fear."

"And how, pray tell, did you make your way from a royal English birth to the torture chamber in a Spanish prison?" he demanded of Arthur.

"'Tis a long story, sir, but if you have the patience and your scribe has the ink, I shall tell you everything you wish to know."

Forty-five

I had met with King Philips English secretary for five days running, and his interrogation of me had been not only painless but at times almost pleasant. Francis Englefield was a strange peacock of a man, skeletally thin with thick spectacles which did him no good whatsoever, and attired in the most outrageous costumes — enormous starched ruffs, a parrot green doublet one day, sulphur yellow with scarlet hose the next. I wondered that a blind man should choose such flamboyance which he could not himself enjoy, and I wondered also how an Englishman — even a Catholic — could choose to live in service to the King of Spain.

I was a storyteller by nature, and whilst at times I merely related the facts of my life, at others I fabricated and twisted them to suit my purposes. Really there was only one purpose — to save my own neck. I had determined there was little I could do to further damage England. True, she had lost a loyal agent for the moment, but the invasion was a foregone conclusion, and I knew that alive there was some further chance of service to perform. I was no good to anyone dead.

I told Englefield and his scribe Randall the truth of my birth and upbringing and the odd incident of my arrest by the Privy Council Guard at Milford Haven beach when I was fourteen. I spoke of my military service in the Netherlands War, and even my presence at the assassination of Prince William of Orange. I explained that I had been called home to the deathbed of Robert Southern, there to be told of my true lineage. I even described my journey to London and the meeting with Lord Leicester, taking great pains to describe his lodgings at Greenwich in order to lend authenticity to my account.

Twas at this juncture, however, that adherence to the whole truth left off, and the spinning of the tale began. I said that Leicester had been utterly convinced of my story — in deed had blanched upon hearing the details of my birth and kidnapping by Kat Ashley and William Cecil, and also at the evidence of my Grandmothers black eyes and sixth finger. But whilst he had embraced me as his son and heir in the privacy of his lodgings, Leicester had thereafter schemed to rid him self of me for ever. He had explained that my Mother could not yet be told of my existence, but begged me to spy for England. Then I had been sent with his secretary to the home of Walsingham where I was issued a passport, and hustled aboard a ship bound for Calais. I related my shock and rage when I comprehended that I had been cut off altogether, that Leicester refused to answer my correspondences, and that I had been officially barred entrance to England for the rest of my natural life.

I had peppered the tale with enough names and places and details to give him pause, and urged him to verify them all. But twas not till I began to expound on the hurt and angry betrayal I felt at Leicesters rejection of me, that Englefields interest became truly piqued. I said that whilst my adoptive Father had been a Protestant, my Mother Maud had been an ardent Catholic, and that my personal sufferings of the past two years had revealed to me my real religious inclinations, bringing me back to the True Faith.

By now I could see the hook lodged in the cheek of this fish, and so I began to pull him in. I spoke of Ambassador Stafford — whom Englefield knew, of course, to be a double agent for England and Spain. I invented a superb yarn surrounding my meeting and association with the ambassador in Paris, and my apprenticeship to him. I described the Staffords hatred of Lord Leicester for his past treatment of Lady Stafford, formerly Douglas Sheffield, and the embarrassing pamphlet about them now circulating the Continent. I even claimed to have met Ambassador Mendoza on several occasions, and got Englefield laughing about the Spaniards lisp. I knew that telling such tales was dangerous, but I knew also that a communication confirming the information from Madrid to Paris and back, could take up to two months travelling time. I would surely be a free man by then, else a dead one. I knew quite well that I was treading upon thin ice, but was required never the less to stride boldly upon it, or I could never hope to save my life.

I pointed out that born the only natural child of Elizabeths body, I had a stronger claim to the English throne than the Scots King James. His Mother was dead at my Mothers hand. I suggested that after the conquest of England I finish the job, assassinating the heretic James, leaving the throne of Scotland conveniently empty and easily annexed to Catholic England. My own claim could then be determined by Philip, to whom I would of course pledge my whole allegiance.

I could see Englefields agitation growing, his blind eyes darting every which way behind the thick glass spectacles, the trembling of his body causing the huge ruff to vibrate round his head. He began firing questions at me. What was the name of Lord Leicesters secretary who accompanied me to see Walsingham? Fludd, I answered. "Humph," he muttered, then nodded in silent concurrence. What did the inside of Walsinghams house in Throgsneck Street look like, Englefield demanded. I said that the house was not in Throgsneck Street at all, but on the Strand, then proceeded to describe it in some detail. He questioned me in several languages and I answered fluently in each of them. He smiled and nodded, muttering, "Like Mother like son . . ." Finally picking up my left hand he pinched and stroked my extra digit as if it were a valuable jewel. Suddenly he hooted with delight, an entirely unnerving sound to be coming from so peculiar a character.

"Randall," he snapped, "take Mister Dudley to the bath house and have him . . . washed. Then have Parenta outfit him with a new suit of clothing. Something subtle, grey perhaps with touches of copper. And Randall," he added, "take several guards with you everywhere you go."

Englefield smiled at me with a mouthful of surprisingly good teeth. "Prepare your self, Sir. You shall soon have the privilege and honor of your young life — an audience with the King of Spain."

Escorted by Englefield and Randall I strode down the endless corridors of El Escorial. Never in my life had I witnessed such grandeur, from the varicolored marble floors and walls and columns, to the exquisite statuary, to the colossal altars which seemed to drip with gold. Nor had I ever been so elegantly attired. The Kings own tailor had outfitted me in a velvet and satin costume in shades of grey and black and white, with knitted silk hose and the most extraordinary boots of Spanish leather I had ever seen, much less worn.

Everything round me seemed very bright and sharply in focus. I felt unaccountably strong and sure of myself. I was walking to meet my destiny. Philip of Spain awaited me.

Finally we arrived at the intricately carven and inlaid door to the throne room. The guards uncrossed their halberds and allowed us entrance. I had imagined an immense throne and a resplendent and overbearing sovereign, arrayed with gold and precious gemstones. What I found was a small, jutjawed and greying old man in a dull black doublet and hose, hunched on what appeared to be a simple campaign stool. I quickly stifled my shock and after my presentation by Francis Englefield, fell into the many obeisances he had instructed me to make, then waited silently, head bowed on bended knee to be released from my prostrations.

"Let me see you," the King said finally in a thin and petulant voice.

I stood and rose to my full height and felt his pale eyes boring into me, searching my face and form and soul. But I did not tremble in that moment and instead regained the surety of my position. I reminded myself I was the son of a Queen and therefore as Royal as he. I reminded myself also, as I strode thro the convoluted maze I had carefully constructed from the truth and lies and outright fantasy, that one misstep, one false turning could be the end of me.

Forty-six

"Let me see the finger," commanded the King of Spain.

The tall, handsome man purporting to be the Queen's son raised his left hand and turned it outer side up. Philip beckoned for him to come closer. He approached slowly and Philip gazed down at the deformity with pursed lips.

"It is nothing but a nub of flesh with a piece of nail in it," he said.

"As it was with the whore Anne Boleyn," replied Francis Englefield.

Philip noticed the young man was smiling a small, mocking smile, as if to reassure them he held his grandmother in equal contempt. He might be pretending, of course, thought Philip, but the truth was, this person standing before him claiming to be Arthur Dudley bore an uncanny resemblance to each of the people he swore were his parents. He was built precisely like Lord Robert Dudley in his prime, when he had fought for Philip in the Neapolitan Wars. He moved with the same grace that the King had always found so peculiar in such a large and masculine man — a grace he had secretly envied. And according to Englefield, the man was persuasive. So had Robert Dudley been. Why, he had even persuaded Philip to support his ludicrous pursuit of Elizabeth's hand in marriage!

"So the Earl of Leicester has turned his back on you," inquired Philip coolly.

"He has, Your Majesty, and made it impossible for me to approach my mother."

"Your mother . . ." repeated the King with a cynical downturning of his lip, and suddenly the image of Elizabeth was before him. Elizabeth as she had been in the days of her sister Mary's ill-fated lying-in. Elizabeth the young and exquisite princess with the mother-of-pearl skin, the willowlike slenderness, the wild, burnished gold hair. Elizabeth for whom Philip would have willingly overthrown his Father's dictum regarding passion. "Do not overstrain yourself," Charles had commanded. "It damages the growth and strength of the male body. Stay away from your wife as much as you can. As soon as the marriage is consummated, leave on some pretext and do not go back too quickly or too often." He had obeyed such orders with his first two wives. But if he had had Elizabeth . . .

"I knew your mother," said Philip, recognizing as the words left his lips that he had in effect admitted he believed this man to be Elizabeth's child.

"I met her once when I was eight."

The man spoke with such authority, such confidence! Who would dare to lie so brazenly to the King of Spain? But how could the son of Elizabeth be standing before him now? It was impossible!

"She was a magnificent horsewoman, strong in her seat and altogether tireless," the man went on. "We rode side by side in a wild goose chase — a custom of ours in England — and I tell you the woman was not above cheating!" With that Arthur laughed a great booming laugh which revealed a sunburst smile.

The sight of that smile forced Philip back into the garden at Hampton Court thirty years before. Elizabeth had laughed at one of his small jests, and that smile's memory had lingered for years, warm on the walls of his mind. She had loved him too, he thought, for a brief moment she had loved him as he loved her. Then abruptly, without the King's permission, a heavy prison door crashed shut upon the rogue memory, and he stood naked before God in his shame. "Jesus forgive me," he cried out silently, "I have loved a heretic whore."

Suddenly there remained not a fraction of a doubt. He knew who stood before him bantering and smiling with Elizabeth's smile and Robin Dudley's graceful swagger. And just as suddenly he was overcome with rage. This man, this stranger who had appeared from nowhere, had emerged as his most dangerous rival for the throne of England.

"You have done well, Francis, bringing young Dudley to me."

Englefield was beaming with pride. Perhaps if he had been sighted he would have detected the cold fury behind the King's placid expression.

"Shall I have a suite of rooms prepared for him, Your Majesty?" asked Englefield, already envisaging the luxurious appointments — the hangings and carpets and gold plate, the wardrobe filled with clothing fit for a prince.

"Indeed," agreed Philip mildly. "We must show our new ally our most gracious hospitality. Nothing shall be spared."

As he spoke, the King of Spain became aware that Arthur Dudley's smile had subtly altered. The man had penetrated Philip's mendacious veneer. He knew he was doomed. Their eyes met and held as Englefield babbled on about apartments in the south wing, or the great chamber in the west wing. To his credit, the Queen's bastard stood unflinching under the King's gaze. Philip searched for a sign of defeat, a crack in the dignified bearing, even the equanimity of a gambler whose bluff has been called. He searched in vain. He could see that Arthur Dudley would hold his proud posture as he traversed the thirty miles back to Madrid and into the prison where he would live in obscurity until the day he died.

He was a formidable opponent. A magnificent man. But that was to be expected, thought Philip with cold pleasure. Arthur Dudley was of royal blood.

Forty-seven

Returned to the horrid confines of my Madrid prison I consoled my self with the knowledge that I was still alive, and for the time being ignored by the grim cadre of interrogators and torturers. I own that I was confused. I believed that Philip had accepted the truth of my parentage. Why then had he turned on me and, horrifying poor Francis Englefield, had me clapped in chains? But who, after all, can fathom the mind of a religious fanatic and tyrant like Philip of Spain? Never the less I was glad to be alive and at least able to contemplate the means of my liberation.

It soon became apparent that escape from that Madrid prison was no easy feat. I learnt that no one had managed it for more than twenty years. To make matters worse, prison security had increased as the date of the Armada sailing approached, and preparations for an Auto da Fé in its honor were begun.

Since my removal and return to the prison, the place had filled with dozens of victims of the Inquisition, altogether wretched men and women accused and convicted of secret Judaizing, some repentant and others steadfastly defiant. As the Holy Office itself had no right to inflict physical punishment on those found guilty of their crimes, they were declared "abandoned" to the secular arm of the law. This was merely the polite way of saying they would be given over to the civil authorities to be burnt at the stake. These, then, were the intended participants in the coming "act of faith" and now the stench of fear was added to the other foul odors in the common chamber.

My daily life was filled with mounting helplessness and despair as the day of the Spanish invasion of England inexorably approached, while the woman I loved seemed to lie beyond my reach for ever.

Then one day late in May I was visited by Sir Francis Englefield himself. He made quite a stir in his fuchsia doublet and matching hose, mincing in on the arm of his young scribe Randall. It occurred to me that for once the man would be grateful for his blindness, having enough to contend with in the offensive smell of the place. He had brought from El Escorial the transcripts of my "confession" and now required my signature on them before they were shipped off to the Royal Archives at Salamanca.

Englefield had me taken to a tiny private chamber and dismissed Randall so that we were quite alone. I could see all round the scribes neat handwriting on the document a great many notations in the margins in a strange loopy scrawl. I took my time with the signature and read one or two. They were obviously Philips comments on the content of my story. Near the bottom he had written "It will certainly be safest to make sure of Dudleys person until we know more about the matter."

Then I heard Englefield whisper urgently, "Please hurry, we have little time, my lord."

"My lord?" I replied incredulously. No one had ever addressed me in that way.

"Listen to me, Arthur Dudley. I believe you are who you say you are. And I have reason for seeing you released from this incarceration which must inevitably lead to your death."

"But King Philip —"

"King Philip will win this war and then destroy Spain when he attempts to take the throne of England for himself."

I laughed aloud then, imagining that wizened little creature trying to control the bawdy English commoners and the growing masses of straitlaced Puritans.

"Quiet!" hissed Englefield. "And listen carefully. On Sunday of next week three dozen prisoners of the Inquisition will be marched to the city plaza to receive their punishment. One group — the "reconciliados" — will be burnt in effigy only, whilst two groups found guilty — the repentant and unrepentant — will be consumed by fire. I have contrived to place your name on the list of the reconciled. Once you have stood before the Inquisitors and received your penance and yellow hood, you will be released into society."

I was altogether baffled. "Why are you doing this, Englefield?"

"Because when the war is won I will see to it that you make your way back to England. I may seem nothing more to you than a blind and ineffectual petty official, but in my day I was a master conspirator." Englefield seemed to stand a little straighter and whispered, "I plotted with the Scots Queen against your Mother —"

"I did not know."

"— and I will plot to make you King. And when you have assumed the throne — a Catholic monarch, but the true heir and an <u>*Englishman*</u> *— then I shall reap my reward."*

"And what will that be?"

"Only the rightful return of my lands and fortune which your Father now possesses." He grabbed my arm. "Will you promise me that much?"

I was staggered. Francis Englefield was actually taking seriously my claim to the throne — something I never expected anyone to swallow. I recovered my self quickly and with a congenial arm round Englefields shoulder I confided, "You shall have your lands and your fortune, my friend, and a title too. But listen, will this plan of yours work? My name on a list, and suddenly I am a free man?"

"I have no doubt of it, my lord. There is only one thing that you must provide for me — the name of someone who will fetch you from the Auto da Fé. Someone whom you trust implicitly."

I went suddenly cold hearing those words, and Englefield saw me stiffen.

"You must trust me, do you hear? I offer your one and only hope to escape from this place. I shall not have another opportunity to help you! Look at me, my lord. I am an Englishman who cannot go home, not so different from your self." He pounded his chest and spoke with a passion I had not seen before. "A Catholic exile, yes, but an Englishman all the same!" There were voices outside the door. "You must decide quickly!"

I knew that if Englefield was lying, divulging the Lorca name might be the death of them all. But I felt in my deepest soul that the man was honest and an Englishman, and that I could trust him. The door began to open.

"In the port of Santa Maria across the bay from Cadiz," I whispered. You must seek Don Ramón Lorca. The saddlemaker."

*   *   *

At dawn four days after the Armada had sailed from Lisbon Harbor, a black and white robed monk stood on the high stair of the common chamber and intoned in the voice of the Grim Reaper three lists of names. I breathed easier as my name was amongst the final group called. Taking my place in that somber company we were led, heavily guarded, out the prison gate and into the courtyard of a nearby greathouse. I looked up to the balconied second floor and saw the children of the house watching wide eyed as the heretics were stripped of their clothing, their private areas covered in loincloths, and each outfitted in the grotesque costume of the Auto da Fé. The "sanbenito" was a kneelength sackcloth tunic painted with the Cross of St. Andrew. Those worn by the reconciliados were nothing more than that. But on the front and back of the tunics of repentant Judaizers was painted a pile of blazing faggots, their flames extending downwards to signify that they would be spared actual death by fire and be garrotted first. For those sinners who were unrepentant, however, the flames on their sanbenitos turned upwards, and they were further painted with the gaudy devils and dragons with whom these worst of all sinners would presumably spend Eternity. Tall conical hats completed the humiliating outfit.

When the grim voiced monk handed me my tunic I felt the breath go out of me. There were flames rising upwards and the faces of nightmarish demons grinned back at me.

"This is a mistake!" I cried to the monk who had already moved on to the next person in line. He turned and raised an eyebrow. "I am a reconciliado. You must check your list of names!"

He fixed me with a patronizing gaze, but finally glided away to confer with his superior. Then he returned.

"You are Arthur Dudley?"

"I am."

He lifted the tunic off my arm and examined it. Then he looked up at me. "This is correct, Señor. Please put it on."

The world spun all round me. I had been betrayed by Englefield, tricked into going like a lamb to the slaughter. Worse, much worse, I had betrayed the Lorcas. What a fool I had been! Why had Englefield done this? I had been as blind as he, never seeing how deeply King Philips evil had infected him. Constanza! Don Ramón! Oh God, for my incredible stupidity I in deed deserved to die!

I remember the procession thro the crowded streets of Madrid to Cathedral Square as if in a dream. The Soldiers of Faith led the way, followed by the green cross of the Inquisition shrouded in a black crepe mourning veil. A bellringer preceded a portly priest walking under a brilliant canopy of scarlet and gold, and as he came, the multitudes sank down on their knees and wept, beating their breasts to the clang of the bell. Then came we prisoners, ropes hung round our necks, clutching green candles, each flanked by two serene monks. The robed constables of the Inquisition came next, and finally men bearing on tall poles the grotesque straw and wax effigies, with their sanbenitos and grinning painted faces.

As we marched into the plaza and saw the two high scaffolds draped in black my heavy heart sank further. What a terrible sight it was! The throngs — more thousands of spectators than I had ever seen assembled. The festive and colorful parade of the soon dead. The sickening air of hypocritical piety. How had it come to this, I wondered, that so horrific a ritual was deemed necessary to turn people from their evil ways? Auto da Fé. The Triumph of Faith.

As the priest celebrated the Mass we sinners stood before the scaffolds in three long lines surrounded by crowds of the devout, come to pray for our immortal souls. One by one the penitents ascended the steps to be seated before the agents of the Inquisition who then read out a long litany of their crimes against God, after which, with great ceremony, they received their penances. Those who had been abandoned to the secular arm were set in carts and driven away to the burning fields just outside the city. After two excruciating hours the first scent of charred human flesh wafted into our midst causing several of the convicted to break down into fits of sobbing from which they could not be comforted.

I my self had fallen into a torpor of hopelessness and despair, made worse by regrets for my stupidity, and insupportable remorse for the sure destruction of Constanza and her family. In deed I despised my self infinitely more fervently than did the surrounding throngs of people, much tho they wished me dead. Only the monks on either side kept the hands of the people from clawing at me.

All at once I felt a strange heat at my knees. I looked down. The hem of my sanbenito was aflame! I shouted "Fire, fire!!" trying to rip the burning garment over my head. Chaos exploded all round, people shrieking and pushing in on each other to see the penitent who had not waited for the pyre to burn. Then I felt my feet wrenched out from under me. I fell to the ground, hands grabbing roughly at me, panicked feet trampling and kicking. I was helpless as my body was dragged thro the huge surging mob.

Then suddenly it was over. I was still, gasping for breath, lying face down in what must have been an alley off the plaza. Bruised, skin scorched in some places, I rolled to my back and looked up, astonished to see the faces of Don Ramón and Enrique and several other men I did not know. Enrique quickly lifted me to my feet and Don Ramón threw a cloak over my shoulders.

"Forgive me for setting you afire, my boy," he said, "but it was the only distraction I thought spectacular enough for the occasion."

I threw my arms round him, laughing, murmuring my thanks. Then behind her Father I saw Constanza, her face illuminated with joy. I wished to embrace her, but Don Ramón restrained me.

"We must hurry out of here, Arturo," he said. "They will at any moment find your empty sanbenito and know you have escaped. Are you badly burnt? Can you walk on your own?"

"I was barely singed, Don Ramón." I could not tear my eyes from the sight of Constanza. "I am alive and I am free. I will follow you anywhere."

At a Lorca family greathouse not far from Cathedral Square I found not only cool refuge from my pursuers and the flames of Hell, but reunion with my beautiful Constanza. So overcome were we both with release from the terror of my close brush with death that it was many minutes before we loosed each other from our first embrace.

All who participated in my daring rescue gathered in the bedchamber as, stript to my loincloth, I allowed Constanza to tend to my burns and abrasions which were, given the circumstances, only a minor annoyance. Everyone talked at once, laughing, recalling their own part in the mission.

"I was kneeling in the crowd at your feet," said Enrique. "My job was to set fire to your sanbenito with a long torch. I had only a moment to light it and find the hem of your tunic, but the blasted monk kept getting in the way!"

"You played your part perfectly, Arturo," Don Ramón said to me. "One would have thought you were following prearranged instructions."

"But how did you find out about my predicament?" I asked.

"An anonymous letter arrived three days ago in Santa Maria."

"Francis Englefield . . ." I said quietly. "He told me I would be listed amongst the reconciliados and set free. When I found my self consigned to the ranks of the unrepentant I was sure that he had betrayed me."

"I cannot say, Arturo," said Don Ramón. "All I was told was that you would be found at the Auto da Fé and that a diversion must be devised to snatch you out of it."

"Perhaps," offered Constanza, "your friend thought you would not attempt the escape if its failure meant your burning at the stake."

"Perhaps," I agreed. "In any event, he and all of you are my saviors, and I thank you with all of my heart."

I embraced them, every one, and they filed out leaving me alone with Constanza in the stillness of the afternoon. We did not speak. She began to silently kiss each of my wounds. A light brush of her cool lips to a bruise on my shoulder, a scrape on my chest, a burn on my belly, my knee. She laid her gentle hand over the scar on my thigh. I quickly swept her up into my arms and carried her to the bed where I greedily succumbed to the fires of passion.

By the time darkness fell over Madrids burning fields littered with the ashes of the dead, Enrique and I, reunited with my proud Mirage, were riding hard for the north of Spain. Philips fleet, three weeks out of Lisbon, had encountered freak summer storms. They had been forced to turn back and now lay anchored in Corunna harbor licking their wounds. As I rode thro the night I wondered at the strange destiny that had freed one convict — my self — and made a prisoner of the Armada, so that I could be amongst its numbers when at last it sailed for England.

Our ride north thro Castile had been scorching hot and dry, but as Enrique and I reached the rich farm and cattle land surrounding Corunna we found our selves in the midst of a deluge, and by the time we reached the large sheltered bay the city was cloaked in thick fog. Twas a good thing, the fog, for it helped mute and hide my presence from those in this town who had once betrayed me. In deed we stayed well away from Rodrigo Lorcas house as well as his haunts, and wasted no time in our efforts to see me safely aboard the ships that floated in the ghostly harbor.

The Armada had come limping into Corunna Bay, forty ships at first, the rest scattered by the storm, straggling in over the next weeks. Their stores of biscuit, fish, vegetables and meat had, on their short journey out, been found to be rotten, and their water had leaked away out of faulty barrels or was too foul to drink. Thus the fleet was making great haste to revictualize even as it reassembled, and to repair the vessels damaged in the storm, so that when the freakish summer weather had passed they might set off again for England.

During this time the Admiral of the Armada who was the Duke of Medina Sidonia, concluded that his crew was in dire need of communal confession and absolution. For this purpose he had had every one of his eight thousand men and two hundred priests ferried to a desolate island in the harbor — he being terrified that putting them on the mainland would lead to mass desertions.

This, then, was my entrance point into the enemy camp. Saying a sad farewell to Mirage whom I never in my lifetime expected to see again, I left her in the care of Enrique who promised to keep her and cherish her always, and boarded a rowboat out to the island of penitents. Into that population I had no trouble blending, but felt much trepidation at this new career as a seagoing soldier.

So many of the crew had already fallen ill from the putrid food and water that after taking Communion on the grim little island and lining up to be ferried to the anchored ships, my presence was not questioned, but I was heartily welcomed as a healthy new recruit. I gave my self as a gunner, an Italian arquebusier, knowing nothing of the use of large cannon and certainly nothing as a sailor.

As the rowing boat moved amongst the now almost entirely reconstituted Armada I found my self awed at not simply the number and variety of vessels — from hulking broadbeamed flagships and tall masted warships, to galleons and galleasses, merchantmen, and smaller dispatch boats we called pinnaces — but also the grandiose proportions of the fighting castles aboard them. These castles were high wooden battlements painted with windows and brickwork, used for protection of soldiers and the throwing of missiles. As I glided amidst the vessels it seemed that they were more great fortresses than sailing ships, and that their magnificent facades, as much as their numbers, would strike terrible fear into the hearts of their enemies.

I was taken aboard the San Salvador, a vice flagship of one of the fleets four squadrons — a thousand tonner carrying nearly four hundred men. I was gratified at my luck. Besides being a treasure ship carrying quantities of gold bullion for use upon the Armadas arrival, the vessel also held huge stores of gun powder and shot.

Betimes did thoughts of sabotage come to me, tho for the moment I was forced to do battle with my own fears. Not of battle surely, for I was a soldier at heart, but of a long ocean voyage in seas so vicious they had turned back King Philips Armada once already. I must think of England, I repeated to myself, of my Father, and my Mother the Queen. I would banish fear and use my presence smack in the middle of the enemy to its most maleficent advantage.

But truly, on the day the Armada sailed, sun glittering on the whitecapped water, I was too utterly transfixed by the sight of it to feel trepidation. All I could see was the breeze billowing the bleached sails with their bold red crosses, the lowslung galleys, their long rows of slender oars dipping in powerful rhythm, agile sailors perched atop high masts, wind whipping their hair. A great banner was unfurled on the Admirals ship — a lurid painting of the Crucifixion flanked by the Virgin and Mary Magdalene. Soldiers on their knees on one hundred and thirty boats, voices raised in song at their glorious Crusade.

The first three days out were in one way a joy, for the sea was calm and the breeze perfect for our journey. But I learnt soon of the poor conditions faced by all men on board. The sailors perhaps were less miserable, for they lived and worked on the upper and above decks, and had their jobs to do in fresh air and sunlight. We soldiers were relegated far below to dark airless dormitories lit only by the occasional candle lantern, with no work to pass the time. The stench was unbelievable, for in the first days at sea out of Lisbon the weather had been so altogether foul that seasickness had claimed nearly every soldier. Those not vomiting were racked with diarrhea from the spoilt rations. Even the month in port at Corunna had sweetened those chambers minimally, for the excrement and vomitus had seeped into the very floorboards.

I learnt, much to my surprise, that the crews had been told nothing exactly or officially, tho rumor had so permeated the ranks that all knew their mission was the defeat of England, and that it was Gods divine plan. Soldiers on the whole were encouraged always to stay below decks out of the way of the sailors work, unless they were needed for battle. Most complied, but with my private mission I could not afford such constrictions.

To allay the sailors suspicion of a soldier so frequently wandering the ship, I charmed my way into their good graces, offering my clumsy assistance wherever it was needed, claiming I had only now recognized my error in choosing soldiering over sailoring. Helping weigh the two heavy anchors, hoisting sails, or learning the art of knotmaking, I was soon a welcome and unquestioned figure on deck, in deed wherever I chose to go. It was therefore easy to make a daily round of the decks and holds, perusing the massive stocks of powder barrels, locating lengths of fuse, and setting out a plan in my head to do some mischief to the Spanish fleet without doing damage to my own self.

A brief but terrifying storm hit one night just before we reached English waters. Feeling a wretch and a coward I fled below rather than face the sight of the great black waves. There I stayed curled in my hard berth that whole cruel night, praying for my life and cursing the Fates for casting me once again as a helpless suppliant in a wild Channel tempest.

When day broke I crept up to the deck and the blessed sun. Several of the vessels which had been separated from the rest were making their way back to the fleet, broken masts and shredded sails testament to the fierceness of the storm. In midafternoon the lookout began shouting and pointing off the port bow. I looked to see the sight I dreaded and longed for in equal measure — the coast of England, a point they called the Lizard. Three guns were fired and all hands — soldiers and sailors, grandees and cabin boys side by side — knelt to offer thanks to God for His mercy in bringing them thus far on their holy mission.

Then suddenly with a flurry of trumpet blasts and flag signals the mighty flotilla — as a flock of birds might do — gracefully assumed the shape of a giant crescent moon, the forward sailing vessels forming the bulge, with tapering tips that stretched some five miles apart. From where I stood on the deck of the San Salvador — a part of the southern arm — it looked as tho the ships at center were sailing so close and solid that a man could jump from one deck to the next. And whilst we moved slowly — as slow as our most lumbering craft, as slow as a man walking on land — we were never the less as majestic and awful a sight as had ever before been seen on Gods earth, and I trembled to think of those English villagers looking out to see it.

I prayed ceaselessly that England might be spared the wrath of these terrible enemies on its shores. Oh serene and verdant fields, rugged hills touched with purple heather, rocky headlands sheltering here and there a tiny village! My home! So close were we that had I been a swimmer I would have leapt into the sea and made for that blessed land.

As the sun slid below the western horizon and darkness spread over us like a shroud I saw a sight which caused my heart to leap joyfully in my chest. All along the English shores on highest ground great bonfires were set alight and flared as beacons, one by one, from village to village as far east as the eye could see. Tiny points of light were signaling the approach of the Armada. My mind reeled to think on the speed of that signal, and how quickly all my countrymen should know that the moment of their greatest reckoning had come. I thought of my Mother, how she would be quaking in trepidation for her beloved Kingdoms fate, but knew as well she was a greathearted Prince, and had done all in her power to preserve it.

Under cover of night I made plans for the morrow when I should act, strike my own blow for England and drive fear into the hearts of her enemy.

Forty-eight

On the Channel headlands just north of Dover the bonfire flames leapt and roared, casting eerie shadows down upon the strange creature now dancing round about it. At the fore the head of a huge horse, the long undulating body a train of men, fringes and streamers flying out behind as they moaned ancient incantations. 'Twas a vision, thought John Dee with satisfaction, from another time. Time of the Great Kingdom. On how many occasions had Britons come together in their strength to save the land from invaders?

But would *she* come? Would the Queen of England heed the summons of a mere subject, throw down her most Christian raiments and feed this pagan ritual with the power of her ancient lineage?

Dee knew he risked royal displeasure with his unofficial journey home on the eve of war with Spain. But he knew, too, that whilst the command for his presence here this night had not come from Elizabeth, it had nevertheless emanated from a power more mighty than hers. He was bound to obey the cosmic sources, which had announced their intentions for him in a terrifying display during one of those angelic conversations they had with him — with him and Edward Kelly — in Prague. The message could not have been clearer: *The Magus to the High King of Britain must attend to the needfires on the eve of the Battle, and invoking the Great Powers, make the spells of Encompassing which shall shield and protect all of England.*

"Good Doctor."

Dee turned to find a countrywoman in a plain hooded cloak standing before him. Her naked face glowed in the firelight, her eyes twinkled, and it was a moment before he realized with a start that he stood before the Queen.

"Make no ceremony of me, John. My disguise fooled you for a little, so I presume it will work with these good folk who have never laid eyes on me before."

"Oh, Your Majesty, you have come!" he whispered fiercely.

"How could I do otherwise? You made it sound as if the very stars in Heaven summoned me." Her tone was wry but not angry, and Dee was certain she had forgiven him his impetuous journey home. "What are you looking for? I see your eyes darting every which way . . . Ah! Yes, I've brought him," she said with a more playful tone than Dee imagined she would have on this occasion. "Lord Leicester takes longer to get from place to place than he once did."

"Now you make fun of your crippled old friend, do you?" The Earl, looking similarly common in simple fustian breeches and a short jacket, had come up behind Elizabeth and was smiling at Dee. It had been years since he and John Dee had clapped eyes on each other, and indeed the Earl looked alarmingly unwell. But there was no time for reunion. There was a ritual to be seen to.

"Your Majesty," Dee began. But the Queen laid a hand on his arm.

"For tonight I am Bess. All right?"

Dee nodded his assent. He saw that Elizabeth was riveted to the sight of the horse beast making another round of the fire, its streamers whipping the three of them as it passed. "Have you never seen Beltane celebrated? Midsummers?"

Elizabeth shook her head. "I was raised most strictly Christian. I know nothing of pagan worship."

Dee smiled. "The Hobby Horse bestows luck on all those whom it brushes in passing. The Law of Opposites has it that good luck for the English means bad for the Spanish."

Elizabeth could not tear her eyes away from the dancing men. "This is happening in other places, then?"

"All over England, I would guess," replied Dee. "This endless fight between Catholics and Protestants seems to have usurped all of our religious energies, but the truth is, Your Majesty . . . Bess . . ." Dee smiled, thinking of all they had shared, and the sweetness of such familiarity on this fateful night. "The truth is, the wyrd ways have never been forgotten by a great many of your people, and in times of greatest danger, there is no substitute for the old prayers. Now if you would, please go and stand on the other side of the fire. We shall begin presently."

Dee and Leicester were silent as they watched Elizabeth walking through the crowd of celebrants, perhaps for the first time in her whole life unrecognized and ignored.

"Have you heard from Arthur?" Leicester asked the moment Elizabeth was out of hearing.

"I have not." Dee placed a sympathetic arm round his old pupil's shoulder.

"I fear he's dead, John. I fear I've lost him once again."

"I do not feel him dead, my lord."

Dudley searched the old wizard's eyes. "Do you not?"

"I feel him alive." Dee's mouth quivered. "And I feel him near."

"O God!" Tears had sprung to Leicester's eyes.

"Come now," said Dee. "We must begin. Conserve your energy, my friend, for I must call upon you and the Queen to be strong, give forth all your life forces combined. You are Mother and Father of Arthur, who I tell you lives! Arthur, heir to the throne of the once and future British Empire . . ."

"Will we have a victory, John?"

"The stars say yes, yes!"

"Then come, teach this old Puritan the wyrd ways and let us drive the evil forces away from England's shores," said Dudley, then muttered, "And may God forgive me."

"Ram ry goll neheneit, As guyar, Honneit," chanted John Dee, eyes closed. He seemed not of this world but lost in the hoary mists of time. *"Dydoent guarthvor, Gvelattor aruyddion, gwydveirch dyavor, Eingyl ygh ygvor, Gvelattor aruyddion."* His eyes flew open. "Strength to our defenders!" he shouted and thrust his staff at the gyrating horse beast which shook its long tail in the direction of the Channel. "Thrice round the needfires bound, Evil sink into the ground. Round the pyre, three times three, Sink the foe beneath the sea!"

Whilst round and round the roaring fire danced the Hobby Horse, the Queen's magician, tall and somber and fully infused with the power of ages, intoned his prayers that the realm and its sovereign's blood should endure for eternity. When he was satisfied the countryfolk were lost in their dancing and incantations, Dee strode across to Elizabeth, now transfixed and trembling at the strength of the confluent energies, and took her by the hand. She gazed at him questioningly, but he did not meet her eyes, simply moved round the fire to Leicester who was likewise transfixed, and took him on his other hand. He led them, altogether silent, beyond the light of the fire to a small grove of oaks and turned to face them.

"This night," uttered Dee with the authority of Heaven itself, "ye two shall marry, and Robert Dudley shall become your king and consort." He heard simultaneously Elizabeth's sharp intake of breath and Dudley's stupefied exhalation. "In this sacred grove, ye shall lie down together and consummate that marriage. Elizabeth, Queen of England, your body shall this night *become the land* and you, King Robert, shall spill your fertile seed upon it. Then . . ." he continued, never taking his eyes from Leicester's, "ye shall go out and lead England's armies against the invaders. Die, if need be." Then to both of them, "This is the ancient ritual and most powerful. What say you to its celebration?"

"Yes," spoke Dudley without hesitation.

Dee saw Elizabeth staring wonderingly at her old lover, perhaps comprehending the irony that his life's dearest wish should finally be granted, but only in private, for magic's sake alone.

"Yes," she said, her eyes afire. "Marry us. Marry us!"

They spoke not at all as they moved together, finding the familiar places where their bodies knew to join. She who had been bereft of a man's touch for so long, and he who had been bereft of a woman's true love, now discovered in each other's arms, besides the deepest solace, a well of forgotten passion. As they found the rhythm of pleasure Elizabeth and Robin Dudley did never unlock their gazes, the years between them melted like spring snow, and their weary faces grew beautiful in each other's sight. The sweet sensation began to grow and build and they reveled in it, knowing that she was the land and his seed spilled upon it was the fecundity of their kingdom. With the song of the mythic horseman drifting across the cliffs, they clung one to the other, rocking, rocking, and then as if blessed one last time by the stars, they came together, cried out together and rejoiced, not only for their friendship undaunted by all that had befallen it, but for England, their beloved England.

"Cum rage!" shouted John Dee, glaring out to the moonlit Channel. The horse dancers had ceased their motion for his final benediction, and they too stood gazing seaward with countenances as fearsome as curses.

"Be wynd an doom be men
Whose stormwracked ships
Astride Epona's prancing dream
Stayn redde, mare's tails wi furies flame
Lend sweet wynd te Anglisc flags
As seadogs ravish sails to Spanish rags!"

Then with a savage cry as old as man itself they began to dance again, and John Dee knew, as sure as the Earth flew round the sun, that no harm would come to this blessed land, and that England would thrive for a thousand years.

Forty-nine

Twas a good thing I had done my secret works on that previous evening, for when day broke thick and rainy we had not only our first sight of the English fleet, but engaged them in battle. I am anything but a seaman and speak from ignorance in all things nautical, but my common sense observations were these. Side by side with the Armada, Englands navy was small, maybe half the number of the Spanish fleet. In deed, the English ships themselves were small — narrow and lying low in the water. But, good Lord, they were fast! Agile as a two year old filly, and powerful in their maneuvering.

Ten of these vessels, guns blazing, beat in for their attack on several ships on the northern end of the crescent. The Spanish, slow and lumbering, had barely returned the cannonade before the English came about and sped away out of range. I heard much grumbling in the ranks of the soldiers, for their enemy confounded them, never coming close enough to be grappled and boarded — the only kind of sea warfare known to them. The Spanish ships with their high castles were huge and ponderous, sitting ducks to these swift hawks who could swoop down, unleash their artillery and disappear, leaving the proud Spaniards frustrated in their search for a proper fight.

Twas in this moment of weakness and disgruntlement that I made my move.

On the stern deck I located a particularly bellicose Spanish sailor and whispered in his ear that I had overheard a burly soldier, now sharpening his sword in full view, call the sailors wife a "puta." I watched only long enough to see the first blow fall, hear the scuffle ensue, know that men from all parts of the ship were running to witness a fine brawl.

I stealthily made my way below to the stern hold which stored all the powder barrels and more than half of the shot on board. I flattened my self into a cranny as the two munitions guards ran past to the fight, and with not a moment to spare laid down the long fuse, its end buried in an open half barrel of powder. The other end I sparked with a candle lantern. Laying it carefully on the floor I prayed quickly that it should not fizzle out before finding its fiery home, and bolted.

By the shouts and crashing about I knew the fight was in full swing. Moving calmly in the opposite direction I headed for the fore deck, careful to avert my face from other men racing to witness it. I had barely made my way forward and crouched behind a bulkhead when the world exploded. The blast blew me into the railing, nearly tumbling me over into the sea. The whole thousand ton ship lifted from the water and fell back with a splintering roar. A moment later, as the concussion faded, I heard men screaming, others moaning piteously and survivors shouting orders for assistance to help the wounded.

I righted my self and, determining that aside from some bruises and a few scrapes I was unhurt, ran to the stern to witness the mayhem I had wrought. Nothing prepared me for the sight of carnage and horrible destruction. The whole of the stern was blown to Heaven. The poops two upper decks were in ruins. Dead and mangled men lay all round. Men afire shrieking in agony leapt overboard to their deaths.

The hold was altogether exposed, and inside many fires raged. Twas Hell afloat, and I had in deed created it. The ship listed sharply but seemed never the less miraculously in no danger of sinking, which had been my intention. Nearby ships of our squadron sped to the rescue, taking us in tow. I worked alongside soldiers and sailors trying to quench the stubborn fires, cowering when some unblown cache of powder exploded with a mighty sound. Wounded men were removed to other ships and, to my extreme displeasure, the gold bullion went as well. I had wished to send it all to the bottom of the Channel waters, but had to make do with the gruesome results of my sabotage — one ship destroyed and two hundred dead.

Finally the fit survivors were lowered into boats sent from other vessels. I made sure I found my way to one bound for the San Martín, and it was in this way that I came to spy on the high admiral, Alonso Pérez de Guzmán el Bueno, the Duke of Medina Sidonia.

Soon after the survivors of the San Salvador were lifted aboard the flagship, commanders of the other squadrons were ferried aboard as well. I watched with interest as they were greeted by the Admiral himself, a small, compactly built man of forty who seemed to lack the dangerous swagger of his visitors. I supposed they had come to confer after their first engagement with the English. Recalde, a tall, handsome man with piercing dark eyes, was well known as the officer with the greatest experience of the sea. He seemed taciturn as he went below to join Medina Sidonia for the war council. The cousins and bitter enemies Don Diego and Don Pedro Váldez, who I imagined would normally strut with confidence and Spanish pride, now wore expressions of frustration and bafflement. The others — de Levya, Moncado, Oquendo — were equally somber. For in deed, the English maneuvering had taken them quite by surprise.

Twas my intention to learn all I could of their plans, and so to that end I sought to befriend the one man whose access to the highest authority was the greatest, and whose position in the naval hierarchy was the lowest — the Dukes cabin boy Jorge Montenegro, a tall skinny and graceless boy with a pimply face as flat as a shovel. In our first conversation, only hours after my arrival on board, I learnt he was the third son of a Castilian hidalgo. Jorge had begun his Armada service as cabin boy under the previous high commander, Santa Cruz. Jorge told me that the Admiral had, after struggling for two years to mobilize the Spanish fleet, inconveniently died several months before it had been set to sail. His replacement, Medina Sidonia, was no naval man, and did not come with his own servant for that job. So young Jorge had stayed on.

I recognized him at once as a third son, lacking the confidence of the first or the studied indifference of the second. I was able to scratch the thin veneer of Spanish haughtiness with a shared bottle of fine sherry I had stolen from the Captains pantry before I abandoned ship. When Jorge had been dismissed by Medina Sidonia, he took me to his berth, a tiny hole in the wall which was at least private. Crushed together like sardines in a barrel we drank and gossiped. He was fascinated by my descriptions of the devastation aboard the San Salvador.

Tho time was of the essence, I needed to be cautious and altogether delicate in my questioning, so he should never suspect he was talking to an English spy.

"I have seen a pinnace leave the fleet and sail on ahead every day since we left Corunna, but I have never seen one return. Where are they bound?"

"To Dunkirk," he replied easily.

"Why Dunkirk?"

"That is where the Duke of Parma is, he and his thirty thousand land soldiers. When we meet up with them," said Jorge, his voice beginning to slur — the Spanish were not known for heavy drinking, and their daily ration of wine was pitifully small — "we will have cleared the Channel of all the English ships, and then Parma will cross and make the invasion."

I felt my heart freeze. "It is a brilliant plan," I said, hoping to sound enthusiastic. "The English coastal defenses are known to be weak. We will slaughter them."

"God willing," he added.

"God willing," I agreed.

"But Parma," said Jorge, grabbing the bottle out of my hands, "Parma does never answer the Admirals dispatches. The Duke is becoming anxious. He must know if Parmas troops are ready, if his fleet of ships is prepared to ferry them across the channel."

"I wonder why Parma does not answer," I mused, swigging from the bottle.

"So does Medina Sidonia wonder. But he is honor bound to follow the Kings orders which are very strict. I think that they irk him."

"What is it about the orders that irks him?" I probed.

But Jorge was silent, and his eyelids drooped. I feared losing him.

"Perhaps we should leave some for another day, my friend," I said, stashing the bottle under my jacket. "It would not do to have you stumble drunk into the Dukes war council."

Jorge giggled at the thought, then became serious. "He is a very fine man, the Duke. Very dignified. Very kind. Too kind. He did not wish for the admiralty of the Armada. He is not a sailor. He is not even a soldier."

"I thought —"

"He enjoys the governorship of his Andalusian lands." Jorge leaned closer and whispered, "I heard him tell Recalde he wrote to King Philip and begged not to be forced to take command. The letter was never answered."

I pulled young Jorge Montenegro to his feet. There was barely room for the two of us to stand. I straightened his jacket and had him blow into my face.

"Phew! You had best eat something to hide the sherry. Think of your Fathers disgrace if you lost your position."

This seemed to sober him immediately. "I shall find some biscuit," he said as I turned to go.

"Maybe a few bites of strong fish too," I added.

"Thank you, my friend," said the boy as I opened the door. "It is easier to face the day with a touch of fine sherry in the veins."

I tapped the bottle under my jacket. "Perhaps we can find a moment to finish the bottle before we reach Dunkirk."

He grinned and I left him, then made my way below to the soldiers quarters, altogether pleased with my new informant. As I lay in my berth that night, rocking with the rhythm of the sea, I pondered the next move.

One whole day passed whilst both fleets floated becalmed. I watched men aboard the San Martín who were gazing nervously out at the English vessels no doubt wondering what was in store from this strange, godless enemy and their devilishly swift ships.

I my self was racked with indecision regarding my future exploits. No other person was more perfectly situated to wreak havoc within the Spanish fleet, yet I was one man alone, a horse soldier without a horse, and afraid of the sea at that. With only secondhand intelligence from a pimply faced cabin boy, my choices were limited. Most ironic was that I was more in danger of losing my life at the hands of my own countrymen than of the enemy.

I was, in a gruesome way, satisfied with my act of sabotage aboard the San Salvador. We all watched as the English took possession of her sinking hulk, tho I regretted there would be few spoils to take off her. One possible plan repeatedly insinuated itself into my head — assassination. I might murder the High Admiral, the Duke of Medina Sidonia, or I could wait until the next war council again brought the squadron commanders aboard, and dispatch them all at once with a well timed explosion. This would leave the enormous fleet in a leaderless condition. But as often as I contemplated such an act, I found myself resisting it. Memories of Prince Williams death came unbidden into my head. Assassination was a much used tool amongst the great powers, but I personally found it a repugnant and cowardly act. Still, I had no better plan, and forced my self to look for an auspicious moment to carry it out.

That night in my cramped berth I dreamt of making love to Mary Willis, then lying side by side in that summer glade staring up at the trees talking companionably, and woke longing for the feel of dry solid earth that had been beneath our backs. I pondered the mystery of dreaming — how a man so in love with one woman could dream of another — and found my self wondering suddenly what the dreams of a man like John Dee might be. If he dreamt fantastically — of stars or magic machines or mythic creatures. If he dreamed of futures and prophecies. Or if his nighttime visions were as mundane as my own.

Suddenly a cry went up that the wind had risen and a battle was afoot. We leapt from our plank beds, swallowed some barely edible rations on the run, and grabbing our weapons hurried to our posts. Mine was on the upper deck, but the shortest route to it took me thro the long narrow gundecks where I saw soldiers readying their cannon, ramming their powder and ball, and laying down a trail of more powder to the touchhole. They would wait to learn the position of the enemy and, with wedges and crowbars, turn and elevate or lower their guns into position to fire. Then they would stand clear of the recoil with their fingers in their ears. Still, amongst the heavy gunners were the largest number of deaf men aboard.

I found my place behind the castle facade and primed my arquebus. Peering out from my window of the High Admirals ship I was fortunate to be positioned on the front line, with good view of the oncoming English fleet, now led by a flagship. I did long to know who commanded her. Was it Drake, Frobisher, Hawkins? As they sailed closer they appeared to be forming into a long line, one behind the other. The San Martín turned sidewise for the attack, and lowered her topsails.

Then the assault began.

The English flagship came marvelous close, turned and fired her broadside at us, as we did the same. But whilst we were stationary in the water with hardly room to maneuver, the English vessels peeled off to make way each for the next in line, which similarly discharged its ordnance with bright flashes from its gunports. Then the next came, and the next. Of course I and my fellow small armsmen were called upon to fire our weapons, but they were clearly useless.

Even our heaviest cannon could not seem to touch such fastmoving targets. But English artillery coming so hard and continuously was doing damage to the San Martín — our flagstaff and the stay of our mainmast were splintered. Bits of their wood made deadly projectiles which slew several Spaniards aboard.

On deck the dignified presence of the Duke of Medina Sidonia kept the Spanish spirits high, and truly I did never see the man duck or flinch or exhibit anything but bravery and sound leadership.

The noise of that battle was the most terrible I had heard in all my years as a soldier, the cannon fire so constant it might have been a land battle with small weapons. But for all the English speed and firepower, and so close as they came, I admit to hearing only the occasional thud of a cannonball on our hull, and the San Martín did never seem in danger of being sunk. The attack continued for two hours, I so marvelling at the sights and sounds that I forgot everything of my fear of the sea, and concentrated on firing wildly into the sky, wasting as much powder as possible, making sure no Spanish soldier observed my folly.

Finally the English retreated, leaving the Armada to lick its wounds. Tho the ships were not greatly damaged, the morale of the men was badly shaken. Twas all too clear that the English would never come close enough for the Spanish soldiers to swarm aboard the heretic ships, use their ferocious skills in fighting hand to hand with pikes and swords. They were, for all the magnificent planning and tireless training, utterly useless, and miserable in that knowledge.

But none was more miserable, it seemed, than Medina Sidonia. On the morning after the battle, the two fleets again becalmed off the Isle of Wight, I sought Jorge Montenegro as he came out from the Admirals cabin. The look on his face was terrible grim, and I escorted him silently as he climbed the stairs to the upper deck. Plying him with spirits was not needed this day, for he desired to unload his heavy heart. There had still been no word from Parma, not a whisper. But intelligence reports had come back that the English fleet which they had so far encountered — already nearly half the Armada in number — would be joined by a second contingent of fresh ships at the Straits of Dover. A force equal to the first.

"The Kings orders," said Jorge, "they are killing the Duke."

"How so?" I pressed carefully. "Were they not provided by God Himself?"

"That is the problem. The Duke knows they came from the Almighty, but believes even God Himself would have difficulty carrying them out. How, in the face of such a mighty offensive, can we remain wholly defensive?"

"Defensive? What do you mean?" I was honestly baffled.

"On the Kings orders we may not instigate any attacks on the heretics, nor take any of their ports, despite our stores which are pitifully depleted, not to mention our powder and shot. We must only continue up the Channel, firm in our formation, to our rendezvous with Parma. The other commanders are furious with the Admiral. He is ashamed of what looks like weakness, tho it is merely the strictest adherence to the Kings orders."

"But we will meet with Parma and make the invasion?" I said, trying to sound hopeful.

Jorge brightened. "Of course. And when the two forces are joined there will be no power on Earth to stop it! Ah, friend, you do cheer me. I had best go."

"God be with you, Jorge," I said.

"And the same to you, Arturo."

In the next days of small skirmishing in the Channel I did think more about God, and life and death and destiny, than I had in my whole life previous. Tho I wished fervently to live — to meet my Mother, and my Father again, and most of all to hold Constanza in my arms — I could not see the way clear to those wishes. I was stranded aboard an enemy ship bound to do battle with my own countrymen whom I longed desperately to be amongst, but from whom I was separated by that which I feared most — the sea.

My mind returned again and again to Prince William and his creed of tolerance. Had he still lived, he would have suffered horribly to see how King Philips unholiest of holy wars had come to encompass England too. And I could not for the life of me believe that the true God would disallow a love so fine as mine and Constanzas for our simply worshiping in different temples.

But most pressing was my decision for the assassination of Medina Sidonia and his commanders. I had so far been denied the chance for a mass killing, as all the captains had never again come aboard the San Martín for a war council. If I dispatched anyone, twould be the Duke alone, and I knew that in case of his death, de

Levya or Recalde, both more able seamen than he, would replace him. But in my present state of mind, twas more the wondering of the right and righteousness of assassination that haunted me. I was a soldier, and in my career I had killed many hundreds of men. As a saboteur I had ruthlessly dispatched two hundred more. Perhaps Jorge Montenegros description of the Admiral as a kind, peaceable man, and the sight of his brave and manly deportment in battle, had thrust some unsoldierly thoughts into my head. But more, memories of the repulsive and cowardly crime that had ended Prince Williams life made me shudder to think of my self as the perpetrator of such an act. The Duke was surely my enemy, but was it my duty, my fate to murder him? My doubts and hesitation continued as we sailed on towards the Straits of Dover and our rendezvous with Parmas enormous army. The invasion of England was only days away.

Fifty

With the boom of guns signaling the arrival of the royal barge, the Earl of Leicester allowed himself a rare moment of satisfaction. Despite the ominous warning by her council that the Queen's life should be put in the gravest danger by going amongst her armed troops, Elizabeth had, on Leicester's urgings, come this day to the camp at Tilbury. She had shunted aside all talk of madmen and evil Catholic assassins, allowing herself to be swayed one more time by her Revels Master, who had pleaded for her participation in this event more fiercely than for any before it. Dudley knew in every nerve of him that this moment of England's greatest peril could be, for the Queen, her finest hour.

He watched as the door of the glass and gilt cabin opened and dainty music wafted out on the perfumed air, mixing with the raucous military fifes and horns and drums blaring out their welcome. Elizabeth's gorgeously attired ladies emerged first, causing a ripple of excitement amongst the soldiers at quayside. Then she came, splendidly, and stood for her first look at the ground forces standing to attention, ten thousand strong.

The site was tidy now, the barrack huts of pine posts and green branches swept of the filth and detritus of a makeshift army camp, and the men as well scrubbed as possible. Leicester gazed about and found himself startled by the great waves of adoration and awe flowing equally from the fresh-faced boys and hardened men toward this strange and paradoxical woman. She had somehow managed it, he thought with amusement. She had attained what had been her most daunting challenge and her dearest wish in life — the absolute love of her people.

Leicester was satisfied too that, if the peers of England still counted him the most hated man in the kingdom, the enlisted men under his command, both here and in the Netherlands before, liked and respected him.

He had fought for their good against Elizabeth's neverending impecuniousness, seen to it that they were fed and paid, even if it meant using money from his own coffers. He knew too well that should the fleet fail to stop the Armada, these hastily assembled and trained soldiers would not last long against Parma's land forces. But he was proud of his army, proud of this commission, and in thanks he would present his beloved Elizabeth with the greatest pageant of her long career.

Now with a hand shielding her eyes from the midday sun the Queen gazed downriver at Giambelli's specially built fortification, which stretched across the Thames from Tilbury to Gravesend. 'Twas a great mass of cables, huge chains, and ships' masts laid end to end, all tethered to a line of small boats anchored in the river. It had been an ingenious plan but, though Elizabeth could not detect as much from where she stood, the barricade had already begun to fall apart. It was, Dudley realized suddenly, only for his belief in John Dee's heavenly assurances that no harm would come to England, that he could allow himself to rejoice in this occasion.

When both her feet were planted on solid ground, a single trumpet blast gave signal, and in the same moment every company raised its brilliant ensign high into the air. Elizabeth's face blossomed into a smile of the purest joy and gratitude, a smile the likes of which Leicester had not seen in far too many years, and in this moment he stepped forward and saluted her. The look she then bestowed upon him warmed and made suddenly painless every joint and bone and sinew in his aging body. He offered his hand and led her to a coach and four which he had had specially painted chequerwise to look as though it was encrusted with diamonds, rubies, and emeralds. Thus the Queen and Her Majesty's Lieutenant Against Foreign Invasion rode through the sea of soldiers who chanted ceaselessly "God save the Queen" and "God save good Queen Bess!"

"Oh! Oh Robin," was all she said, punctuated by tiny gasps of delight. But she seemed, he thought, altogether unprepared for the sight of two thousand uniformed horsemen astride their mounts waiting at the center of camp. Unprepared for the shape of her army spread out before her eyes, the prospect of which had always been her worst nightmare, now England's only salvation, Elizabeth began to weep. Her silent tears were all the thanks that Robin Dudley required.

She had changed her clothing, was all in white velvet, silver breastplate and plumed silver helmet glittering in the sun. The Queen went amongst the troops in her review first on foot, striding almost manlike down the rows of men, commenting with pleasure on their strength and comeliness. Then Leicester lifted her on a high horse, white with hindquarters in dappled grey. He knew as he took the reins and led her to the head of her army that the stallion had been trained to prance, and when it began its highstep an unexpected laugh escaped Elizabeth's throat.

On a small rise he turned the horse so she could face the crowd and gaze out over the mass of upturned faces. The sincerest shouts of "God save the Queen!" were so thunderous that she bade them stop, but they would not. Leicester had told her a good speech was the order of the day, and now as he watched her, heard the voices finally quieting, he knew the words Elizabeth had chosen could not fail to be rousing. She was magnificent. Tall and strong. The best of her father Henry. Bright as the sun itself.

"My loving people," she began in a hale and steady voice. "I have been cautioned by my many advisors that I should have fear for my life coming here amongst yourselves, the armed multitudes. But as you can see I have refused to take heed of them!"

It was true, thought Leicester. Elizabeth had indeed let men love her but never ever rule her. So it had been since the earliest days of her reign.

"I believe my subjects to be loyal," she continued, "my strength and not my weakness, and bearing me only peace and good will. And so I come here in the heat of battle to live or die amongst you all, and to lay down my honor and my blood, even into the dust!"

Leicester steadied the reins, for her horse too was aflame under her. By God, he thought, she thrills *me* with the words I bade her speak!

"I may have the weak and feeble body of a woman," Elizabeth went on, her voice rising almost to a cry, "but I have the heart and stomach of a King, and King of England too!"

A great roar went up then, soldiers shouting for joy and pride and love, and Leicester, that most reserved of men, found himself shouting along with them.

"How does Parma or Spain or any Prince of Europe dare to invade my realm?!" she roared, raising her truncheon over head, stabbing at the sky. "Let me take up arms and I shall fight them myself!"

Cries of "No, no, Majesty, preserve your life!"

"Good people, I already know of your valor in the field, how deserving you are of reward, for I have been told of it by your Lieutenant General!"

As another roar of approval went up from the crowd Leicester felt himself flush with pride.

"I tell you now that I have never commanded a more worthy subject than he, and by your obedience to him, and by your valor on the field of battle *I promise you* we shall shortly have a famous victory over these enemies of God, my kingdom, and my people!"

Fifty-one

Jorge, whose love and admiration for Medina Sidonia was growing in the same proportion as the Dukes woes, kept me well informed of all the many unanswered dispatches to Parma. One was a request for forty flyboats — strong and efficient flatbottomed warships — to join up with the Armada as quickly as possible. Another was for powder and shot to be delivered at their Dunkirk meeting, necessary to help the fleet clear the seas of the English so Parma might cross. But by this time, with nothing but silence from the Netherlands, Medina Sidonia was despairing of ever making contact with the commander of the land forces. Jorge told me, pity in his voice, that the Duke repeatedly reviewed the Kings written orders to assure himself Parmas part in the invasion had not been a figment of his own imagination. His worry was growing that even if we did meet up with him, how we would clear the channel of English ships when ours were so slow and heavy, and theirs so fast and light?

Then came the report from the Armada pilots that the rendezvous with Parma could not under any circumstances be made at Dunkirk, with its dangerous sandbanks extending twelve miles from shore. Other Flemish harbors were too shallow for our meeting, and Calais was held by Spains ancient enemy, France. Such dire news provoked bitter arguments, the captains and the pilots each looking to blame the other for a blunder of such enormous magnitude.

By 12 July of a breezy Saturday afternoon, the Spanish Armada dropped anchor off the coast of Calais. The Duke, grim and ill, climbed slowly aloft to see what incalculable disaster the Kings or-

ders had inflicted upon his fleet. He stared bleakly out at the English flotilla which had dropped anchor upwind of them, not more than a quarter mile away. Then he turned landward to see the French hordes who had gathered on Calais beach, to gawk at the spectacle of a great battle come to their shore. Soon a rowboat was seen splashing its way towards the San Martín. With great show, fruit and cheese and wine were borne aboard, gifts from the Mayor of Calais — a known Catholic — who pledged all support save that most desperately needed. Powder and shot.

But three hours hence came the most horrible spectre to Medina Sidonias eyes — reinforcement for the English fleet, bringing its numbers nearly equal to the Spanish Armada. Now, fully aware of the enemys greater speed and agility — and not doubting the English artillery holds were as full of ordnance as ours were empty — the Duke could no longer hide his desperation. At that moment I was overcome with a great presentiment that it was lost for the Spanish, and I would not have to murder the poor man after all.

Later he had climbed slowly down again and gone below, beckoning to Jorge to follow. Within the hour the cabin boy reappeared, orders in hand for a pinnace captain, who departed immediately up the coast towards the Netherlands. I met Jorge in a lower corridor. At first he would not even meet my eyes, as tho the Dukes own despair had infected him. So I stayed there quietly with him, not pressing him to speak, but pretending my own sadness.

"It is finished," he said after a long while. "Until the Spring at least."

"Finished?" I said.

"There will be no rendezvous with Parma. No invasion of England."

"Do we sail for home then?" I asked trying heroically to stifle my joy.

"No," he said. "This last dispatch, it begs Parma" — Jorge could not hide his contempt — "begs him to at least send us Flemish pilots to guide the Armada into a safe harbor for the winter."

"But we will strike again in the Spring?"

"Of course. But such a disgrace for the Duke . . ."

"No greater than for Parma," I said. "Why has he sent no word, do you think, Jorge?" My respect for this ungainly lad had grown in the past days thro the sheer level of kind compassion I had seen him show his commander.

"I have heard my Father say that the Duke of Parma has ambitions of his own. Royal Portuguese blood. I know it sounds mad, but he may wish the invasion to fail. He has been negotiating with the heretic Queen for years. Perhaps . . ." It was as tho the thought was forming as he spoke. "Perhaps she has offered him something better than the King has."

In all my musings in days past I had given little thought to Parmas motives, but now I was intrigued. "You think he may have betrayed Spain?"

"No!" Jorge went suddenly pale. Confusion and panic clouded his eyes, for he was casting aspersions on one of Spains highest lords. "I have said too much. I must go!" He turned to leave but I held his arm.

"Jorge, have faith. We have not won, but have not lost either. Surely Medina Sidonia will lose face, but there is always next Spring for our victory."

He looked unconvinced but never the less grateful for the encouragement. He managed a wan smile and went below.

Part of me wanted to shout at the top of my lungs the joy and relief I felt for England's deliverance. But I knew that with these two great navies anchored but a cannon shot apart, there was no power under Heaven could keep them from battle, and in that fight lay the next turning of my own destiny.

Fifty-two

Yo el Rey. I the King, wrote Philip with a grandiose flourish. He did enjoy affixing his signature thus to each and every document which left his council chamber desk. This last was perhaps the final one he would write to the Duke of Medina Sidonia before the battle of the Great Enterprise was joined. He knew it would not reach the admiral in time, but he still had much good advice to bestow, and it gave the King pleasure to think the letter would one day be placed amongst his state papers in the vast archives at Salamanca.

Still, as he called his secretary in to seal the letter, the King of Spain found himself in a state of great annoyance. Things were not at all working as God had so carefully designed. Men dared to question his orders and offer "better" solutions to the task at hand.

Philip had thought when the opinionated old Santa Cruz died it had been a blessing. The man he chose to replace him, Medina Sidonia, would accede unquestioningly to all royal commands. But from the moment the Armada left Lisbon Harbor, the King had been challenged. Rendezvous points had been disputed, warnings about attempts to join land and sea forces in the presence of the enemy had been issued, requests for reinforcements, which all knew did not exist, had been presented. Medina Sidonia had complained about fighting with no harbor behind him, and harped on the Duke of Parma's unending silence. This troublesome communication had flowed onto Philip's desk in a foul and unceasing torrent.

And Parma had proven worse yet, begging for more and more time for the building of his fleet of low, flat boats, claiming that anything but the most perfect weather would rule out the rendezvous with the Armada, prohibit the crossing, and quash the invasion altogether.

It was this lack of support from the men upon whom he most

depended that had forced him to author the Secret Orders — the one document in his long career that Philip regretted having written. The thought of that parchment, now lying in a sealed box in Medina Sidonia's cabin, caused the King to rise suddenly from his chair. He must move, despite the pain in his knees, must walk the thought of that dreadful letter out of his mind. He left his council chamber and made for the Church of San Lorenzo el Real where he would pray once again for forgiveness, beg for understanding. For the Secret Orders were nothing less than an affront to God.

He must hold fast to his faith, thought Philip. Surely, despite this lapse, the Almighty would reward him for his devoted service. The invasion would succeed as planned, and the letter would never have to be opened at all. Its contents were to be revealed to the Duke of Parma only in the event that by some awful miracle the English gained the advantage, and the invading army found itself stymied or stalemated on the heretic queen's island. If that happened, read the orders, Parma should negotiate three points with Elizabeth. Religious freedom for English Catholics. The return of his cities in the Netherlands. And reinstatement of the English exiles. A cash payment would be nice if it could be arranged, but it was less important.

It was a dreadful document, a shameful capitulation, he knew. Parma would probably say that if Philip would settle for so little, no invasion had been needed in the first place. And damn Medina Sidonia! If the two of them had simply abided by God's divine plan, had had faith in his Great Enterprise, the Secret Orders would never have been necessary. And he would not, every day of his life till he died, be forced to his knees seeking forgiveness for his humiliating lapse of faith.

The King of Spain could only pray, and pray he did, that his great Armada would overcome all worldly obstacles and human fallibility, bring glory to his kingdom, to Rome, and to God Himself.

Fifty-three

"Hellburners!"

"Jesus save us!"

These were shouts and cries I heard from sailors and soldiers of the San Martín, and from ships surrounding us, and in eerie echoes from vessels at the far tips of the Spanish crescent, still anchored off Calais. Men were falling to their knees, clutching at the robes of priests as they scurried to tend to their flock. No one could tear their gaze from the line of English fire ships, masts and sails ablaze, now heading slowly towards the central bulge of the Armada.

I saw Medina Sidonia stride to the rail, calm and braver than he had a right to be. That very morning, I learnt from a livid Jorge, he had had confirmation that Parma would never meet him, in deed could never meet him. That the flat bottomed barges he had been bound to build and provision were nowhere near ready. That Parma had never bothered to oversee the work done on the boats, thus allowing the Dutch shipbuilders he had hired to sabotage their own efforts. Such bad news, of course, was allowed no circulation amongst the Spanish troops, for morale was already very low, and mutiny a hairs breadth away. Instead, from the time of the message ships arrival, I had heard rumors that Parma was already on his way with one hundred and fifteen vessels to add to our own.

As night had fallen the Armada had found itself trapt tween the Calais shore and the English fleet, upwind and uptide of them. The Duke and every man under his command had known without a doubt that the enemy would turn fire ships against them. There was nothing new in such a strategy. Twas the very device used against Drake at Cadiz. Medina Sidonia had in deed been so confident that the English would attempt using fire ships, that even now several of his own patrol vessels with grapnels were rowing out to meet the enemy before they reached the Armadas first line. But now the Duke and the men of his fleet could see that the fireships were more in number and very much larger than they had imagined. And the real terror that gripped them came not from the mere sight of eight tar and pitch covered vessels, flames licking their masts and rigging, but from a terrible knowledge — for some a memory — shared by them all.

In Antwerp not three years before, the Dutch had especially refitted a fire ship with all cannon double loaded with shot, and all holds filled to brimming with gunpowder. Then they had turned it on the Spanish trapt on shore. The flames had reached the powder, and an unimaginable explosion had blown burning wreckage a mile round the harbor, slain one thousand Spaniards in an instant. Now it was rumored that Giambelli, the very same engineer who had designed this monstrous "hellburner," was in the service of the Queen of England.

The fully engulfed fire ships — gun ports spouting flames, fountains of red hot embers from each of them rising high into the night sky — flowed inexorably with the tide and wind towards our giant mass of timber and canvas vessels. I heard prayers and hopeful murmuring round me as we watched our patrol boats with their grappling hooks and lines, divert one ship on either end of the mile long line. Then with a terrible and sudden volley of blasts, red hot cannon began exploding, scattering shot in all directions.

Shrieks of terror. These were the dread hellburners! And the patrol boats had failed to stop them. Here on the front line I stared openmouthed to think that death by burning had, for the second time in one month, become my probable fate. As the cannonade grew louder and the glow of the fire ships brightened the sky and water before us, as the cries of panic rose all round, the Duke of Medina Sidonia, still calm, began to call his orders.

"Slip your anchors and buoy them! Ride out clear of the fire ships path and reassemble with the change of tide at your buoys at morning light!"

But the vessels, so tightly crowded, could barely turn. Sailors scrambled up rigging in the dark to make sail. Ships collided with ships. On one vessel I saw a frenzied mob gathered round a sailor trying to slip the anchor cable as ordered — the crowd screaming at him to cut the thing and be done with it! Finally he was shoved aside and a soldier with an axe severed the cable with a few blows. Within moments the ship was moving. I wondered as I clutched the rail, watching clusters of vessels round me leave their anchorage, how many of them had cut the cables in their panic, and wondered, too, if we on the San Martín would escape before the boats from hell blew us into oblivion.

Suddenly the wind took our sails. The way had come free and we tacked away at a good speed. Twas only then, with a cool wind on my face and the six monstrous balls of fire drifting towards the now empty anchorage, that it occurred to me — the ships could not possibly have been hellburners, for fully engulfed in flames as they were they would by now have certainly exploded. They were simple fire ships and from the looks of things, not one Spanish vessel had suffered damage.

But something else had. The Armadas protective crescent formation, for the first time since its assemblage, had been dispersed. We had scattered, lost the awesome strength of our tight bound phalanx. I knew little about warfare on the sea, but logic told me that the Spanish fleet, finally broken apart, was a better target for the English captains. So I fixed my mind on the morrow and prayed with all my heart that dawn would see the battle which would banish these God obsessed creatures from our shores, and that I would live to tell the story.

Six great galleons straining hard against their anchors in the bright windy dawn were all that was left of the once mighty crescent. None of the soldiers or sailors of the San Martín had slept below, but out on deck or at their posts. Some had been lulled to sleep where they sat, exhausted from terror of the fire ships which, in the light of day, showed as smoking skeletons scattered on sandbanks and the southern Flemish shores. The other Spanish ships — one hundred and thirty of them — lay studded like far flung pearls in the moving fabric of greyish green water, some as far as ten miles to the north, others as far out to sea. We saw dozens of hulks and galleons carefully skirting the dangerously shallow Dunkirk banks. The vice flagship of Moncado, the San Felipe, lay stranded upon Calais Beach, her oars and cannon poking helplessly skyward, her men at the ready to defend her against all comers.

I rejoiced to see the English fleet strong and altogether intact, lying southwest of us where they had last been anchored at the time of the fire ships. Medina Sidonia had spent this desperate night in the high lookout. I can scarce imagine the torment he felt to see his great Armada so sundered, weakened by distances and the panic which had caused them. Most ships, he now knew, had in deed cut both their anchors and with a south westerly wind blowing, would find it impossible to reassemble round their Admiral.

Finally the Duke descended from the nest, allowing Jorge to help him down the last rung, and they passed by me on the way below. Since the wind would not allow the Armada to come to the Duke, he had decided the San Martín and five other nearby galleons would go to the Armada. Perhaps thirty of their number were sailing hard to join us when the English, not wishing to let their advantage slip away, charged.

Medina Sidonia spoke quietly to his pilot. Then trumpet blasts rent the air, and the six warships came into a line side by side. As I hurried to my own post high in the castle I saw the other Spanish vessels sailing hard to overtake us. More warships came up to flank the line, and the weaker craft fell in behind. Astonishingly, the captains had recreated a semblance — diminished tho it was — of the original crescent formation.

The English were coming with the wind and coming fast. A pretty flagship raced towards the San Martín. We held our fire — we were on our last day's supply of heavy shot and could not afford to miss — till the ship was at such close range I could read its name, Revenge. I felt like cheering. This was Drake, I knew it was!

He opened fire and so did we. Twas a cannonade to shake the Heavens! Thunderous explosions. Cannonballs flying and crashing, tearing into rigging and deck, holing the sides of both ships. The barrage of small artillery made a fearsome noise, and in this melee I shot wild, or shot down at the deck of the San Martín, picking off what sailors and soldiers I could without detection. Once delivered of its load, the Revenge swooped away and another ship took its place. And another. Their lengthwise attack formation levied formidable consequences upon us, the men of the Armada now recognizing with growing alarm that this, the English captains original and most daring maneuver, would be used again and again as morning dragged on into afternoon.

Our ship was a shambles, and the English had a clear advantage, yet I found my self urgently thinking there was more I must do!

The San Martín's heavy shot was still coming hot and fast, and I worried at the damage it was doing to the English ships. Several arquebusiers round me lay dying or dead. With a loud cry I fell back, and dipping my hand in another mans blood, smeared it heavily on my forehead. No one saw me or cared, but thus disguised as a badly injured man, I stumbled down the castleworks and made my way — dodging bullets and falling debris — to the lower gun deck.

That dark and deafening place was a Hell, but I aimed to make it more of one. All gunners were either hard at work at their posts, dead or wounded. A man lay sprawled halfway out a great gaping hole in the hull where a fifty pound ball had crashed thro. Another sat, back to the wall, alive but noise maddened and entirely paralyzed but for his chattering jaw. I grabbed a handful of powder and kneeling low, strewed it behind the gunners. Another handful and another. I was forced to suddenly slump against the wall and play dead as several new gunners came to replace those downed on the gun deck. They shoved away the fallen, began their tasks, and I renewed my surreptitious efforts. Now I found splinters of wood, bits of canvas and dry rope, and tossed them amidst the powder. Then I set it alight and it burst into smokey flame.

"Fire, fire in the gun deck!" I shout. Gunners turn to see a wall of flame behind them, never knowing how brief a conflagration it will be, and run for their lives. I have no time to lose. Grabbing hammer and half a dozen iron posts I race to the first culverin and pound the post into its touch hole. When it is firmly imbedded I break it off low, move to the next cannon. The next and the next. I have thus spiked five big guns rendering them useless when I hear angry shouts behind me. The fire quenched, the gunners have returned to find their mate in an act of outrageous sabotage.

They rush me shrieking Spanish curses. I bolt, the door blessedly clear. I fly up the steps to the deck. Thick smoke. Screaming. A stray bullet parts my hair, pings off an iron fitting. No time to stop, think, plan. The gunners at my heels. I run aft, dodge a falling sail, shards of the castle wall. I slow to grab a rope which uncoils as I quickstep across the deck, alive with sound and fury. Pull taut the rope. Hear the angry grunts of gunners tripping, cursing. "Traitor!" they scream. "Kill him!" Come face to face with Jorge, eyes hurt and unbelieving. Shove him aside. Stand frozen, back to the rail. See them coming thro the smoke, coming. Death at the hands of my enemy . . . or else the sea. A choice from Hell. Tis not my moment to die. I vault the rail, am suddenly airborne. Flying. Tumbling. Falling towards the maw of the great churning beast of my blackest nightmares.

How long have I been floating in terror, the thick of the battle raging all round and above me? Half drowned, clinging to a raft of broken hull, deafened by the cannons roar. Helpless, praying that I not be crushed amidst the hulking galleys, battered by wild swinging oars, bombarded by cannonade and potshots leveled by English small armsmen.

It seems for ever, that ocean siege. I have floated away from the San Martín, amidst some other fights. I see scuppers running with blood. Bodies by the dozens thrown overboard into the sea. Two ships, Spanish and English, sail so close to one another they crash together, two shuddering wooden behemoths. Out of large shot, only their arquebusiers and musketeers can carry on. I see an Englishman, puffed with some insane bravado, actually leap upon the Spanish galleons deck, only to be hacked to death in an instant.

Is it wishful thinking? The English vessels appear somehow less damaged. How can that be, fired upon at such close range? The Armada is battered. Every sail in tatters. Masts toppled, rudders smashed. Badly holed between wind and water. Once I call up to an English sailor, "Help me! I am an Englishman!" He cannot hear me over the roar. But he sees my uniform. A moment later a musketeer appears at the rail. Fires at me. Shatters the corner of my makeshift raft.

Then suddenly the weather changes. A squall. Violent. Fierce wind. Chop becoming churning waves. Higher, louder. The English turn and sail away. "No, don't leave me!" I cry but they cannot hear, disappearing into the distance leaving me to clutch my raw ark, rise with the crests and drop into the troughs. Waves crash down upon my back. I choke and spit. My hands bleed as I claw at the slippery, splintering wood. O God, is this how I shall die? Is this how I shall die!

It ends suddenly, as it began. The sea flattens. Tis night still. A moon flits in and out of clouds. I am dead exhausted. Lying face up staring at the stars. The stars. Those heavenly orbs which rule our destiny. They glitter down on me, a poor dying man.

Something bumps the raft, drags a corner down. I turn to shove it away. But what I see stays my hand. Tis an English uniform! A headless body wearing an English uniform!

I somehow heft the gruesome corpse aboard. I strip my self naked. Pull off the Englishman's clothes. Struggle into his shirt, breeches, jacket. Say a prayer for his soul. Push him off the raft. I am sick with pain and fatigue. There is nothing to do but wait for the dawn. But I am again in the uniform of an English soldier and I am content with that blessing.

When day comes I am greeted by a sight more beautiful than I could hope to dream. The ships of the Spanish Armada, mangled and limping, are strung out along the Flemish shores. Closer and closer are they driven to their doom on the sandy shoals. Finer still is the sight of the English fleet, smart and tidy and entirely intact. Now with the wind at their backs they are making for the Spaniards to harry them from their waters altogether. And God be praised, on their present course they will easily intercept me. I feel my rescue close at hand.

But I am weak, battered, and in questionable circumstances. I know no details of the English fleet except what I have seen from a distance, nor whom I should claim to be. I fear I may blunder in my weariness. Still, I have not come so far and suffered so greatly to be denied acceptance by my own.

When I believe they are within hailing distance I cry out in my native tongue, wave my arms, determine I have been spotted, then feign a collapse into unconsciousness. In good time I feel my body gently lifted aboard ship, and still pretending to be dead to the world, celebrate the sound of my countrymens voices. I swear, the swoon is half real, so overcome am I with grateful relief that I will live to see England once again. I am going home. I am going home.

Fifty-four

As her carriage rumbled through the London streets thronged with cheering celebrants Elizabeth found herself pleasantly plagued by a giddy lightheadedness. Her return to London in the wake of the Armada's defeat was in all ways triumphant, greeted as she was by her people's wild outpourings of joy and relief.

Reports from the English fleet had come slowly. Drake and Lord Howard were at first unsure that they had even *had* a victory with their fire ships, and the following day at Gravelines. But their confidence had grown as they chased Philip's devastated ships into the North Sea, assisted by the freakish storms prophesied by Doctor Dee, and by Regiomontanus a hundred years before.

Elizabeth thought, I have a right to be giddy, for I have met the Dragon on the field of battle and slain it — I, a woman. She leaned back onto the soft down and satin cushions and smiled with satisfaction. Her mother would have been proud. She had not died in vain. *"A Tudor sun shall rise from your belly and shine over England for four and forty years,"* the Nun of Kent had said. Elizabeth calculated. She had only ruled for thirty years and would therefore live to see her grandfather's dynasty into the new century. One hundred years of Tudor rule. A brilliant accomplishment indeed. Only a child of her body, an heir, was lacking for perfection. But then, she thought with a wry smile, life itself was imperfect. Always imperfect.

Outside her carriage window a clutch of Morris dancers danced, their leg bells jingling merrily, and suddenly Elizabeth was gone from the carriage, gone from the year 1588, flown back to another time. She was a small child carried high in her father's arms, wearing yellow satin to match his own. He held her close as they watched the Morris dancers doing their jig amidst a huge celebration, up close to his wide, handsome face, so handsome when he smiled. She tugged at his red-gold beard. He laughed a belly-shaking laugh and she squealed with delight, for she had pleased him. Oh, she loved her father! Adored him. He was the hero of her young life. And the beast of her mother's.

The sobering thought snatched Elizabeth back to the present, though not from thoughts of her father. She wished to forgive him his vile and murderous rages, and she prayed daily that the madness in his blood would not infect her own. How could he have ordered the arrest of a woman he had loved so desperately? Ordered her beheading? And how could he have left that little girl in yellow so terrible a legacy? Knowledge that her mother had died because Elizabeth had been born a girl.

"Well, Father," came the sudden defiant retort, "this girl has gone and saved England." She allowed herself a smile. She *would* forgive Henry, and she would honor Anne. Together they had made her, and from their places in Heaven and Hell they were watching her now. She would allow no more painful memories nor mournful wishes that the past had been different. For it was altogether the proudest day of her life, and she meant to savor every moment of it.

"The Earl of Leicester, Your Majesty."

Elizabeth could not help wincing as her old friend walked across the Presence Chamber floor to her throne. His limp had worsened considerably in the days since Tilbury, and his usually florid complexion seemed more grey than high pink.

"Robin, don't," she commanded as he began to kneel. "Just come and sit by me." She gestured for a page to bring a chair and place it next to hers. They both ignored the stares and whispering of the courtiers. What others thought of their behavior had long ago ceased to matter.

"I heard your processional into London was very grand indeed," she said. "Fit for a king."

"I *am* the King," he said, grinning mischievously. "Have you already forgotten?"

Elizabeth chuckled. "And where is your good wife?"

"With her lover at Wanstead," he replied evenly. "But I assure you she will appear presently to reap the accolades due her famous husband."

"*Infamous* husband," Elizabeth corrected.

"Indeed."

She noticed a whimsical smile playing about Leicester's lips. "What is it you find so amusing, my lord?"

"How they come and go. The courtiers. The beautiful ladies . . ." He nodded down at the small clusters of men and women engrossed in their conversations and gossip. There was his wife's son, the handsome and eminently charming Earl of Essex to whom the Queen had taken quite a fancy. And William Cecil's son Robert, dwarfish and deformed but terribly bright, who had of late taken over his father's role as Elizabeth's secretary. "And how we two endure, despite the plots and romances, illnesses, wars, furies."

"Dine with me tonight, Robin," said Elizabeth suddenly.

"Of course I will."

"And tomorrow night. And the night after."

He looked at her curiously. "So you desire the company of this creaky old man even now?"

"More than anyone in the wide world, my love." She drew her long fingers gently along his cheek, down the once angular jaw gone soft, and tickled him playfully in the hollow of his neck. "And more than ever."

Fifty-five

I had always believed my self to be tolerably brave. No hero, but a man who could face that which life offered up to him in challenge, refusing to live in fear of the future, or the unknown, or those who were different from my self. But on the day I was rowed down the Thames into London, still weak from my long immersion in the sea and weakened further by the dysentery which had struck nearly every member of the English crew of my rescue ship, I found my self beset by an almost paralyzing fear.

I had come to London with only one purpose — to reunite with my parents. To embrace my Father once again and humbly lay my self at my Mothers feet. Twas a simple thing really, and I was bound by truth and fairness to us all to do it. But despite these last years of dreaming and rehearsing the moment, as it approached I felt unprepared and worse than that, a charlatan. I had convinced Lord Leicester of my story, and no doubt he would convince the Queen of its veracity. But in my weaker moments — which were coming upon me with terrible frequency — I hardly believed it my self. I, the son of Elizabeth. I, a Prince of Royal Blood. Twas laughable. My real Father, Robert Southern, must somehow have learnt of the Fulham House kidnapping, and maddened by an intolerable life with his wife, fabricated and twisted the story in his mind to make me the Queens child.

Even it were true, what words could I possibly conceive to introduce myself into Her Majestys life? She would have me thrown out on my ear. Arrested for treason. Tortured. Executed!

Many times in that rowboat as it touched onto docks and landings on its way to London did I consider hopping off and waiting for the tide to turn, going back the way I had come. But something stopped me. Memories of the deep and inexplicable love I had borne Elizabeth and Leicester from the time we had first met and, too, that strange knowledge of my own destiny which, even as a young boy, I perceived to be great.

Now I could see Saint Pauls Cathedral looming beyond London Bridge, and I knew my destination was Saint Jameses Palace where the Queen was holding Court. I could only pray that Lord Leicester would be close by for the celebrations. So girding my self against fear I pulled my self tall and straight and forced regal bearing into my posture. I forced my self to remember all that I had accomplished in my life, those great people and Princes who had recognized my qualities, so by the time I had set foot on Three Cranes landing and started up the street to Saint Jameses, I had nearly convinced my self again that I was in deed the Queen of England's only son.

Fifty-six

Elizabeth and Leicester had been stricken by an uncontrollable fit of childish giggles. On this, their third consecutive evening closeted together in her private apartments, both of them tipsy on French wine, she had prescribed for him an evil-smelling potion for what had become a chronic flux. He sniffed it suspiciously.

"Here," he said. "You look ashen, Bess. Have a little sip yourself." He pushed the bottle under her nose and she caught a good whiff of the stuff.

"Augh!" she cried in disgust.

"I think you have a grudge with me you have not admitted, for this will kill me more surely than the flux will. Come along, a small draught . . ."

"Robin, take it away, I tell you!"

"Just a weeee nip!"

Once begun, their laughter soon grew far beyond the bounds of the original jest. They were still clutching their sides and wheezing when the door opened and Lady Hunsdon entered. Eyes downcast, she curtsied and handed Leicester a folded letter, then exited hastily. Elizabeth watched Leicester's smile crumble as he read its contents.

"Robin, what is it? Has there been a death?"

He was very still. A hand went to his chest and his breath became a series of shallow gasps.

"You must tell me, please!"

But he could not speak. Could not find the words to explain. All he could do was raise Elizabeth to her feet and enfold her in a long and forceful embrace.

* * *

She had asked Robin over and over again who it was he was bringing to meet her, but he'd refused to answer. Now instead a tall, broad-shouldered but rather thin man in the uniform of her navy was kneeling at her feet. As he'd approached her she'd seen that the skin of his face and hands was sunburnt and weathered, and she guessed he was somewhat younger than he appeared. Still he was quite handsome, she thought, square-jawed with a high unblemished forehead and strong, even features. The hair was reddish brown and the eyes were very dark, almost black.

She could feel Leicester at her side trembling with emotion. "You look ill," she heard him say to the younger man, who gazed back at Leicester with what seemed to Elizabeth a look of longing, though she could not guess for what.

"I'm recovering from some wounds I received fighting in the Channel," he said.

"You were there? Aboard one of my ships?" said Elizabeth.

The young man did not immediately answer, but looked mildly confused. Elizabeth was growing irritated. She looked back and forth between him and Leicester. The two men could not tear their eyes from each other.

"Why do you look so familiar to me?" she suddenly demanded of the stranger.

"We met once, Your Majesty. At Enfield Chase."

"Enfield? Enfield . . ."

"In Surrey, Madame. Many years ago. I was eight years old."

She looked more closely at him. "Did we ride a wild goose chase together through your father's wood?"

"We did."

"Robin, this was the young boy who performed the manège so beautifully for us that day!" But when she turned to Leicester she found his face wet with tears. Then suddenly the two men fell on each other with shouts and embracing.

"I demand to know what is happening here!" Elizabeth thundered. "I order you to stand down from Lord Leicester, young man, and tell me who you are!"

She watched the pair of them move apart and saw the man come to attention before her. With one last glance to Robin he pulled his gaze forward and fixed the Queen with his eyes.

"My name is Arthur Dudley, Your Majesty. I am Lord Leicester's natural son . . . and your own."

Elizabeth opened her mouth instantly to object, but closed it again when she realized she had no sensible words to utter. She thought to turn her head and look at Robin for counsel, but found every part of her frozen in place.

"Elizabeth . . ." She heard Robin's gentle voice in her ear and prayed that he would say something that would clear the confusion in her head, unlock her paralyzed limbs, loose her jaw so that she might speak, respond to this . . . this . . .

"He *is* our son. He is our own flesh and blood."

"Our son died," she whispered hoarsely.

"Our son was stolen from us. That poor dead child we held between us was some other woman's babe. Kat Ashley and William Cecil —"

"No! They couldn't have! They would not have dared!"

"Oh, they dared."

Elizabeth stared at the stranger, fury darkening her eyes. "Prove it!" she shouted shrilly.

"He has, Elizabeth. To me," said Leicester quietly. "He knows too much about that terrible night at Fulham House to be an impostor. His adoptive father and Kat were longtime friends —"

"I thought she was a friend to *me!*" Elizabeth cried, her face contorted with anger.

"Kat is dead now. But your son is alive and standing before you."

"He is not. He is *not.*"

"Show her, Arthur."

Slowly the man lifted his left hand and held it up to Elizabeth's face. There in front of her eyes was the tiny nub of flesh and nail. She could only stare at the extra finger and then at the face. The eyes. The black, fathomless eyes. Her mother's eyes.

"Dear God, dear God!" she wailed and suddenly her arms went round the young man, and she wept. In anger and love and for lost dreams found. Then laughed. And with the feel of her son's tentative arms finally twining about her waist, she wept again. Leicester embraced them both, kissing first Elizabeth's face and then his son's. And there they stayed for some good time, whispering and crooning comfortably each to the other, and finally seeking words to begin healing the great wound of their terrible separation.

Fifty-seven

I stayed closeted with my Parents for several days more, meals delivered by nosy servants desperate to know who this stranger amongst them was. Leicester and I slept in his apartments adjoining the Queens chamber. I think that except when we slept we did never stop regaling each other with the stories of our lives, details of adventures, truths learnt and tall tales made taller. Tis said lost time can never be found, but we put forth a valiant effort. The two of them sat riveted by my exploits as a boy, a soldier and a spy, my Mother especially keen to hear all about King Philip, her worst enemy whom she had not laid eyes on for thirty years.

And I begged to hear their stories. My Mothers fearful childhood, her terrifying road to the Throne, her joys and woes as the ruler of England. But I was most greedy to hear of their love for each other, their childhood courtship, the passion which had created me, the sad reality of my Fathers loveless married life. Tho it was not spoken, I knew my Mother had in her way begged my Fathers forgiveness for never marrying with him. I found joy in their indelible friendship and Leicesters service to the Crown, both of which had endured thro every tribulation. I saw they still held tender secrets tween them and even, to my surprise, a flame of sexual love.

But in the end, of all the storytelling nothing compared to my saga of sailing incognito with the Spanish Armada. They sat spellbound as I told of the terrible privations, religious mania. The foul betrayal by Parma of the goodhearted Medina Sidonia, and the terror of the English fire ships, the daylong battle of Gravelines. I recounted my close brush with death that stormy night in the Channel on my lonely raft, and the headless corpse, and my final ruse which earned me my rescue by the English vessel.

But whilst I saw my Mother grow stronger and more cheerful with every passing hour, my Father, despite an heroic effort to hide it, became ever more pale and sickly. Finally the Queen bade him go and rest. He agreed, saying he was headed for Buxton to take the waters there. He embraced me soundly, and with promises to meet up again in a months time, he went to my Mother who stood at a window overlooking the Thames. I saw such love and so sweet a caring tween them that had not so many tears already been shed in previous days I might have wept. When, however, the Queen sternly pressed an apothecarys bottle into Leicesters hands the pair of them suddenly burst into peals of raucous laughter which I did not understand, and which they did never explain. With a final kiss and the deepest of courtly bows that his poor old body would allow, my Father departed.

I was alone with the Queen. From across the chamber I saw her fix me with a steady gaze which was at once completely disbelieving and altogether accepting.

"Come here to me, Arthur."

I obeyed and stood with her at the window for a long while, silently watching the river traffic below. Finally she spoke in an intimate and softly edged voice. "Since you walked in my door I have never ceased thinking about you. I have listened to you, I have wondered about you. I have even dreamt of you." She lowered herself into the window seat and gestured for me to do the same. "When I was pregnant with you I was a full grown woman in my body, but in my mind I was hardly more than a girl. I had just taken the Throne, you see, and believed I could do exactly as I wished in all things. I believed that I could whisk you away into seclusion, conceal your existence entirely until the time I decided it was safe to reveal you to the world."

She laughed, I think at her own naivete.

"Knowing what I do now about my treacherous and backstabbing Court, tis certain that my bastard son would not have stayed long a secret. My name was already sullied. It would have sunk as low as the Scots Queens had, and we both know the swift and brutal punishment her people visited on Mary for her amorous indiscretions. I think I might well have lost the Throne altogether. Even had

I managed to retain my Queenship, you your self would no doubt have become a pawn. Bloody rebellions to determine the succession would have been fought in your name, both to raise you to the Throne and to see you discredited. Too many men wished for a male sovereign — still do. They would have wheedled me ceaselessly to abdicate to you, driving a terrible wedge between us." She touched my face then, and I thought I saw a flicker of the beauty that had once been hers. "You might even have been assassinated as your friend Prince William was."

She sighed deeply. "Oh, I have cursed Mistress Kat Ashley and William Cecil for taking my flesh and blood from me, but I look at you, Arthur, and see as fine a man as I have ever known. You were raised and educated as a commoner and I think had you been raised as a Prince of England you would not now be so fine as you are. Royal children are pampered and spoilt, ruined in their heart and soul, and hardened, as I was. You might even have come to hate me."

"I could never have hated you," I said, taking her hand. "We have lost a great deal of time between us, but just know, Mother . . ." The word caught in my throat. "Know that from here after you are ever, <u>ever</u> beloved by me till I die."

We embraced once more, but then she pushed me to arms length and said, "There is something we must speak of now, something urgent." She looked away from me as tho, despite all that had passed between us she could not now look me in the eye. "I have never yet named my successor. . . ."

"Your Majesty," I began as if to silence her, for suddenly I was seized by the most terrible misgivings. I had come here seeking my Parents and never seeking the Crown.

"You are the only natural child of my body," she continued, ignoring my interruption, "and therefore rightful heir to the Throne of England."

I did not wish her to go on, but she now turned, emboldened by her own words spoken, and silenced me with her eyes.

"I am the Queen and so I shall continue while I have breath left in my body. But I am prepared to acknowledge you as my successor, come what may, and from this day forward begin the education you will need to prepare you to rule."

I fell wholly silent, without even the attempt of a reply. For whilst such a notion had, of course, occurred to me since learning of my lineage, it had never once seemed even remotely plausible. I, King of England . . .

She must have taken my silence as assent because she began then to enumerate the course of my studies — the understanding of warfare on a grand scale, diplomacy, currency and taxation issues, the workings of Parliament, the problem of state religion, the personalities of each of her Privy Councillors, the management of her many households.

But as she went on describing the myriad skills I must needs master, the etiquettes and protocols I must learn, and the limits — no, the obliteration — of my very privacy, I felt the blood pounding in my head until finally I could be silent no longer.

"Forgive me, Mother!" I blurted.

The Queen, in midsentence, was taken aback to be interrupted so rudely, but she stopped and waited for me to continue, with a look of parental indulgence that bordered on bemusement.

"I . . . I do not wish . . . the Throne."

"You do not wish the Throne," she repeated mildly, as if the meaning of the words had not yet impressed themselves on her. Then her white face and painted eyebrows knitted into a frown. "You say you do not wish to succeed me, to become King of England?"

"Yes."

Her laugh was a high bark. Then she grew silent as she sought comprehension of the idea. Finally she said, "Pray explain your self, Arthur, for I have no way to understand this."

"For these past days," I began, "I have heard the story of your life and of Fathers, of the Court and especially of your Royal upbringing and circumstance. And I have reviewed my own life as well. And I cannot help but think — with all due respect, Madame — that I prefer my own."

Her arched eyebrows rose even higher, but I forged on.

"Since I was a boy I have loved adventuring. I dreamt of it when I was too small to leave home, but soon as I was able I rode out seeking it. And oh, I found it. In towns. In wooded glades. On storm tossed ships, in foreign lands, on battlefields. In the company of great men, brave women, matchless horses. I have seen marvels and mysteries, beauty, misery. I have been tested again and again. I have known freedom, Mother . . ."

I could see she was listening intently, but still seemed

unconvinced. I went on. "Then I looked round me at this courtly life. It feels so small to me, yet dangerous in a way I fear I could not endure. You were born a Princess, and it brought you very low. When you became Queen, people wished to murder you."

She began nodding in agreement with my words, her eyes faraway, as if remembering those occasions.

"And this life has been cruel to my Father as well. I know he is not a blameless man. He freely admits to the sin of ambition. The lengths to which he went to win your hand . . . even I might call them scurrilous. But we both know Lord Leicester is a good man and loved you faithfully, Mother."

"That he did," she agreed with a small smile.

"Tis my belief that he was so reviled only for the faithful love you bore him in turn, and the rewards you heaped upon him, and not for any real evil in him. There were no bounds to the jealousy those petty courtiers felt, knowing you loved him best, knowing you could never be steered from your course of devotion to him."

My Mothers lips began to tremble then, and her eyes suddenly filled with tears. I put my hand on hers.

"I recall," she said, "another monarch and the love for which he moved many mountains. And the jealousy which brought his lover down. But go on. I think I have not heard the best part of this explanation yet."

"If I were acknowledged Prince of Wales tomorrow," I said, "then all of my wanderings would come swiftly to an end. I would be stuffed into the clothing of a dandy and expected to assume an array of fine manners. My person would be diligently guarded, every ache and pain discussed. I would never again be free to don disguises, assume false names, nor just ride out into the countryside by my self for the sheer pleasure of it. I would have the fate of nations hanging on me! You were brought up on a diet of such responsibilities, and you craved to rule. I crave adventure!"

I stopped then, for I wondered if what I would say next might lay well or ill with the Queen. She skewered me with her eyes, allowing me no escape from finishing what I had started.

"There is a woman . . ." I began.

"Ah." That was all my Mother said, though every harsh line of her face suddenly softened.

"I had sought her my whole life. I found her not so long ago. She consumes my every thought and emotion."

"Then you should have her," said the Queen quickly. "I, of all people, could never ask you to sacrifice love for a political marriage."

"You do not understand, Mother. She is a Spaniard. A widow with two children. This life, Court life, would only ruin her."

The Queens smile began to fade.

"And she is a Jew."

"A Jew!" she cried. This last revelation had been altogether unexpected. She stared at me with such a look of confoundment that I thought she had finally reached the boundaries of her patience and understanding. Then she said, "Good Christ, Arthur, you have gone to great lengths to excuse yourself from taking this throne."

I sagged with relief. "Then . . . then you understand?"

"I think I have no choice. Are you sure you cannot live without her?"

I laughed mirthlessly. "I'm not sure I can even find her again. She and her family are running from the Inquisition, still one step ahead, I pray."

"So," said my Mother with the sound of finality, "my only son would willingly give up the Crown of England for a woman and a life of adventuring."

"Do you forgive me?"

"No, I do not forgive you. This displeases me in the extreme. But you are young still. And I am not very old. I shall reign for a good many more years, and in that time you may grow weary of your adventuring — tho if you are anything like your Father," she added with a wry smile, "you may never grow weary of your woman. I shall not give up hope that you might change your mind. I shall therefore continue refusing to name my successor. I think my men have all ceased to expect it anyway."

With that she gave me her blessings, and a good purse to go on with, and promise of all the monies I should ever need my whole life long. Before she gave me leave to go she stood and walked to a large carven chest at the foot of her bed. Kneeling before it she dug deep into it and removed a worn old book. Its red leather cover was faded, and the gilt trim round its edges was nearly faded away. She held it to her heart for a long time before thrusting it into my hands.

"This is for your eyes only, Arthur. And you must guard it diligently. Promise me."

"I promise, on my honor."

"Go now," she said with a sharpness that liked to cover the tenderest heart. "Go find your love."

I knelt and kissed her hand, holding it to my cheek. She said no more, not even goodbye.

When I first found a moment of privacy I opened the book to its first page. Twas not a printed volume as I had expected, but instead was written in an old fashioned hand. Its title "The Diary of Anne Boleyn" startled me altogether. I had never before read a journal, tho I knew such things existed. To be in possession of my ancestresses history thrilled me beyond measure.

So, I mused, I had been gifted with books of great import by both my Mother and my Father. Perhaps twas that thought which has led me to the writing of my own life. In any event that very night, by candlelight, I began to read my Grandmothers secret diary.

Fifty-eight

Robin Dudley gazed across the bubbling stream at his brother Ambrose struggling with gouty fingers to bait his line, and thought with more resignation than bitterness that the body's aging was perhaps the most unredeemable curse of life. There were some joys in growing old, and death was many times a blessing. But the inexorable march of decrepitude on the human form seemed wholly cruel to him. His once handsome and vigorous brother was now stooped, and he wheezed when he walked. The war wound of his younger days had never ceased to plague him, and in the last years had given him excruciating pain in the chill of winter. Leicester himself was not much better off, with his malarial fevers and constant dyspepsia. And then there was vanity. He would be lying if he did not admit that the sight of his bloated and discolored old flesh repulsed him. He could barely look at the portraits of himself as a vital young man which hung in his many residences. Perhaps, he considered, he should have them all removed.

"Have you given more thought to speaking to the Queen on James Croft's behalf?" called Ambrose as he cast out his line in a graceful arc across the water. The salmon had so far evaded them both this day.

"He's a devious, scheming old bugger," Leicester called back. "On King Philip's payroll in '82. Last year making Parma offers to return Dutch cities to him on no one's authority but his own. . . . And when Elizabeth has him thrown in the Tower for his actions, he cries foul."

"He does. And he blames you."

"As does everyone for everything. I have become used to it by now."

"His son Edward is fit to be tied. Murderous against you. He vows revenge."

"Ah well, what can he do to me that time has not already begun? Listen, do you know of a lawyer in Buxton?"

"A man called Doughtry," replied Ambrose. "What for?"

"I am thinking to change my will."

"Cutting me out of it, are you?"

Leicester laughed good-naturedly. He'd said nothing about Arthur to his brother. He and Elizabeth had concluded that revealing their son's existence for the present would serve no good purpose. But he would make sure that the boy was remembered in his will. He could imply the mother was dead. Arthur would be just another acknowledged bastard, as his son Robert was.

Dudley threw his own line into the sparkling water with a fisherman's prayer. He would savor a fine salmon for supper tonight. The warm sun beating down on his shoulders, and the sound of rushing water a balm to his soul, he suddenly realized that aside from his annoying and unalterable decrepitude, he felt more contented with his life than ever before. This golden summer had seen England's glorious victory, had seen him drawn back into the warmth of Elizabeth's love, and delivered to them their long lost son.

He was so proud of the boy, saw how well he pleased his mother. Surely they would spend good time together in the coming years. Leicester smiled a private smile. Arthur would be a comfort to him in his old age. Not only for the beauty and fullness of his person, but as a sweet and constant reminder of his long and blessed presence in the life of a great queen.

He felt the salmon strike and cried out in excitement. Ambrose turned to watch his brother tug to set the hook and begin the fight. Suddenly the great fish shot skyward, twisting energetically, its silver scales glittering in the sun. Both men shouted with the size of him, his power, and the joy of the struggle. And in that moment, it seemed to Robin Dudley that no man's life could ever have been so fine.

Young Essex gave the Queen a leg up onto the chestnut gelding. Nothing was more satisfying, thought Elizabeth settling herself in the saddle outside the royal stables, than to find a handsome new riding partner. Though she loathed the mother, Lady Leicester, the Queen could not help her unreserved enjoyment of the son. She had moved him into his stepfather's apartments adjoining her own, and tongues had begun wagging immediately. She cared not a whit. She simply wished the tall, dark-haired young man to attend her, and attend her often. Essex. She would see to his future.

"Forgive me, Your Majesty," he said, "but my horse seems to be lame. I shall be a few minutes more." He bowed with that particular combination of grace and masculinity which she found utterly irresistible, and strode away into the stalls.

A few moments to spare. She had tucked the note from Robin in her bodice and now took it out to reread. In the strong September sunlight the words were clear, even without her spectacles. 'Twas a short thing, written from Robin's rooms at Rycote as he made his way to Buxton Baths, inquiring after her own aches and pains in his familiar and affectionate way, and praying for her good health and long life. *I continue still the medicine you so kindly proffered on our last meeting, and find that it amends me much better than any the doctors have prescribed.* That foul brew! thought Elizabeth, amused. The revolting tincture that had elicited so much giddiness and laughter. *Thus hoping to find a perfect cure at the baths, and ready to continue on my journey there, I pray continually for your happy preservation, and most humbly kiss your foot. By Your Majestys faithful and obedient servant. R. Leicester.*

"I humbly kiss your foot," she repeated in a whisper. Dear Robin. There was no one like him. Not Raleigh, not Drake, not this new young stallion.

A page hurried across the gravel yard just as Essex returned with a fit horse. The boy looked at the Queen and then at the young lord as if he did not know whom first to address.

Well, what is it?" demanded Elizabeth impatiently.

"Lord . . . Lord . . ." he stammered. "Lord Leicester is dead. At Cornbury."

"He is not dead," said Elizabeth matter-of-factly. "I have a letter from him." She waved the note in the air as proof.

The page shifted uncomfortably from foot to foot. "Begging your pardon, Your Majesty. 'Twas a sudden fever took him, though there is some talk of . . . murder."

Elizabeth had become very still. Essex, who had not yet spoken, pulled the messenger to face him. "Where is my mother?"

"With her husband, my lord. She was with him when he" — the boy looked quickly at the Queen and then away — "died."

"Madame." Essex turned to Elizabeth in confusion. For a moment neither of them spoke.

"My deepest condolences, Lord Essex," she finally uttered. Nothing but her lips had moved.

"And mine to you, Your Majesty. May I . . . would you . . . ?"

"You have leave to go to your mother immediately."

Altogether shaken, Essex rushed away. Elizabeth waved the page to follow him. She sat quite still in the saddle, gazing round her at the stables, St. James's Palace, the river beyond.

The world has suddenly changed, she thought simply. Altogether changed.

The horse moved beneath her, eager to begin their ride. But she felt odd. Hollow, like a long metal pipe. If someone had struck her now, she thought, she might chime like some discordant bell. He was dead. It was over.

I humbly kiss your foot.

Elizabeth hooked her knee round the horn and tapped the gelding's side with her boot. He knew somehow to go gentle with the woman on his back. She rode slowly from the gravel yard toward the yellowing heath. Her back was straight as a rod, her chin high, eyes dry.

Robin.

Christopher Hatton and Robert Cecil had had the locked door of the Queen's bedchamber broken down on the third day after the Earl of Leicester's death. She lay still on her bed, fully clothed, though she had loosened her stays, and one sleeve hung off her bodice by a single lace. She wore no wig, and her grey-red hair clung to her ghostly skull. In her hand was clutched a small folded parchment on which she had written in her own hand the words "His last letter." She gazed with glassy eyes at the men who stood fussing and clucking over her, but did not quite see them, for she was elsewhere.

Fulham House of a stormy evening in late summer. She had given birth and lay encircled in Robin Dudley's strong arms. The newborn babe lay snug between them, mewling and squirming, his face even now losing its angry red for a sweet, pale pink. Their son, Arthur, lived. He lived! Robin leaned down and kissed the boy, looked up, kissed Elizabeth's damp cheek. She smiled at her lover and her beautiful son with immeasurable serenity, for here was a child of her body, of Tudor blood. The world, at last, was full and altogether perfect.

Fifty-nine

Few mourned my Fathers lonely death. His wife wasted no time in marrying her young lover, and even the writers and poets on whom he had bestowed his faithful patronage and who had lauded him in his life, were silent. Only one, Edmund Spenser, dedicated this verse.

He now is dead and all his glory gone
And all his greatness vapoured to naught,
That as a glass upon the water shone
Which vanished quite soon as it was sought
His name is worn already out of thought.

My Mother, who did mourn him deeply, was soon called back to her duties and could not refuse them. The Spanish threat to England was ended, but only for the briefest moment, and it was evident that there would be no real peace whilst Philip still lived and breathed.

I returned to the south of Spain for Constanza, only to find her, with her Father and children, gone. The saddle factory had been boarded up, the Lorca residence inhabited by a local Bishop. The family, he told me, had decided to emigrate to the New World. The wealthy conquistadors, soldiers and caballeros were numerous, and Don Ramón believed he could grow very rich. They had gone under a grant from King Philip to Nuevo León, a great tract of land in northern Mexico, its Governor General a distinguished hidalgo named Carvajal. Nothing more was known.

In Lisbon there was difficulty finding a ship bound for the New World, so many had been impounded for the Armada. Every day battered remnants of that once proud fleet came limping back from their hellish journey round Scotland and Ireland. But I prowled the docks daily till I found a merchantman newly mended and sea-worthy — so they said — and bound for the New World. That land of promise. The Atlantean land of Doctor Dee. And tis from that journey, in search of my love and my destiny, that I write.

The weather is turning ugly, and soon I shall pack up my ink and quill and journal and go below. I should like to say that I have conquered my fear of the sea, but this would be a lie. I have found a means of comfort, however, when the terror of the waves threatens to overwhelm me. I hie to the hold where my sweet Mirage is stabled, and sit with her. The Lorcas had left her with the Bishop, saying that one day an Italian named Reggio would return for her. The sound of my voice seems to soothe Mirage, as her scent and strength and beauty soothe me. Together, thus, we have ridden out many a storm and banished fear, if only for a time.

Tho I have suffered the twin griefs of loss and separation, yet there is thanksgiving every day in my heart for the love and many blessings with which I have been gifted. The wide world is mine to explore, and hope is my constant companion.

My Father is dead, but never in my life forgotten. And my Mother is Queen of England.

ARTHUR DUDLEY

A Historical Perspective

That a man claiming to be the son of Elizabeth and Leicester, and calling himself Arthur Dudley, lived in the late sixteenth century is indisputable fact. Whether he was who he professed to be is a matter of conjecture. Though this problem is, to my way of thinking, one of the great unsolved mysteries of the Renaissance, and while there are numerous references to illegitimate children born to Elizabeth and her horsemaster, Robin Dudley, Earl of Leicester, during the first years of her reign when the love affair with Dudley was a generally accepted fact, specific mentions of Arthur Dudley are scarce.

Contemporary explanations of how the closely watched Queen could get away with such a thing ran thus: Every summer Elizabeth would depart on her summer progress, which lasted for up to five months. During this time, it was suggested, she would, using proxies and feigned illnesses and specially designed clothing, "disappear into the countryside" for the final months of pregnancy and lying-in.

Such rumors might of course be no more than idle backstairs gossip, but I found as I researched *The Queen's Bastard* that while Arthur Dudley's story had many gaps in its chronology, the scenario was entirely plausible. In fact, nothing in his story conflicted with any part of Elizabeth's or Leicester's minutely documented lives. I began wondering why biographers of Elizabeth, with only a few exceptions, had ignored so interesting a personage, or at best relegated him to a footnote in history.

I reasoned that most writers subscribed to the hypothesis that Elizabeth was, in the strictest sense, the Virgin Queen she purported to be. If this were true, anyone claiming to be her offspring must, of course, have been an impostor. But recently several Tudor biographers have examined the possibility that the Elizabeth-Dudley relationship was indeed a carnal one. My own opinion is that the two were intimate in the fullest sense of the word. It is a fact that during the first year of her reign, when William Cecil was away in Scotland negotiating the Treaty of Edinburgh, Elizabeth and Dudley were closeted together day and night for weeks on end. This behavior was so scandalous that when Cecil returned he sternly rebuked her for it.

If one considers heredity a factor, it should be remembered that Elizabeth was the child of two outrageous and passionate parents, Henry and Anne, and was herself a vigorous and healthy young woman with a great appetite for many physical pleasures including dancing, hard riding, and hunting. She was decidedly willful. She was queen and reveled in the fact that she could do as she pleased. And she was deeply in love with her childhood friend Robin Dudley. Even after the scandal of his wife's suspicious death, Elizabeth had the audacity to move him into apartments at Greenwich Castle adjoining her own. These do not seem to me the actions or the attributes of a chaste woman.

My search for the story of Elizabeth's and Dudley's illegitimate child began when I came upon a reference to him in Carolly Erickson's *The First Elizabeth* that was so brief and dismissive that it hardly registered: " . . . in the 1580's a boy representing himself as their son was making himself known at Catholic Courts abroad." A few allusions to Arthur Dudley in other books were similarly brief, with one as long as a paragraph, and all of them parroting the notion that he could not have been anything but an impostor.

Imagine my delight upon finding an entire page devoted to him in what had become my bible on the relationship of the Queen and her horsemaster, Elizabeth Jenkins's *Elizabeth and Leicester.* While admitting that the early part of Arthur Dudley's story, which rested "entirely on his own assertion . . . had been got up by somebody with considerable knowledge of the events of twenty-five years before," she ultimately rejected his claim to royal blood on the basis of his age. "Dudley was said to be twenty-five years old, and 1562 was the year in which Elizabeth had nearly died of smallpox. An illness of the Queen's was there established in the probable year of his birth." Carol Levin in *The Heart and Stomach of a King* concurs. "We know that Elizabeth was seriously ill in 1562 with smallpox; this was not a cover for her having given birth to a child." I agree with that, but from my reading, his age being twenty-five was approximate. Much of the dating from that part of history is imprecise. It cannot tell us, for example, the exact year of Queen Anne Boleyn's birth. If, in fact, Arthur Dudley was twenty-*six* at the time of his arrest in Spain, his year of birth would have been 1561, and during that year Elizabeth's summer progress is completely undocumented from the middle of the month of June till the end of October — a huge hole in history. Plenty of time for her to "disappear into the countryside."

The bulk of what we know of young Dudley comes from a deposition he gave to Francis Englefield, Philip II's English secretary in 1587, the year that Arthur, disguised as a pilgrim, was arrested in the north of Spain as a spy for England, the year before the Spanish Armada. The document, gleaned from five days of interrogation by Englefield, complete with Philip's handwritten comments in his loopy scrawl, survives among his *State Papers* in the archives of Salamanca. Englefield clearly believed Dudley's account.

Certainly the story is sketchy, but it was sufficient to serve as a skeleton for the plot of *The Queen's Bastard.* Arthur claimed to have been born to the Queen, and handed over as an infant by Kat Ashley to Robert Southern, who became keeper of Enfield Chase. He was brought up by Southern in ignorance of his true lineage. At age fifteen he ran away from home and was inexplicably brought back from Milford Haven by a warrant from the Privy Council. Later he fought for the Protestants in the Netherlands War until he was recalled to England when his father lay dying. On his deathbed Southern revealed Arthur's true identity, after which the young man took himself to confront his birth father, Lord Leicester. Arthur claimed Leicester acknowledged him as his son, then sent him with his secretary, Mr. Fludd, to Walsingham's house for a passport. Not wishing to be interrogated by the head of Elizabeth's secret service, Arthur fled to the Continent. Leicester is said to have observed of his son, "You're like a ship under full sail at sea. Pretty to look at, but dangerous to deal with," a statement that David Howarth in *The Voyage of the Armada* claims "has a ring of truth to it." Once in Spanish custody Arthur apparently suggested that he assassinate the Scottish king James, and implied that he himself was the true successor to the English throne.

Another superb "hole in history" that I discovered was the explosion aboard the Spanish vessel *San Salvador* during the voyage of the Armada. It was, at the time, believed to be an act of sabotage by a disgruntled foreign mercenary, but the actual identity of the saboteur has remained a mystery and I used this, happily to my advantage, in Arthur's story.

Howarth's account of the Armada from the Spanish perspective was the last piece on Arthur that I discovered, fully halfway through the writing of *Bastard.* The author's analysis of Philip's motivations and behavior surrounding his Great Enterprise was the most detailed and well observed of any I'd read, and I was gratified by the seriousness with which the author regarded the person of Arthur Dudley. The King of Spain, he wrote, was — though no one was then aware of it — planning to take the crown of conquered England for himself and his daughter the Infanta Isabella. When he was confronted with Arthur, Philip took him seriously enough to consider him having "a stronger claim to the throne than anyone else." The King therefore saw him as a potential rival and someone who, for reasons of national security, needed locking up. "It will certainly be safest," Philip wrote in the margins of Englefield's report, "to make sure of his person until we know more about the matter." Arthur was clapped in a Spanish prison and from that moment on was lost to history.

I was struck by the realization that if the King of Spain as well as Francis Englefield, each of whom knew both parents personally, considered that the young man might be telling the truth, then perhaps readers of history as well as historical fiction should finally be made aware of Arthur Dudley's existence so that they might decide for themselves if he was, in fact, the bastard child of Lord Leicester and the Virgin Queen.